Sequel to the novel Azure Bonds!

FORGOT

FANT

Book Two: The Finder's Stone Trilogy

THE WYVERN'S SPUR

D0052837

BK06133389

Kate Novak and Jeff Grubb

A beam of light passed through a chink in the pile of grain sacks, reminding Olive of her peril. Dropping Giogi's gold, she fumbled again in the darkness for Jade's magic pouch. Her hands felt heavy and awkward, and she was dizzy from the excitement. When she finally touched the pouch it took all her concentration to grasp and lift it.

The footfalls halted right in front of her hiding spot. Automatically Olive slipped Jade's pouch in her vest pocket and pressed her eye to the chink in the sacks, just as a shadow blocked the light streaming through. The halfling looked up, her eyes wide with terror.

Jade's murderer looked down at her with anger. His right hand held a translucent ball of light, which limned his face. Despite the cruel, twisted smile, the sharp features were unmistakable. It is the Nameless Bard, Olive thought with anguish. He used to be a Harper. How could he become a murderer? We were allies and friends. How can he murder me?

"Beshaba's brats," he cursed.

Olive felt much the same way. The goddess of ill luck seemed to be following her tonight. She tried to stand, but her knees were too weak. She looked up, prepared to deliver what she suspected were her last words. She started to say, "You'll never get away with this. Alias will find out, and she'll—" but all that came from her mouth was a hoarse bray.

Nameless turned away from her as if she didn't exist, and began searching the horse stalls.

He had me dead to rights, Olive thought. How could he miss me? She tried to scratch her head in puzzlement, but all she could manage was a twitch of her fuzzy muzzle, a swish of her bushy tail, and a pricking of her long, pointed ears. In panic, the halfling looked down at herself. Instead of her black vest, breeches, and furry feet, Olive discovered she was covered with short brown fur and had four delicate hooves.

Sweet Selune, Olive thought, I'm an ass!

Also by Novak and Grubb:

AZURE BONDS

FANTASY ADVENTURE

THE WYVERN'S SPUR

KATE NOVAK AND JEFF GRUBB

Cover Art
CLYDE CALDWELL

TSR, Inc.

To Tracy and Laura—
our family in Wisconsin

THE WYVERN'S SPUR

Distributed to the book trade in the United States by Random House, Inc. and in Canada by Random House of Canada, Ltd.

Distributed in the United Kingdom by TSR Ltd.

Distributed to the toy and hobby trade by regional distributors.

FORGOTTEN REALMS, PRODUCTS OF YOUR IMAGINATION and the TSR logo are trademarks owned by TSR, Inc.

First Printing, February, 1990
Printed in the United States of America.
Library of Congress Catalog Card Number: 89-51883

9 8 7 6 5 4 3 2 1

ISBN: 0-88038-902-8

TSR, Inc.
P.O. Box 756
Lake Geneva, WI 53147
U.S.A.

TSR Ltd.
120 Church End, Cherry Hinton
Cambridge CB1 3LB
United Kingdom

The Wyvernspur Line

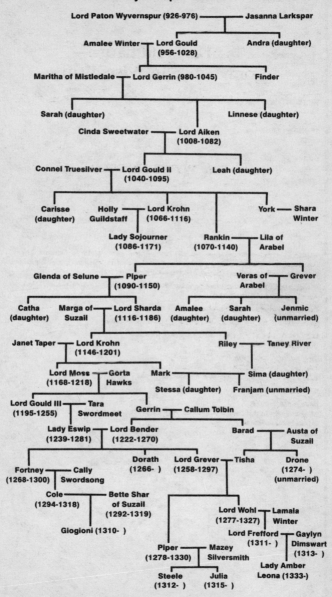

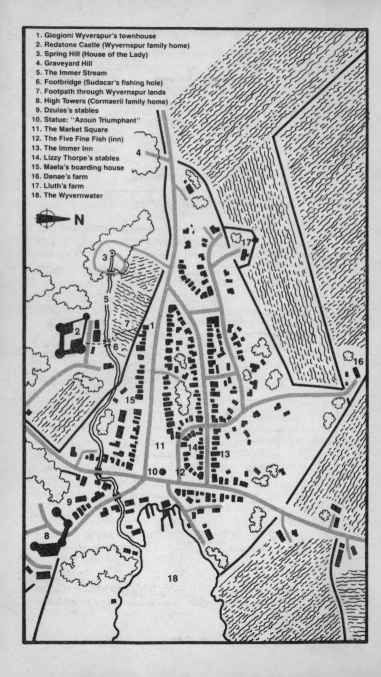

1. Giogioni Wyverspur's townhouse
2. Redstone Castle (Wyvernspur family home)
3. Spring Hill (House of the Lady)
4. Graveyard Hill
5. The Immer Stream
6. Footbridge (Sudacar's fishing hole)
7. Footpath through Wyvernspur lands
8. High Towers (Cormaeril family home)
9. Dzulas's stables
10. Statue: "Azoun Triumphant"
11. The Market Square
12. The Five Fine Fish (inn)
13. The Immer Inn
14. Lizzy Thorpe's stables
15. Maela's boarding house
16. Danae's farm
17. Lluth's farm
18. The Wyvernwater

N

❧ 1 ❧

Homecoming

From the journal of Giogioni Wyvernspùr:

The 19th of Ches, in the Year of the Shadows

Late last night I returned home from my duties as royal envoy, to find my kin in a greater uproar than the southern city I had left behind. Ten months of Westgate's problems shrivel to insignificance when compared to the tragedy that has befallen the clan of the Wyvernspurs of Immersea.

How could the flattening of an entire neighborhood by a dragon corpse, followed by an earthquake and an underworld power-struggle, hope to compete with the theft of a family heirloom no larger than a zucchini and uglier than three-week-old sausage?

"A hunk of junk" is what Uncle Drone has always called the wyvern's spur (said heirloom), and, considering all the trouble it has been, I am inclined to agree with him. No doubt the family would have donated it to a church rummage generations ago if not for the detestable prophesy that came with it.

According to family legend, the wyvern who presented it to old Paton Wyvernspur, way back when, promised that the family line would never die out as long as we held on to the gruesome chunk of mummified beastie. Logically it doesn't follow that losing the dratted thing guarantees our demise, but we've always been a superstitious lot, we Wyvernspurs, so there is a family conclave tonight in Aunt Dorath's lair at Redstone Castle. Although I have not yet unpacked from my journeys on behalf of the crown, I am expected to attend.

Someone will need to comfort Aunt Dorath. An oldest nephew's lot is never easy.

Giogi laid his quill pen on the writing table and left the journal open for the ink to dry. He didn't feel it necessary to add that his great-aunt would find his presence comforting only insofar as it would give her something else to criticize. He planned to leave his journal to posterity someday, and there were some things posterity just didn't need to know.

As far as Aunt Dorath was concerned, Giogi had dishonored the Wyvernspur family last year with his disgraceful—but, as Giogi would put it, dead-on—imitation of King Azoun IV, which had resulted in Giogi's near assassination by the cursed sellsword Alias of Westgate and the disruption of an entire wedding reception. Nor had Dorath, the matriarch of clan Wyvernspur, been impressed by her nephew's tale of his subsequent hair-raising encounter with a red dragon named Mist. To her mind, any young man who could not avoid entanglements with assassins and monsters needed to be sent far away for an extended period. Aunt Dorath had assumed that His Majesty Azoun had exiled Giogi in disgrace for those transgressions.

What Dorath, and most of the general population, had not known, was that King Azoun actually had assigned Giogi a secret mission, to discover the whereabouts of Alias of Westgate, the king's potential assassin.

Not that I needed to be assigned, Giogi thought. I seem destined to run into the woman—or her relatives—wherever I roam. Yet, after Giogi had spotted her near Westgate that summer, she seemed to have vanished from the Realms entirely.

Giogi rose from his writing desk and stretched. His fingertips brushed against one of the overhead chandeliers. He was a very tall young man, a legacy from both his father and his mother. Last year he'd been slender and clean-cut, but his travels had left him gaunt and his hair in desperate need of a trim. His sandy-brown locks straggled down his sunburned neck in back and into his muddy brown eyes in front. His long face made his features seem less plain than they were. He bore no resemblance, however, to the other living members of the Wyvernspur family, who all had thin lips, hawklike noses, blue eyes, pale skin, and dark hair.

Taking up his goblet of mulled wine, Giogi crossed the parlor to the fireplace, where he warmed his fingers by the flames. It would take a day or two of blazing fires to chase the last of the winter chill and damp from the parlor. Uncertain as to his master's return, Thomas, Giogi's manservant, had decided not to waste wood and effort heating an empty house. Giogi shuddered to think of the effect that ten months of such neglect had on the plush wool Calimshan carpeting, the brilliant Sembian satin furniture coverings, and the Cormyrian duskwood paneling. At least, it being the month of Ches, the returning spring sunshine kept ice from forming on the leaded glass windows. It had come as quite a shock to Giogi, though, to find no candle burning in those windows upon his return, neither literally nor figuratively.

The young noble wondered whether a mere fire laid in the hearth could burn off the strange and unwelcome feeling he now sensed in his home. Everything was familiar and in its proper place, but the townhouse felt empty. After months spent at inns, aboard ships, and in traveling with strangers, now being alone left Giogi disquieted. He took a long swig of wine to shake off his gloom.

On the mantlepiece lay the most interesting souvenir of his travels: a large yellow crystal. Giogi had found it in the grass outside Westgate, and he was sure there was something special about the stone besides its beauty and financial value. The crystal shone in the dark like a great firefly, and Giogi felt quite comforted whenever he held it. He considered showing it to his Uncle Drone, but he decided against the idea, afraid that the old wizard would tell him the stone was dangerous and take it away.

Giogi polished off his drink and placed the empty silver goblet on the mantlepiece, then picked up the yellow crystal. Cradling it in both hands, he flopped back into his favorite stuffed chair and propped his feet up on a cushioned footstool. He turned the crystal over in his hands, watching the firelight sparkle in each facet.

The crystal was roughly egg-shaped but far larger than any bird egg—smaller, though, than a wyvern's egg. It was the color of the finest mead and faintly warm to the touch. Where the facets met, the edges were not sharp but beveled smooth. Giogi held the stone at arm's length, closed one eye, and tried to divine if it held some secret within its depths, but he could make out only the firelight shining through it and his own reflection broken by the facets.

"Now, what would be the best way to display you?" he asked the crystal. There was no sense in having a case made for it, he realized. Taking it out every time he wanted to handle it would be a bother, but it was too large to wear from a neck chain. On the road, he had kept it tucked in the top of his boot, where most adventurers kept their daggers.

The boots would have to suffice this evening, he decided at last. Although he didn't plan to show it to Uncle Drone and the rest of his family, he very much wanted to show the stone to his pals at the Immer Inn. With any luck, Aunt Dorath would dismiss him from the family gathering early enough for him to slip back into town before closing hour.

That matter resolved, Giogi bounced back to his feet and wandered from the parlor to his home's entrance. With the stone tucked awkwardly in his belt, he rummaged through the hall closet under the stairs. He'd left his boots in the front of the closet, but they had somehow vanished. He rustled about the cloaks and capes hanging from their separate hooks, and kicked through a number of shoes that littered the floor. Then he began pulling from the closet all manner of walking sticks, abandoned clothing, and curios—which were gifts from relatives, and so could not be thrown away, but which were too ugly to place anywhere but in the relative darkness of the closet.

Finally, having moved half the closet's interior into the hall, the young noble gave up and let out a bellow.

"Thomas!" he shouted toward the back hallway. "Where are my boots?"

Alerted by the sound of chests, shoes, and walking sticks being thumped about, Thomas had already decided to investigate the racket and had put aside the silver tureen he'd been polishing. He was just coming out from the kitchen as Giogi called his name. Beneath the archway separating the front hall from what Giogi termed "Servant Land," the gentleman's gentleman paused.

Thomas looked askance at the closet's contents strewn about the hallway and tried not to blanch. He wasn't more than three years Giogi's senior, but many more years of responsibility had given him an aged, wiser-than-thou look. It was a look that the servant used now on his employer.

"Is there something that Sir requires?" Thomas asked evenly.

"I can't find my boots," Giogi declared. "I know I left them in here."

From the chaos before him, Thomas drew out a pair of recently polished black boots with narrow heels and sharp, pointed toes. "Here you are, sir," he said without a trace of annoyance.

"Not those things. I won't wear them ever again. They pinch my feet. Take them away and burn them. I want the boots I bought in Westgate. The knee-high, brown-suede clodders with wide brims. They're the most comfortable boots in the Realms."

Thomas raised a single eyebrow. "Comfortable they may be, sir, but they are hardly a gentleman's boot."

"Tish! I'm a gentleman, and they're my boots, ergo, *argumentum ab auctoritate*," came Giogi's riposte. "Et cetera," he added.

"I thought, sir, now that your travels are through, that you would wish to dispense with the accoutrements of your journey. I have already retired the boots."

"Well, bring them out of retirement, and please hurry. I need to leave for Redstone."

"I understood that your Aunt Dorath was not expecting you until after supper."

"That's right, and since I thought I would walk to Redstone and would like to arrive on time, I need to leave now." Giogi sat on the hall bench and kicked off his silk slippers, anticipating that Thomas would produce his boots out of thin air.

Thomas surveyed his master with disbelief. "Walk, sir?"

"Yes. You know, one foot in front of the other," Giogi explained patiently.

"But what about your own supper, sir?"

"Supper? Oh, sorry, Thomas. Write supper off. After that magnificent lunch and all those wonderful raisin cakes at tea, I'm completely full up. Couldn't eat another thing. Thanks anyway."

Thomas's look of incredulity turned to one of concern. "Are you feeling all right, sir?"

"Splendid, except that my feet are getting cold," Giogi said with a grin.

Without another word, Thomas spun about and disappeared through the archway into Servant Land.

Giogi twisted sideways on the bench to keep his stockinged feet off the chilly floorboards. He ran a finger along the smooth parquetry worked into the wooden bench's high back. One of his earliest childhood memories was of his father explaining to him the picture in the bench. It depicted the moment the family had gotten its patronymic, "way back," as his father used to say, "in the days before we knew which spoon to use for the soup course." In the design, Paton Wyvernspur, the family founder, stood before a great female wyvern. Two tiny hatchling wyverns played at the monster's feet, and behind her lay the corpse of her mate. Bandits had killed her mate and stolen her eggs from her nest, but Paton had tracked down and vanquished the thieves and restored the young wyverns to their mother. In gratitude, the female wyvern had sliced off her mate's right spur and conferred it upon Giogi's forefather with the promise that his family line would never dwindle while the spur remained in the family's possession.

Later, when he was older and had learned that wyverns weren't considered very nice beasts, Giogi often wondered why Paton had helped the female wyvern. By that time, though, Giogi's father and mother were both dead, and Giogi couldn't bring himself to ask Aunt Dorath or Uncle Drone. He sensed instinctively that it would be branded a question only a fool such as himself would ask.

He wasn't fool enough to part with the bench, though. It had been a wedding gift from his mother to his father, and while the other Wyvernspurs scorned the wealthy carpenter's daughter that Cole Wyvernspur had wed, they all coveted the bench. The carpentry was solid, and the parquetry picture positively hypnotic. Aunt Dorath had suggested a number of times that the bench ought to sit in the hall of Redstone, the family manor, and last year, before his marriage to Gaylyn Dimswart, Giogi's second Cousin Frefford had hinted it would make a lovely wedding gift, but Giogi declined to part with it.

Bored by inactivity, Giogi bounced to his stocking feet and began tossing back into the closet all the things he'd tossed out.

Thomas appeared in the archway, holding out the knee-high, brown-suede clodders, which, by his master's own declaration, were the most comfortable pair in the Realms. "Please, sir," the servant requested, "don't trouble yourself with putting those things away. I'll be happy to do it."

Giogi halted in midtoss of a lone wool mitten. Something in Thomas's tone revealed the servant's anxiety. Giogi noticed that the inside of the closet was now as untidy as the outside.

"Sorry, Thomas," he apologized meekly.

"That's quite all right, sir," Thomas said, setting the boots beside the bench.

"Ah, my boots! Excellent!" Giogi sat back down on the bench and pulled the right boot on, then slipped the stone into the brim.

"Are you certain, sir, you wouldn't rather ride?" Thomas asked.

Giogi, one foot still unshod, looked up at his manservant. "It may surprise you to know, Thomas, that when I was on my mission for the crown, I often walked great distances." Giogi did not feel it necessary to add that he had walked great distances whenever forced to because some scurrilous cove had stolen his horse or some equally evil beast had devoured his mount.

"Indeed, sir. I did not mean to suggest you weren't up to the task. I just thought that after your strenuous journey you might prefer the luxury of riding. If not in the carriage, I can saddle Daisyeye."

"No, thank you, Thomas," Giogi said, finally pulling on the other boot. "Daisyeye deserves a good, long rest, and I really want to walk." He rose, whipped his cloak about him with a flourish, and stomped to the front door. "Don't bother to wait up for me," he suggested. "I expect I'll be quite late. Good night," he called out before he plunged outside.

In town, everything was brown; the buildings, the grass, the muddy roads, the wooden carts, even the horses and oxen, were shades of umber and tan. Townhouses blocked out the late afternoon sun and cast long chocolate shadows on the earth. Women shouted out the windows at dirt-caked children in the streets. It was as if the gods had run out of other colors by the time they reached that part of Immersea, left it etched in one shade, then hadn't bothered to mix new paint to fill in the color.

Giogi walked east, away from the center of town, then turned south onto a trail that led from town to the Wyvernspur estate. A low wall surrounded the land, and the lanky noble swung his legs over it easily and entered another world, one that the gods had colored. Stalks of winter rye glittered like jade in the setting sunlight; purple-specked crocuses sparkled with gemlike raindrops; a great flock of wild geese honked overhead in the deepening blue sky. Giogi felt his spirits rise and shook off the gloom that had gripped him in his own house.

He struck out along the path through the fields. As the town founders, the Wyvernspurs held title to nearly all the land south of town. Most of the land was set aside for hunting and riding. The highest hill was dedicated to the goddess Selune, and the temple at its peak was left to the administration of her priestess, ancient Mother Lleddew. The Wyvernspurs resisted, however, cultivating much of the land, felling many trees, or clearing many fields for cattle. They were nobles, not farmers or foresters or ranchers. The Cormaerils—the only other titled family in Immersea—regularly planted nearly a hundred acres, but had been nobility for only four generations. Giogi feared that, after fifteen generations, the Wyvernspurs were too entrenched in relying on the family fortune as their only source of revenue.

As Giogi emerged from the fields of rye, the sun was no more than half a palm's width from the horizon, and the air was already turning chill. The path wound down into the valley of the Immer Stream. The noble kept up a quick pace to keep warm, but as he approached the northern bank of the stream he was forced to proceed more cautiously. The trail grew marshy, and he picked his way from one tuft of dry grass to the next. His boots were reasonably waterproof, but he didn't want to arrive at Aunt Dorath's looking a mess.

Finally, after a long period of testing footfalls and doubling back, he reached the footbridge that crossed the stream. To the west of the trail, the Immer Stream flowed down from the hill dedicated to Selune. To the south of the stream, the trail climbed onto drier ground and up to Redstone Castle, ancestral home of the Wyvernspurs.

Just as Giogi clomped onto the bridge, a fine white strand of something whipped out in front of him. With a shriek the nobleman leaped backward with visions of giant spiders and a sudden irrational belief in the curse of the wyvern's spur. The white strand was not followed by others, though, giving Giogi the opportunity to clutch his chest in relief and spot the silhouette of a man on the southern shore.

"Cole?" the silhouette gasped. "No, of course not. It's Giogioni, isn't it? You gave me a fright, boy. Looked for a moment just like your old man in that getup."

Giogi squinted in the gloomy light. The sun had nearly set, but he could make out the tall, broad form of a man on the far bank. The man's erect stance and bearing reflected a military background. His dark hair was short and just beginning to gray at the temples. He had a warm, perfect smile, which set Giogi at ease. "Sudacar? Samtavan Sudacar, is that you? What are you doing out here?"

"Getting in a little casting. Sorry about the line. My technique's gotten a little rusty over the winter." Sudacar tugged at the string hanging from his fishing rod until it slipped off the footbridge and into the water with a small splash. As he jerked the line through the water, tiny minnows chased after the lure.

Giogi crossed the bridge and picked his way along the south bank until he stood beside Samtavan Sudacar, the man appointed by none other than King Azoun himself to defend Immersea, dispense the king's justice, keep the peace, and, of course, collect taxes. "Taking a break from your pressing administrative duties, eh?" Giogi asked.

Sudacar snorted. "Keeping out of Culspiir's way is more like it. Behind every local lord, my boy, is a trained herald making him look good. As long as I keep delegating authority to Culspiir, I'll be a great success at this job." Sudacar continued casting, watching his lure all the while.

"Why isn't Culspiir the local lord, then?" Giogi asked meekly.

"If he had my job, who would we get to do his job?"

"Good point," Giogi admitted.

"Besides, Culspiir never slew a giant."

"Is that a prerequisite for your job?"

"Got to make a name for yourself at court. Slew a frost giant that was terrorizing merchants in Gnoll Pass. That's how I got into politics—a service like that has to be recognized officially."

Giogi nodded in agreement, though he knew not all the other members of his family felt the same way.

Samtavan Sudacar had not been born to nobility, nor was he a native of Immersea. Nonetheless, King Azoun had named Sudacar Lord of Immersea when that position fell vacant by the death of Giogi's father's cousin, Lord Wohl Wyvernspur. Wohl's son, Frefford, had still been a boy, so the family had accepted Sudacar graciously enough. They'd even invited the middle-aged bachelor to make his home with them in Redstone Castle.

When Frefford reached majority, though, His Majesty hadn't assigned the young Wyvernspur to the post. That's when Aunt Dorath had begun to consider Sudacar not just an upstart, but an interloper and a usurper as well. Giogi knew, though, that Frefford had been secretly relieved. Aunt Dorath and Cousin Steele had taken the most offense. Pride and loyalty to the king prohibited the family's asking Sudacar to leave Redstone. When Giogi had left Immersea last spring, an uneasy truce had existed between the Wyvernspurs of Redstone Castle and the Lord of Immersea.

Giogi, since he chose to live in town instead of at the castle, had never really gotten to know Sudacar very well. They didn't travel in the same circles. Now, though, Giogi realized, he had to learn something more about Sudacar. "If you're from Suzail originally," he asked, "how did you know my father?"

"Cole? Met him at court a few times. Slew his share of giants, your father did."

"He did?" Giogi asked with surprise. His father had died when Giogi was only eight, so he hadn't known him very well. But he was certain no one had ever mentioned that Cole had slain giants.

"Served His Majesty with honor, like generations of your family before him," Sudacar said, pulling his dripping line from the water and adjusting it behind his back.

"Aunt Dorath told me he was a trade envoy."

"He might have been that as well," Sudacar said, whipping the line out over the stream again.

"As well? As well as what?"

"He was a warrior adventurer. Your aunt never told you that?"

"No," Giogi admitted. Loyally, he added, "It must have slipped her mind."

Sudacar snorted. "Wouldn't have considered that a proper occupation for a Wyvernspur, would she? I'm surprised Drone never mentioned it."

So was Giogi, though he did not say so aloud.

Drone Wyvernspur was Giogi's great-aunt Dorath's cousin and therefore Giogi's first cousin twice removed, but out of respect and affection, Giogi called him Uncle Drone. When Giogi's mother had died a year after her husband, Aunt Dorath had taken care of Giogi, but Uncle Drone had been assigned the task of completing the masculine aspects of Giogi's education. An unmarried wizard of sedentary habits, Uncle Drone had not exactly been the most useful source of information about women, hunting, or horses.

Drone knew a good deal, though, about wine and gambling, and something of politics and religion, and, armed with this learning, Giogi usually managed to hold his own in taverns and after-dinner conversations. The wizard had told Giogi plenty of stories about his mother, Bette, and her father, the carpenter, even though Aunt Dorath had never approved of Cole's wife's family. Why, though, Giogi wondered, hadn't Uncle Drone told me Cole was an adventurer?

"Would you care to walk back to Redstone with me?" he asked Sudacar, hoping to hear more about his father, something he could confront Uncle Drone with.

The lord shook his head. "Everything's at sixes and sevens up there. Culspiir and I offered our assistance, but your Aunt Dorath as much as told us to keep our noses out of Wyvernspur business. She doesn't want an interloper like me involved. I'll tucker in at the Five Fine Fish and creep back to the castle in the small hours. Safer for all involved that way."

"Oh." Disappointed, Giogi stood beside Sudacar, racking his head for something else to say to keep the conversation going. His wits failed him, as they were wont to do, so he stood wordlessly beside Sudacar as the shadows lengthened. Sudacar cast his line twice more. Farther upstream there was a hooting and a sudden flurry of wings, followed by a splash. An owl fished the waters as well.

Finally Sudacar spoke. "Thought I'd seen a ghost when I saw you on the opposite bank, in those boots with that cloak. You haven't got Cole's face, but you have his shape, his stance, his walk." Sudacar cast his line again. "If you'd care to talk about your father," he offered, "stop in at the Fish later, and we'll raise a mug in his honor."

Giogi grinned with pleasure. "If I can escape Aunt Dorath's clutches, I'll do just that," he agreed. Just then, a sudden chill made him realize the warmth had gone with the sunlight. He pulled his cloak closer to his body. "I'd better be going. They're expecting me up at the castle."

Sudacar nodded without taking his eyes off the lure he tugged through the water.

Giogi left the Lord of Immersea by the water and hurried up the trail. It was dark and cold by the time he reached the walls surrounding Redstone Castle, but he still didn't relish the thought of entering. The castle was wrapped in shades of gray and black. The reddish pallor of its stonework, which gave it its name, was absent in the darkness. The castle squatted on the low hill overlooking the Immer Stream, the town of Immersea, and the Wyvernwater—a great lake east of Cormyr—beyond, like a dragon watching a merchant road.

Looking up at the brooding monstrosity as he approached, Giogi was reminded again of the dragon that had fallen on Westgate and the earthquakes and underworld power-struggle that had ensued. Having dealt with all those things, Giogi assured himself, coping with this family crisis shouldn't be too difficult.

❧ 2 ❧
Family

Giogi circled the castle walls to the front gate, strode into the courtyard, and tapped on the hall door. An unfamiliar footman opened the portal a crack and peered out at the shaggy, gangly noble dressed in yellow pants and a red-and-white striped shirt covered with a black tabard. The tabard was emblazoned with the Wyvernspur coat of arms, but the man who wore it looked more like a traveling juggler than an Immersea noble. The servant stood waiting impatiently for the man to speak.

Giogi was unaccustomed to having to announce his business at the doorstep of his own family's ancestral home. He, too, stood in silence, waiting to be recognized.

Finally the footman spoke. "Well, what is it?" he asked, his face creased with irritation.

"I'm here to see my Aunt Dorath."

The footman opened the door an inch wider. "And you are?"

"Giogi. Giogioni Wyvernspur."

The footman's facial creases retreated just a fraction. "Oh," he said without enthusiasm. He held the door open so that Giogi could enter the main hall. As the noble clomped in, the footman eyed Giogi's clodders; his attention was not lost on Giogi.

"Great boots, aren't they? Bought them in Westgate."

The servant maintained his stoic expression and did not comment on the boots. He held out his arm for Giogi's cloak and said, "The gentlemen are still in the dining room having their brandy. The ladies are in the parlor. I presume you know the way."

"Yes," Giogi replied, handing over his cloak.

Laden with Giogi's outdoor gear, the footman disappeared through a small door.

Left alone again, Giogi felt hesitant to return to the bosom of his family. There had been a reason he'd moved from Redstone to his parents' old townhouse. His family thought him a fool and made a habit of reminding him of it. He was branded for life just because, as a boy, he'd accidentally let an evil efreet out of a bottle in Uncle Drone's lab and had once tried to fly off the stable roof with pigeon feathers—and had gotten himself locked in the family crypt—which had really been Cousin Steele's fault.

If only he could get them to forget the foibles of his youth and judge him on his behavior as an adult—except for when he'd lost Aunt Dorath's pet land urchin in the provisions wagon of the seventh division of His Majesty's Purple Dragoons and the time he'd gone skinny-dipping in the Wyvernwater on Midwinter Day. After all, he had no idea a land urchin could eat so much, and no one as inebriated as he on that Midwinter Day would have passed up such a profitable wager.

He hadn't done anything that foolish since—well, not since last spring, when he'd done his impersonation of King Azoun and ended up in a brawl with the crazy Alias of Westgate, knocking down a tent on top of two hundred people and nearly breaking up Frefford's wedding reception. He hadn't wanted to do the impersonation, but his girlfriend, Minda, had nagged him into it. If his family could only forget that incident, and if no stories of his exploits in Westgate reached their ears, they might just begin treating him like a normal person. Granted, that was more luck than the goddess Tymora usually dealt anyone, but it was still possible.

Prepared to make a fresh start with his family, Giogi considered whether to go straight to the parlor to pay his respects to Aunt Dorath, or to join the gentlemen in the dining room for some brandy. If he entered the parlor while the ladies were still discussing "female things," his Aunt Dorath would be annoyed with his intrusion. He did want to speak with Uncle Drone, but the old wizard would not be alone in the dining room. Giogi's second cousins, Frefford and Steele, would be with him, and, while Frefford might tease him a little about the wedding reception fiasco, Steele's taunts would be as mean and vicious as possible.

Giogi liked a room full of people to serve as a buffer between Steele and himself. Of course, Steele's sister, Julia, would be with the ladies. She could be mean, too, but she wasn't so bad when she wasn't in Steele's company. Giogi decided that he might as well break in on the ladies. That way, Aunt Dorath couldn't accuse him of lapping up her brandy whenever her back was turned. Besides, Frefford's new wife, Gaylyn, would no doubt be with the ladies, and she was the cheeriest, most amusing woman Giogi had ever met.

The nobleman knocked timidly on the parlor door, just in case they were discussing petticoats or something equally personal, then he entered.

Redstone's parlor had not changed since Giogi's last visit, nearly a year ago. It was warmer and drier than the parlor in Giogi's townhouse, but it was quite a bit shabbier. Faded tapestries depicting ancient events covered the flaking stone walls. The once-rich carpets were stained. The furniture coverings were worn thin. Giogi's mother's money had refurbished his townhouse, but the Wyvernspur fortune was shrinking, and servants, horses, and clothing had a higher priority than Redstone's fashionable appearance. Some generation soon, the family would need a new source of revenue, though the decision to find one was unlikely in Aunt Dorath's lifetime.

Aunt Dorath sat perfectly erect in her chair by the fire. She looked up from her knitting and squinted at Giogi. She was a tall, robust old woman with the classic Wyvernspur face, thin lips, hawklike nose, and all. Her black hair, which she wore in a severe bun, was streaked with steel-gray strands. More streaks had appeared since Giogi had last seen her, and her squint had grown more pronounced, but, otherwise, time had not touched her much. It wouldn't dare, Giogi thought.

Gaylyn and Julia were immersed in a game of backgammon and did not notice him until a gasp from Aunt Dorath alerted them.

"Giogioni! Sweet Selune! Just what are you doing in those ridiculous boots?" Aunt Dorath demanded. Her voice boomed like the thunder of a god's wrath. That part of Dorath had not changed in the least.

"These boots?" Giogi replied, his voice cracking slightly. "They're just something I threw on to walk over."

"You should consider throwing them away. Whatever did you walk for? What happened to your carriage?"

"Nothing. I just felt like walking."

"The idea! Sinister forces have dealt our family a tragic blow while you've been gadding about the Realms. I summon the family together, and you just stroll over here as if nothing's wrong. It's just like you. You are a fool," Aunt Dorath chided.

Giogi stood frozen, afraid that anything else he might say would only dig him deeper into his great-aunt's contempt.

"Well, don't just stand there," Dorath ordered. "Come take a seat."

Giogi bowed before Gaylyn and Julia and positioned himself in a chair where he could attend to Aunt Dorath as well as address the younger women, should they address him.

Giogi glanced at his Cousin Julia. Her tall, well-proportioned body was clad in the latest velvet fashions, jewels glistened in her silky black hair, and gold rings flashed from her long, slender fingers. She, too, had the aristocratic Wyvernspur features, which were more striking on her youthful face than they were on Aunt Dorath's. In addition, she sported, from her mother's side of the family, a tiny mole to the right of her mouth. As far as Giogi was concerned, though, Julia was too haughty to be beautiful.

The nobleman preferred to gaze on Gaylyn. Her golden hair lit up the room, and her pink, glowing complexion reminded him of a wild rose. Her gown and jewels were as remarkable as Julia's but Giogi didn't notice them. It was impossible, though, for him to miss her swollen abdomen. According to Thomas, Freffie and Gaylyn's firstborn was due any time now. So, Giogi thought, the family is going to continue another generation despite the loss of the wyvern's spur.

Gaylyn, unaware that the tradition of her new family was to generally ignore Giogi, turned her sweet smile on him and asked, "How was your journey home, Cousin?"

"Just marvelous. Very exciting," Giogi replied, grinning back at the young woman.

"Exciting," Aunt Dorath scoffed. "Traveling is never exciting. Only tedious. Waits, delays, ruffians, strangers, and highwaymen. Only someone as foolish as yourself would revel in it. You'll end up like your father," she added darkly.

Giogi debated asking his aunt exactly what she meant by that, trying to work in some reference to what he'd just learned from Sudacar, but just then the parlor door swung open and the gentlemen entered. Frefford made a beeline to Gaylyn's side and took her hand in his own, looking down on her with solicitous devotion. Uncle Drone scuffled over to a tomcat in the window seat and began feeding it drippy tidbits of venison from his cupped hand. Steele remained in the door-way, leaning against the jamb and sizing up Giogi with an evil grin.

Like his sister, Julia, Steele had the Wyvernspur face with a mole to the right of his mouth. Many people would have called him tall, dark, and handsome, but his grin reminded Giogi of the red dragon Mist—an impression heightened by the way the firelight caught Steele's blue eyes and made them glint red. As he had in Mist's presence, Giogi winced when Steele spoke.

"So the exiled family jester has returned. Everyone in Suzail was talking about your remarkable impersonation at the wedding last season. And, of course, about the "duel" that followed. I trust you have fresh entertainment lined up for us this year. Maybe you can debut at Gaylyn's baby's blessing ceremony."

Giogi winced again. It didn't look as though the family was going to forget the wedding incident any time soon. Wondering if Gaylyn could ever forgive him, Giogi shot her a guilty glance. The bride had the most right to be angry.

Gaylyn laughed, though. "I thought I would just die when that tent collapsed on all of us," she said. "Remember what fun we had crawling out from under it? It was such a relief to have an excuse to leave that stuffy old canvas and just revel in the garden."

Steele squinted with annoyance at Gaylyn, and Aunt Dorath raised an eyebrow at the woman's frivolous attitude, but Lord Frefford smiled at his wife's high spirits.

A stranger might have guessed Frefford and Steele were brothers and not just second cousins, because Frefford, too, sported most of the Wyvernspur features. Frefford's face was always softened by a friendly smile, though, and his eyes were more hazel than blue. He whispered something in his wife's ear, and she giggled.

Giogi smiled at the couple with gratitude.

Aunt Dorath sniffed. "Now that we're all here, it's time to get down to business," she announced imperiously. "Drone, leave that infernal cat and join your family."

It was hard to believe, watching Uncle Drone shuffle across the room, that Aunt Dorath's wizard cousin was eight years her junior. If time had avoided Dorath, it made up its loss by visiting Drone twice over. His black hair and beard, besides being shaggy and unkempt, was splotched with gray and white, much more so than Aunt Dorath's hair. His blue eyes were rheumy, and his Wyvernspur features were lost in the cracks and wrinkles that lined his face. Magic had taken its toll on him.

Years of puttering in his lab, brewing magic potions, had also left Drone a little careless of his appearance. Forgetting he did not wear a lab apron, he wiped his hand on his chest, leaving a venison blood stain across his yellow silk robe. He offered his hand to Giogi, saying, "Welcome back, boy. Heard you've been jousting with red dragons."

Giogi held out his own hand nervously, afraid he was about to be censured again. A cloud of Tymora's blackest luck seemed to hang over him this evening. It hadn't been his fault that he'd been kidnapped by the red dragon Mist. Giogi then saw that his uncle's eyes twinkled with amusement. The young man relaxed and jokingly replied, "Uh, actually, it's a little difficult jousting with them, don't you know, because they tend to eat your horse first."

Dorath, Steele, and Julia glared frostily at Giogi for treating the incident so lightly, but Drone wheezed out a cackle and plopped down beside Dorath.

Giogi used his handkerchief to wipe the blood from the hand Uncle Drone had shaken.

"Did you really joust with a dragon?" Gaylyn asked, her eyes shining with excitement.

"Well, actually I—"

"Of course he didn't," Aunt Dorath snapped. "Giogi could no more joust with a dragon than he could match his own stockings. Enough of this nonsense. Drone, it's time you explained to all of us what happened to the spur."

Uncle Drone sighed a deep sigh, like a bellows letting out all its air. When he spoke, it was in a measured, professorial voice, his tone as dry as the ancient paper scrolls he kept in his lab. "Last night," he began, "an hour before dawn, someone got into the family crypt, where the wyvern's spur has been stored for years. Awakened by a magical alarm, I immediately attempted to scry into the crypt, but a powerful darkness obscured my vision. I teleported to the graveyard and found both the mausoleum door and the crypt door within locked. There was no sign that anyone had broken in or out. All the magical wards I had placed to keep spell-casters from by-passing the locks were intact. However, both the spur and its thief were gone."

"Why was the spur kept in the family crypt?" Gaylyn asked. "Wouldn't it have been easier to guard it in the castle?"

"The guardian lives in the crypt," Frefford explained softly to his wife.

"What's 'the guardian'?" she asked.

"The spirit of a powerful monster, which will slay any being in the crypt that is not a Wyvernspur by blood or marriage," Aunt Dorath said.

"So it had to be a Wyvernspur who stole the spur," Gaylyn reasoned.

"One of us," agreed Uncle Drone, pausing for a moment to let the thought sink in. Then he added, "But probably a long-lost relative. We've never been able to discover any before, but that doesn't mean there aren't any."

"Why steal the spur? What good is it to anyone?" Giogi asked.

"It's said to have powers beyond that of ensuring the continuance of the family line," replied the wizard.

"I never heard about that," Giogi protested. "What sort of powers?"

Uncle Drone shrugged. "It isn't in any of the family history books."

"What makes you think it was a long-lost relative?" Julia asked. "Why not one of us?"

"Well, firstly," Drone explained, "I was able to ascertain through magical means that none of the keys entrusted to the keeping of Frefford, Steele, and Giogioni—" Uncle Drone waved an arm at each of the men in turn— "were used to open the crypt."

"What about your own key?" Aunt Dorath interrupted. "Are you certain you haven't mislaid it somewhere?" Her emphasis suggested the unspoken word "again."

In reply, Uncle Drone held up a large silver key hanging from a chain about his neck. "As everyone here but Gaylyn already knows," the wizard continued, "besides the mausoleum entrance, the only other entrance to the crypt is from the catacombs below, and the only other way into the catacombs is from a secret magical door outside the graveyard."

"But you told us that that secret door only opens every fifty years," Steele snapped peevishly, "on the first of Tarsakh. That's still more than a ride away."

"Twelve days. That's a ride and two days to spare," Gaylyn corrected.

Steele scowled at the woman's exactness.

"Well, I seem to have miscalculated," Drone said. "Apparently the door opens after three hundred sixty-five days multiplied by fifty. In other words every eighteen thousand two hundred fiftieth day. The family records weren't so precise and rounded the interval off to a half-century."

"What's the difference?" Steele growled.

"Shieldmeet," Gaylyn cried excitedly, like a woman playing charades.

"Exactly," Uncle Drone said. "Shieldmeet, every four years, adds an extra day. After fifty years, the extra days add up, so the door opened earlier than I had expected."

"By twelve days," Gaylyn added.

Gaylyn, Giogi guessed, was one of those women who were good with figures.

"Fortunately," Drone continued, "I had the notion to check out that door within minutes of the theft. Sure enough, it stood open. I sealed it with a wall of stone and left magical guards to tell me if anyone tries to break out by that door or the door from the crypt to the mausoleum. No one has. The would-be thief is still stuck in the catacombs. So, you see, none of us can be the thief, since none of us are missing."

Giogi wondered idly, if he hadn't managed to return to Immersea before that evening, whether his family would be sitting around suspecting him of the crime.

"Since only a member of our family can enter the crypt, it's up to us to deal with this thieving rogue Wyvernspur," Aunt Dorath said. "No one else need know about this notorious incident. All we need to do is search the catacombs," she announced. "First thing in the morning."

"And will you be leading us, Aunt Dorath?" Steele asked with a smirk.

"Don't be absurd. This is a job for healthy young men like yourself and Frefford."

"And Giogioni," Uncle Drone said. "Can't leave him out."

"That's all right, Uncle Drone," Giogi insisted. "I can guard the crypt door or something, in case the thief gets past Steele and Freffie."

"Nonsense," Steele said. "We need you, Giogi. Besides, don't you want to renew your acquaintance with the guardian?"

"Actually, no," Giogi retorted sharply, glaring at his cousin. If looks could kill, the rest of the family would have to have summoned a cleric for Steele.

Aunt Dorath gave Giogi a cold look. "Giogioni, I won't have you shirking your family responsibilities. You can help by carrying the water flasks or something."

"Yes, you can be our provisions officer," Steele said. "But leave the land urchins behind—and don't forget your key. It'll remind the guardian that you are a Wyvernspur after all."

Giogi began breathing a little too deeply, and the room seemed to tilt. Steele's taunts were wasted on him—he was too busy fighting off a rising panic. Frefford moved to his side and clamped a reassuring hand on his shoulder. "It'll be fine, Giogi. We'll all be down there together."

"You can't possibly still be affected by that scare you had as a boy," Aunt Dorath insisted.

Giogi did not answer. His mouth moved, but no words escaped.

"Well, that's settled, then," Aunt Dorath said. "I suggest you all get a good night's sleep so you can get an early start. That includes you, Giogioni. Don't spend the rest of the evening carousing in town. You must be at the crypt at dawn. This is not a duty any of you dare take lightly. Until that spur is back in the crypt where it belongs, none of us are safe. You may scoff all you want, but I know for a fact that the spur's curse is no silly superstition. Its absence will bring evil upon us."

Giogi shuddered, anticipating meeting the guardian again. Gaylyn lay her hand nervously on her belly. Frefford returned to his wife's side to comfort her. Julia watched Steele, who fidgeted with impatience. Uncle Drone studied the stain on his robe.

Everyone remained speechless for several moments until Drone said, "I'll see you to the door, Giogi," and held an arm out for help in rising.

Still in shock, Giogi stood automatically and helped Drone to his feet. He held the parlor door open as the old man shuffled through, and he followed his uncle out.

After the door had closed behind them, the old man patted Giogi's arm and said softly, "Dory's right, you know. It's time you were over that fright you had as a child."

"Aunt Dorath wasn't locked down there," Giogi objected as they descended a staircase to the main entrance hall.

"Well, actually she was once, but that's neither here nor there. Listen, my boy, I have something very important to tell you, something I couldn't tell you in front of the others."

Suddenly reminded of Sudacar's revelation, Giogi shook off his anxiety over the coming expedition. "And I have a question for you that I couldn't ask in front of the others. Why didn't you ever tell me my father was an adventurer?"

"Found that out, did you? Who let it slip?"

"It makes no difference," Giogi retorted. "Why didn't you tell me?"

"Your Aunt Dorath made me swear not to."

"How could you agree to something like that?" Giogi demanded. "I thought you liked my father."

"I loved your father," Drone whispered angrily. "I had my reasons. Now hush up and listen."

When they'd reached the bottom of the staircase, the new footman popped out of an alcove and asked, "Shall I fetch Master Giogioni's things, sir?"

"Yes, yes," Uncle Drone snapped, annoyed at the interruption. He watched the footman's back until the servant disappeared from sight. Drone swiveled his neck in all four cardinal points, making sure he and Giogi were alone in the hall before he spoke again. "Now, where was I? Oh, yes. The spur and the thief aren't in the catacombs."

"What! Then why did you tell us all—?"

"Shh! Keep your voice down. I had good reasons, but Dory would never understand. You must go down into the catacombs anyway to keep up the charade, and tell me everything that happens there."

From the hallway upstairs they could hear Aunt Dorath bellow, "Drone!"

"Look, I'll explain it to you tomorrow night when you return. In the meantime—"

The footman returned with Giogi's cloak. Drone took the cloak and waved the servant away. As the old wizard wrapped Giogi up in the garment, he whispered, "In the meantime, watch your step. Your life could possibly, just possibly, be in danger." He opened the front door, and cold air rushed into the hallway.

"Because of the spur, you mean?" Giogi asked.

"Not because of the spur—well, maybe because of it, but not the way you might think—"

"Drone!" Aunt Dorath called out a second time.

Uncle Drone pushed Giogi out the door, saying, "I'll explain tomorrow. Remember—watch your step." The wizard closed the door on Giogi before he could protest further.

My life could possibly, just possibly, be in danger, Giogi thought. He shuddered, not just from the cold. A wizard such as Drone said "just possibly" only in cases where anyone else in the Realms would say, "most definitely."

A hearty spring wind, fresh off the Wyvernwater, danced around the side of the castle and tore through Giogi's cloak. He shuddered again and wished that he'd stayed in Westgate, where all he'd had to worry about were dragons, earthquakes, and power struggles. They really were insignificant compared to these family crises.

❧ 3 ❧

Olive and Jade

The halfling hid in the shadows—even though there was no one presently on the streets for her to hide from. Hiding in shadows was an art, and the halfling's mother had always warned her, "Never neglect your art, Olive-girl," so Olive hid in the shadows. Besides, sooner or later someone would come along the street.

That's what makes the natives of Cormyr a great people, Olive thought fondly. While citizens of other nations would cower indoors on a cold spring night like this, Cormytes will brave anything to visit the taverns of their choice. At this hour, there were usually just enough pedestrians to offer her a selection, but not so many that she need worry about any witnesses to her light-fingered larceny.

While she watched the street, Olive twiddled a platinum coin across the tips of her slender, dexterous fingers. A gust of wind from off the lake swirled around the corner and into the alley, blowing a strand of her long, russet hair into her green eyes. Olive pocketed the coin and pushed the strand up into her wool cap. She was bundled against the cold in a pair of breeches, a knee-length tunic, a bulky quilted vest, and the hat.

Besides keeping her warm, all the extra clothing hid her slim waist and curvaceous figure, so that she looked almost as plump as a typical town-living halfling. She was shorter than most adult halflings, though—well under three feet. She might have been mistaken for a human toddler, except for her fur-covered bare feet with their tough, leathery soles.

She would never even consider stuffing her feet into a pair of shoes and disguising her race, though. For one thing, there was always someone who made it his or her business to discover what a human child was doing wandering the streets alone, especially in Cormyr; or worse, there were people, even in Cormyr, who were ready to accost such children. For another thing, Olive found shoes just too uncomfortable, not to mention exceedingly awkward for running in, and she never knew when she might need to run. Most important of all, Olive felt that conducting business by passing as a human child was demeaning. Only a very untalented or very desperate halfling would resort to such a measure.

Down the street, a tavern door opened and sounds of laughter spilled out into the lane. Olive tensed for action. A fat youth in an apron came puffing along, carrying a jug of ale. A servant, Olive guessed, sent to fetch ale for a guest. Probably charged the ale to his master's tab, so he won't have any money on him. She stood motionless.

A minute later, two older men in heavy, dusty jackets shuffled by, arguing over whether or not it was too soon to plant peas. Farmers, Olive conjectured, no doubt carrying nothing but copper coins—and only enough copper at that to buy three rounds of ale. She remained motionless.

A skinny fop, attired in bright-colored raiment and wearing the most unusually large boots, strode down the center of the street. Dressed as he was, he might have been an adventurer or a merchant, but from the way he hadn't bothered to conceal the bulging coin purse in his cloak pocket, Olive judged him to be a noble. He looked sober and pretty alert, which made him just the sort of challenge Olive had been waiting for. She took her hands out of her pockets, intent on following him. As he passed the alley, though, a feeling of recognition tickled at the back of Olive's brain, and she held back.

"Are you watching a parade, Olive, or are you just screwing up your courage to make a grab?" someone behind her whispered.

Olive's heart pounded in her chest, but no visible sign betrayed how startled she was. She did not turn to look at her taunter; she did not need to. She could picture the person in her mind: a human woman, nearly six feet tall, slender, with a mop of short hair the rust-red color of bugbear fur, bright green eyes twinkling with merriment, and a face identical to one of Olive's previous companions—Alias of Westgate.

Olive kept her attention on the fop and whispered, "Jade, where in the Nine Hells have you been for the past ride? I've missed you, girl."

"It hasn't been ten days, only six," Jade whispered back. "I've been visiting family," she explained. Olive could hear the playful smile in her voice.

Olive furrowed her brow in puzzlement. For six months Jade had been her protegee, her partner, and her friend, and Olive knew things about Jade that not even Jade knew. Furthermore, as far as the halfling knew, Jade had no family. Jade herself had told the halfling she was an orphan. "What family?" Olive whispered, her eyes following the fop's progress down the street.

"It's a long story. Look, are you going to pluck this pigeon?" Jade asked, indicating, with a toss of her head, the dandyish noble now moving away from them. "If not, I'd like a crack at him. He looks ripe."

"Wait your turn, girl," Olive replied. "Age before beauty, and I win on both counts," the halfling added with a smirk. She then slipped away from her partner and padded silently down the street after the fop. She swiveled her head nonchalantly to the right and left to make sure she and her target were alone on the street.

He's not only a fat pigeon, Olive thought, once again focusing on the nobleman, but an easy pluck, too. You'd think someone would warn him about letting his purse strings dangle out of his pocket.

Ordinarily Olive would have offered such an easy job to Jade. The human woman was just getting started in business and really depended on it for her living. Olive, on the other hand, didn't need the money; her adventures the previous year had left her almost as wealthy as her wildest dreams. She had to have a closer look at her mark, though. Where have I seen him before? she wondered.

As she closed the gap between herself and her target, her furry feet as silent as cat paws, Olive could hear the fop half singing, half humming softly to himself. Good sense of pitch, Olive critiqued silently, but no sense of rhythm.

"Oh, listen to the story, of the scandal of the wyrms, red Mistinarhm-hmm-hm-hmm, rumored mad and quite infirm—"

Olive stopped dead in her tracks. He's singing one of my songs! she realized. That piece I composed on the spur of the moment to distract the old red dragon and save Alias's life.

A small flower of pride blossomed within Olive, and for half a moment she thought of just walking up, tapping the fop on the shoulder, and introducing herself as the song's creator.

Then she remembered that Jade was watching from the

shadows. If she backed out, the younger thief would never let her hear the end of it. Olive prodded herself forward again. After all, she thought, in a few more years, everyone will be singing my songs.

Now the fop was muttering something to himself and motioning with his arms outward, palms upward. He forced his voice into a lower, more resonant range, added a slight burr, and said, "My Cormytes. My people. Harumph." He cleared his throat and dropped his voice another half-octave. "My Cormytes. My people. As your king, as King Azoun, and as King Azoun the Fourth—" He returned his voice to it's normal pitch and congratulated himself, "Yes, that's it. Haven't lost the old skills."

Olive stopped dead again as the feeling of recognition stopped tickling at the back of her brain and hit her with the force of a runaway cart. Could it really be him, she wondered. Out of all the pigeons in the world, I pick Giogioni Wyvernspur, infamous imitator of royalty?

Olive had sung at the wedding reception of one of Giogioni's relatives. During her performance, the young Wyvernspur noble gave an impromptu imitation of the king of Cormyr, and Alias of Westgate had tried to murder him. It wasn't that Alias had felt any loyalty to the crown, nor had she been offended that the youth had interrupted Olive's singing. With her body controlled by sinister forces desiring Azoun's death, Alias had been unable to stop herself, even though she could see that Giogi was not the king of Cormyr.

He's a little scrawnier and shaggier than he was last spring, but it's Giogioni all right, Olive decided. Not that surprising really. This is Immersea, after all, the Wyvernspurs' home. Poor boy, Olive thought with a sympathetic smile as she resumed stalking her prey. First Alias tried to commit regicide on his decidedly unregal person, and now, here I am, about to steal his purse.

Some people are just born unlucky, the halfling thought with a grin. Giogi halted at the door of the Immer Inn. Olive passed within inches of the young noble, and with a deft snatch she tugged the sack of coins from his cloak pocket. She gave the bag a flamboyant spin by its string as she hurried off. Centrifugal force kept the coins secure and unclinking.

Unaware of his loss, the nobleman pushed open the door to

his favorite tavern and burst inside, crying, "What ho!" There were hearty cries of greetings from within, to which Giogioni responded with the voice of King Azoun IV, "My Cormytes. My people . . ."

Three buildings beyond the Immer Inn, Olive ducked into an alley, circled around the block, and sneaked behind Jade.

Jade turned and smiled, though, before Olive could surprise her. For a human, she had good hearing and excellent night vision. "You hesitated before the snatch, Olive," Jade noted. "Were you having trouble sneaking up on him, or were you having pangs of conscience?" she taunted.

Olive shook her head. "Did you see those boots he was wearing?"

"Those earth-shakers?" Jade asked with a nod.

"I was trying to figure a way to get them off his feet without him noticing. I thought they might just fit your hulking hooves."

"And if they didn't fit my feet," Jade teased back, "I'd give them to you. You could buy an acre of land, roof over them, and live in them."

The two women, halfling and human, leaned against the wall and chuckled softly. Olive spun the stolen purse by its string one last time and tossed it in the air. She caught it casually in one hand. The coins within gave a hearty clink.

"Now, really. Why did you stop like that?" Jade asked earnestly, her green eyes flashing with curiosity.

"I recognized the mark. Giogioni Wyvernspur. Remember the swordswoman I traveled with last year, Alias of Westgate?"

"The one you said looked like me?" Jade asked, stifling a mock yawn. Jade generally found Olive's professional exploits amusing, but she had no interest in people who worked outside her field. Also, Olive's preoccupation with her supposed resemblance to this Alias person disturbed Jade. She sometimes feared Olive liked her for who she looked like, though Jade was careful not to show it.

"That's the one," Olive said with a nod. "Only she doesn't just look like you, girl," she reminded Jade, "she looks just like you. She could be your sister."

Jade shrugged.

The halfling sighed inwardly at her partner's attitude. Olive had hoped all her stories about Alias would somehow magically spark Jade into remembering who she was and where she came from. Each story had failed, though, until there was only one tale left untold, one that Olive could not bring herself to tell her new friend.

It was the tale of how Olive and Alias had discovered twelve duplicates of Alias in the Citadel of White Exile, duplicates not dead but not alive either. When Alias had slain the evil master of the citadel, the duplicates had vanished. Olive had supposed that the images had returned to their elemental origins—until she'd met Jade More, that is.

Jade had to be one of the duplicates, Olive realized. Not only did Jade resemble Alias, but the irrefutable proof was carved into her flesh. On her right arm swirled the remains of the magical brand—a blue river of waves and serpents set there by her creator. Just as with Alias's brand, the creator's sigil was missing from the design—the azure bond of servitude had been broken when Alias had killed the monster. Finally, set at the base of the design on the underside of Jade's wrist was a blue rose, just like the one with which the gods had favored Alias in honor of her love for the music of the Nameless Bard, the man who had designed her.

If it hadn't been for the telltale brands, though, Olive might not have been so sure of Jade's origin. Her personality was very different from Alias's. Granted, Jade exuded the same confidence and competence as the sell-sword, but that was the mark of any experienced adventurer. Jade was relaxed, though, where Alias was driven, humorous where Alias was solemn, and larcenous where Alias was upstanding. Moreover, Jade seemed not to care about her inability to recall much of her own history. Rather, she seemed content practicing her art and getting on with her life without wondering, as Alias had, about her missing memories or true origins.

It was that trait of unreflective self-satisfaction that endeared Jade to the halfling and made it impossible for Olive to tell the human woman that she was a copy of Alias. Olive feared that Jade might lose her joy of life if she learned she'd been created by an evil denizen. She also feared that Jade might hate her for telling the truth.

Jade broke through Olive's reverie. "What's this Alias got to do with JoJo Whatever?" she asked.

"Giogioni Wyvernspur. We've been here all winter, Jade.

You must have heard something about the Wyvernspurs. They founded this town. They're big favorites at court. They're supposed to have some sort of ancient artifact, some spur for riding wyverns, that gives them power beyond mortal men. At least that's the story they tell in the taverns. Anyway, what I was getting at was that Alias once tried to assassinate Giogioni."

"Olive, you really should be more careful who you travel with. These violent types'll get you into trouble."

Olive nodded. "It's true. She did."

"Lucky you've got me to look out for you, now," Jade said in mock earnestness, waving a slender finger.

"And who's going to look out for you?" Olive teased.

"I don't need looking out for. I never get into trouble."

"You will if one of Sudacar's men sees you with Giogioni Wyvernspur's purse hanging from your belt," Olive warned, an impish smile barely contained on her face.

"I don't have—" Jade swung her hand down to her hip. Knotted around her belt were the strings of a yellow velvet bag embroidered with a green "W" and bulging with coins.

Olive grinned. "Don't you think you'd better tuck that out of sight? I'll collect my cut later."

Giving a low whistle of appreciation for the halfling's dexterity and sneakiness, Jade teased the knot out of the purse strings. From her belt she drew a second, smaller pouch. She opened the smaller one and dropped Giogi's larger, unopened purse into it. The money-laden purse disappeared into the pouch without making a bulge.

It was Olive's turn to whistle. "How'd you do that?" she gasped.

"Isn't it great?" Jade said as she knotted the smaller pouch's strings and tucked it back into her belt. "It's a miniature magical bag. You can really stuff it. Want to know the best part? It was a gift."

"Well, well, well. Who gives you such magical gifts, and when are you going to introduce us, girl?" Olive asked.

"Later, Olive. That's what I've been up to for the past few days. He said not to say anything until it was all over, but a girl can't be expected to keep this kind of thing from her best friend, now can she?"

"Of course not," Olive agreed. "What kind of thing?"

"Well, it all started that night you caught cold and went back to your boarding house to rest your voice. After you left, I plucked this servant— Hello, what's this?" Jade interrupted her story to turn her attention to a cloaked figure coming down the street.

It was hard to identify the figure as man or woman, since the cloak fell in voluminous folds about the body and the cloak's hood shadowed the face. From the figure's size and heavy, measured stride, Olive guessed it was a man. An unpleasant man. Jade leaned forward, a feral glint in her eye. Olive tugged her back by the hem of her tunic. "Not this one, girl."

"Olive, what's gotten into you?"

"I don't know. He feels . . . dangerous somehow." A new feeling of familiarity tickled at her brain, but this one was mixed with an inexplicable fear.

Jade's nose twitched with annoyance. "He feels rich to me." She tugged the hem of her tunic out of the halfling's hand. Still, Olive's words had shaken her confidence. She slid the magic pouch out of her belt. "Hold onto this for me, then I'll have nothing to lose if he's ticklish and calls out the watch."

"Nothing but your freedom," Olive sniffed. "Lord Sudacar hand-picked those guards himself. You don't want to take them on, believe me."

Jade grinned. "As long as they don't find that purse on me I can talk my way around them, and if not, my new friend can handle Lord Sudacar."

"So certain, are you?" Olive asked as she slid the pouch inside her vest pocket.

"Got a name for myself in this town now," Jade whispered. Before Olive could make the woman explain what she meant by that, Jade padded off after the new pigeon.

Left in the shadows, Olive sighed. It was hard to get angry with her protegee's exuberance. With all her wealth, Olive might have retired from the business and just stuck with music, but she couldn't bear to see Jade's talent wasted. The woman really needed someone to advise her. She's just going to have to learn the hard way, though, if she won't take my advice, Olive thought.

Silently the halfling critiqued her partner's performance. Jade had a nice natural style of walking after her pigeon, which didn't betray her intent to anyone who might be watching the street. She also had the quietest tread of any woman Olive had ever known, and marks never heard her coming. She had one trait, though, that could betray her.

Jade was tall, even for a human woman. While this would not ordinarily be a great handicap, it was here and now, because Immersea was one of those civilized towns whose cobbled thoroughfares were lit at night with lanterns hung from poles. The illumination posed very little problem for Olive, but Jade's shadow shot out before her whenever she passed a lantern pole, right across the path of whoever she followed.

Olive had warned Jade about that before, but either the human had forgotten or had chosen to ignore the warning. To Olive's relief, though, the pigeon bundled in the heavy cloak seemed oblivious to Jade's presence.

Jade got close enough to run her hands gently through the curves of the pigeons' cloak and then fell back a few steps. She examined whatever it was she had snatched. Olive frowned. First rule is take cover, then examine the booty, the halfling chided silently. Whatever Jade had grabbed excited her greatly, and she broke protocol again by turning around and holding up her prize for Olive to see. It appeared to be a fist-sized crystal of black glass that did not reflect the streetlight. At least Olive presumed it was glass. It didn't seem possible that anyone would carry around a valuable gem that size in an outer pocket.

Olive waved Jade away, afraid that the human thief might forget everything she'd been taught and walk back directly to their shadowy base of operations. Jade pocketed the item and strolled behind the pigeon another several yards—which was even worse. How many times, Olive wondered with a scowl, do I have to tell her never go back for seconds? Why do you always push Tymora's luck, Jade-girl? Still, the street was otherwise empty, save for the two figures.

Luck broke badly for Jade all at once. Whether she had made a noise or the pigeon had spotted the human's shadow, Olive couldn't tell, but something alerted him to the thief's presence. He stopped and turned slowly, the front of his hood fixed in the direction of Jade's approach. As cool and calm as a frozen pond, Jade passed the pigeon, looking for all the Realms as if she were another Cormyte searching for a warm tavern, but

Olive saw the mark rummage through his cloak pockets. The thief's charade had not fooled him.

The human woman had only gotten four paces beyond the cloaked figure when he shouted in a deep, rich voice, "Treacherous witch! You've escaped, and now you try to steal what you have not earned!"

The thief's ice-cool composure cracked. Without looking back, Jade made a dash for the unlit alley. Once the darkness folded around her, no pigeon would ever find her.

Before Jade could reach the alley's shelter, though, the cloaked figure raised an arm and pointed a slender, ringed finger at her fleeing form. A line of emerald light emanated from the finger.

The beam sliced through the darkness, striking Jade squarely in the back. She froze in midstride, her mouth open, but, like some horrible pantomime show, her scream was never heard. The emerald light outlined the woman's body and burst into a searing brilliance. Olive's eyes shut instinctively against the glare.

When she opened them again, the light had died and there was no Jade, only a collection of glittering green dust motes drifting lazily to the ground. Jade More had ceased to exist.

"No!" Olive screeched in horror.

The cloaked figure whirled about at the shout. The hood fell away from his face. Lantern light illuminated his visage: sharp, hawklike features with piercing predatory blue eyes.

Olive recognized the face immediately. She knew the man. Unbidden, warm memories sprang to her mind: fighting beside him at Westgate, learning new songs from him, accepting his silver Harper's pin. Yet, in her fury, her hand reached automatically for her dagger.

"You!" she spat through clenched teeth. Anger and anguish overrode her common sense, and she stepped from the shadows to confront the man, her screams increasing in volume and pitch with every step. "How could you? You killed her! Can't you keep from playing at gods' games? You fiend! You disgust me!"

Apparently unconcerned with the halfling's opinion, the cloaked figure pointed a ringed finger in her direction.

Olive froze, suddenly realizing her own peril. The halfling sprang back into the alley, just as a second lance of green light shot from the man's finger. The ray sizzled into the cobblestones, leaving a pothole where Olive had stood a moment before.

The halfling did not turn to inspect the damage. She dashed down the alley without looking back. She could hear the level, thudding strides of the man behind her, like an inhuman heartbeat.

He doesn't need to dash to keep up with me, Olive realized. Time to disappear into thin air, she told herself, or face the prospect of literally disappearing forever.

She always prepared a bolt hole when she worked the streets. Along the right side of the alley ran the stable where she boarded her pony, Snake Eyes. There was a loose plank in the rear wall that pivoted on a single nail. At the end of the alley Olive dodged right, slid the plank up, and slipped into the stable. She let the plank slide back into place and stood trying to gasp for air as quietly as possible.

The thudding footfalls of her attacker approached her bolt hole, then ceased. Olive held her breath, hoping to determine in which direction he would head. The killer did not move away, however, but stood near the stable wall, muttering to himself. Pick a direction and move away, you murdering fiend, Olive willed silently.

Snake Eyes, her pony, sensed his mistress's anxiety and moved toward her, nuzzling her ear. Irritated, Olive pushed the animal's muzzle away. The pony whickered softly in annoyance. Keep quiet, Snake Eyes, Olive willed, there's a very crazy man outside trying to kill me.

Olive scratched the pony's back, and it grew calm. Olive calmed as well; her breathing became more regular. She tried to deny she'd seen the murderer's face so clearly. He could not be who he looked like. She had to be mistaken.

The halfling's heart skipped a beat as something knocked on the stable wall behind her. Her pursuer had not given up! He was searching for an opening. Olive stumbled backward in panic and knocked over Snake Eyes's water pail. The man outside began mumbling again, and Olive realized with horror that he must be chanting a spell.

Olive pushed on the stall's door, but it was bolted on the other side, and she hadn't the time to use her skills to slip it open. Fortunately the walls to the stall did not go to the ceiling, and, with an effort born of desperation and a great deal of scrabbling, the halfling was able to climb to the top. She dropped down into the stable's center aisle and dashed for the building's main entrance. Snake Eyes whinnied in terror as his mistress pushed on the front door—only to discover that it, too, was bolted from without.

Olive whirled around, looking for another place to hide. A pale glow of yellow light and more muttering emanated from Snake Eyes's stall. He's inside! Olive thought, terror grabbing her insides and giving them a quarter-turn. He disintegrates, detects secret doors, and walks through walls. How can I hide from him?

The muttering stopped, and Snake Eyes's stall door rattled. A series of sharp thumps followed, and the stall door's hinges began to give way.

Stifling a sob, Olive dodged behind a large pile of grain sacks and crouched, cowering miserably in the dark.

There has got to be some way out of this, Olive thought feverishly. I'm too talented to die. Her eyes lit on an empty sack on the ground and she pulled it over her head, hoping to masquerade as a bag of feed. It was only a thirty-pound sack, though, and she was a fifty-pound halfling.

I'll never stuff myself into this, she realized as she heard the sound of screws ripping out of wood. Uttering the word "stuff" and staring at the useless bag, a fresh idea sprang to the halfling's mind.

Jade's magic pouch! she thought. Akabar the mage had once told her a story of a southern prince who kept an elephant in his magic pouch. Jade said the pouch was a miniature one, Olive recalled. I'm hardly an elephant, she reasoned, so the thing ought to accommodate me.

Her sweaty fingers pulled the small sack from her vest. All I need to do is get my head and shoulders in, and the rest should tumble after, she thought. Her hands trembled as she tugged on the purse strings. In her haste, she dropped the bag, and it clunked to the dark floor. Her fingers groped through the straw and grain until they snagged one of the strings. She fumbled with the knot and yanked open the mouth of the sack, ignoring the sound of approaching footsteps rustling through the straw and the light illuminating the wall behind her.

KATE NOVAK and JEFF GRUBB

A queasy feeling came over Olive as she opened the pouch. An ancient, dry voice whispered, "He who steals Giogioni Wyvernspur's purse makes an ass of himself."

Nine Hells, Olive cursed. I've opened the wrong sack. Giogioni's must have fallen out when I dropped Jade's. The fop had a magic mouth cast on his purse to warn him if someone else opened it. Usually, Olive knew, those sorts of spells shouted aloud to embarrass and reveal the thief. Why did this one only whisper? the halfling wondered. Lucky for me it did, but why? Stop thinking about stupid things, girl! she snapped to herself. Don't you realize that you're about to die?

A beam of light passed through a chink in the pile of grain sacks, reminding Olive of her peril. Dropping Giogi's gold, she fumbled again in the darkness for Jade's magic pouch. Her hands felt heavy and awkward, and she was dizzy from the excitement. When she finally touched the pouch it took all her concentration to grasp and lift it.

The footfalls halted right in front of her hiding spot. Automatically Olive slipped Jade's pouch in her vest pocket and pressed her eye to the chink in the sacks, just as a shadow blocked the light streaming through. The halfling looked up, her eyes wide with terror.

Jade's murderer looked down at her with anger. His right hand held a translucent ball of light, which limned his face. Despite the cruel, twisted smile, the sharp features were unmistakable. It is the Nameless Bard, Olive thought with anguish. He used to be a Harper. How could he become a murderer? We were allies and friends. How can he murder me?

"Beshaba's brats," he cursed.

Olive felt much the same way. The goddess of ill luck seemed to be following her tonight. She tried to stand, but her knees were too weak. She looked up, prepared to deliver what she suspected were her last words. She started to say, "You'll never get away with this. Alias will find out, and she'll—" but all that came from her mouth was a hoarse bray.

Nameless turned away from her as if she didn't exist, and began searching the horse stalls.

He had me dead to rights, Olive thought. How could he miss me? She tried to scratch her head in puzzlement, but all she could manage was a twitch of her fuzzy muzzle, a swish of her bushy tail, and a pricking of her long, pointed ears. In panic, the halfling looked down at herself. Instead of her black vest, breeches, and furry feet, Olive discovered she was covered with short brown fur and had four delicate hooves.

Sweet Selune, Olive thought, I'm an ass!

❧ 4 ❧

Night on the Town

The Immer Inn catered to an exclusive clientele. It was patronized by only those travelers and members of Immersea society who were able and willing to pay exorbitant prices for board, drink, and lodging. Giogi, who had on occasion slept off one too many drinks at the inn, could attest that the guest rooms were very nice. As a local resident, though, he was generally more familiar with the board and drink aspects of the inn.

The decor of the dining hall was the inn's biggest attraction, though. The floor was covered with plush carpeting, the walls lined with elaborate tapestries, and the ceiling hung with crystal chandeliers. The room was warm and dry and furnished with tables covered with elegant linen and surrounded by the most comfortably cushioned chairs in Cormyr.

Giogi had patronized the Immer Inn since he'd come of age six years before, but, after being away nearly a year, he thought the dining room seemed as strange as his own home had felt. He thought that perhaps it was because the inn was nearly empty this evening, but his friends were there, and their company was strange, too.

They'd welcomed him back heartily enough, but they had cut short the tale of his travels with their pointed lack of interest, insisted his yellow crystal must be ordinary quartz, and teased him about his boots. In addition, he no longer understood half the things to which they alluded in their conversations and jokes. So, though he was not really keen on it, he'd accepted their offer to play a game of *Elemental Empires.* The game, at least, was familiar.

Giogi began drinking too much and losing lots of money, habits that also were familiar. With a roll of a pair of ivory dice on a felt-covered gaming table, Chancy Lluth had just vanquished all Shaver Cormaeril's troops. In response, Shaver sacrificed all his leaders to protect a hidden card.

"Primary of flames—that's a guarded assassin," Giogi announced when Shaver revealed the card to Chancy. Giogi grinned. One could always count on Shaver to do something vindictive just before he lost.

With a scowl, Chancy tossed one of his knights into the discard pile. Shaver surrendered his unused cards to Chancy and signaled a servant to bring him a fresh drink.

Shaver drew a priest from Chancy's unused cards to replace his murdered knight.

"How many cards do you want, Giogi?" Lambsie Danae asked. Lambsie had folded much earlier, as usual, unwilling to risk as much money as the others. Lambsie's father, while one of the wealthiest farmers in Immersea, kept Lambsie on a strict gambling allowance, and Lambsie never exceeded his limit.

Giogi stared at the crystal chandelier hanging over the game table and tried to calculate the odds of his drawing a card he could use. His element was earth, and there weren't too many stone cards left in the deck. Nor were there too many major cards he could use without the minor stone suit cards to act as armies to protect them. Each unused card he held doubled the price of a new card, but he could not afford to discard those he held—they were mostly wave cards, which Chancy, whose element was water, would snatch up and use against him.

"First card will cost you sixty-four, and if you can't play it, the second one will cost a hundred twenty-eight," Lambsie said.

"I can multiply by two, thank you, Lambsie," Giogi said with an insulted sniff, though after the last brandy he'd downed, he probably couldn't.

Giogi counted out sixty-four points' worth of his yellow scoring sticks. Lambsie dealt him a card, a jester—nearly useless, but playable. Giogi turned it over and sifted it into his single army line.

"You've got a two-strength army stacked with a sorceress, a bard, and a jester, Giogi," Chancy said. "Are they leading your troops or entertaining them?"

Ignoring Chancy's taunt, Giogi paid another sixty-four points. "Another card, please," he asked Lambsie.

Lambsie dealt him a four of winds, unplayable, but safe to discard, except, once he discarded, Giogi could buy no more cards. He slid the card into his unused pile. "One more," he said sliding one hundred twenty-eight points' worth of sticks across the table to Lambsie.

Lambsie dealt him a third card.

Giogi drew a priest out from his unused stack and played it with the new card.

"The moon!" Shaver exclaimed. "How lucky can you get?"

"You know what they say," Lambsie said, "Tymora looks out for fools."

"The tide goes out, wave troops retreat," Giogi said.

Visibly annoyed, Chancy picked all his minor Talis cards off the table and slipped them into his unused stack of cards.

"I think my leaders will challenge yours to personal combat," Giogi said. "My sorceress against your priest and my rogue against your warrior."

"That doesn't leave anyone to command your troops," Chancy pointed out.

"Jesters can command troops when the moon is in play," Giogi said.

"That's right," Lambsie agreed.

Confronted with the possibility of losing big, Chancy asked. "What kind of surrender terms are you offering?" he asked.

"Half your debt," Giogi offered magnanimously.

"Accepted," Chancy said, offering his knight and priest to Giogi.

"Earth wins," Shaver declared. "You let him off too easy, Giogi."

"It's getting late," Giogi said. "I have to be going."

"So soon?"

Giogi nodded, signaling a servant for his check.

His friends counted up their scoring sticks. Lambsie paid out his eight silver pieces' worth of debt while Shaver and Chancy wrote out IOUs. Shaver would be good for his before a day had passed. As head of the second noble family in Immersea, Shaver's father was always keen to prove to any Wyvernspur that the Cormaerils had no problem meeting their obligations. It would take some time before he could wheedle Chancy's money out of him, though. Chancy's father, like Lambsie's was a very wealthy farmer, as well as a successful merchant. He lavished his money on Chancy, but Chancy had more gambling debts than Cormyr had trees, or so people said.

Bottles, the inn's owner, came up to their table and presented the tab without a word. People didn't generally argue over a check presented by Bottles. The retired soldier's massive physique discouraged the timid, and his gruff, unsophisticated manner indicated to his haughtiest customers that he was not a man one could intimidate.

Giogi glanced at the check for the total and reached for his purse. Then he began patting down his pockets frantically while Bottles cleared away their glasses.

Chancy smacked him on the back and asked, "Something wrong, Giogi?"

Giogi turned to his drinking buddies and muttered, "I seem to have mislaid my purse."

"Oh, dear. We'll have to call out the sheriff now," Shaver announced in a deadpan voice. "Bottles doesn't take anyone's chits. Cash and carry only."

Giogi swallowed hard. When Bottles had married the inn's previous owner's widow, the inn had been debt-ridden. The business thrived under Bottles's management, not just because he kept the same staff as had his predecessor, but because he had a shrewd head for business—in other words—no credit. His policy was renowned throughout Immersea, as were the two youths he kept on retainer for dealing with deadbeats and other heavy lifting.

The young Wyvernspur rummaged through his pockets again, then checked his boots for good measure. He pulled out the yellow crystal, which glittered in the chandelier light.

It would be impossibly hard to let the stone out of his hand, let alone out of his sight, but he had announced he was hosting the evening's revelries, and the humiliation of reneging on friends would be even more unbearable.

Giogi laid the crystal on the table. "Will you take this as collateral, Bottles? I haven't had it appraised, but I'm sure it's worth a great deal. It is to me, anyway. I'll ransom it back tomorrow."

"No, Bottles," Lambsie cried, "hold out for those boots. They're the most comfortable pair in the Realms."

Giogi flushed. Why doesn't anyone like these boots? he wondered. They're so sensible.

"Already got a pair of them kind," Bottles said.

Shaver, Lambsie, and Chancy broke into laughter.

Bottles eyed the three "gentlemen" with disdain. He pushed the yellow crystal away. "Keep your stone, milord. Your credit's good here."

"Whoa!" Shaver exclaimed. "Is that the breaking of a tradition I hear?"

"How come my credit isn't good here?" Chancy demanded.

"'E feels bad about it. You don't," Bottles replied.

Giogi smiled gratefully. "Thanks, awfully, Bottles. I'll have Thomas stop by to settle up first thing in the morning."

"See that you do," Bottles said, and walked off.

"First thing in the morning for Giogi, isn't that somewhere around noon?" Shaver joked.

"For your information," Giogi replied with a haughty tone, too inebriated to consider what he was saying, "I'll be up before the crack of dawn tomorrow, crawling through the family crypt."

"Whatever for?" Chancy asked.

"Someone's stole the spur and he's trapped down there," Giogi explained in a conspiratorial whisper. "Or not," he added, still confused by Uncle Drone's mysterious confidence to the contrary.

"Not really?" Shaver gasped.

Lambsie and Chancy looked up with horror.

Too late Giogi recalled that Aunt Dorath hadn't wanted outsiders to know about the theft.

"But the spur's supposed to ensure your family's success," Chancy said.

"No," Shaver corrected, "his family succession. Right, Giogi?"

"That's just a superstition. Look, do you think you might keep this between the four of us?" Giogi asked. "It's best if it doesn't get around."

"Of course," Shaver said. Lambsie and Chancy nodded in agreement.

Looking at his friends' faces, Giogi did not feel reassured. They were all too blank. One of Uncle Drone's little sayings popped into his head: Nothing flutters so frantically when caged like a secret, nor flies so fast when released.

Giogi didn't like to imagine Aunt Dorath's reaction if, when she sat down to breakfast tomorrow, she were to find a letter of condolence from Lady Dina Cormaeril, Shaver's mother. At least I'll be in the catacombs by then, Giogi thought. Maybe Aunt Dorath will have calmed down by the time I come out. No, he realized, Aunt Dorath could stew for hours and still be boiling mad by sunset.

With a feeling of doom, Giogi took leave of his friends and wove his way out of the Immer Inn. He headed west, toward the Wyvernwater. "A bracing sea breeze would fit the bill," he said aloud, though there was no one present to hear him, nor did it matter to him at that moment that the Wyvernwater was a freshwater lake, not a salty sea.

He grew less anxious walking in the fresh, cold air, and by the time he'd turned south on the main road, he'd reasoned himself out of his fear. If Aunt Dorath finds out I babbled about the theft, he thought, I can always go abroad again. Maybe, though, if I find the spur, she'll forgive me and I can stay home.

A stiff gust of wind off the lake blew right through his cloak. He shivered and suddenly felt very tired. What am I doing walking around in this cold? I could be home sleeping in my warm bed.

He quickened his stride, but before he turned down the road leading home he remembered the duties facing him in the morning. His desire to sleep vanished, and he slowed his pace. If he stayed awake, it would be hours before he had to go into the crypt with Freffie and Steele and face the guardian.

Somewhere nearby Giogi heard the strumming of a yarting and the jangle of a tantan. He turned toward the music to find the door to the Five Fine Fish standing open as a crowd of travelers squeezed its way in.

"Sudacar," Giogi whispered, suddenly remembering the local lord's invitation to stop by the Fish to talk about Cole.

The Fish was renowned for its ale and very popular as a meeting place among adventurers who passed through Immersea. Giogi's friends all patronized the Immer Inn, so Giogi, who had never felt very comfortable among strangers, had not been in the Five Fine Fish very often. It would be full of strangers tonight, but Sudacar, while not exactly a friend, could hardly be considered a stranger—not if he knew things about Cole that Uncle Drone hadn't even spoken of.

Determined to learn more about his father's adventuring life, Giogi strode purposefully toward the inn. He slipped through the front door behind the last of the travelers and squeezed his way past them into the common room.

The room was packed with people. Five musicians in the corner struck up a reel, and several people began dancing on the wooden floor. The dancers' shadows swayed against the wall whenever someone bumped into one of the oil lamps hanging from the low ceilings. The tables and chairs of the Fish's common room were built for durability rather than style, not carved, but hewn, and polished, not with wax, but by generations of oily hands and elbows. Lem, the inn's owner, was tapping a fresh keg of ale, banging the spigot into the barrel in time to the music. He looked up at Giogi and gave him a wink.

Giogi searched the room for Sudacar while people coming in and out jostled him. Finally the young noble spotted the local lord in a corner opposite the musicians. He was seated with a few members of the town guard and some adventurers Giogi did not recognize. Sudacar rose to greet one of the travelers who'd just come in—a wool merchant. The two men gave each other a hearty handshake. Sudacar offered the newcomer a seat and signaled for more drinks before sitting back down himself.

Giogi suddenly felt very nervous. True, Sudacar had invited him, but the local lord was obviously very busy with friends and associates. Uncertain as to what sort of reception Sudacar would have for him, Giogi turned about and left the inn.

Once outside again, Giogi felt aimless. He meandered toward the market green with his hands stuffed deep in his cloak pockets and his head tilted back toward the stars. At the near end of the green stood a statue of Azoun III, grandfather of the present king. The stone monarch sat on a granite stallion frozen in the act of rearing and trampling rock-carved bandits. Giogi leaned against a stone bandit and sighed loudly.

"This was not the homecoming I expected," he explained to the bandit.

The wind, chill and damp, blew from the lake. Giogi sighed again and watched the ghosts of his breath drift east toward his own home.

"The house felt like a tomb when I got in last night," he told the bandit. "I have to spend my second day back, tomorrow, visiting the family crypt. Shaver says I missed the best summer regatta in ten years. His yacht, *The Dancing Girl*, came in second against four hundred-to-one odds. And Chancy says that his sister, Minda, did not wait for me. She married Darol Harmon, from over in Arabel. Not that there was anything official between us, mind you. I thought we had an understanding, but I guess a year is a long time for a girl to wait."

Giogi studied the bandit's grimace. "I suppose, though, that you have your own troubles."

The bandit did not keep up his end of the conversation, so Giogi continued. "Everyone laughs at my boots, and no one wants to listen to the tale of my travels. I'll admit, there aren't any princes or elves or casts of thousands in it, but it does have a whopping big dragon, and an evil sorceress, and a lovely, but quite mad, lady sell-sword. Wait. There was one person who was interested," Giogi amended. "Gaylyn, Freffie's wife. Nice girl, and pretty, too. Olive Ruskettle, the renowned bard, wrote a song in honor of their wedding—Freffie and Gaylyn's wedding, that is. Now, how did it go?"

Giogi began singing snatches of the song: "Something, something, syncopated breath. Something, something, love transcends even death."

"Giogioni!"

Giogi was so startled, he slid off the stone bandit.

Samtavan Sudacar had to grin at the sight of the young nobleman lying beneath the hooves of the stone monarch's stallion as if he were being trampled with the bandits about him. "That's no sort of company for you to keep, boy," Sudacar said, offering him a hand up.

Giogi accepted the assistance gratefully, and as Sudacar hefted him to his feet, he could easily imagine the well-muscled arms slaying giants. "What are you doing here?" Giogi asked.

Sudacar laughed. "Coming to fetch you. Lem said you came in but left. Couldn't find me in the crush, eh?"

Giogi nodded, then shook his head. It would be too difficult to explain that he was afraid he wouldn't be welcome.

"I came out to bring you back inside, unless you're too busy rendering assistance to Azoun's granddad. Getting to be a habit with you, I hear."

"What?" Giogi asked, wondering if Sudacar meant that rumors abounded that he drank heavily and often collapsed beneath town monuments.

"Lending the royal family a hand. Someone told me tonight you weren't just abroad, you were on a mission south for His Highness."

"Oh, that," Giogi replied. "It wasn't much, really. Just a messenger job."

Sudacar chuckled at the nobleman's modesty. "You'll have to

tell us all about it inside. If you're not too hoarse or too tired to tell it again."

Giogi grinned. Someone wanted to hear his story. He stood up straighter. "Love to oblige."

The two men walked toward the Five Fine Fish, but just outside, Giogi hesitated. "I just remembered. I, uh, seem to have mislaid my purse."

Sudacar looked at the nobleman darkly. "You, too, eh? A lot of that going around lately. Seems we have a new element in town. I've got to have Culspiir look into it. Don't worry. Tonight you're in my hands. We've got to raise that glass in honor of your father."

Entering the Fish with Sudacar was very different from entering it alone. Sudacar knew everyone, and everyone in turn seemed to know and like Sudacar. The crowd parted for him. He had the best table in the house. He sat Giogi down at his right-hand side and introduced him around as Cole Wyvernspur's son. Many of the older merchants and their even older adventurer bodyguards nodded in approval. Giogi saw some of the younger adventurers whisper a question to their elders, and when the veterans whispered back the answer, the younger adventurers turned friendly smiles on the nobleman.

As the tavernkeeper set fresh mugs of ale down in front of Giogi and Sudacar, the local lord asked, "Lem, Mistress Ruskettle come in yet?"

"Not yet," Lem replied. "Odd thing. You know, usually you could set the town clock by her stomach."

"I'm looking for that woman she goes around with, Jade More."

"So's Rusketle. Been asking all week if anyone's seen her."

Sudacar knitted his brow. "Jade leave town?"

Lem shook his head uncertainly. "Her packs are still up in her room, not stuffed with rags, either. I checked. Full of nice clothes, and plenty of money. I'm holding it for her return."

"Business must be good, whatever it is she's in."

"Aye," Lem agreed with a smirk.

When Lem had left their side, Sudacar gave a toast, "To Cole Wyvernspur, a brave adventurer."

Giogi drank to his father, but his curiosity was suddenly running in another direction. "This Mistress Ruskettle," he said. "Is she Olive Ruskettle, the bard?"

"Yes. She's been wintering here. You know about her?" Sudacar asked.

"She sang at Freffie's—um—Lord Frefford's wedding to Gaylyn. In a way, she's responsible for my being sent on my mission for the king."

"Oh?" Sudacar said encouragingly.

"She had this bodyguard with her, named Alias, you see. Very pretty but quite mad. Alias, that is."

"Yes, Ruskettle's told us all about her. Wait a minute!" Sudacar said, his eyes sparkling with amusement. "Are you the noble whom Alias attacked after doing an impression of Azoun?"

Giogi nodded. "Guilty as charged," he admitted, relieved to see that Sudacar did not seem to be offended that he'd done an impression of His Highness. "Anyway," Giogi continued, "on my way home after the wedding, I was waylaid by this dragon who ate my horse—a monstrous, ancient red beast—the dragon, that is, not my horse. A good horse, too. Then this dragon sent me to His Majesty with the offer that she would leave the country if he could tell her where Alias was."

Sudacar's brow furrowed. He didn't like the idea of making deals with evil red dragons. "What did His Majesty do?"

"His Majesty didn't want to have anything to do with it, but Vangy told him that Alias could be an assassin and convinced him to settle with the dragon."

"Sounds like Vangerdahast," Sudacar muttered.

"Yes," Giogi agreed, taking a sip from his mug. The young Wyvernspur had no love for the court wizard, who was an old chum of Aunt Dorath's. In his few interviews with the wizard, Giogi felt more than a little intimidated by the man's magic powers and overweening certainty that he was always right.

"Still," Sudacar sighed, "the old mage keeps our king safe, and for that we should be grateful. The king's health," he added, raising his mug.

"Long live the king," Giogi agreed, raising his drink.

They both took a pull on their ale and sat quietly as it ran down their throats.

"So why did you travel to Westgate?" Sudacar asked.

"Well, Vangy never really did know exactly where this Alias was. Seems she couldn't be magically detected, but she was supposed to come from Westgate. So His Majesty sent me down there to inquire of what the authorities knew about her, and to see if she showed up there. She did. I spotted her outside the city. I spent the rest of the season in Westgate trying to find her again, or some information about her, without luck. I wintered there and came back as soon as a safe sea crossing could be made."

"According to Ruskettle, Alias is up in Shadowdale now," Sudacar said.

"Really? Maybe I ought to bop off a letter to His Majesty about that," Giogi said.

"Let me handle it. According to Ruskettle, Alias was working for Elminster. Vangy ought to know that before he tries making any more trouble for the lady."

Giogi grinned. He wondered if a wizard as powerful as Elminster could make Vangerdahast as nervous as Vangerdahast made him.

"So how'd you like Westgate? I noticed you got yourself a pair of clodders. Won't get a better pair of boots anywhere in the Realms, not even in Waterdeep."

"Got one of these, too," Giogi said, pulling out the yellow crystal from the top of his boot.

Sudacar sat up more attentively. "Boy, where did you get that?" he asked.

"Found it lying in the mud just outside Westgate."

"Found it lying—" Sudacar's words halted. He looked flabbergasted. "Boy, that's a finder's stone. I know, because Elminster himself loaned me one once."

"What's a finder's stone?"

"It's a magic crystal. It helps the lost find their way."

"But I'm not lost," Giogi said.

Sudacar gave the nobleman a queer look. "Maybe you better hang onto it, just in case."

"Oh, I intend to. I like it. It makes me—this is going to sound silly—"

"It makes you feel happy," Sudacar said.

"Yes. How'd you—oh, right, you said you had one once." Giogi tucked the crystal back into his boot.

"Tell me more about Westgate. Things are shaking down there, I hear."

Giogi nodded. "A dead dragon fell on their city just before I arrived, followed by an earthquake the day after. Then there was a power struggle going on for the property and business of some sorceress and her allies. A woman named Cassana, the Followers of Moander, and the Fire Knives all were missing after the earthquake."

"The Fire Knives. Now that is good news. I remember the year His Majesty broke their charter for the murder of that scullery maid. Ever since Azoun sent the thugs packing they've been a threat to him. May they stay missing," he toasted and took another swig of ale.

Giogi did likewise. The warmth of the ale augmented the warm, comfortable feeling he had in Sudacar's company.

Giogi and Sudacar drank and compared stories about Westgate until Lem stood over them and coughed politely. Giogi looked up and realized that the other tables and booths were empty, and Lem's waiters were stacking the chairs and benches.

The two noblemen were the last customers in the tavern, and Giogi suspected Lem had stayed open well after hours just to oblige Sudacar. Sudacar left a small pile of gold lions on the table, stood, and led the way to the door. Giogi stumbled after him.

Many of the streetlamps had burned all their day's oil and expired or been blown out by the wind, but the waxing moon gave the two men plenty of light to see their way. They crossed the market green together and halted beneath the statue of "Azoun's Triumph."

"You know," Giogi said, "you let me babble on so long, you never had a chance to tell me about my father."

Sudacar grinned. "It's part of my fiendish plot. Now you have to visit me another night," he said.

"I'd like that," Giogi said.

"We'll keep an eye out for your purse, too. You really ought to get yourself an enchanted one, you know. The kind that makes some noise if it's touched by someone else."

"It *was* enchanted. Trouble was, I kept leaving it places, so whenever the servants found it anywhere and touched it, there was a big fuss. Uncle Drone fixed it so it would do something only if someone besides myself actually opened it."

"What was it supposed to do?"

"I think Uncle Drone said it would make a fool or something out of the thief."

"Well, I'll tell my men to keep an eye out for any fools."

Giogi giggled. "I'd hate to end up arrested for the theft of my own purse."

Sudacar gave a disapproving frown and pointed a finger at Giogi. "You shouldn't put yourself down like that, boy. His Majesty wouldn't have entrusted you on a mission for the crown if you weren't competent. As a matter of fact, now that you and your cousins are grown, Azoun will soon be relying on the services of all three of you, just as he did with your father and his cousins. Once you get this spur nonsense cleared up, it'll be time for you to take up the responsibility of nobility—serving your king."

"Me?" Giogi gasped.

"You," Sudacar replied, chuckling at the shocked expression on the young man's face.

Giogi had assumed he'd only been sent to find Alias in Westgate because he would recognize the sell-sword. It had never occurred to him that the king would ever require him on other missions. Apparently, finding the spur was no guarantee that his life would return to normal—the way it had been before last spring. "Wait a minute. How'd you know about the spur?" Giogi asked Sudacar. "You said Aunt Dorath wouldn't tell you what was going on?"

"I have my sources," Sudacar replied with a wink. "It's getting late. Time to go." He gave Giogi a pat on the back and strode south from the market square toward Redstone Manor. He called out, "Good night, Giogioni," before he disappeared into the darkness.

Automatically Giogi called back, "Good night, Sudacar." Sudacar had left him feeling bemused and astonished, but not in the least bit anxious. He headed west down the side street that led to his townhouse.

Tired and inebriated, the nobleman did not remember Drone's warning that his life might "just possibly" be in danger. Nor did he notice the sound of clattering hooves on the paving stones made by the angry beast following him.

❦ 5 ❦

Mistaken Identities

After failing to recognize Olive in her transmuted condition, Nameless continued his inspection of the stable. He searched methodically in grim silence, slamming each stall door a little harder than the last. Olive could sense the anger and frustration building in him. Pulling a needle-thin dagger from his belt, he jabbed it into any bag of grain or stack of hay large enough to hide a halfling.

Finally, when Olive began trembling at the thought that he might study her bestial form more carefully and realize he had her at his mercy, she heard the sound of someone unbolting the stable's front door. Nameless cursed and began muttering another spell.

The stable door opened, and a young woman carrying a lantern strode in. Olive recognized her as Lizzy Thorpe, the stable's owner. Whether Lizzy was aroused by the noise or was just checking on the animals wasn't clear, but when she spotted the cloaked figure in her stable without permission, she gave a shout. The cloaked figure vanished. Lizzy ran out, still shouting for help.

Olive noticed a peculiar churning of straw where Nameless had stood, and it moved down the center aisle to the stable's front door. Olive also sensed the floorboards shift slightly and heard them creak from the weight of a human.

He's gone invisible, she realized, but at least he's leaving.

Lizzy returned less than a minute later with two of the night watch. "He was standing right there when I came in," she told them, pointing to where the cloaked figure had turned invisible. Lizzy and the watchmen began to search the barn as methodically as Nameless had, though without his intense desperation.

Still hiding behind the sacks of grain, Olive heard Lizzy cry out, "Look what he's done to my wall. Left a bloody huge hole in it, big enough to ride a paladin's mount through!"

The two guards made their way back to Snake Eyes's stall.

"Wood's just vanished, edges left smooth as butter cut with a hot knife," the older night watchman noted. "Looks like mage work to me. If it is magic, it'll fade, and you'll get your wall back, probably in an hour or two."

"You're lucky this pony had the good sense to stay put," the other watchman said. "Any horses missing, Lizzy?"

Before Lizzy noticed the addition of one small donkey to her stable, Olive snatched up Giogioni Wyvernspur's purse in her teeth and slipped quietly out the open stable door.

The halfling waited what seemed an eternity for Giogi to come out of the Immer Inn. Olive wondered if she were succeeding at hiding in shadows in her new four-legged configuration or if the people passing by simply weren't keen on donkey-snaring this late at night. Whichever was the case, no one approached her.

For a while she savored the irony that the noble's cursed purse had saved her life, but as the hour grew later and the night colder, she became annoyed. Now that she was no longer in immediate danger, her situation appalled her. By the time the young Wyvernspur finally emerged from the Immer Inn and wobbled down the street, she slunk after him, feeling considerable animosity.

She realized, however, that the streets were too open for a confrontation and that she would have to follow him home. Unfortunately, Giogi seemed to have no interest in going back. He wandered along the lakefront. Then the sound of music from the Five Fine Fish attracted his attention. He hurried over to the inn and disappeared inside.

Olive imagined with longing the fish and chips and ale the Fish served, but apparently the same things did not interest Giogi. He came out only a few minutes later and wandered over to the market green and began talking to one of the stone bandits.

That's just great, Olive thought sarcastically. My fate is in the hands of a man who talks to statues. She hung back in the shadows, and she was glad she had, for just as the fop began serenading the statue—with another one of her compositions—Samtavan Sudacar came out from the Fish and called out to him.

The local lord had never shown Olive anything but the utmost courtesy when she entertained in the Fish. There was something about Sudacar's thoughtful gaze, though, that convinced Olive he suspected her of something. It wouldn't do to be seen holding Giogi's purse in her teeth, even if she were an ass.

Sudacar talked Giogi into re-entering the Fish, and Olive was forced to wait for a second eternity before they came out again. They were the last patrons to leave the inn, and Lem locked the door behind them when they left. The moon had begun its descent as they crossed the market square to the statue of Azoun III. They lingered, chatting, beside the stone carving. Olive considered creeping closer to eavesdrop on their conversation, but she was still wary of Sudacar. Finally, the local lord left Giogi and strolled south.

Giogi watched Sudacar walk away, then headed west. Olive, her spirit by now burning with a righteous wrath, trotted after the long-legged Cormyte, her hooves clattering on the cobblestones. She no longer bothered to avoid his detection. She was determined to give the Immersea fop a healthy piece of her mind. "Only an irresponsible, thoughtless fool," she planned to say, "would leave a cursed purse lying in the gutter where it would be found by some poor, defenseless halfling," namely herself. First, though, she had to get him to change her back into the lovely, talented halfling she'd been born and bred to be.

Giogi stopped in front of a large, well-kept townhouse surrounded by a high iron fence. The noble hummed to himself as he fumbled with the gate latch and pushed his way into the front yard. Before the gate could close, Olive nudged her way through, right behind the oblivious Giogioni. The gate swung shut behind her, its latch engaging with a sharp clang.

Olive found herself in a small, formal garden. Straw mulch covered the square, raised beds and dormant vine stalks clung to wooden trellises along the path to the front door. The sight of the dead garden in the moonlight gave Olive the shivers.

It's time, she decided, to announce myself.

Olive opened her mouth so Giogi's sack of coins fell with a clink, and she gave a loud, annoyed bray.

Giogi whirled around with a shriek of terror. Upon spotting the beast that had been stalking him, though, he gave a cry of delight.

"What an adorable burro," he said with a smile. He put his hand out to pet her, but Olive backed out of reach. With a forefoot, she kicked Giogi's purse forward.

"What's this?" Giogi bent over. "My purse!" he cried, picking it up and brushing the dirt off it. "It wasn't stolen at all. It must have fallen out of my pocket before I even got to the street." Giogi pocketed the sack of coins, once more leaving the strings dangling in full view.

No! Olive thought with alarm. I just brought it to you, you idiot. You have to change me back to a halfling. She tried to snatch at the purse strings with her teeth, but Giogi gave her a swat on the muzzle, and she missed.

"Silly creature. Mustn't chew on them," he said tucking the strings all the way into his cloak pocket. "They're not good for you, you know. Now, what are you doing roaming loose in my garden? Hmm?"

Olive glared at the nobleman in frustration.

"Thomas must have had a reason for procuring you," Giogi said. "Not the sentimental type, ol' Thomas. Very responsible. Always spends my money wisely."

Olive tried to protest that Thomas had not bought her, but, of course, she could only bray angrily. This she did, at a volume that would put a banshee to shame.

"Shh. You'll wake the neighbors. Thomas wouldn't have left you untied. He's responsible, you know. You must have chewed through the rope, eh? Maybe we'd better tuck you in the carriage house." With those words, he unclipped the buckle fastening his belt and slid his belt from his waist with a whiplike snap.

Olive's eyes widened, and she backed away from the nobleman. She brayed now with fear. Her tail and hindquarters banged against the iron gate, which rattled but remained securely fastened, blocking her escape. She dodged to the right, but before she could maneuver around him, Giogi had fashioned his belt into a noose and slipped it neatly over her head.

Olive jumped away, hoping to jerk the noose free of Giogi's grip, but the noble's grasp was too firm. The sudden choking sensation broke her spirit immediately.

This had been the worst night of her life. Watching her best friend murdered had been awful. Recognizing the murderer had been a shock. Fleeing for her life had been terrifying. Being mistaken for a beast was completely humiliating. More miserable than she'd ever been in her life, Olive walked docilely alongside Giogi as he led her to the carriage house.

"Daisyeye," Giogi called out softly as he opened the smaller of the carriage house's two doors and led Olive inside. "I've brought you some company, Daisyeye."

Giogi lit an oil lamp beside the door. In the light, the carriage house looked warm and cheery. From her burro's-eye-view, Olive could see a buggy painted vibrant yellow and green and two horse stalls, one occupied by a chestnut mare.

The other stall was empty, and Giogi led Olive into it. He fussed about her—the perfect host trying to make his guest comfortable. Olive realized he meant well, but she could have wished he weren't trying so much in his drunken state. He laid only half the amount of bedding straw she needed, but left her with twice as much hay as a horse could eat in a day and sloshed more water on the floor than in her water trough. Ignoring the hay, Olive dipped her muzzle in the water and gulped thirstily, thinking how much she really needed something stronger to drink. When she finally came up for air, her gaze wandered idly around the walls of her stall.

Hanging on the outer wall was a portrait of a man with bird-like features, silky black hair, and piercing blue eyes. His powerful hands rested on a seven-stringed yarting. A silver brooch glistened on his tabard. The eyes in the portrait seemed to stare right at Olive, boring into her soul, so that she imagined the man was watching her, undeceived by her magical disguise. Instinctively Olive backed away, braying with alarm.

Giogi looked up at the wall where the burro's gaze was fixed. He seemed startled by the portrait, too, for a moment, at least. Then he laughed, reached up, and took the painting down.

"Nothing to worry about," he murmured soothingly. "Look, silly," he said, holding the frame up to her muzzle so she could sniff at the painting. "It's only the picture of some old, dead ancestor. Completely harmless."

Wrong, Olive thought. He's not dead, and he's not just some old ancestor, and he's not harmless. He's the Nameless Bard, and he's a mad murderer.

"His name should be on the back somewhere," Giogi muttered, searching the canvas. "How odd. The name's been blotted out."

Naturally, Olive thought. The Harpers went to a great deal of trouble wiping his name from the Realms.

"Doesn't matter," Giogi said. "He could be any Wyvernspur. Wyvernspurs all look alike. Except me, of course. I take after my mother, you see."

Giogi hung the picture back up and offered Olive a handful of oats, sweetened with molasses, from a wooden bucket. "See what I have? Num-nums," he said.

The halfling-turned-burro declined to even sniff at the grain.

"Not hungry, eh? Well, we'll leave them for you as a midnight snack, in case you get peckish."

Giogi dumped the oats back into the bucket and left it against the wall. "Nighty night," he said, scratching Olive between her ears before she had a chance to dodge away. He slipped his belt off her and left the stall, closing and latching its door behind him. Before he left the stable, he blew out the lamp.

Left alone in the dark, Olive tried to make plans. I have to think of a way to get out of here, she thought. I have to get someone to turn me back the way I belong. I have to avenge Jade's death. All she could think about, though, was Jade.

Olive had benefited from her association with Jade, as with no other person. Of course, there had been the practical benefits. Like Alias, Jade could not be detected magically, and this protection extended to her companions. Jade had also been an appreciative audience for all Olive's songs—unlike Alias, whose habit of performing better songs had constantly pricked Olive's jealousy. Most importantly, though, Jade had simply been the best friend Olive had ever had.

Jade had been a perfect companion. She had enjoyed all the things Olive did: practicing her craft, celebrating with food and drink, gossiping, traveling—but only in fair weather—and meeting new people. Olive had once wondered if, instead of getting a spirit and soul from a paladin, as Alias had, Jade's spirit and soul had been cleft from the halfling's own. That would have explained why Olive felt so drawn to the human. Whether it was true or not, Olive knew for a fact that the last six days without Jade had been the loneliest she could recall in her lifetime.

Not only had she missed the woman, but secretly she'd been worried sick about Jade. Olive had been able to think of only one reason why Jade would disappear, but she could hardly go up to Lord Sudacar and ask, "Have you arrested my friend Jade for picking someone's pocket?" It certainly wouldn't have helped Jade any. Olive had searched through Immersea as subtly as she could. She didn't want Jade to think she kept tabs on her, but the halfling had felt responsible for the human.

She'd felt that way ever since she'd spotted Jade in the streets of Arabel—picking the pocket of a purple dragoon. Jade's technique had been superb, but, of course, purple dragoons were never paid in anything but royal script, which civilians were not allowed to have. If someone doesn't warn her about that, Olive had thought, she'll end up a bonded servant, and those talented fingers will be wasted scrubbing floors.

Right then Olive had realized she was the perfect candidate to look after the girl, train her, and offer her guidance, just as Alias had a saurial paladin to keep her safe. Who better, Olive had thought, than I? Not only do I know more about her than she probably knows about herself, but we share the same craft.

Nonetheless, Olive had been surprised at how easily Jade had accepted her offer to become her apprentice, how quickly Jade had come to depend on her, and how completely the human had trusted her. Because of all this, Olive had come to think of Jade as a daughter. An overgrown daughter, but a beloved daughter.

When Jade had said she'd been visiting family, Olive had felt an unreasonable flare of jealousy. Now she wondered angrily, Who was this phony family member who'd kept her Jade away for six days, tempting her with magic sacks and the gods knew what else? A fat lot of good he'd been to her when she'd been murdered on the street.

A fat lot of good you'd been to her, Olive derided herself. You failed her. You knew there was something evil about the mark she went after. Why didn't you stop her? If you'd insisted harder, she would have stayed. Why did you let her go? You'll never see her again, now. Never, ever.

Unable to weep in her burro body, Olive found herself banging her head against the stall door in a mindless fury. Daisyeye nickered nervously, upset by the noise Olive made.

With some effort, Olive controlled herself. She took a deep breath and another drink of water.

Its not all my fault, she thought with a flash of anger. Nameless killed her, though why he should murder one of Alias's copies is a mystery. Face it, Olive-girl, she told herself, he's never been completely sane. He could have a reason, albeit a twisted one.

The first thing that had occurred to her, because of what Nameless had said to Jade on the street, was that he'd judged Jade to be unfit because she was a thief, and that he'd taken it upon himself to destroy her because he'd been partly responsible for creating her.

"You've escaped," he'd said to Jade. Had he kept her prisoner for the past six days? Was that what Jade had meant when she said she'd been "visiting family"? In a way, Nameless was kin to Jade. He thought of himself as Alias's father, and Alias was Jade's older sister, sort of. Who else could she have meant?

Of course! Olive thought with a start. She could have meant one of Nameless's relatives! If the portrait on the wall of Giogi's carriage house was Nameless, as Olive was sure it was, and if, as Giogi claimed, the man in the portrait was some ancestor, then Nameless was a Wyvernspur, and Jade would be kin to all the Wyvernspurs, at least in as much as she was kin to Nameless.

Even better than that, though, was the inevitable conclusion that if, as Giogi also claimed, the portrait could have been of any Wyvernspur, since they all looked alike, then Jade's murderer might not have been Nameless at all, but some other Wyvernspur.

With the realization that Nameless wasn't her only suspect, a feeling of relief swept over Olive. She hadn't wanted to believe he would murder anyone. From the day she'd freed him from the sorceress Cassana's dungeon, Olive had respected his talents as a bard, and he had gained her sympathy with his tale of being stripped of his name and exiled to another plane. Of course, Olive had not approved of the callous way Nameless had risked people's lives in order to satisfy his egotistical desire to create an immortal vessel to sing his music. On the other hand, his treatment at the hands of the Harpers had been nothing short of tyrannical. Exiling him had been cruel enough, but repressing his songs was unforgivable. The halfling could not help but admire the way Nameless had defied the Harpers a second time. His scheme had been mad, but it had ended in the creation of Alias and Jade. On the whole, Olive had really liked Nameless.

She was pretty sure he'd liked her, too. After all, he'd spent hours teaching her new songs on his yarting, possibly the same yarting he held in his portrait. He'd also given her his Harper's pin, the same silver brooch he wore in the portrait. The piece of jewelry fashioned in the shape of a harp and crescent moon was pinned somewhere in Olive's vest pocket—wherever that was beneath her burro hide. Some might have interpreted his presenting the pin to a halfling thief as an act of defiance against the Harpers, but Olive chose to think of it as a reward for helping Alias gain her freedom.

Now that she thought about it, Olive recalled that there had been something about Jade's murderer that was different from Namelooo. The murderer's hair was as dark and silky as the hair in Nameless's portrait. The portrait was done two centuries ago, though. The last time Olive had seen Nameless, his hair had been splotched with gray and was somewhat luster-less. So it couldn't have been Nameless who killed Jade, unless he'd found some potion of youth.

Olive shook her head, unwilling to believe Nameless capable of such treachery as long as there were other possibilities in the Wyvernspur family. Giogi might know who those other possibilities were, she realized. Remaining with him would be my best opportunity to discover the identity of Jade's murderer.

And when I find out which Wyvernscum murdered my Jade, Olive thought, I can avenge her death.

Having settled her mind about Nameless and realizing that her transformation and captivity might have some tactical advantage, Olive's thoughts turned to more mundane matters. Her stomach was rumbling. She'd missed dinner, and her appetite had not diminished upon her transformation. She sniffed experimentally at the bucket of oats.

* * * * *

Giogi tossed uneasily in his sleep. He was dreaming that he was soaring over a meadow on a spring morning. He knew that he was asleep. He hadn't the ability to soar over anything except dream things. Besides which, he'd had this particular nightmare before. That's why he tossed uneasily. While most people would find the beginning of this dream enchanting, or even exhilarating, Giogi was too well acquainted with the ending to appreciate the soaring part.

His chestnut mare, Daisyeye, galloped into sight beneath

him. Giogi swooped down on the horse more silently than an owl on a rabbit. He sunk his talons into the mare's haunches and his fangs into her neck and snatched his prey from the ground. Daisyeye neighed in terror and pain as Giogi beat his wings harder and faster and climbed back into the air. The horse writhed in his grasp for a few moments, then went limp.

Giogi landed back in the meadow. Blood flowing from Daisyeye's neck and haunches steamed in the cool air. Her bones snapped as Giogi began swallowing her whole.

Giogi awoke with a gasp, trembling with fear. "Why me?" he moaned.

That was the question he'd been asking himself since he'd come of age and he'd started having the dream. At first, the prey in his dream had been wild creatures: stags and boars and mountain goats, and while the dream had disturbed Giogi greatly, at least he was accustomed to hunting such creatures for real—with a bow, of course. Ever since the dragon who'd waylaid him last spring had eaten the first Daisyeye—not Daisyeye II, who was safe in the carriage house—the prey in Giogi's nightmares had become Daisyeye. Like all Cormyrian nobles, he loved his horses, and the idea of slaughtering and devouring them appalled him.

Just to reassure himself, Giogi padded barefoot over to his bedroom window to look out at the carriage house, where Daisyeye was stabled. Giogi could make out the silhouette of the carriage house and see that nothing had burned it down or broken in looking for an equine snack. The moon had set, but the sky was not completely dark. The sun would be up soon.

"Oh, my gosh. I have to be at the crypt," Giogi remembered aloud.

* * * * *

Thomas was awakened by a thumping noise followed by the clatter and clash of metal on metal, like the sounds made by gladiators battling in an arena. Thomas listened more intently, trying to determine if the noise wasn't coming from outside the house, created perhaps by a band of drunken adventurers with no respect for the conventions of town living—such as sleeping at night. A second thump and more bashing noises reached his ears. Now he was able to tell for certain that the disturbance came from within the house. The noise originated from his own kitchen.

It was early dawn, the sky just beginning to lighten to iron gray. Presuming the noises had been made by some very careless burglar, the servant picked up the poker from beside his fireplace and carefully eased open his bedroom door. A bright light shone across the hall. A very brazen, as well as careless, burglar, Thomas thought as he tiptoed to the kitchen door and peeked around the doorjamb.

His kitchen was in complete disarray. Serving trays and mixing bowls lay scattered about the table and floor. All the cabinets stood open—most of them emptied of their contents. One stack of plates sat balanced so precariously on the edge of the linen chest that it appeared as if a passing breeze could send them plummeting to the stone floor. In the midst of the chaos stood the intruder—a lean young man who scowled at the tabletop with a long, sharp knife in his hand. Thomas gasped in surprise.

Giogioni looked up from the kitchen table at Thomas, who stood in the doorway with a raised poker clenched in his fist and his mouth hanging open. "Ah, good morning, Thomas," the young noble greeted him and smiled. "Didn't mean to wake you. Just getting together some tea. Why are you waving that poker about?"

"I—I—I thought you were a burglar, sir," Thomas explained, carefully leaning the iron rod against the wall.

"Now why would you think that, Thomas? You know I have scads of money. Why should I become a burglar?"

"No, sir, I meant that I heard a sound, sir, and that I thought at this hour down in the kitchen, it must have been made by a burglar. Couldn't you sleep, sir?"

Giogi snorted. "With all I had to drink last night?" he replied. "I went out like a snuffed candle."

"Bad dreams again?" Thomas guessed.

Eager to forget the dream, Giogi denied it with a shake of his head. "I am awake at this ungodly hour," he explained, "because Aunt Dorath has condemned me to crypt-crawling with Steele and Freffie. They've put me in charge of provisions, so I've boiled water for tea and now I'm hacking at this cheese for sandwiches. I made a bit of a mess looking for that earthenware tea jug. Sorry. I seem to be having trouble with this knife.

Since you are up anyway, would you oblige, please?" The young Wyvernspur waved the knife at the servant, handle first.

Thomas picked his way across the kitchen to the table—carefully pushing the stack of dishes back from the edge of the linen chest on his way. Large crumbs and chunks of cheddar littered the table, but none could be even charitably described as a slice. Thomas took the remnants of the wheel of cheese and carved through it neatly six times. "Will that be sufficient, sir?"

"Excellent," Giogioni said, stacking the cheese slices between chunks of bread. He lay each sandwich on a piece of oiled paper. "And would you slice them into those cute little triangles like you always do for tea?"

Automatically Thomas quartered the sandwiches, wrapped them in the oily paper, and stuffed them into the waterproof sack Giogi held out. Finding his master not only awake at this hour, but fully dressed, shaved, and alert was enough to confuse Thomas; discovering Giogi also making an attempt at self-sufficiency in the kitchen had left the servant dazed.

"I swiped those leftover tea cakes and some apples. Is that all right?" the nobleman asked.

"Yes, of course, sir." Thomas replied.

"Oh. I told Bottles you'd stop by the Immer Inn first thing this morning and pay my tab from last night."

"Very good, sir," Thomas replied.

Giogi packed the waterproof sack, the earthenware jug, some teacups, teaspoons and a jar of tea leaves into a picnic basket. He strapped on his fencing foil, pulled on his cloak, and unlatched the back door. "By the way," he said, pausing in the doorway, "I thought I'd take the burro with me to carry my supplies. That won't be any problem, will it?"

"Of course not, sir," Thomas said automatically as he nested a set of mixing bowls and stacked them back into a cupboard.

It wasn't until Giogioni's servant had finished tidying the kitchen and had his morning cup of tea that he was sufficiently awake to wonder to which burro his master was referring.

❧ 6 ❧

The Guardian

"Rise and shine, my pretties," Giogi called softly as he entered the barn.

Olive stirred awake. Without meaning to, she'd fallen asleep on her feet. She shook herself, feeling her mane tickle her neck and her tail slap against her hindquarters. Still a burro, she realized with annoyance.

Giogi stopped to pat the chestnut mare. "Would you like some apples, Daisyeye?" Olive could hear the horse chomping away on Giogi's offering.

Then the nobleman entered her enclosure. He looked into her bucket of oats. "Good, you've eaten," he said.

Olive could feel herself blushing beneath her furry hide. After all she had suffered last night, going without dinner would have been unbearable. The oats' molasses coating had rendered them almost tasty, actually better than some of the things she'd eaten at inns outside of Cormyr. After a few experimental nibbles, Olive had polished the remainder off without thinking.

Now confronted with the empty pail, though, she worried that she might grow too burrolike and forget that her favorite meal was not grain, but roast goose, and that she might come to prefer water to Luiren Rivengut.

"How about a little treat," Giogi said, holding out a quarter of an apple.

At least that could be considered halfling food, Olive decided. She muzzled the fruit from the nobleman's hand. Giogi's other hand slid something up over her ears. The feeling of leather straps about her muzzle caused Olive's nose to twitch. Nine Hells, she thought. I fell for the apple and the halter trick.

Olive brayed and tried to back away, but Giogi held fast to the halter he'd just slipped on her. "Whoa, girl. Easy, now. We're just going into the catacombs beneath the old family crypt to look for the thief who stole the wyvern's spur."

KATE NOVAK and JEFF GRUBB

The wyvern's spur? Olive thought with astonishment. The Wyvernspur family's most precious heirloom? It's been stolen? Olive looked up at Giogi with puzzlement. How can you be so calm about a thing like that, boy? she thought.

As Giogi began brushing her coat, he briefed her in soothing tones. "The catacombs aren't so bad," he said, "except for the kobolds, stirges, bugbears, and occasional gargoyles. Of course, first we have to get past the crypt guardian. The guardian shouldn't bother us, though. I think. We're old friends. Last time I saw her, she said I was too small—I presumed she meant too small for her to eat. Her idea of a joke, I suppose. You know how perverse those crypt guardians can be."

Able to distinguish the meaning of his words, Olive had no trouble sensing Giogi's nervousness as well. A shiver went up her long spine. Giogi patted her reassuringly and laid a blanket over her, then a set of packs. As he pulled the cinch under her belly and knotted it through the buckle, Olive considered trying to get out of the little jaunt by lying down or rolling over, but she decided that the floor was just too dirty. Besides, she thought, I won't learn anything more about the Wyvernspurs in a horse stall, but if Giogi keeps babbling, I might pick up quite a bit.

"Actually, she's probably not as terrible as I remember," Giogi continued with his reminiscences of the guardian. "It's just that I was only eight back then. My father had just died, you see, and I inherited his key to the crypt. My Cousin Steele was so jealous that I had a key and he didn't that he badgered my other cousin, Freffie, and me into sneaking into the crypt. Then he, Steele, that is, swiped the key from me and locked me in there all alone and left with Freffie.

"Freffie had an attack of conscience and told Uncle Drone, but I ran into the catacombs to get away from the guardian. I spent the good part of a day wandering through them and missed supper before Uncle Drone found me."

There, Olive thought. I have three murder suspects already: jealousy-ridden Steele, guilt-ridden Frefford, and nephew-ridden Uncle Drone. I can rule out Giogi's father, though—unless he's undead.

Giogi strapped the picnic basket atop the packs, balancing it on either side with a pair of full water skins. Olive groaned under the weight, but the noise came out as a testy bray.

The water and tea things, however, were only a beginning. Into the packs Giogi loaded oil, torches, a lantern, a tinder box, rope, a rope ladder, spikes, a portable stool, a blanket, a heavy mallet, several sealed vials, a can of white paint, a brush, and a large map. He then added a small sack of feed for the burro. "Can't have you missing lunch," Giogi said, patting Olive's rump.

Don't worry about me, Olive thought. I'll collapse from exhaustion long before then. She brayed again in protest.

"You're a very musical little creature," Giogi said. "Maybe I should name you Birdie. Come on, Birdie." Giogi led Olive out of the stall and from the carriage house.

The pair of them clomped through the garden and out into the street. Wagons and carts loaded with hay and seaweed and fish and firewood crammed the road. Servants and field hands and fishermen and foresters edged around each other on the plank walkways. Oblivious to the immediate flow of traffic, Giogi led his burro down the center of the street, while he studied the movement on either side of him with intense curiosity. Olive was hard-pressed to avoid stepping on his feet when he wandered too close to her hooves.

"I had no idea how busy this town was so early," Giogi muttered.

So why don't we go back to bed and wait for the traffic to clear? Olive thought, but Giogi guided her westward through the crush.

The sky, which last night had been clear and starry, was blanketed by slate-gray clouds, and the air was no longer crisp, but was moist with impending rain or snow. Olive's breath steamed from her nostrils, and Giogi puffed vapor from his lips as he strolled along whistling, in tune if not in tempo.

Near the edge of town, the pair turned onto a path heading south up a steep hill. I'm not making this ascent, Olive thought, planting her feet firmly in the road. A swat on her rump from the nobleman got her moving in spite of herself.

The path led to a rocky graveyard bordered by a low wall and surrounded by pine and oak trees. The trees cast dark shadows on the already gloomy setting, and the carpet of pine needles and oak leaves muffled the sounds of their footsteps. Most of the headstones within the yard were weathered and broken with age, reminding Olive of the stumps of an old giant's teeth.

Very near the entrance stood a large stone mausoleum, as worn-looking as the rest of the graveyard's monuments but still intact. Thick stalks of ivy ran up its walls. The dead ivy leaves looked black in the shadows and rattled in the breeze. Small, ornately carved stone wyverns perched all along the mausoleum's roof and looked down on them with glass eyes. Giogi avoided looking at them, knowing all too well their long reptilian bodies, batlike wings, and scorpion tails. He shuddered as he approached the mausoleum's entrance. The Wyvernspur coat of arms was carved into the walls on either side of the door, and the Wyvernspur name was carved into the lintel.

Smaller markings were cut into the door, lintel, and jamb— invocations to Selune and Mystra to protect the crypt from trespassers. For good measure, magical glyphs were scrawled in a spidery hand on every wall.

This must be the place, Olive thought.

"This is the place," Giogi said. "It's so deadly quiet."

Wonderful choice of words this boy has, Olive thought.

"Giogioni, you're late," a woman's voice snapped behind them.

Olive might have jumped at the sound, but she was too loaded down to do more than jerk her head up. Giogi, not so limited, whirled around.

A beautiful young woman in a dark fur cape popped out from behind a ruined tomb. She tossed her hood back with an ungloved hand, revealing long black hair and sharp, familiar features.

One of the Wyvernspur brood, Olive realized immediately.

"Julia!" Giogi said, "What are you doing here?"

"Steele told me to wait here to tell you about Frefford."

"What about Freffie?" Giogi asked. His expression clouded with concern.

"Gaylyn's gone into labor, so he's still at Redstone. You were late, so Steele entered the crypt without you. He said you could follow him in and try to catch up."

"Catch up. Right," Giogi muttered, pulling out a silver key that hung from a chain around his neck.

Olive studied Julia curiously. Something about her, besides her Wyvernspur face, interested the halfling. Olive sniffed the air. She could smell something mingled with Julia's sweat. The human woman was nervous. She might not be lying, but the halfling could tell she was up to something. An expert herself at the art of deception and guile, Olive could not be fooled, especially not by an amateur like this woman.

Giogi turned toward the mausoleum door.

Julia appeared to be wringing her cold bare hands. Even hampered by the vision of a beast, though, the halfling caught the surreptitious twist Julia gave to one of the rings on her right hand.

As Giogi inserted the silver key in the mausoleum door, his cousin reached toward his neck. Olive saw the gleam of a tiny needle jutting from the cousin's ring. A drop of something clear dripped from the tip of the needle.

Instinctively Olive lunged forward, butting her forehead against the woman.

"Agh!" Julia cried, leaping backward. She took notice of Olive for the first time. "Giogioni, what sort of creature is that?" she screeched angrily.

"Birdie, cut that out. You're scaring Cousin Julia," Giogi said, yanking Olive's head down with the halter. To his cousin, he said, "It's just a burro, Julia."

"A what?" Julia asked.

"A burro. It's a pack animal. They're very useful in mines. Haven't you ever seen one?"

"I should think not," Julia said with a sniff. "I thought it was an ugly pony."

Giogi turned his back again to work the lock, and Julia edged forward, her right hand poised in the air as if to swat a fly.

Olive placed a hoof down on the train of Julia's gown. The woman tripped as she stepped toward Giogi and dropped to her knees on the pine needles. "Damned creature," she whispered.

Giogi turned around and looked at his kneeling cousin with surprise. Before he could help Julia to her feet, though, Olive managed to tangle her lead rope around the woman and butt her again. Without thinking, Julia slashed at the burro with her right hand. Olive felt a sharp scratch on her neck, then a fire burned through her blood, starting at the wound and racing to her extremities. Her knees wobbled and Olive sank to the ground.

"Birdie!" Giogi gasped. "What's wrong, girl?"

"That beast attacked me!" Julia cried, untangling herself

from Olive's lead rope, leaping to her feet, and backing away quickly.

"She was probably just playing. Julia, what did you do to her?"

Olive stretched her neck out so Giogi couldn't miss the small trickle of blood from her wound.

The young noble gasped. He turned toward Julia and snatched at her cloak, yanking her toward him. He caught her by the wrists. All the meekness he'd ever felt in his female cousin's company was dispelled by the alarm he felt for his pet's safety.

He investigated Julia's rings with a frown. "What is this?" he demanded, spying the ring with the jabber. "Where did you get this ring? How could you poison such a sweet, little animal?"

"It's not poison, only sleeping sap," Julia protested.

Thank Tymora, Olive thought through the fog. That'll teach me to stick my neck out for anyone.

Barely containing his anger, Giogi yanked the offending ring off Julia's finger. "I think I'd better hang on to this for you before you hurt someone with it," the nobleman said, pulling out a handkerchief, wrapping the ring up in it, and stuffing it into a pocket. He thrust Julia away and bent over Olive's prone body. Pulling two vials out of a pack on her back, he poured the contents of one over Olive's cut and the other down her throat.

"Why are you wasting potions on that stupid creature?" Julia asked.

"Because she's not a stupid creature. She's a perfectly lovely burro."

"I told you it was only sleeping sap."

"Sleeping sap can do a lot of damage if you use too much. What were you doing with it, anyway?"

Julia did not reply.

Olive felt suddenly cool and strong as the potions quenched the flame that ran through her body. She stumbled to her feet with Giogi's help. The young noble made sure the burro was steady, then turned again to face his cousin. Olive could see a spark of comprehension gleaming in his milky brown eyes.

"Julia!" Giogi barked sternly. Olive stood by his side, trying to look as menacing as possible. "You meant that ring for me, didn't you? This is one of Steele's ideas, isn't it?" Giogi asked, grabbing Julia by the shoulders and giving her a firm shake.

"No!" Julia protested. "It's . . . just something I carry to protect myself."

"Attacked by a lot of burros on the streets of Immersea, eh? Don't bother to lie, Julia. You always did what Steele told you. What did he have in mind?" he asked hotly. "Leave me down there with the guardian again? Hmm?" Giogi gave his cousin another shake.

"You are a fool," Julia said. "Steele isn't interested in child's play anymore. He wants—" Julia bit off her words and paled visibly, obviously afraid she'd said too much.

"What does he want?" Giogi demanded.

Julia shook her head. "I can't tell you," she insisted. "Steele would be furious."

"You will tell me," Giogi said, shaking her harder.

"You're hurting me," Julia whined.

Giogi released his cousin suddenly, ashamed of bullying a woman, and so young a woman as Julia. I have to know what Steele's planning, though, he thought.

"Julia," he said, trying to reason calmly with the woman, "I won't tell Steele that you told me anything. Now, what's his game?"

"Why should I tell you?" Julia asked haughtily.

"If you don't tell me, I'll—" Giogi hesitated. He wasn't sure what he could do to threaten Julia.

"Run and tattle to Aunt Dorath," Julia taunted, "like you always did when we were children."

Did I? Giogi wondered. Yes, I suppose I did, but only because Steele and Julia were such naughty children. He looked at Julia with annoyance. "Yes," he said. "That's exactly what I'll do. I'm sure she'll be very disturbed to hear that her grandniece was running around with an assassin's ring. I'll give her the ring so she can have Lord Sudacar check that it's not poisoned."

"No! Don't tell!" Julia begged, obviously more anxious to avoid Aunt Dorath's wrath than she'd been as a child.

"Then spit it out, woman," Giogi demanded. "Everything."

"Steele wants to find the wyvern's spur without you," Julia explained, "so he can keep it for himself. He wants the power."

"Power? What power?" Giogi asked, surprised that Steele and Julia would know something about the spur that not even Uncle Drone could tell him.

"Steele doesn't know what the spur's power is yet," Julia said, "but when he gets hold of the spur, he'll find out."

Giogi laughed. "Steele's going to be in for a big disappoint-ment if he finds the spur," he predicted, shaking his head sagely. "It's nothing but a hunk of junk."

"That's not what Uncle Drone said last night."

"Julia, I love Uncle Drone like—like an uncle, but you may have noticed that he's not all together up here," Giogi said, tap-ping his forehead. "The stairs run to the top of the tower, but there are no landings, don't you know."

Julia stood defiantly before him with her hands on her hips. "The spur does so have some power," she insisted. "That's why Cole took it with him whenever he went tramping around the country like a commoner."

"My father? What are you talking about? The spur's been in the crypt since Paton Wyvernspur died."

Julia shook her head vehemently. "No, it hasn't. Your father used to steal it whenever he wanted to use it. He was Uncle Drone's favorite, so the old fool never told anyone. No one found out about it until Cole died. Uncle Drone was forced to tell the family, because, otherwise, they wouldn't have gone to so much trouble to bring back his remains. Cole was wearing the spur when he died."

"Wearing it?!" Giogi asked incredulously.

"It's true," Julia said with a scornful sniff.

"Why hasn't anyone ever told me any of this?"

"Aunt Dorath said that she would never have approved of your father using the spur if she had known, and no one would ever use it again. We children weren't to be told about it."

"Then how did you find out?"

Julia hesitated for a moment, then saw the look in Giogi's eyes.

"Steele and I were listening at the keyhole when she ex-plained all this to our father."

Just what I would expect from a sneaking little witch like you, Olive thought.

Giogi shook his head, trying to reconcile Julia's story with his own memories. Whenever Giogi tried to picture his father, though, Cole always looked like his portrait, which hung in Giogi's bedroom—a portrait that could have been interchanged with nearly every other portrait of Wyvernspur menfolk, in-cluding the painting hanging in the carriage house. All Giogi could remember clearly was a tall man who'd tried to teach him to ride, took him swimming, and loved to sing.

The nobleman sighed. Everyone in the Realms except me knew that my father was an adventurer. Most of the members of my family knew he used the spur, but I didn't. Maybe I should have tried listening at a few keyholes. Giogi turned back to the mausoleum, unlocked the door, and pushed it open.

"Giogioni," Julia continued, "Frefford has the family title. You have all your mother's money. Why shouldn't Steele get the spur?"

Giogi turned around thoughtfully. It wasn't hard to come up with an answer to that question. "Julia," he said, "do you know what Steele said to me when Uncle Drone gave me my father's key to the crypt? He said he wished your father would hurry and die so he could have his own key. Steele was a jealous, mean little boy, and as far as I can tell, he's grown into a jealous, cruel man. Did it ever occur to you that he doesn't deserve the spur?"

"What have you done to deserve it?" Julia asked with venom.

"Julia, I don't want the spur. I just want to return it to the crypt, where it belongs."

"Then why has Uncle Drone been secretly nagging Aunt Dorath all winter to let you have it?"

"Listening at keyholes again, are we?" Giogi asked, using the question to hide his own surprise.

"I have servants to do that for me now," Julia said coolly.

Too lazy to do your own dirty work, eh? Olive thought.

Giogi sighed again. "Look, this whole argument is moot if we don't find the spur. I'm going into the crypt after Steele. You should be back helping Aunt Dorath and Frefford with Gaylyn."

"Steele will find the thief before you do. He's an hour ahead of you, and he knows how to use his weapon. He isn't bogged down by some overgrown pack rat, either."

Olive brayed loudly, jerked her halter from Giogi's hand, and charged at Julia.

Not used to being charged upon by burros, the noblewoman retreated with a yell and almost toppled over a headstone. Olive herded Julia out of the graveyard and waited at the entrance until the woman had fled down the path.

Giogi grinned as the little burro trotted back to his side. He scratched behind her ears. "Don't you pay any attention to her,

Birdie. Julia's too foolish to see what a superior burro you are. She doesn't even realize I'm better with a foil than Steele is. Steele only used to win by thwacking at me with the flat of the blade. That's cheating, you know."

Giogi picked Olive's lead rope off the ground and pulled her through the door into the family mausoleum. He closed and locked the door behind them. Olive shivered. It was colder inside than out, and, naturally, as dark as a tomb.

Giogi drew a shining crystal from his boot. Olive stared at it with astonishment. It was a finder's stone, just like the one Elminster had given Alias. Olive had spent many hours guessing at its value before it was lost near Westgate. Olive remembered now that Alias had run into Giogi again, outside of Westgate. If this is the same stone, Olive thought, then there are more coincidences in my life than in one of those bad operas in Raven's Bluff, the Living City.

Whatever its origins, the finder's stone filled the mausoleum with a warm, rich glow. The twinkle of precious metal attracted Olive's attention to the tomb itself. Giogi was busy lighting torches set in gold-plated sconces. The flames' reflections danced on every surface around them. The floor was checkered with black and white squares of polished marble, and the walls and ceiling were covered with solid plates of a dull gray metal, which Olive presumed was lead. Two white marble benches, inlaid with runes of gold and platinum, were the only other decor in the room. The husks of long-dead flowers lay on one bench. Olive could see no other exit besides the one Giogi had just locked.

Giogi finished with the torches and began hopping like a child along the squares of marble laid out on the floor. Right foot on white, left foot on black, two jumps diagonally on white with the left, then back one jump with both feet.

Olive was just thinking how Uncle Drone might not be the only Wyvernspur "not all together upstairs," when a large section of the floor at the far end dropped a foot and slid silently beneath the rest of the floor. A narrow staircase led down into the dark hole revealed by the secret door. Nice workmanship, Olive thought. Invisible, quiet, no vibrations.

"Come on, Birdie," Giogi said, taking Olive's lead rope. "The secret door doesn't stay open very long."

Olive grudgingly followed the nobleman down the steps.

Giogi used the finder's stone to light their way. The walls on
either side were of rough-cut stone fitted together by expert
masons. The stone was cool but dry. The air was less chill than
in the mausoleum and grew even warmer as they descended.

Olive tried counting the number of steps, but she got confused by her extra feet. There were three landings where the
staircase turned, but the steps were all even and not too steep
or narrow for her hooves. Olive caught glimpses of shimmering lines on the walls, but whenever she looked directly at
them, the lines disappeared. More magical glyphs, she realized.
I must be immune to their power because I'm in Giogi's company. Or because I'm just an ass, she added.

Finally they reached the bottom. Their way was blocked by
another door plated with the same gray metal used in the
mausoleum. Emblazoned across the door was a painting of a
great red wyvern. The words, "None but Wyvernspurs shall
pass this door and live," were inscribed in the Common tongue
over the door.

Once again Giogi pulled out his silver key. He stared at it for a
moment, took a deep breath, then exhaled, puffing out his
cheeks. "Now, don't be frightened, Birdie," Giogi said as he
turned the key in the lock. "I'll protect you from the guardian."

Much obliged, Olive thought, but who's going to protect you?
The halfling burro could smell fear on the nobleman.

Giogi took another deep breath, gathered his courage, and
pushed open the door. He took a step into the room, then another. Olive followed alongside him, which Giogi took as an in-
dication that the little burro was a fearless creature. In reality,
Olive was simply anxious to stay within the finder's stone
sphere of light.

"Hello, hello," Giogi said, at first softly, then with more volume. "Steele, are you here?" the nobleman called out. His voice
echoed back, but there was no living response. Giogi pushed
the door closed behind them and locked it.

They stood in the Wyvernspur family crypt—a vast tunneled
chamber with straight walls and a vaulted ceiling. Both walls
and ceiling were lined, as the staircase had been, with fitted,
cut stone. Every so many feet, in place of a stone, was a block of
marble engraved with the name of a Wyvernspur, with—so
Olive presumed—the remains of a Wyvernspur buried behind
it.

In the center of the crypt was a single cylindrical pedestal ringed with concentric circles of letters carved into the floor. Each circle repeated the same warning in a different language. Olive couldn't read all the tongues, but the outer and most prominent warning was written in Common. The words, "painful, lingering death," stood out clearly in the finder's stone light. Olive did not feel compelled to read any more.

The pedestal stood higher than Olive's line of sight. She could see only the swatch of black velvet draped over the top of the pedestal and which hung down about a foot all around.

Giogi, from his adult human height, looked down on the top of the pedestal. "It's missing, all right," he muttered.

"Giogioni," a voice whispered from the other end of the hall. The echo repeated the whisper.

Olive shivered. She was willing to bet that that wasn't Giogi's Cousin Steele. The voice had a sensuous, husky quality, but it also conveyed to Olive the unpleasant sensation of something sawing at her bones. The voice had to belong to the guardian. Olive understood immediately Giogi's childhood terror of the creature.

Giogi froze, like a man held by magic. He moved his mouth, wetted his lips, and moved his mouth again, but no words came out.

Patches of darkness broke through the edges of the light cast by the finder's stone and swirled together until they coalesced into one large shadow, which sprouted legs, a serpentine neck and head, a sinuous tail, and huge reptilian wings. The shadow spread out against the far wall, covering the detail of the stonework in an inky pool.

Olive had no trouble recognizing the silhouette as the shadow cast by a monstrously large wyvern. Yet, there was no wyvern in the room. Olive began to back up slowly. She had had frightening ordeals with dragons before, but at least those dragons had been visible and alive. The creature dwelling in this place, Olive realized, was neither.

"Giogioni," the disembodied voice whispered again. The shadow of the wyvern head moved as the voice spoke. "You've come back at last."

"I'm only passing through, guardian," Giogi said. "Don't bother—" Giogi's voice cracked. He swallowed hard to wet his throat before continuing. "Don't bother yourself on my account."

"Is this little morsel for me?" the guardian asked as a shadowy talon elongated and traveled across the ceiling and down the wall toward Olive.

Olive could've sworn the air grew colder as the shadow claw drew near her.

Giogi interposed himself between his burro and the darkness. "This is Birdie, and I need her to search the catacombs, so I would appreciate it if you would leave her undisturbed."

The voice laughed. "Not too little anymore, are you? I shall respect your wish. But you've come too late, my Giogioni. The spur has been taken."

"I know that," Giogi said. He could feel a bead of sweat trickling down his face as he mustered all his courage and asked, "Why didn't you stop the thief?"

"My charge is to let Wyvernspurs pass unslain," the guardian replied matter-of-factly.

"So which of us took the spur?" Giogi demanded.

"I have no idea. Wyvernspurs are all alike to me. Like shadows on a wall."

"Great," Giogi muttered.

"Except you, Giogioni. You are different. Like Cole, like Paton. Kissed by Selune."

"What is that supposed to mean?"

"Do you remember what we spoke of when you were here last?"

"I've been trying to forget it, actually."

"You can never forget the death cry of prey, nor the taste of warm blood, nor the crunch of bone."

Olive's ears pricked up at the unusual pattern of words. Wyvern poetry? she wondered.

"I have to go," Giogi insisted. He tugged on the burro's halter. Olive needed no further coaxing. She trotted across the chamber at the nobleman's side, keeping him between her and the silhouette. As the only source of light in the room—Giogi's finder's stone—moved, the shadow did not shift position but remained looming on the far wall.

In that wall, beneath the shadow of the guardian's wing, was a small archway opening onto a downward staircase. As they neared the arch, Olive again felt the chill of the guardian. They passed through the archway unharmed, though, and the chill did not extend beyond the crypt. They had passed out of the guardian's realm.

Behind them, the creature called out in its bone-grating whisper, "You will always dream of these things, Giogi. You will dream of them until you've joined me forever."

Giogi hurried down the stairs, but at the first landing he slumped against the wall, trembling, with his hands covering his face.

Olive nuzzled him gently, concerned that he might go to pieces if she didn't keep him moving, and anxious to put another flight of stairs between them and the guardian.

Giogi pulled his hands away from his face, took a deep breath, and looked down at the burro. Olive could see tears in the corners of his eyes. "I was wrong," he said. "She is just as terrible as I remembered. It's her horrible dream. If I could just stop dreaming that damned dream."

❦ 7 ❦

Cat

Giogi stood up straight and took a few deep breaths to compose himself. He was over the worst of it. While the catacombs were no doubt more deadly, they did not hold the same terror for him as the crypt. "Come on, Birdie," he said, heading down the next flight of steps.

Olive let out her breath in relief and followed.

The passage descending into the catacombs was hewn out of the rock. No marble or cut and fitted stone lined it, and the bare rock was rough and dirty. Water dripped from the ceiling, seeped from the walls, and trickled down the stairs. The steps were crumbling in places and were slick with mud and slimy fungus. Someone heading down the stairs had left large, deep boot impressions in the muck.

"Steele's footprints," Giogi muttered unhappily as he plodded down the stairs alongside them. He didn't really want to join his cousin. Steele didn't want his company, and if, as Uncle Drone had said, the thief wasn't down here, Steele was very likely to lose his temper with Giogi. He had to join Steele, anyway, because Uncle Drone had insisted on it. Giogi was just now beginning to suspect why—considering the old wizard's confession last night and Julia's revelation this morning.

It looks as if Uncle Drone has been up to skullduggery on my behalf, Giogi thought uneasily. He wants me to pretend to look for the thief so no one blames me for the theft.

Giogi sighed, and the sound echoed up and down the stairway. "Have you ever noticed, Birdie," he asked philosophically, "that as soon as one's life has settled down, when there's nothing but clear sailing ahead, one's relatives steer one into the shoals, so to speak?"

Olive, whose concentration was riveted on descending the broken, slippery stairs while carrying enough provisions for an adventuring party of twelve, naturally did not reply.

"Take Freffie, for instance," Giogi said. "Two years ago, he decided I needed a career, and he talked me into joining the army. Me, a purple dragoon. Imagine! Fortunately, I was dismissed from service after accidentally releasing Aunt Dorath's pet land urchin into the provisions wagon." Giogi broke off detailing his family's interference in his life to concentrate on climbing down an especially crumbled section of stairs. He took care that the burro had sure footing each step before pulling on her lead rope.

After they'd overcome that obstacle, the nobleman continued his monologue. "Then last year, Aunt Dorath decided Minda Lluth was just the girl for me. Minda talked me into all sorts of foolish things, then abandoned me while I struggled to extricate myself from the trouble she'd gotten me into. She convinced me to do my impersonation of Azoun at Freffie's wedding, then, after I nearly got killed, she went and married someone else," Giogi griped sullenly. He kicked a chunk of stairs down ahead of them.

Unable to ignore Giogi's last comment, Olive suddenly realized, That's the wedding I sang at last year. Giogi's Cousin Freffie must be Lord Frefford Wyvernspur. Olive had sat right in front of the wedding party table, but for the life of her, she could not remember the groom's features. The man had been eclipsed by his bride, three hundred wedding guests, and the excitement of watching Alias try to assassinate his Cousin Giogi. I'll have to get another look at Frefford, Olive decided, before I can rule him out as Jade's murderer.

It took Giogi a few minutes to overcome his disappointment with Minda and focus on his current problem. "Now, Julia tells me that Uncle Drone has been trying to arrange for me to use the wyvern's spur," he said.

I know. I heard her, Olive thought. I was there, remember?

"Did I ask him to do this?" Giogi asked the burro, annoyance creeping into his voice. He answered his own question with an indignant tone. "I most certainly did not. Did he ask me if I'd mind him acting on my behalf? He most certainly did not!"

More calmly, Giogi stated, "I love my family," then he shouted, "but why can't they all just leave me alone?"

"Alone, alone, alone," the stairway echoed up and down.

Disturbed by the sound of his own voice reverberating through the dank corridors, Giogi continued his descent in silence.

Finally given the quiet to think, Olive tried to analyze the possibility that Steele could be Jade's murderer—based on all that Giogi and Julia had said about him. Steele Wyvernspur possessed a streak of cruelty and ruthlessness. That matched the murderer. Steel was supposed to be competent with a sword. The murderer could cast powerful spells, and, while it was unlikely he would also wield a sword well, it wasn't impossible. Every now and then, one came across a wizard proficient with a weapon besides a dagger. Steele wouldn't be too old, but he might be too young. If his sister, Julia, is anything to go by, he'll have the Wyvernspur face, Olive thought, but I won't know anything for sure until I get a good look at him.

It was at this point that Olive noticed a second set of footprints. They were smaller and less deep, apparently made by a woman or a small man wearing soft-soled slippers. The prints went up toward the crypt and back down to the catacombs. The thief's? Olive wondered excitedly.

Curious now to see this thief and eager to get a look at Giogi's cousin, Olive clomped down the stairs with more speed. Before she reached the bottom, the burro was walking ahead of Giogi and the lead rope, like a bloodhound on the hunt.

Finally, man and burro reached the bottom of the stairs. They stood in a small anteroom paved with rough stones. The light of the finder's stone revealed corridors leading away in three directions. Two of the corridors were heavily webbed over, but strands of torn spider silk wafted in the subterranean breeze of the third tunnel. Scattered at the tunnel's entrance was the hacked-up remains of a large spider. A heavy boot heel had left its imprint in the smeared spider ichor.

"Easy to see where Steele's been," Giogi said matter-of-factly. The noble unsheathed his foil for the first time. "At least he's brushed all the cobwebs away for us."

No, Olive thought. The thief would have done that. Steele's just following the culprit's trail.

Giogi led the way cautiously down the web-cleared corridor. There was nothing outstanding about the passage. Water had created it, and Giogi's ancestors had widened it. No jewels or precious metals glittered in the walls, no delicately carved stone columns towered over them. The surfaces all about them consisted of well-packed dirt, pockets of sand, pebbles, and rocks, and magically hewn stone. The corridor had been excavated for utility, not for show.

The sound of dripping water and their own footsteps echoed around Giogi and Olive. The air was moist and cold. Large, ugly spiders, chittering like angry squirrels, scrambled away from the light of the finder's stone.

The corridor continued straight for almost a thousand feet. The spiders and torn cobwebs ended abruptly. A short distance farther, the corridor began to twist and branch. In the absence of broken webs, Steele's route was no longer obvious.

At the branching, Giogi halted, sheathed his foil, and began rummaging through Olive's packs. He lightened her load by the weight of the portable stool, the picnic basket, the blanket, the sack of grain, and the map. After sprinkling a little grain on the blanket, he set up the stool, sat down, and poured himself tea in a tin mug.

This boy can really rough it, Olive thought sarcastically. No linen, no china, no butler.

Steele will have headed for the outer door, to see if the thief is sitting by it, Giogi decided. As he munched some old tea cakes, he examined his map for the quickest route to the door. When he looked up, his burro had its nose buried in his picnic basket. "Bad Birdie," he said, pushing Olive's muzzle away. "That's your food over there." He pointed to the grain on the blanket.

Olive pleaded with her eyes.

"Oh, very well," Giogi sighed. He drew out a cheese sandwich and fed it to her in pieces, then spoiled her with another slice of apple.

I wonder if I can get him to pour me some tea, too, Olive thought with a mental chuckle.

"No more, Birdie," Giogi said, rising suddenly to his feet. He packed up everything in a flurry and loaded it back on Olive. Before they continued, the nobleman drew out from the packs a jar of paint and a paint brush.

At every intersection, the nobleman consulted the map and painted a number on the wall. Several times, he had to turn the map or turn himself to get his bearings. Twice they retraced their steps to check a previous number. Their progress slowed to a crawl.

With their tedious pace and the sound of dripping water percolating through the stonework, Olive felt as if she were being tortured. She fought her irritability by reminding herself, You need the boy to get you out of this pit, Olive-girl. You can't afford for him to get confused.

They were halted in an intersection when Olive detected something flutter softly past her long ears. Giogi, intent on his map and paints, seemed not to notice it. Olive felt a prick near her haunches. She swished her tail automatically. She was just thinking, Useful things, tails, when a bloated crow-sized shape swooped down behind Giogi's head.

For a moment, Olive thought it was just a bat, but as it hovered by Giogi's neck, she saw it had feathery wings. Then she caught sight of its mosquitolike proboscis.

Olive brayed in terror, suddenly realizing what the prick she'd felt earlier had been.

Giogi whirled around at the sound. The light from the finder's stone flared, outlining a stirge nearly as large as a tomcat. Giogi leaped backward with a shriek, dropping the map, the paint can, and paint brush. Recovering his nerve quickly, though, he drew his foil and lunged at the creature. Too fat to gain altitude quickly, the startled creature swooped down and away, and Giogi's foil stabbed at empty air. The flying monster disappeared into the darkness.

Meanwhile, Olive was smashing her haunches against the uneven rock walls, trying to squash the bloodsucker she knew must be attached to her. She felt something solid catch between her body and the wall and rupture. Something wet seeped through the blanket between the packs and her back.

Was that the stirge or a water bag? she wondered. Not taking any chances, she kept on swinging her back half against the stone. The tea basket tumbled to the ground and things in the packs clattered against one another.

"Take it easy, Birdie," Giogi said. "You'll hurt yourself."

Take it easy, he says, while something's sucking my lifeblood away. In her mind Olive imagined a swarm of stirges hanging from her fuzzy belly like bats did from the ceilings of caves.

With a look of grim concern, Giogi raised his foil and lunged at the burro. Olive closed her eyes and held her breath.

She never felt the prick of the foil, but in less than a few seconds, Giogi was patting her back, whispering soothing words.

"It's all over now, girl. I got the lot."

The lot! Then there was more than one, Olive thought queasily. She opened her eyes. Skewered on the nobleman's sword, like cornish hens on a spit, were half a dozen stirges, the largest no bigger than a squirrel.

Mercifully the finder's stone's light had dimmed back to its normal soft glow, so she didn't get a good look at them. Nonetheless, Olive had to fight back her nausea.

"Disgusting creatures, aren't they?" Giogi commented as he slid the bloodsuckers off his weapon and kicked the corpses against the wall. From the pallor of Giogi's face, Olive could tell he was not inured to battle. The young noble wiped his foil clean with a silk handkerchief, grimaced at the gore and stains on the fabric, and dropped the cloth over his kills.

He wasn't boasting after all, Olive thought with relief. He is competent with that foil. He managed to skewer the enemy without harming a hair on my head—or the other end, for that matter. We may live through this little jaunt yet.

After sheathing his foil, Giogi bent over to retrieve the supplies he'd dropped. He salvaged as much of the spilled paint as he could by mopping it up with the brush. Murmuring reassuring words to the burro, he reattached the picnic basket to Olive's packs and checked the security of the other supplies. He took another few moments to consult the map, picked up Olive's lead rope, and led her down the left-hand passageway.

They hadn't gone five paces when Giogi seemed to stumble. He toppled sideways, slumped against the wall, and slid to the floor. The map, paint brush, and jar tumbled out of his hands again, but his fingers remained clasped about the finder's stone.

Olive was at his side at once. Frantically she searched over his body, nuzzling and pawing at his cloak, looking for a stirge that might have attached itself to the nobleman without his knowing it. Her search yielded neither bloodsucking monster nor wound. Moreover, Giogi did not appear in any shock. He was breathing quite naturally and snoring softly. How can he fall asleep at a time like this! Olive thought.

A tongue clicked behind her to attract her attention. Olive whirled about. Her eyes widened in astonishment at the sight of the human woman who stepped from the shadows.

"Nice burro," the woman whispered, taking a cautious step toward Olive with her hand out for the burro to sniff.

The woman's bright hair hung freely about her shoulders like burnished copper wire. She was dressed in a shimmering, flowing robe smeared all about the hem with muck, and the cloth slippers on her feet were equally grimed. Ordinarily, Olive's first thought would have been that the slippers must have made the smaller footprints going up to the crypt, but it was the woman's face that held her attention and excited her.

She has Alias's face! Olive thought while her heart raced. She's another copy of Alias!

"Don't fret, little one," the woman said soothingly. "I put him to sleep with magic. We'll just get his key before he wakes up, and we'll be out of here in no time."

Ordinarily, Olive might have found the offer irresistible, but the woman set Olive's nerves on edge and brought to the half-ling's mind Cassana, the sadistic, vain sorceress in whose image Alias had been created. Cassana had often addressed the half-ling as "little one" in the same condescending tone and had put her into a magical sleep. There's nothing to guarantee, Olive realized, that just because she looks like Alias, she isn't as evil as that witch, Cassana, had been.

Then, of course, there was Giogi to consider. She couldn't leave the nobleman in the foul place, unprotected while he slept, prey to stirges and gods knew what else. Even if he lived to awaken, he wouldn't be able to escape unless he found his Cousin Steele. She had to stay with him, and she had to protect his key. Olive positioned herself fully between the woman and Giogi, bracing her legs against possible assault.

"My, but aren't you fierce," the woman said with a nervous laugh—not as cruel a laugh as Cassana's had been, but taunting enough to get Olive's blood boiling. "I will have that key," the sorceress growled, reaching down and picking up a fist-sized rock.

The halfling burro charged. The load on her back pitched and threw off her balance. The human woman sidestepped her with remarkable ease. Burdened by the weight of all Giogi's equipment, Olive hit a wall before she could skid to a halt.

As Olive turned around, she saw the woman kneeling over Giogi's prone body, reaching for the key chain about his neck.

As it had earlier when the stirge attacked, the finder's stone light flared again. It filled the corridor with a radiant brilliance centered on Giogi. The woman fell back with an anguished cry. Olive rushed to Giogi's side and nipped at his arms and legs.

"Not now, Thomas," the nobleman muttered, rolling over on

his side. "I'm having the nicest dream."

No time for subtlety, the halfling realized. She turned and gave him a sharp kick in his rear end.

"I'm awake, Aunt Dorath! Really!" Giogi exclaimed, sitting up suddenly. He looked around in confusion at the burro hovering impatiently over him and the strange woman whimpering on her knees a few feet away. He rose shakily to his feet, still clutching the finder's stone.

Giogi bent over the woman and touched her shoulder gently. "Are you all right?" he asked.

"Of course I'm not all right," she snapped, squinting up at him with watery eyes. "Your damn light-rock nearly blinded me."

"You!" Giogi gasped, instantly recognizing the woman's resemblance to Alias of Westgate. "No," he said after a moment, "you're not Alias. Your hair's all wrong."

"Would you turn that dratted light down?" the woman growled, shielding her eyes with an outstretched hand.

"Um, I'm not sure I know how," Giogi said, examining the finder's stone with confusion. "If you just give your eyes a minute to adjust, I'm sure they'll get used to it."

"I've cast a spell so I could see in this dark pit," the woman snapped. "Any light is annoying."

"Oh." Giogi tucked the stone in his cloak and allowed just a little light to peek out. "You can't be Cassana of Westgate, either," he mused. "You're too young. She's dead, anyway. Just who are you?"

"I'm Cat of Ordulin," she said, lowering her hand from her eyes. "I'm sorry my age and my eyes and my hair don't suit you," she continued, her tone dripping with sarcasm, "but you might at least thank me for saving your life from a stirge." She held out her hand imperiously, expecting assistance to stand.

Giogi helped her to her feet. "I didn't intend any insult," he said. "It's rather nice hair, and your eyes look fine now that you've stopped squinting, and, of course, it's none of my business how old you are. Really, though, you do have the most remarkable resemblance to Alias of Westgate. Is she a relative of yours? Or Cassana of Westgate?"

"I've never heard of either of them," Cat declared.

"Oh." Giogi tilted his head in puzzlement. Cat had the same green eyes, pert nose, shapely mouth, high cheekbones, and pointed chin as Alias. It was strange enough that two apparently unrelated women should have the exact same beautiful face. It was just incredible that he should meet both of them. Finally, remembering his manners, Giogi said, "Well, thank you for rescuing me. Funny, though, I don't remember any stirge."

"Stirge saliva numbs the flesh around the bite," Cat explained. "If you don't notice the prick when it attaches to you, it can drain all your blood without you feeling a thing. It had drained nearly all the life from you. I only brought you back to consciousness with a potion. It was an especially powerful potion, so you shouldn't be feeling any weakness."

"You're right. I don't feel weak," Giogi said with surprise. "Thank you again."

"You're welcome," Cat said, her tone softening pleasantly. She smiled at Giogi.

Olive tried to sneer, but it wasn't in the burro's repertoire. She didn't know which annoyed her more, the female mage's bald-faced lies about rescuing Giogi or Giogi's gullibility.

"Really, though," Giogi said, "I must ask what you're doing here."

Good thinking, Giogi, Olive thought. A little slow, but good thinking.

Cat's manner became suddenly formal. "I don't know that it's any of your business," she replied haughtily. "Who are you, anyway?"

Giogi drew himself to his full height. While his gaunt frame was not very imposing, he did tower a good six inches over the woman. "I am Giogioni Wyvernspur," he declared, bowing slightly as he spoke, "of the Wyvernspurs of Immersea. These catacombs lie beneath my family's crypt. They're our catacombs."

"Do you have a deed for them?" Cat asked coolly.

"Well, no, but the only way into them is through our family crypt and—"

"And the secret, magical door, just outside the graveyard, that opens once every fifty years," Cat concluded impatiently. "I used that secret door to get in here. I was going to use it to get out, but some idiot blocked it while I was still inside the catacombs. I've been stuck here for days."

"Uncle Drone just sealed that door yesterday morning, so you can't have been in here for that long," Giogi objected.

"All right. I've been stuck here for hours," Cat amended her story with annoyance. "I'm starving just the same. You wouldn't happen to have brought food, would you?"

Giogi stared at Cat with considerable perplexity as he reached inside the picnic basket and produced a cheese sandwich.

"Wonderful," Cat said, snatching it out of Giogi's hand. She unwrapped it halfway, sniffed at it once, shrugged, and took a large bite.

Olive stared at the nobleman in amazement. Don't you realize she's got to be the thief who stole the spur? Olive berated Giogi mentally. How can you stand there calmly feeding her cheese sandwiches? "I don't understand," Giogi said. "Uncle Drone said I wouldn't find the thief or the spur down here."

Olive huffed, wishing she could tell Giogi, Shake this woman down for the spur and turn her over to Lord Sudacar. Uncle Drone's made a mistake.

Cat held up her finger, chewed faster, and swallowed. Then she said with a grin, "Your uncle was right. You didn't find the thief or the spur."

"What are you doing in the catacombs if you aren't the thief?" Giogi demanded.

Cat took another large bite, chewed, and swallowed before answering. "Wishing I were the thief. You see, my master sent me here after the spur, but when I got up to your stupid family crypt, the thing was gone. Someone else took it. The door from the crypt to the upper mausoleum was locked, so I had to come back through the catacombs, and, like I said, some idiot—that'd be your uncle—blocked the stupid door to the outside."

"He's not my uncle, really," Giogi said. "He's, well, he was my grandfather's cousin, so that makes him my first cousin twice removed. We all call him uncle, though, because he's so very old." The young noble frowned suddenly. "You have a lot of nerve, you know, admitting you came to steal my family's most precious heirloom, and then insulting my relatives to boot."

"Well, I didn't steal your heirloom, now did I?" Cat pointed out defensively. "And if your uncle knew the thief with the spur wasn't in the catacombs, it was pretty idiotic to seal me up in here, wasn't it?" she asked before popping the remainder of the sandwich in her mouth.

"Uncle Drone is a sweet, gentle old man," Giogi declared with indignation.

"If you say so," Cat mumbled with her mouth still full. When she'd managed to swallow, she asked, "Do you have anything to wash this sandwich down?"

"There's tea," Giogi offered. He began reaching into the picnic basket for the tea jug but stopped short upon noting the disgusted look on Cat's face.

"Would you prefer water?" the nobleman asked.

"Haven't you got anything stronger?" the sorceress asked with a sly grin.

Feeling rather odd, Giogi drew a silver hip flask from his back pocket and held it out. He'd never offered hard liquor to a woman before. "It's Rivengut," he warned. "Quite strong. Would you like me to water it down for you?"

Cat took the flask, unscrewed the lid, and took a long swallow. "No, thank you," she said with a cheerful smile. "It's just right."

Giogi blinked twice in astonishment, then he shook himself mentally. "Why did your master send you after the spur?" he asked.

Cat shrugged. "I have no idea. I just follow his orders. One doesn't ask men like Flattery to explain themselves. It's a good way to get oneself killed."

"But you could have been killed, anyway. The catacombs are full of dangerous creatures, and the guardian is supposed to slay anyone in the crypt who isn't a Wyvernspur. Did you really go into the crypt?"

"How else could I know the spur was missing? I never saw hide nor hair of any guardian. Are you sure your guardian's not a myth your family uses to frighten would-be thieves?"

Giogi shook his head. "She's not," he insisted. "If she didn't kill you, that must mean you're a Wyvernspur. We've always suspected there were missing members. What branch of the family are you from?"

"I'm a mage, not a family historian," Cat said with a sniff.

You're too proud to admit that you don't know, aren't you, girl? Olive thought slyly. You think you're an orphan, just like Alias and Jade. Somehow, though, the guardian must have realized that you're connected to the Nameless Bard, who is a Wyvernspur.

"If your master, this Flattery person," Giogi said, "told you that the guardian wouldn't bother you, then he must have known you were a Wyvernspur."

Cat's brow furrowed with some thought. She looked down at her hands, as if to examine them for proof. "You could be right," she admitted softly.

Giogi lifted the mage's chin so that her eyes met his own. "Why do you serve him if he sends you out to steal for him?"

"I was just beginning to wonder about that myself," Cat said, smiling weakly.

Giogi dropped his hand from the mage's chin to her shoulder. "You should leave his service," he advised.

"I may have to," Cat said, lowering her green eyes again. So softly that Giogi could barely hear her, she whispered, "Flattery will be furious with me for failing my mission."

"Don't go back to him," the noble suggested, giving her shoulder a friendly squeeze.

"I wouldn't," Cat said, looking up at Giogi through her long red eyelashes, "except—" Cat looked down and hesitated. Then, as if she could barely contain her misery, she looked back up at Giogi and burst out, "except I have nowhere else to go, and he's sure to find me, and when he does he'll be even angrier that I tried to leave." Her voice quavered slightly with fear.

Bravo! Olive thought cynically. Excellent performance.

"I see," Giogi said solemnly.

Don't be a fool, Giogi, Olive though .

"I shall offer you my protection, then," Giogi said.

What a sap, Olive thought, shaking her burro head.

"That's very kind of you, Master Giogioni, but I can't accept your offer. Flattery is a very powerful mage with a violent temper. I don't dare risk your life as well."

Think about it, Giogi, Olive pleaded silently. She's just vying for your sympathy, old boy. Make it backfire. Accept her refusal. You don't really want to interfere with the business of powerful mages with violent tempers.

"I insist," Giogi replied staunchly.

I knew he'd say that, Olive thought.

"After all, you saved my life. You must come with me," Giogi continued. "Uncle Drone is a powerful mage, too. He can help protect you. He'll probably want to know all about this Flattery, anyway."

Olive pricked up her ears. Giogi might consider his Uncle Drone a sweet, gentle old man, but if he was a powerful mage, he was another suspect for the man who'd disintegrated Jade. Except, according to Giogi, he was very old. Wizards could disguise their age, though, Olive knew.

"I should accompany you out now, before Steele sees you," Giogi said. "He's my second cousin. He'll think you're the real thief, because Uncle Drone told him the thief was down here."

"That really won't be necessary—" Cat began, but she was interrupted by a crash.

"What was that?" Giogi asked.

"They're your catacombs. You tell me," Cat challenged.

From the same direction as the crash came a blood-curdling scream. A human scream.

"Steele!" Giogi exclaimed. "You wait here with Birdie," he ordered Cat. He drew his foil and ran off in the direction of the scream.

❧ 8 ❧

Steele's Rescue

Olive took only a moment to consider her options. On one hand, she was sure she didn't want to run into whatever had made Steele scream that way. On the other hand, if whatever it was happened to swallow Steele and Giogi, she was stuck in the catacombs—as a burro—with Cat, possibly for the rest of her life, as short as that might be.

Not an amusing prospect, Olive thought. I have to keep the boy from doing something rash. She trotted down the corridor after the shrinking light of the finder's stone.

There was another scream, and Giogi dashed down a narrow side passage to follow it. The ceiling was lower there, and he had to stoop as he ran. Shrill cries of anger and laughter echoed down the hall. The nobleman slowed. There were no further cries from his cousin. The laughter had a sinister tone, which chilled Giogi to the marrow. He stopped.

Olive bumped into the nobleman. He gasped and whirled around. "Birdie, you naughty girl. You were supposed to wait with Mistress Cat."

Cat drew up behind the burro. "What is it?" she asked.

"You should have stayed with the burro. It could be very dangerous," Giogi chided.

"I am with the burro," Cat pointed out. If it's dangerous, why don't we leave?" she asked.

"That was Steele. He's my family. I have to help him."

"But if you don't come back, I'll never get out of here. I'll die down here," Cat said. Her lower lip quivered.

What she said, only without the dramatic touches, Olive thought.

"If Steele and I don't come back, my Cousin Freffie will come down looking for us. If you wait in the crypt for him, he'll let you out."

Cat frowned with displeasure. Olive thought, She doesn't want to take a chance on Freffie. He might not fall for her story as easily as Giogi did.

"I'm not leaving you," Cat insisted.

Giogi sighed with defeat. "Then you'd better stay behind me," he stated, holding an authoritative finger up to her nose. He turned about and crept down the passage.

The corridor turned, and there Giogi halted, peering around the edge. Cat stopped behind him and peeked out from behind his back.

The passage opened into a larger chamber ten feet farther down. Inside the room, a tangle of white-horned, black-scaled creatures smaller than halflings jumped up and down on a massive mahogany tabletop. The monsters wore nothing but raggedy red shifts with belts of rope and dagger sheaths.

The table rocked on the splintered stumps that had once been its legs, and on a prone human body. Protruding from beneath the table were Steele's head and shoulders; the rest of him was pinned by the tabletop and the weight of the creatures swarming on top of it. A moan escaped Steele's lips and his head lolled to one side. From Steele's stillness and closed eyes, though, Giogi guessed his cousin was mercifully unconscious.

"Kobolds," Cat said with scorn. "Just a few stupid kobolds."

Giogi counted at least twenty, which ranked slightly higher than a few, in his estimation, but he kept his growing sense of alarm in check. He could hardly convince Cat that he could protect her from her master, he realized, if he cringed from a battle with kobolds.

"Right. You wait here," he ordered. "And I mean right here." Having laid down the law, Giogi plunged into the room, foil drawn in his right hand, finder's stone raised high in his left, shouting an inarticulate battle cry.

"What does he think he's doing?" Cat muttered.

Proving himself, obviously, Olive thought.

"Idiot," Cat said, pulling something out of one of her robe pockets. As Cat dangled it in front of her, Olive got a closer look at it: a finger bone. Cat began chanting softly. Motes of light began to sparkle about the bone.

The burro pulled back quickly. Don't want to get in the way of a spell that involves anyone's finger bone, Olive decided.

Oblivious to the magic being cast behind him, Giogi rushed to his cousin's side. The kobolds, alarmed by the sudden loud intrusion and the finder's stone light, scattered before him.

Their surprise gave way to rage, however, when they realized they were beset with only a single foe armed with nothing but an oversized skewer. With cruel smiles on their muzzles, the kobolds drew sharp daggers, which glittered in the light of Giogi's stone. The beasts began encroaching on him in groups of three or four, snarling like dogs set to bait a bull.

Assuming a combat stance, Giogi pivoted about his left foot, lunging with his foil in the direction of any kobold who came within range.

Back in the corridor, Cat ceased her chanting and the bone she held crumbled to dust. Suddenly, the kobolds surrounding Giogi fell back in terror. Impressed with the effect his prowess seemed to have had on the creatures, Giogi jabbed his foil a few times in their direction to test their reaction. The kobolds cowered like whipped dogs.

The nobleman didn't have the heart to skewer any of them. Keeping a wary eye on the little monsters, he bent over to examine his cousin. Steele's breathing was shallow and his face pale.

Cat padded into the room, smiling with pleasure at the effect her scare spell had on them. The creatures trembled at her gaze. Olive stood watching from the shadows near the room's entrance. According to common adventurer lore, pack animals were seen as a delicacy among kobolds and other underground races. She didn't want to take the chance that the sight of dinner on the hoof would prick up the monsters' courage.

"I thought I told you to stay put," Giogi whispered to the mage.

"They won't hurt me with you to protect me," Cat insisted. When she looked down at Steele, she gasped softly. "This is your cousin?" she asked.

"Yes. Why?" Giogi asked.

"Nothing," Cat said, shaking her head.

"Well, now that you're here, I suppose you can help," Giogi said with a sigh. "Take these," he ordered, handing Cat his foil and the finder's stone so he could use both hands to lift the table off Steele. He strained under the weight, unable to shift the massive piece of furniture.

"How did they move this thing on top of him in the first place?" Giogi gasped, sweat beading on his forehead.

"Look up," Cat suggested, holding the finder's stone over her head so he could get a better look. A great length of rope ran from the table to a pulley mounted in the ceiling twenty feet above, to a second pulley at the edge of the room, and finally to a spool controlled by a winch.

"Keep an eye on them," he ordered Cat. He crossed the room to examine the winch. Whimpering kobolds backed away from him. It took him a minute to find and operate the toggle that engaged the spool's gears. He cranked the rope taut, then began lifting the great table off the floor. Even with the ingenious machine, it was hard work. Sweat trickled down the sides of Giogi's face by the time he'd raised the table a few inches.

"That should be enough," Cat said, peering under the table at Steele's body.

Giogi returned to her side and slid Steele clear of the crushing weight. "I wonder how these little monsters managed to get this table in here," Giogi said aloud. "I think it used to be in the anteroom beneath the crypt."

"No doubt they bribed something bigger to do it for them," Cat guessed. "So, unless you want to meet whatever that thing is, I suggest we leave now."

"Good idea," Giogi agreed. "Just as soon as Steele recovers. I need to fetch a healing potion from Birdie's pack."

Cat placed a slender hand on Giogi's sleeve. In a soft but urgent voice she said, "If you bring him around now, he'll see me down here. Didn't you say he'll think I'm the thief?"

Giogi nodded. "Yes. He'll make a tremendous fuss, too. Steele can be quite vicious when he has his heart set on something, as he does on the spur. I'll have to carry him."

"But that will slow us down awfully," Cat argued. "Why don't you load him on the burro and wait until we're back out in the graveyard before you use your potion?"

Oh, no, you don't, Olive thought from her hiding place in the shadows.

"Birdie's got a full load, and even if I unpacked her, Steele would weigh too much for her."

Cat gave an annoyed sniff. "I might be able to manage a spell to handle him," she offered.

Handing Giogi his weapon and the finder's stone, she drew a vial of silver liquid and unstoppered it. Murmuring a chant, she tilted the vial so a drop of the liquid fell from it. Just before it reached the ground, the droplet spread out into a shimmering disk, rose three feet, and hovered there. "We can lay him on that," Cat said.

"Are you sure it will hold him?" Giogi asked.

"Hurry," Cat whispered, putting away the vial, "before the kobolds begin to lose their fear of you."

Even before Giogi looked back at the little monsters cowering in the cavern, some of them had begun making muttering, discontented sounds. He lifted Steel up and laid him on the disk. It held the wounded man off the ground without sinking. Cat headed slowly for the doorway. The disk and its cargo followed her.

Giogi followed, too, walking backward, his weapon at the ready. If the kobolds attacked en masse, he was sure he would not be able to hold them off.

Suddenly, one of the grimy creatures stepped from around the table and began shouting angrily. Its weapon was sheathed, but its tone was hostile. Cat stopped by the entrance and turned around. The disk hovered beside her. She listened with some interest to what the creature had to say.

Giogi backed into the mage. "Do you know what he's gibbering?" he asked in a whisper.

"She says," Cat explained, "that it's not fair. Your cousin captured and tortured her, but she hasn't had her chance to give as well as she got."

Aghast, Giogi asked, "Why would Steele do such a thing?"

Cat made a series of hissing and growling noises, which Giogi could not begin to comprehend. The belligerent kobold answered in kind.

"To find out about the spur and the thief," Cat explained. "She convinced him to follow her into this booby trap."

"Can you tell her I will take him away so he can't hurt any of them again?"

Cat spoke again in the tongue the kobolds understood. The lead kobold growled and chittered some more, and Cat snarled back at it. The gaze of both, human woman and kobold female, locked onto one another with a long, menacing glare.

After a minute, the staring contest ended. The kobold looked down, spat on the ground in Cat's direction, and ran off into the darkness. The other kobolds followed.

"She would have preferred that you left him here. I think you spoiled their fun," Cat said with a wry smile.

Giogi shuddered. "Let's get out of here."

When they'd rejoined Olive, Giogi pulled a blanket out of the burro's saddlebags and covered his cousin's unconscious body. Then the party began carefully retracing its steps using Giogi's map and the numbers painted on the walls.

Olive plodded beside Cat's magic disk and took advantage of the time to study the unconscious Steele. He had the Wyvern-spur face, all right. Considering Steele's sadistic streak, which Cat had just revealed to them, he seemed even more likely to be Jade's murderer. Unfortunately, while the murderer had looked far younger than Nameless, he had also looked some-what older than Steele. Steele wasn't any older than Giogi. Be-sides, Steele had a mole by the right side of his mouth, which Olive was certain the murderer had not possessed.

Of course, that left the possibility that Steele might have been disguised. It was hard to imagine, though, that a young man foolish enough to walk into a kobold ambush was really a pow-erful mage. Ruling out Steele left the halfling with Frefford and Drone, and any other male relatives Giogi might have who he hadn't yet mentioned.

Plodding along behind Giogi and Cat, Olive hadn't paid much attention to their progress. They'd crossed or turned at six in-tersections when Giogi looked up from his map with a puzzled expression. "We can't have come this far already," he said, reaching out to touch the numbers on the wall. His fingers came back with paint on them. "Odd. This should have dried by now."

From one of her robe pockets Cat drew out her own crudely drawn map.

A sinister giggling echoed around them.

"The kobolds," Cat whispered with alarm. "They've tricked us with false markings."

Giogi held the finder's stone up high to see if he could catch a glimpse of the monsters. The light sprang out down one corri-dor of the intersection, but left the other three in the dark. Giogi spied no kobolds, but he did spot a piece of paper on the floor. He led them toward it and picked it up.

"This is from your cheese sandwich," he said. "I can find our way from here." He rolled up his map and slipped it back in one of the burro's packs. Remembering what Samtavan Sudacar had told him about the finder's stone, the nobleman followed its light with confidence. Whichever way it shone the brightest, he turned.

"Are you sure you're headed in the right direction?" the mage asked uncertainly.

Giogi nodded with a sly grin.

Olive, aware of the finder's stone's powers, thought, The boy's smarter'n he looks, girl. Take his word for it.

Giogi's party wasn't too far from the stairs to the crypt when a huge shadow blocked the corridor ahead.

"Bother!" Cat growled. "Not him again."

"What is it?" Giogi asked nervously, trying to make out the great shape's identity by squinting.

"Bugbear."

"Right," Giogi said with a gulp. Maybe if I charge with a yell, he thought, I can send it running, as I did with the kobolds. He raised his foil and took a deep breath.

Cat put her hand on Giogi's sleeve again. "Let me handle this," she said. She pulled out Giogi's hip flask—which she had never returned—and unstoppered it. With two fingers on her tongue, she gave a shrill whistle and held up the flask.

The bugbear looked up at the newcomers, then came lumbering down the corridor at them.

Giogi froze with fear, and the burro tried to press her heavily loaded bulk flat against the wall. If she has a death wish, Olive thought, I wish she'd leave us out of it.

The halfling couldn't tell for sure which smelled worse, the bugbear's matted red fur or the lice-ridden wool sweater it wore. Its fangs were a dull yellow, but its eyes shone bright red. It stood much taller than Giogi. Giogi grabbed at Cat's arm to pull her behind him, but she evaded his grasp and walked right up to the bugbear.

"Wine?" the mage offered with a smile. "More wine?"

The bugbear snatched the flask from Cat's hand and poured its contents down its throat.

Cat stepped back.

"That's not wine," Giogi whispered. "It's straight Rivengut."

"I know, but he doesn't. In another moment, he won't care," Cat replied, smiling.

The bugbear roared once, wobbled, and passed out.

"See?" the mage asked. She stepped over the monster and continued down the corridor with the disk and Steele floating after her.

Giogi and Olive hurried to catch up.

"I bribed him a few hours ago with a skin of wine," Cat explained.

They reached the anteroom and slowly climbed the stairs back to the crypt. Olive felt her stomach rumbling. She thought longingly, too, of the Rivengut that Cat had given the bugbear.

When they reached the top of the rough stairs, Giogi peered into the crypt, but the guardian was silent.

Giogi crept across the crypt without a word. Olive needed no warning to step as softly as she could, but Cat couldn't leave well enough alone.

"So where's the guardian?" the mage asked as they waited at the crypt door for Giogi to pull out his key.

"She's here," Giogi muttered as he inserted his key in the door and unlocked it. "Please, don't disturb her."

"Giogioni," the guardian's voice whispered. "Not long now, my Giogioni."

Cat whirled around and saw the huge wyvern shadow on the far wall. "Mystra's mysteries!" she whispered excitedly. "There is a guardian."

Giogi flung the door open and smacked Olive through. The burro needed no further encouragement. She clomped up the stairs.

"What does she mean?" Cat asked. "Not long until what?"

"Don't ask, please," Giogi whispered, tugging on the mage's arm to pull her through the doorway with him. As soon as the disk floated through, too, he slammed the door shut and relocked it.

"Why shouldn't I ask what she meant?" Cat demanded.

Giogi closed his eyes. "Because I don't want to know," he whispered.

They trudged up the last four flights of stairs. Giogi hopped hard on the tenth step from the top, and the secret door slid open. He ushered them through the mausoleum and out into the graveyard beyond.

The noon sky was a cold steel gray laced with low clouds, but the trio blinked in the open air as if they had been prisoners exposed to full sunshine for the first time in months.

Giogi reached into one of the burro's packs and pulled out a vial of healing potion. As carefully as he could, he poured it down Steele's throat. His cousin stirred and sighed, but remained unconscious.

"That's the best I can do," Giogi said. "We'll have to get him to a cleric. How much longer can you carry him like this?" he asked Cat.

"As long as you need me to," the mage replied with a gentle smile.

"Thank you. For everything," Giogi said.

What about me? Olive thought. I've pulled more than my share of the weight, too, you know.

As if reading Olive's thoughts, Giogi scratched between the burro's ears and said, "We'll be home soon, Birdie. You'll get your lunch then, and with any luck we'll get an explanation from Unce Drone before teatime."

Yes, Olive thought. Uncle Drone's one mage I want to meet.

Their party hadn't gone halfway down the graveyard hill when a man wrapped in a green cloak came rushing up to meet them. He was calling out Giogi's name. As he approached, Olive realized he was another Wyvernspur. He had the same face as Steele, Nameless, and Jade's murderer. Good grief, Olive thought, how do Wyvernspurs tell one another apart?

Now, that has the makings of a good joke, the halfling mused. She studied the newcomer. He didn't have a mole like Steele, but he was just as young. His eyes weren't the right shade. Jade's murderer had ice-blue eyes, like Nameless's eyes. The eyes of the man before them now were definitely hazel.

Beside her Olive felt Cat start for a moment and gasp softly. Funny, the halfling thought, that's the same reaction she had when she got a good look at Steele. I wonder why.

"It's just my Cousin Frefford," Giogi explained. "Let me do the talking."

Cat relaxed instantly.

So, this is Frefford, Olive thought. Well, he's not the murderer. That leaves me with Uncle Drone.

"Good morning, Freffie," Giogi greeted his kinsman when they stood face to face.

"Good morning, Giogi. What happened to Steele?" Frefford asked.

Giogi sighed with exasperation. "He went in without me. I found him under a kobold trap. I thought I'd better get him back before exploring further. This young woman was in the graveyard. She offered to give me a hand with him. He'll be all right, I think. Freffie, how's Gaylyn?"

"She's fine," Freffie replied. "Mother and daughter are both fine." His grim tone, however, did not match his good news.

Giogi broke into a grin. "Congratulations! I'm so happy for you. But shouldn't you be with them?" Frefford's hard expression finally registered with Giogi. "Freffie, what's wrong?"

"Aunt Dorath sent me to fetch you and Steele," Frefford explained. He took a deep breath and put a comforting hand on Giogi's shoulder. "It's Uncle Drone," he said. "Aunt Dorath said he went to his laboratory to cast some awful spell. We looked everywhere for him, but he's disappeared. On the floor of his lab we found," Frefford's voice broke. He swallowed and continued. "All we found were his robes, his hat, and a pile of ash. Uncle Drone is dead, Giogi."

❧ 9 ❧

Drone's Last Message

Giogi felt as if he'd been pole-axed. The color drained from his face. He did not reply to Frefford's news at once, but stood looking out at the lake in the distance. Wind whipped his hair about his face, but he seemed not to notice.

"Giogi, are you all right?" Frefford asked, squeezing his cousin's shoulder gently.

"No," Giogi said. "There has to be some mistake. He can't be dead."

"I'm afraid it isn't a mistake. I'm sorry, Giogi. We all cared for him very much," Frefford said. "Come on, let's get off this cold hill," he suggested, pulling on his stunned cousin's arm, leading him down the hill.

Olive and Cat followed, with the disk carrying Steele trailing behind them. Frefford's and Giogi's cloaks whipped out behind them in a wind that swept up the hill. Olive glanced sideways at the mage and was surprised to see she wasn't shivering with only her satin robes to protect her from the weather. Cat was deep in thought.

I'll bet she's weighing her chances with Giogi without his Uncle Drone to protect her from her master, Olive thought.

What are the chances, she wondered, that Drone killed Jade and retribution caught up with him the very next morning? Olive shook her head. It hadn't seemed very likely that the old man Giogi had described as sweet and gentle would be Jade's murderer. Now I won't be able to identify Drone for sure, Olive realized, since he's been turned to a pile of ash.

A pile of ash—like Jade! Did Drone meet his fate at the same hands? Was the murdering Wyvernspur running around killing all of his kin? Olive trotted closer to Giogi and pricked up her ears to eavesdrop on the two men's conversation.

"How could this have happened?" Giogi asked, rubbing tears from his cheeks.

"We think he used a gate spell to bring in something dangerous and evil, then lost control of it, and the thing killed him."

"But he hated gating things," Giogi protested. "That spell always ages him horribly. Why would he do a thing like that?"

"To help him find the spur," the Wyvernspur lord explained. "You see, after the baby was born, Gaylyn and Aunt Dorath both wanted me to lend a hand in the crypt. Gaylyn was worried for you, and Aunt Dorath, of course, is frantic to have the spur returned. Uncle Drone said that there was no sense wasting my time, because once you got past the guardian, you'd be fine, and the thief and the spur weren't in the catacombs anyway."

"Oh," Giogi murmured listlessly. He thought that if he hadn't been wasting his time saving Steele's miserable hide, he might have been with Uncle Drone.

"Oh? Is that all you can say?" Frefford asked. "Giogi, did you know about that?" he asked, suspicious.

"Uncle Drone told me last night," the noble admitted, "but he wouldn't tell me why he misled us all. He said I was supposed to go down to keep up the charade, and tell him later everything that happened."

"Well, when Uncle Drone told us this morning," Frefford said, "he claimed it was some sort of ruse to see what Steele would do. Aunt Dorath hit the ceiling. She demanded Uncle Drone return the spur. Uncle Drone swore he didn't have it and didn't know where it was. Aunt Dorath said he had darn well better find out. Uncle Drone said he darn well would. Then he went stomping up to his lab with orders that he was not to be disturbed—that it would be dangerous to interrupt him."

Frefford took a deep breath, let it out slowly, then continued his grim tale. "When he didn't come down for morning tea, Aunt Dorath sent me after him. Both doors to his lab were locked and bolted. Aunt Dorath insisted I force one of them. It looked like there'd been a fight when we got inside. Papers were scattered about. Furniture was overturned. Then we found the ashes beneath his robes and hat."

Frefford's word hung on the cold air with the vapor of his breath. Then he asked his cousin, "Giogi, did you talk to the guardian? Did she say anything?"

"Freffie, I'd really rather not talk about her right now," Giogi replied.

Frefford put his hand on his cousin's shoulder again. "Giogi, it could be important," the Wyvernspur lord insisted, giving

Giogi's shoulder a squeeze. "You know you're the only one she communicates with."

Giogi kicked at a rock on the path. The guardian spoke to only one member of each generation of Wyvernspurs. Giogi wished she would have picked someone else—someone like Steele. Steele didn't believe in her. He had teased Giogi about her since they were children, when Giogi had first admitted hearing her voice.

Frefford believed, though. And he was right, it could be important. Giogi said, "I asked her why she didn't stop the thief, and she said that she's supposed to let Wyvernspurs pass unslain. I asked her who had taken the spur, and she said she couldn't tell—that we're all alike—except me."

"Nothing about the curse?" Frefford asked.

"Freffie, that's just superstition," Giogi said.

"Aunt Dorath doesn't seem to think so," Frefford said softly. "Maybe she's right. Uncle Drone and Steele both risked their lives because of it, and Uncle Drone—" Frefford broke off his sentence. There was no need to say it again.

They reached the bottom of the hill and stepped out onto the road, where Frefford's carriage waited. A wedding gift from Gaylyn's father, the carriage's gilded surface still sparkled, even in the gray light. Giogi and Frefford transferred Steele from Cat's magical disk to the carriage's back seat.

"Steele must see a healing cleric right away," Frefford said, "but I can drive you into town, at least."

Giogi excused himself, using Birdie as an excuse. Cat explained she had business with Giogi.

"Stop by later and see the baby," Frefford invited as he climbed into the carriage, beside his wounded cousin. Steele moaned softly in his sleep.

"Thanks. I will," Giogi promised.

Frefford signaled his driver, who clucked the horses into motion. As the carriage rattled down the road, Giogi felt a sense of relief. He didn't want to be around when Steele fully recovered and found out Uncle Drone had deceived them. Frefford could handle Steele's rage far better than Giogi could.

"Perhaps I'd better leave," Cat suggested, "now that your uncle is no longer here to aid you."

Good idea, Olive thought, nodding her burro head in agreement.

"No," Giogi said. "Uncle Drone's death doesn't change anything. You're still in danger; you must stay with me. After all, if the guardian let you pass, you must be a Wyvernspur, and we Wyvernspurs look out for one another."

Cat bowed her head. "Very well. I accept your kind offer, Master Giogioni."

"Wonderful." Giogi smiled at Cat, feeling excessively pleased with himself. "Gracious Tymora. I never even noticed. You haven't a cloak. Here, you'd better wear mine. I insist," the noble said, ignoring the mage's protests as he wrapped her in his own cloak.

Humans are such fools, Olive noted, especially human men. All this chivalry nonsense and family duty could get a person killed. Like Uncle Drone.

"Come along, Birdie," Giogi chided, giving the burro a tug on the lead rope. "Stop daydreaming. We want to get home before the weather turns ugly. Ugh. Make that uglier."

Olive looked up. The clouds overhead had gone from steel gray to black. Olive felt the first sharp, cold needles of sleet pierce through her fur. She began trotting alongside the two humans as they hurried down the road toward Giogi's home.

The traffic in Immersea was lighter than it had been earlier that morning. A few grimy urchins chased one another through the streets, but the foresters had returned to the forest, the field hands to the fields, and the fishermen to their beds. Servants were busy eating their noonday meals.

By the time Giogi's party reached his townhouse gate, the drizzling sleet became a heavy freezing rain, which hid the townhouse behind a curtain of water. The nobleman, mage, and burro dashed through the garden and hustled into the carriage house. They all stood shaking water and ice from their hair, clothes, and fur for a minute.

"Just as soon as I get Birdie settled, we'll have our lunch," Giogi promised Cat as he lit the lantern by the door.

"Haven't you got a servant to take care of that?" Cat asked.

Giogi nodded. "Yes, Thomas usually handles it, but I like to look after them, too. I like animals," he explained.

Cat climbed into the parked buggy and sank into the cushioned seat with a sigh.

Giogi unloaded all the equipment from the burro's back and led the beast back into her stall. He unclipped the lead rope but left the halter on. He rubbed her dry with an old blanket and brushed the worst of the catacomb dust and cobwebs from her hide and the mud from her little feet. Olive submitted to the grooming philosophically. After all, she thought, how many halflings get their feet washed by Cormyte nobles?

"Some fresh water, more grain, and hay." Giogi pointed out all the provisions he'd brought in for the burro. "You should try the hay, Birdie. It's very good. Just ask Daisyeye."

Daisyeye can have my share, Olive thought.

After shutting the burro in, Giogi took a few moments to stroke the chestnut mare. Finally he picked up the picnic basket and turned to Cat. "Shall we go?"

Cat held out her hand. Hastily Giogi transferred the basket to his left hand to help Cat down with his right. The mage leaned on him heavily as she dismounted and landed very near him, so that her forehead brushed against his chin.

"Excuse me," Cat whispered. "It's just that I'm so tired. I was afraid to sleep in that awful place."

Giogi stood, momentarily stunned. A feeling came over him even more odd than the one he'd felt offering Cat his liquor flask. He'd never stood this close to a woman before, not even Minda. It took him a moment before he could collect himself enough to step back and say, "You poor thing. I think right after lunch we should tuck you up in the guest room for a nap." Then he blushed, aware that his words could be misinterpreted.

In the dim lamplight, Cat seemed not to notice his embarrassment, nor did she object to his offer. "You've been so kind," she said.

"Not at all," Giogi replied.

Giogi offered Cat his arm as he led her to the door and blew out the lantern.

"We could share this cloak," Cat suggested before he opened the door.

Through a knothole in her stall wall Olive watched as Giogi slid his arm around the mage's shoulder, beneath the fabric of his cloak. The two humans dashed from the carriage house, slamming the door behind them.

Olive's burro eyes squinted suspiciously. That woman is up to no good, she insisted to herself, and, while Giogi is a nice boy, he's no match for the machinations of a mage. What's a burro to do?

Keep up my strength for one thing, the halfling thought, sniffing daintily at her bucket of sweetened oats.

* * * * *

"Why don't you make yourself comfortable by the fire while I go see about lunch," Giogi suggested as he ushered Cat into the townhouse parlor.

Cat sat on a satin-covered chair, carefully keeping the muddy hem of her robes from the expensive fabric, and kicked off her dirty slippers. She curled her feet beneath her and closed her eyes to slits. The noble scurried out with the picnic basket and headed back for Servant Land.

Thomas looked up from his lunch with astonishment. Giogi, as wet as a river rat, stood in the door, looking very apologetic.

"Sorry to disturb you, Thomas," his master said, setting the picnic basket down on the table, "but the catacombs jaunt didn't quite go over as expected. Do you think you could manage lunch for myself and a guest—just a little nourishment, preferably something warm?"

"Of course, sir," the servant replied, rising from the table. "Um, sir. You have heard the news about your Uncle Drone?"

"Yes," Giogi said. "Lord Frefford told me."

"My condolences, sir."

His voice cracking with emotion, Giogi replied, "Thank you, Thomas." Giogi turned, about to leave, then, remembering that his lunch guest's stay was to be more permanent, turned again. "One more thing, Thomas. When you've finished your lunch, could you spark up the lilac room fire and turn down the bed?"

"The lilac room, sir?" Thomas replied with confusion.

"Yes. My lunch guest will be staying with us for a while, and will need to rest immediately after lunch."

"You wouldn't want to offer anyone the lilac room, sir," Thomas replied. The servant actually looked a little alarmed, though Giogi could hardly tell why, it wasn't as if Thomas didn't keep the lilac room in pristine condition. "The red room would be far superior," Thomas said.

"I thought the lilac room would be—well, it's more suitable for a lady, don't you think?"

"A lady, sir?" Thomas asked, his eyebrows disappearing into his bangs.

"Um, yes, a lady." Giogi's voice quavered slightly and he felt a trace of alarm. He had forgotten how provincial people were in Immersea, especially the servants. "I know it's irregular, but it's an irregular situation—not one we need mention, though, to Aunt Dorath."

"I would imagine not, sir," Thomas agreed. "Still, the linen in the red room is in better condition. Your guest would be much more comfortable there."

"Very well," Giogi agreed, dissatisfied but not wanting to antagonize the man on whose discretion he must depend. "The red room. The lady's name, by the way, is Cat. She's a magic-user. She may be able to help me find the wyvern's spur."

"Ah, I see." Thomas nodded. "Oh, sir. About two hours ago, a servant from Redstone delivered a package for you. I left it on your writing table in the parlor."

"A package? Hmm," Giogi mused, wondering what sort of package would be sent down from Redstone. "Well, thank you, Thomas. We'll be in the parlor until you announce lunch."

"Very good, sir."

Giogi turned about again and nearly ran over a large, fat black-and-white tomcat, which meowed up at him with annoyance.

"Thomas, is that Spot?" Giogi asked.

"Yes, sir," Thomas said. "He appeared on the doorstep about an hour ago. I didn't have the heart to turn him away."

"No. You were quite right," Giogi said. "He'll need looking after now that Uncle Drone is gone. Aunt Dorath always threatened to turn him into a muff someday. Can't have that, can we, boy?" Giogi bent over and picked up the heavy feline.

Cradling Spot in his arms, Giogi returned to the parlor and his guest. Spot leaped from the noble's arms, sat by the fireplace, and began washing himself.

Giogi looked over at Cat. Her eyes were closed, and her head rested against the overstuffed wing of the chair. Her face was relaxed now that her fear and pride had drained away in sleep. Actually, Giogi thought, she's much prettier than Alias of Westgate.

Giogi crept quietly over to his desk so as not to disturb the young woman. A bundle of red velvet cloth wrapped with twine lay upon the blotter. The noble sat at his desk and picked up the parcel. Something hard, nearly two feet long, eight inches around, and quite heavy lay within the cloth. Giogi picked away the knot in the string.

Giogi unwound the velvet cloth carefully, revealing a gleaming black statue of a beautiful woman. Her lithe and scantily clad form was slightly arched, and her shapely arms were swept up over her head in a circle. Her face was round and pretty. Her lips were parted slightly, and her eyes were closed, like a woman waiting to be surprised. The rest of her physical features Uncle Drone had once described as ample, though Aunt Dorath had argued they were scandalous.

"Sweet Selune," Giogi whispered, recognizing the statue immediately.

"What's wrong?" Cat asked sleepily.

Giogi started and turned in his chair. "I'm sorry. I didn't mean to wake you."

"That's all right," the mage said, rising from her chair. "I was just napping. Oh! What a beautiful statue," she said, padding over to Giogi's side. "Where did you get it?"

"It's Uncle Drone's—well, it was Uncle Drone's. Thomas says a servant brought it over this morning. It's a carving of Selune by Cledwyll."

"Really? I've never seen a Cledwyll before. It must be worth a fortune."

"I suppose. Not that we'd ever sell it. It was a gift from the artist to Paton Wyvernspur, the founder of our family line." Giogi set the statue on the writing table and idly stroked the glistening black stream of hair that flowed down its back.

Why did Uncle Drone send me this? the nobleman wondered. I wouldn't have thought he'd have ever parted with it. Unless he had some premonition of his death and was afraid Aunt Dorath would lock it away from sight. Giogi took his hand off the statue to search the cloth wrapping for a note of explanation.

"Down, Spot. Naughty boy," a wheezy voice suddenly chided.

Giogi sat up and stared at the statue. The lovely lips of the carving of Selune moved, and from them issued an old man's voice—Uncle Drone's voice. The voice spoke again, saying, "Giogi, listen. The wyvern's spur is your destiny. Steele mustn't get it. You must find it first. Search for the thief."

The statue's mouth froze back into its normal alluring shape and was silent. The room was quiet, except for the wind and rain on the windows. Spot jumped up on the desk and sniffed at the statue.

Cat's brow furrowed in puzzlement. There was something very unusual about the magical message. She did a quick mental calculation. Yes, she realized, something's missing. "Who's voice was that?" she asked.

"Uncle Drone's," Giogi replied. An ache settled in his heart. That's the last time I'll ever hear his voice, he realized.

"And who's Spot?" the mage asked.

"His cat. This beast," Giogi explained, reaching out to stroke Spot's fur. Spot pushed Giogi's quill pen off the desk to the floor and leaped down after it.

"What did your Uncle Drone mean," Cat asked, "by the wyvern's spur being your destiny?"

"I'm not sure. I suppose it has something to do with my father. He used the spur somehow. I guess Uncle Drone expects me to, as well."

"How can the spur be used?" the mage asked curiously.

Giogi shrugged. "I don't know."

Cat sank down onto the thick Calimsham carpeting and sat cross-legged beside the writing table. "Do you think your uncle was telling the truth when he told your aunt he didn't have the spur or know where it was?"

"Oh, Uncle Drone would never lie," Giogi said.

"But he told your family the thief was in the catacombs," Cat pointed out with a skeptical smile.

"Actually, what he said was the would-be thief was stuck in the catacombs. He was right, wasn't he?" the nobleman asked. He meant the question to be a chastisement, but he couldn't help grinning at the mage.

Cat blushed with embarrassment and stared down at her lap.

"It's possible," Giogi admitted, "that Uncle Drone knew more about the real thief than he let on. I don't see how he expected me to find the spur without telling me more about the thief, though," he added irritably.

Cat looked back up at the nobleman. "He may have meant to include something more about the thief in his message, but it got cut off," the mage conjectured.

"Cut off? What do you mean?" Giogi asked.

Cat repeated the message, holding up a finger for every word. " 'Giogi listen. The wyvern's spur is your destiny. Steele mustn't get it. You must find it first. Search for the thief.' That's twenty-one words. The spell he used to send the message only has magic enough to send twenty-five words. That leaves four words."

"Four words," Giogi mused. "He could have told me the thief's name and city, at least. Why didn't he?"

"He probably did, but he used four words at the beginning of the message, probably by accident. Remember?"

" 'Down, Spot. Naughty boy,' " Giogi said with a sigh. He looked at the tomcat chewing on his quill pen. "You are a naughty boy, too," the noble said, pulling the feather from the cat's mouth and setting it back up on the desk. "Well, that's that."

"A priest might be able to try speaking with his spirit," Cat suggested.

"Aunt Dorath would never allow that. Not even to find the spur. We don't disturb the dead in our family."

"Then you're back to scratch unless there's anything else you can think of that your uncle might have mentioned. Is there?" the mage queried.

"He told me to watch my step, that my life could be in danger," Giogi recalled.

"From whom?" Cat asked.

Giogi shook his head uncertainly. He considered Julia's attempt to drug him at Steele's request. Steele wouldn't have killed me, he thought. The guardian would never harm a Wyvernspur, even if she is always talking about cracking bones. Uncle Drone wouldn't have bothered to warn me about the disgusting stirges or the awful kobolds or the bugbears—he knew I already knew about them. The only other person down there was Cat.

Giogi looked at the lovely mage. Her face was still pale and drawn from exhaustion, but her green eyes glittered. She saved my life in the catacombs, he thought, so it couldn't have been her that Uncle Drone meant. She must have been freezing down there, Giogi realized, noting the way the firelight shone through Cat's shimmering robes, outlining her slender figure. Her long, shining copper hair would have kept her warmer than that foolish frock, he thought.

"Master Giogioni? Who are you thinking of? Who would want to kill you?" Cat asked, noting the faraway look in the young noble's eyes.

Giogi snapped out of his reverie. "No one. I haven't got any enemies."

"Does the guardian know about your fate? Is that what she meant by 'not long now'?"

"I don't know."

"You said before that you don't want to know. *I* would want to know if it were *my* fate. Why don't you want to know?"

Giogi shuddered. "Because it has something to do with dreaming about the death cry of prey, the taste of warm blood, and the crunch of bone." The words just tumbled off his tongue before he could hold them back.

"Do you dream about those things?" Cat asked in an awed whisper. Her eyes widened with excitement.

"No," Giogi said, then he amended, "not often."

"How interesting," the mage said. "What kind of prey?"

Giogi shuddered, a little shocked by Cat's reaction. There was a knock at the parlor door. Giogi felt a flash of relief that the conversation was interrupted. "Come in," the noble called.

Thomas stepped one pace into the room. "Luncheon is served, sir," he announced, then he retreated hastily. The sight of the beautiful woman seated at his master's feet flustered him. He withdrew from the parlor hurriedly.

Giogi rose and bent to help Cat stand. She placed her hand in his own and used it to steady herself as she stood. Her thankful smile warmed the young noble. He led her from the parlor and into the dining room.

Thomas had whipped up a simple meal: cheese fondue, venison broth with noodles, fish poached in wine, and crepes with boysenberry jam. Cat seemed delighted with each course, which pleased Giogi, but the young man didn't feel very hungry.

When I was younger, he thought, I had no trouble devouring a meal this size and asking how soon until tea. What's happened to my appetite? he wondered.

Conversation was suspended briefly while they ate, but Cat resumed her questions as they finished off the lemon tea. "If I must be a Wyvernspur because the guardian let me pass, then the spur's thief must be a Wyvernspur, too, right?" she asked.

Giogi nodded.

"How many of you are there?"

"Well, there's me and Aunt Dorath and Uncle Drone and Fref-ford and Steele and Julia, oh, and Frefford's wife and new baby

daughter. That's all that's left of Gerrin Wyvernspur's line—
that's old Paton's grandson. There must be other lines of the
family. Gerrin had a brother. I can't remember his name, but,
anyway, none of his descendants have kept in touch with the
Immersea branch. We didn't even know if there were any, but
the real thief must be one of them. You must be one of them,
too," Giogi explained.

"I wouldn't know," Cat said with a disinterested shrug. "I'm
an orphan," she explained.

Giogi gave the mage a sympathetic look. "I'm so sorry," he
said.

"Why should you be?" Cat asked sharply, annoyed by what
she thought was pity.

"Well, it's pretty awful being an orphan," Giogi replied sin-
cerely. "I know. I'm one myself. My father died when I was
eight. My mother died a year later, of a broken heart, they say. I
miss them both."

The nobleman's tenderheartedness disturbed the mage. She
explained hastily, "I don't remember my parents." She stifled a
yawn.

"I shouldn't be keeping you from your nap," Giogi said. "I'll
show you to your room."

"What will you be doing this afternoon?" the mage asked.

"Well, I'd like to visit Frefford's new daughter. Then—" Giogi
hesitated, trying to decide what he could do. "I think I need to
speak to someone who knows more about the spur."

"Who's that?" Cat asked, stifling another yawn.

"I don't know," Giogi replied. "There has to be somebody."

❧ 10 ❧

Cat's Master

From the journal of Giogioni Wyvernspur:

The 20th of Ches, in the Year of the Shadows

My Uncle Drone died this morning, apparently a victim of his own magic. No one will mourn his passing more deeply than I. Yet, I can't help feeling cross with him at the same time. It seems apparent he was involved somehow in the theft of the wyvern's spur. Since his very last message to me enjoined me to find the thief, however, I must assume he did not steal the spur himself.

It would have been an easy matter, though, for Uncle Drone to disengage the magical alarms that warn of intruders in the crypt, giving his accomplice the opportunity to sneak in.

The theft might have gone undiscovered for some time had it not been for the presence of a second thief, who did set off an alarm.

Since Uncle Drone was desperate enough to cast a dangerous spell to locate the spur, it's probable that his accomplice betrayed him. A disturbing idea, that, since the thief must have been another Wyvernspur.

Besides the problem of discovering the thief, I'm also left with the worry that my life still "might possibly be in danger," as Uncle Drone warned me last evening. That danger might be past now that I've returned safely from the crypt, but, somehow, I doubt it. I've just taken into my protection a young woman, Cat, whose former master, Flattery, is, according to Cat, "a powerful mage with a violent temper."
Flattery also wishes to obtain the spur.

I can't help thinking that to find the spur, I'll need to find out about its alleged powers. The guardian spirit in the family crypt might know, though I don't relish the idea of asking her. Aunt Dorath might know, too. I'm not certain I relish the idea of asking her, either.

Giogi leaned back in his chair and waved his quill idly in the air. Having settled his guest in her room, he'd returned to the parlor to make a quick entry in his journal before heading off to Redstone.

As usual when he wrote in his journal, there were things he thought it best not to record. Aside from keeping secret his Cousin Julia's scandalous behavior in the graveyard, he couldn't bring himself to reveal that Cat was the second thief. She hadn't actually stolen anything, after all, and she'd apparently left Flattery's evil influence.

Giogi realized he could not mention that he knew Cat to be a Wyvernspur, either, since that would put her under suspicion of the theft. That meant he could not mention a speculation he'd formed regarding the identity of the thief.

As he'd been writing in his journal, it had seemed an awfully unusual coincidence that both Flattery and Uncle Drone had found unknown Wyvernspurs to enter the crypt for them. This had reminded him of how unusual it was that he'd run into two women who looked like Alias of Westgate. That's when it had struck him. Perhaps Alias was a Wyvernspur, too.

If that were the case, the swordswoman could be the thief. Last night, Sudacar had said she was supposed to be in Shadowdale working for Elminster the sage, but perhaps Sudacar was mistaken. There was one person who might know for sure: Alias's friend and patron, Olive Ruskettle, who happened to be in town.

Giogi laid his quill down. He would go see Frefford's new baby first, he decided, then speak with Aunt Dorath about the spur. There was no point, he realized, in trying to get in touch with Mistress Ruskettle before sunset. All entertainers slept in the day. After supper, he could stop in at the Fish to see if the famous bard was in.

* * * * *

Mistress Ruskettle, the famous bard, stirred uneasily in her sleep. She was plagued by nightmares of Cassana, the evil sorceress who'd created and tried to enslave Alias. In the current dream, Cassana was not destroyed, but had transformed into a lich, an undead magic-user. Cassana wore, as she had in life, the most expensive clothing and jewelry. All her finery could not hide her emaciated form, nor distract Olive's gaze from her withered skeletal face, which had once resembled Alias's.

In Olive's dream, the Cassana lich had captured Jade, but Olive, in her halfling form, was too frightened to rescue her. Instead, she fled from Cassana. As often happened in dreams, though, no matter how fast Olive tried to run, she seemed to stand still. She heard a horse whickering. If I could just find the horse, catch it, and mount it, Olive thought, I could ride to safety.

The horse whickered again. Olive started awake. She was back in Immersea, in Giogi's carriage house, still a burro.

"Silly mare. Here, have some oats," a familiar voice said.

Olive peered through a gap in her stall wall. Cat stood outside Daisyeye's stall with her hand extended out to the mare. The mage had successfully routed the horse's instinct to raise an alarm by bribing it with more of the sweetened grain. The beast sniffed curiously, nuzzled up the treat, and lost its distrust of the woman.

Sleet still splashed and skittered on the roof overhead, but some gray daylight trickled into the carriage house from a window. Late afternoon, Olive guessed.

What's she doing here? the halfling wondered. Maybe she's decided to leave Giogi, after all, Olive thought, and she's here to steal Daisyeye to escape. It occurred to Olive again that Giogi's Uncle Drone might have been wrong about Giogi not finding the spur's real thief in the catacombs. Cat could have had the spur all along and been only waiting for the most opportune moment to run off with it.

Instead of saddling the horse, though, Cat drew out a sheet of white paper from a pocket of her muddy robes. She began folding the paper, over and over, pulling and tucking corners until it resembled a long-winged bird.

She held the bird up to her face and stared at it angrily. With a sudden motion, she crumbled the figure and tossed it into Olive's stall.

Olive watched Cat walk to the outside door, but the mage hesitated with her hand around the door handle. She turned about and walked back to Olive's stall.

Unlatching the door, Cat slipped in beside the burro. She fished about the straw on the floor until she'd found the crushed paper bird. She smoothed the paper out against her thigh and folded it back into shape.

Holding the figure to her lips, she whispered, "Master Flattery, your Cat has information about the spur. She begs thee to come swiftly to her. She waits alone in Giogioni Wyvernspur's carriage house."

The mage walked out of Olive's stall so preoccupied with her paper bird that she left the door open. She walked back to the outside door, opened the upper half, and held the rumpled figure in her palm. The bird twitched, then fluttered its wings. "Fly to my master's throne," Cat instructed. The paper bird sped from the carriage house and disappeared into the sleet.

Cat left the upper half of the door open, climbed up into the unharnessed, open buggy, and settled onto the cushioned seat. She sighed once and sat very still with her hands folded in her lap. She closed her eyes, but not completely, and from her posture, the halfling could tell she was still alert and aware.

Olive trembled with anger. The treacherous witch didn't waste any time, the halfling thought. As quietly as she could, the burro tiptoed out of the stall and slipped into the shadows at the rear of the carriage house. How long, she wondered, would it take for Cat's master to arrive from his throne? Cassana and ol' Zrie Prakis sat on thrones. Mages who sit on thrones always mean trouble, Olive-girl. They take themselves too seriously.

Either Cat's little paper bird had the speed of a dragon, or her master's throne was just on the other side of town. Whichever it was, the woman didn't have too long to wait. In less time than it took to hard-cook an egg, something arrived.

A huge black raven swooped through the open upper door and landed on the buggy's lantern pole. The bird shook its feathers dry and fluttered to the buggy seat beside Cat. At first, Olive thought the bird was some sort of magical messenger, perhaps Flattery's familiar. Then the raven grew monstrously. Its feathers became cloth and hair, its wings turned into arms, and its claws into legs. Cat remained still and silent throughout the transformation.

The raven finished changing into a man. He wore a black cloak of great size. Silky black hair, shinier than raven's feath-

KATE NOVAK and JEFF GRUBB

ers, hung to his shoulders. His face was turned away from Olive, but the halfling had no trouble hearing his words, and there was something disturbingly familiar in his deep bass rumble. "Well, Catling?" he demanded.

Cat trembled and bowed her head. When she spoke, her tone was so meek that Olive cringed to hear it. "Forgive me, master," Cat said. "I failed at the task you set me."

Without a word, Flattery backhanded the woman across her face. The crack of his hand on Cat's flesh startled Daisyeye, who kicked at her stall and nickered nervously. Olive backed up, prepared for an awful fight. Only last month, she'd witnessed Jade slash the finger off some fool mercenary who'd pinched her, and, of course, everyone who'd tried to keep Alias as a slave was dead, by her hand or the hands of her allies. Olive had a momentary fear that the carriage house would not be big enough to contain any magical reaction by the sharp-tongued female mage, sister to both Jade and Alias.

Cat sat motionless. She uttered no sound of protest. Her head remained bowed.

"Since I set you this simple task the spur has twice defied my power to detect it. Your failure could mean we've lost it forever," Flattery snarled.

"The spur was not where you said it would be."

"Are you saying I made a mistake?" Flattery asked.

"No, master. I'm saying someone else stole it before I reached the crypt."

"Who?" Flattery demanded.

"I don't know," Cat answered. She continued hurriedly, "But I may be able to discover that information." She paused as if hoping for some sign of pleasure or excitement from her master, but she hoped in vain.

"Continue," Flattery said coolly.

"I saw no one else in the catacombs that evening," Cat explained, "save the monsters who live there. After searching the crypt and finding the spur gone, I tried to leave the catacombs by the secret door, but it was sealed from without. I returned to the crypt, but the door to the mausoleum staircase was locked. I was trapped inside." The woman's voice quavered with the memory of the fear she'd felt when she'd been imprisoned underground.

Flattery was not as sympathetic to her plight as Giogi had

been. In fact, the wizard was not sympathetic at all. "You should have stayed there and saved me the trouble of listening to your pitiful excuses," he growled.

Cat trembled for a minute. Olive thought the woman might be weeping, but since the halfling couldn't see the mage's face, she couldn't be sure.

"Continue," Flattery snapped.

Cat sniffled once and obeyed. "Giogioni Wyvernspur found me in the catacombs," she said. "I told him what I have told you, that I did not steal the spur only because someone else stole it first, and he believed me completely. His uncle, Drone Wyvernspur, had told him he would not find the thief in the catacombs, and he took the old man's word as prophecy.

"Realizing that Drone must know something more of the thief, I arranged to return with Giogioni, planning to meet Drone and wheedle his information from him. Drone died this morning, however, in a spell gone awry."

"The town heralds announced his death," Flattery said. For the first time, he sounded pleased. "Not that it came as a surprise, did it?" he chuckled.

"I don't understand," Cat replied with confusion. "His family seemed rather shocked by it."

Flattery snorted derisively. "You can be such a fool. I presume," he said imperiously, "that you have an excuse for not returning to me immediately after you discovered Drone Wyvernspur was dead."

"Drone left a message for Giogioni Wyvernspur instructing him to find the thief," Cat explained anxiously. "If I remain beside Giogioni, and he succeeds, I shall have the information you seek."

"By all reports, this Giogioni is an idiot and a fop. How can he succeed where I cannot? You are wasting both your time and my own," Flattery growled.

"Yet, Drone Wyvernspur confided in Giogioni and left the search in his hands. Didn't you tell me yesterday that Drone was shrewd?"

"Yes," Flattery admitted reluctantly. He sat, unspeaking, for several moments, deep in his own thoughts. Finally he asked Cat, "Under what pretext are you remaining beside this Giogioni?"

"I told him I was afraid to return to my master without the

spur. He has offered me protection from you."

Flattery burst into laughter. The sound echoed unpleasantly through the carriage house rafters and made Olive's fur-clad flesh crawl. The wizard leaped down from the buggy, grasped the rear right wheel in his hands, and snapped it in half. As the axle crashed to the ground, Cat lost her balance. Flattery caught her in his arms and spun around wildly. To Olive, his treatment of the woman appeared not like a dancer swinging a partner, but like a vicious dog shaking a rag doll.

When he stopped his mad capering, Flattery fell back against Daisyeye's stall. Still holding Cat in his arms, he whispered harshly, "The Wyvernspur never breathed who could protect you should I find you've betrayed me. Don't ever forget that."

A dim beam of light illuminated his face, revealing the terrifying rictus grin he wore. Olive's heart skipped several beats, and she forgot to breathe for a moment as she stared in horror at Flattery's face. He had cruel ice-blue eyes, a hawk nose, thin lips, a sharp jawline—all the features of a Wyvernspur on a face younger than Nameless's and older than Steele's and Frefford's. The face of Jade's murderer.

"You trust me with so little. How can it be in my power to betray you?" Cat asked.

Flattery's eyes glowered. "Don't nip at me, foolish Cat. What's annoyed you now?"

"You did not tell me of the guardian of the crypt."

Flattery shrugged as he set her down. "What of it?"

"The guardian slays anyone in the crypt who is not a Wyvernspur. You told me nothing of this. You did not even tell me you were a Wyvernspur."

"So you've figured that out, have you?" Flattery laughed. "What difference does it make? I saw to your protection. I gave you my name."

"Is that the only reason you insisted I wed you?" Cat asked. Her tone was meek but expectant.

Flattery laughed again. "Is your pride wounded, Cat?"

"Is that the only reason?" Cat demanded more firmly.

Flattery sobered. "I haven't decided yet," he replied coldly.

"Suppose the guardian hadn't recognized our marriage? You're a Wyvernspur. Why didn't you go after the spur yourself? Why did you send me in your place?"

Flattery's hand shot out with the swiftness of a viper, gathering up the front of Cat's robes and pulling her toward him so that her face was just below his. "You have to do something to prove your worth, you lazy witch," the wizard said.

Moving his hands to her waist, Flattery lifted the woman from the ground and tossed her away from him, but, like her namesake, Cat managed to twist about and land on her feet. Flattery grabbed at her long hair and pulled her back toward him. He yanked her around by her arm.

"You have sworn to serve me," he reminded her.

Cat's stance became submissive at once. Her shoulders slumped. Her head was again bowed. All the fight, what little there was of it, had gone out of the woman. She whispered, "Yes, master."

Flattery smiled. "I will expect to meet with you again tomorrow," he said.

"I will arrange it, master."

"Spur this Giogioni on, Catling. I know you can."

"Yes, master."

Flattery pushed himself away from Daisyeye's stall and walked back toward the buggy. He spun around to keep Cat in his sight, as if expecting her to jump him once his back was turned, but she remained as still as ever. Olive, too, remained frozen, terrified of revealing her position.

Bored by Cat's silence and submissiveness, Flattery let his gaze wander past her. His eyes fell on the portrait of the Nameless Bard that hung in Olive's stall.

The wizard snarled like an animal. "Flame spears," he said, gesturing with his hands toward the stall. Jets of flame sprang from his fingertips and enveloped the painting hanging over Olive's oat bucket. The painting crashed to the floor and spread fire to the straw on the floor. Daisyeye, in the stall next door, whinnied.

"Master Flattery, what are you doing?" Cat cried out with fright.

"What do you care? Curse him. Curse them all. May their homes burn while they dream inside."

"This place is too useful for private meetings," Cat argued, rushing toward the fire, her meekness now forgotten.

"Then you preserve it," Flattery snapped. He flung his arms out from his body and snarled a chant of arcane words. His voice became hoarse and sharp, and his form small and feathered. He cawed raucously in his raven shape, then hurtled out the open window and into the gloom.

Cursing, Cat grabbed the burro's oat bucket and used it to dredge water from the beast's trough to throw on the fire. By the time she had doused the last flame and spark, the mage was as sodden as the straw around her.

Cat picked the portrait up from the ground, but the paint was too blackened for her to make out what there was about it that had so angered Flattery. She leaned the charred frame and canvas against the wall and turned to the next stall to calm Daisyeye. The mare accepted her caresses and reassurances and could not find the heart to refuse another handful of oats from the mage.

Stupid horse, Olive thought.

It was then that Cat noticed the missing burro.

"Birdie?" she whispered. "Little one?"

Olive froze.

"Birdie, I know you're in here. Come out, you silly ass."

Olive held her breath.

Cat rustled her hand in the oat bag. "Want a treat, Birdie?"

Olive felt her nose twitch from the smell of smoke.

"Have it your way," Cat said into the darkness. "Giogioni can think you caused this mess for all I care." After giving Daisyeye a last pat on the rear, the mage returned to the outer door, joined the lower half to the upper, slipped outside, and closed the door behind her.

Olive remained still, hidden in the shadows of the carriage house, until long after the sound of Cat's footsteps faded from her hearing.

She crept back into her blackened stall, keeping a sharp eye out for any telltale sparks Cat might have missed. The mage seemed to have done an adequate job keeping the carriage house from destruction. Too bad she hasn't got the same concern for Giogi, the halfling thought.

Even if she was concerned for the young Wyvernspur noble, Olive couldn't picture Cat standing in Flattery's way should he decide to destroy Giogi the way he murdered Jade.

It was beyond Olive's capacity to understand how Cat could transform from a clever and confident mage, able to manipulate foolish young men into taking her home, to a humble and frightened slave, who watched in silence while someone wrecked carriages and burned down horse stalls. What kind of power did Flattery have over her that he could bully her like a whipped child and had even coerced her into marriage?

Somehow, Olive realized, she had to keep Cat from double-crossing Giogi. Olive snorted derisively at herself. I have as much chance at that, the halfling thought, as I do at convincing her to help me destroy Flattery to avenge Jade.

She would be the perfect choice, though, Olive mused. Flattery trusts her as much as his insanity will allow. It would be so fitting if he were destroyed by someone with the same face as the woman he murdered.

Olive pondered the idea while she munched on hay in the smoky carriage house.

* * * * *

Giogi reached out and stroked his new cousin's tiny left hand. Her delicate fingers opened at his touch, like a moss rose in the sun.

"She's just perfect, Freffie," Giogi whispered. "As pretty as her mother."

"Well, she gets some of her good looks from me, don't you think?" Frefford asked.

Giogi looked up at his Cousin Frefford and back down at the baby girl sleeping in the maple cradle. Then he looked up again at Frefford, then back down at the baby. "Not if she's lucky," he said with a grin.

Frefford chuckled.

"It's so exciting, Freffie," Giogi said. "You're a father now, and I'm an uncle. Wait. I'm not really, am I? Just a second cousin once removed."

"You can be an uncle if you want, Giogi," Frefford said. "Lady Amber Leona Wyvernspur," Frefford whispered to the sleeping baby, "this is your rich Uncle JoJo. Learn to say his name, and he'll buy you all the ponies you want."

Giogi grinned.

"I'm going to check to see if Gaylyn's awake yet," Frefford said. "You can stay here if you like."

Giogi nodded. "Give Gaylyn my regards," he said.

"I will," Frefford whispered. He tiptoed from the nursery, where his daughter lay on display for well-wishers to view

KATE NOVAK and JEFF GRUBB

while his wife slept undisturbed in the next room.

Giogi had the baby all to himself now, since the well-wishers had been few so far. Some, no doubt, had been discouraged by the awkwardness of having to deliver congratulations and condolences in the same breath. The majority, Giogi assumed, had been put off by the awful weather.

The sleet had wrapped everything in a thick coating of ice, and Immersea looked like it had been encased in glass. Unwilling to risk Daisyeye on the slick roads, Giogi had once again hiked up the path to Redstone. It had been rough going, but the fields and marshes had offered his feet far more traction than the cobblestone roads would have. This latest exertion, combined with having risen at dawn after a late night of drinking, followed by walking miles through the catacombs, had left the nobleman exhausted.

Giogi slid a rocking chair up beside the cradle and collapsed into it. "There's nothing I'd rather do than just sit here with you, Amberry," he whispered to the baby. "It's so snug and peaceful here, I could almost forget all the bad things that have happened."

Giogi closed his eyes and lay his head back. His breathing slowed and grew more shallow. Giogi felt himself beginning to soar. He was dreaming again. He opened his eyes in his dream and found the field he soared over covered in ice, like the fields surrounding Immersea. A little burro trotted into view.

Giogi gasped. Not Birdie! he thought. Unable to speak in the dream, the nobleman urged the burro mentally, Run, Birdie! Birdie needed no warning. She began to gallop downhill, but her hooves slid on the ice, and she ended up on her front knees with her back legs splayed out behind her. Giogi swooped down. Birdie brayed pitifully.

"Giogioni Wyvernspur! Just what do you think you're doing here?" a female voice barked.

Giogi started awake. He had no idea how long he'd slept, but if Aunt Dorath caught him napping, a minute would be as bad as an hour. Aunt Dorath was of the opinion that a healthy young person did not need to sleep in the day, and Giogi could hardly offer her the excuse that he was tired because he'd been out late drinking with Samtavan Sudacar.

The young nobleman leaped to his feet. "Good afternoon, Aunt Dorath. I was just having a peek at Amber. Freffie said it was all right if I sat with her a few minutes."

"He did, did he? He would," Aunt Dorath said with a sniff. "Did he also give you permission to slough off your duties? Or have you forgotten that this family is in the middle of a crisis of unimaginable proportions? The curse of the wyvern's spur has already claimed Cousin Drone and nearly took Steele as well, yet here I find you napping."

Giogi meant to point out to his aunt that Steele had brought his injuries on himself by his horrendous behavior, and that he, Giogi, had played no small part in rescuing Steele from the jaws of death, as it were, but he was never given the opportunity. Not even magic could stop the avalanche of Aunt Dorath's harangue.

"Yet, despite his brush with the hereafter," she continued, "Steele went off immediately after lunch in search of a discreet high priest or mage who might help us locate the spur. Of course, you've made discretion rather unnecessary, haven't you? I've just learned that our family's tragedy was the talk of every tavern in Immersea last night. No wonder you can't stay awake—you were carousing in town all night, discussing family business, both of which I specifically forbade you to do."

"But I didn't mean—" Giogi began to say.

"I will not accept your overindulgences with alcohol as an excuse for divulging our family's problems, nor for sleeping when you should be performing some task that will aid in the spur's recovery. The only person with any excuse for resting on this day is Gaylyn. And Amber, of course. Even Frefford has assigned himself a task. He is investigating every stranger in town who might possibly be a long-lost relation and our thief."

Giogi's exhaustion got the better of his temper. "What about Julia? Why not just have her listen at the door of the thieves' guild?" he asked sarcastically.

Aunt Dorath's brow knit in annoyance. Her reaction was a clue to her great-nephew that she already had some inkling of Julia's eavesdropping. The old woman recovered her lost ground quickly, though. "Julia," she replied frostily, "is seeing to the arrangements for Cousin Drone's memorial service. Now, what do you propose to do in what time remains today?"

Well, Giogi thought, straightening up, here goes. "I plan to discover the spur's secret powers," he announced.

"The spur doesn't have any secret powers," Aunt Dorath snapped.

"Oh, but it does," Giogi insisted. "My father used the spur's powers whenever he went adventuring."

Aunt Dorath gave a little gasp and sank into the rocking chair. "Who told you that?" she demanded. "It was Cousin Drone, wasn't it? I should have realized his oath was not to be trusted."

"Uncle Drone didn't tell me, Aunt Dorath," the nobleman insisted. Angry with the old woman for keeping his father's adventuring a secret from him, Giogi felt spite take hold of him. "Actually, it's common knowledge," he taunted. "They talk about it in every tavern in Immersea."

Aunt Dorath leaned forward in the rocker and poked Giogi in the rib with her finger. "This is not a joking matter," she reprimanded him.

"No," Giogi agreed, feeling bad for trying to shock her. "It is a family matter, though." He bent over his aunt and put his hands on her shoulders. "I have a right to know about my father," he said vehemently. "You should have told me."

Aunt Dorath glared up at him. "All right," she replied hotly. "Cole used to tramp about the countryside in the company of rogues and ruffians, and whenever he left, he took the spur from the crypt. Not that I blame Cole. Your Uncle Drone, to his everlasting guilt, aided him, and Cole hadn't the force of will to resist the spirit of that she-beast. She used those awful dreams to seduce him from his family's side."

"She-beast?" Giogi asked. "Do you mean the guardian?"

Dorath's voice rose sharply as she retorted. "Of course I mean the guardian. What other she-beast lurks in our family?"

Giogi bit the inside of his cheeks and fought back his urge to reply.

"Who else," Dorath asked, "is always babbling about the death cry of prey, or the taste of warm blood, or the crunch of bone?"

"She's talked to you, too?" Giogi squeaked in astonishment.

"Of course she's talked to me, you fool," the old woman replied. "You don't imagine that out of fifteen generations of Wyvernspurs you were the only child ever locked down in that crypt by accident, do you?"

Amber gurgled and squawked in her cradle, and Aunt Dorath rose to pat the infant reassuringly. Frefford's daughter quieted.

"Do you have the same dreams, too?" Giogi asked.

For a moment, it looked as if some fearful memory disturbed Aunt Dorath's composure, but she shook her head once, the way a horse would to dislodge a gadfly, and her face grew calm. "I had them once," she admitted softly, then added more sternly, "but I ignored them, as would any well-bred young woman."

"But they don't go away," Giogi whispered.

Aunt Dorath turned from the cradle and put her hands on Giogi's shoulders. "You must keep ignoring them," she insisted, giving him a shake. "You are a Wyvernspur. You belong with your family in Immersea. All that gadding about the Realms with the spur got your father was killed."

"He didn't die from a riding accident like you said, did he?" Giogi accused the old woman. "How did he die?"

"How do all adventurers die? Fell monsters hunt them. Ruthless bandits slaughter them. Evil wizards turn them to dust. It didn't make any difference to me. Cole was dead. He died far too young and far too far from home. Your Uncle Drone fetched his body back. We never discussed how he died. My only concern was that it should not happen again."

"I need to know the spur's power," Giogi said. "It could be a clue to who the thief is."

"No," Dorath answered. "It's not. Even if it were, I wouldn't tell you."

Giogi sighed with exasperation. "Aunt Dorath, I don't want to use the spur," he insisted. "I just want to know what it does."

Aunt Dorath shook her head in refusal. "I'm doing this for your own good, Giogi. I won't watch another member of our family destroyed by that cursed thing." She turned back to the cradle and readjusted the blankets around the baby.

"If you won't tell me, Aunt Dorath, I shall have to find out from someone else," Giogi threatened.

"There is no one else," his aunt said, stroking Amber's hand with her finger.

Giogi racked his brain for an idea of who could tell him about the spur.

"I'm the last member of the family who knows," Aunt Dorath whispered down to the baby.

"Then I'll have to ask an outsider," Giogi said. It came to him suddenly. There was someone who'd known his father, someone who'd promised to talk more about him. Someone his aunt would hate to think of as telling him the family secrets. "I'll have to ask Sudacar," he said.

Aunt Dorath whirled and glared at Giogi. "That upstart?" She sniffed. "What could he possibly know? He doesn't swallow without advice from his herald."

"He met Cole at court. He knows all about Cole's adventures," Giogi answered, hoping it were really true.

Aunt Dorath's eyes narrowed into slits. Giogi could tell she was calculating what Sudacar knew. She called her kinsman's bluff. "Go ahead," she said. "Ask Samtavan Sudacar. You'll be wasting your time, though."

"I will ask him," Giogi retorted. "Right now." He leaned over and stroked Amber's little ear before turning about and striding from the nursery. "Good afternoon, Aunt Dorath," he whispered as he left.

❧ 11 ❧

Selûne's Stair

Samtavan Sudacar finished studying the last document in the cord of parchments Culspiir had piled before him. "Depleting resources necessitate troop inactivity," he read aloud, though he was alone. He ran his fingers through the graying hair at his temples. Reading reports such as this one was turning his dark hair gray, he decided.

He read the phrase over again as if it were a riddle, which indeed it was to him. Suddenly he pounded his meaty fist on his desktop and chuckled with understanding.

"That boy has a way with words," he sighed, shaking his head. While he admired his herald's bureaucratic skills, there were times the local lord felt it would be better if Culspiir weren't so clever that he made himself misunderstood.

In the document's margin, beside the passage he'd just read, Sudacar scrawled: Azoun, I can't send these boys out patrolling in freezing rain with nothing but watery porridge in their stomachs. I need those food rations!!!

Sudacar initialed the notation, scrawled his full signature at the bottom, and rolled up the scroll. He finished by slopping liquefied wax on the seam and pressing his signet ring into the resulting mess.

Stretching out his arms to ease the muscles in his broad shoulders, he muttered, "I've had enough of this stuffy little closet."

The main reception hall of Redstone had been set aside for use by the king's man. Pillars and arches two stories high rose all about him. Archery contests had been held along the length of the room, and the entire town had gathered within its walls in times of crisis and celebration. Sudacar's desk was tucked at one end of the hall, with a view of the entire enormous chamber.

Sudacar, former giant-slayer, was a tall, burly man, though, and anywhere the wind could not blow felt stuffy to him.

Time to indulge in one of the prerogatives of office, he

thought as he pulled on his coat. "Culspiir," he bellowed in his booming voice.

Culspiir slid into the room, closing the door softly behind him. The herald's face appeared so careworn it would have alarmed a stranger. Sudacar was aware, though that Culspiir wore that same expression for all occasions, from weddings to barbarian invasions.

"I've gone over all the reports you gave me, Cul," Sudacar said. "Good work. I thought I'd break for the day," he added, his brown eyes glittered with all the eagerness of a schoolboy asking for permission to play outside.

"I'm sorry, sir, but I've granted someone an interview with you for this hour."

"Now? Culspiir, how could you schedule someone now? Can't you see it's raining? Don't you realize that the fish are out there searching for my lure?"

"I thought, considering the person and the nature of his problem, that you had best see him today, sir. I've kept him waiting more than an hour so you could finish your other duties."

"Show him in," Sudacar sighed. He sat back down, but he did not bother to remove his cloak.

Culspiir slipped out, and a moment later Giogioni Wyvernspur stepped in.

Sudacar's face brightened. "Giogi!" he said with surprise. He rose and extended his hand to the nobleman.

Giogi strode up to Sudacar's desk, accepted the handshake, and returned the smile. Sudacar's welcome was a relief after being made to wait so long by the local lord's herald.

"Culspiir was a dog to make you wait like that," Sudacar said as if reading his thoughts. "Sorry."

"Oh, no. I understand. You've got lots of work," Giogi replied, though he suspected Culspiir had kept him waiting as a snub to the Wyvernspurs. The nobleman didn't resent it too much. After all, the Wyvernspurs had snubbed Culspiir and his master often enough.

"Culspiir just wants to be sure I don't have any excuses to put his boring papers aside," Sudacar confided in a whisper. "He doesn't like me to have any fun." Sudacar's expression became serious. "I'm sorry about your uncle, Giogi. He was a fine man. A good wizard, too."

"Thank you," Giogi replied softly. "It's hard to believe. I don't want to believe it."

"That's only natural," Sudacar said, giving the younger man a comforting pat on the shoulder. "So, tell me," the local lord said more boisterously, "what brings you here, boy?"

"I'm sorry to bother you, Sudacar," Giogi said, "but, well, things have gotten rather confusing about the spur. I realize Aunt Dorath was a little huffy with Culspiir yesterday, not wanting to tell him about the theft, but the truth is, I could use your advice. I thought maybe there might be something you could tell me about the spur."

"Well, whatever advice I have is yours, Giogi, but I'm afraid I've never seen the spur. I've seen others, still on the wyvern, as it were, but not the one you're looking for."

"I thought you might know something about it. You knew it was stolen before I—uh, before it got around town."

Sudacar grinned. "Well, I don't like to brag, but not all women are as immune to my charms as your aunt," he said, giving Giogi the same wink that he had the evening before, when he'd admitted to having his own source of information. Giogi wondered idly if the woman in question was a parlor maid or a lady's maid.

"But, you know some tales about my father," the nobleman said. "Did you know he used the spur when he went adventuring? That the spur has some magical powers?"

"Does it, now? Well, well." Sudacar stared thoughtfully at the ceiling. "I didn't know that, but it might explain some things I've heard."

"Like what?"

Sudacar abruptly stood. "Tell you what. Why don't we take a little walk while we talk about it?" He led Giogi toward the door. On the way, the Lord of Immersea pulled a casting pole out of a rack on the wall.

"What's this for?" Giogi asked.

"We'll need it to defend ourselves, in case we run into any fish," Sudacar explained.

"Oh," Giogi replied as Sudacar held open the hall door for him.

Sudacar hoped to hurtle past Culspiir's station before his herald could find another excuse to keep him confined, but Giogi stopped at the door, his finger to his forehead, trying to dredge something from the back of his mind.

At last it came to him. "Ah, yes," the nobleman said. "You

KATE NOVAK and JEFF GRUBB

know my purse that was stolen?"

"Oh, that," Sudacar said. "Any word on it, Culspiir?" he demanded of his subordinate.

"It still hasn't turned up, Master Giogioni," the herald said as he regarded Sudacar—and his casting rod—with suspicion.

"Well, it won't," Giogi said, "because it wasn't stolen. I'd dropped it right outside home. Found it later," he explained. "Hope I didn't cause a fuss."

Sudacar grunted. "Remind me to let you pick up the tab next time," he said with a grin. "Culspiir, I'll be out for the rest of the day in consultation with Master Giogioni."

"Of course," Culspiir said, his eyes not leaving the fishing tackle as the two men hurried through his office and out the door.

On the front steps of the manor, they bundled up their cloaks and pulled up their hoods against the rain, which was still icy but far less violent than it had been at noon. They left the castle walls.

As they trudged down toward the Immer Stream, Sudacar explained, "I never actually had the honor of adventuring with your father. To tell the truth, when I met him at court he was already a legend and I was just an apprentice sell-sword. By that time, Cole had single-handedly vanquished the hydra of Wheloon—walked into the beastie's lair unarmed and walked out alive an hour later. He was all cut up and bleeding, but, as the saying goes, you should have seen the other guy. His Majesty's troops went into the lair afterward and found the monster everywhere—diced into pieces."

Behind the privacy of his hood, Giogi tried without success to picture the quiet, gentle man he remembered from his childhood killing anything, even something as fierce as a hydra. His imagination remained as gray as the soft sleet falling around him.

Sudacar began regaling Giogi with a tale of how Cole had let himself be kidnapped by pirates. By the time the local lord had reached the part where Cole sailed the pirate ship into Suzail's harbor with all the sea thieves in irons, the local lord and the nobleman had reached the bridge where Giogi had encountered Sudacar the day before. The stream's water was a little faster and the level a little higher. Patches of ice crusted over the stiller shallows near the banks.

Sudacar wasted no time whipping his line out over the water, but he continued with another story about Cole. This story was set, as Sudacar put it, "in 'aught eight," when the gnolls came down from the north. Saboteurs had burned the bridge over the Starwater. The purple dragoons might never have marched to the Cormyr border's defense in time had Cole not managed miraculously—and mysteriously—to repair the bridge overnight with no one to help him but Shar, the master carpenter—who later became Cole's father-in-law.

Giogi's gaze remained fixed on Sudacar's lure as it flew out over the water, slithered downstream and jerked out, over and over again. The noble's thoughts, though, were occupied with trying to figure out why Sudacar's tales sounded so familiar. It wasn't until the older man began a story with Giogi's mother in it, that the reason came to Giogi in a flash.

In the story, Shar, the master carpenter, had come to Cole begging that he rescue Bette, the carpenter's daughter. Bette had refused the mad red wizard Yawataht as a suitor, so Yawataht had kidnapped and imprisoned Bette on top of a glass mountain. He left her there to freeze, high above the tree line, up in the clouds. Cole flew up there—though Sudacar could not say how—but he looked so fierce when he arrived that Bette mistook him for one of Yawataht's minions and smacked him on the head with a hammer.

The name "Yawataht" and the image of a woman striking a man with a hammer finally reminded Giogi why Sudacar's tales sounded familiar. "Uncle Drone's told me all these stories," he said, "but the hero was someone named Callyson, and the woman he rescued on the mountaintop was named Sharabet—"

Sudacar laughed. "Wasn't your grandmother's name Cally?" he asked.

Giogi smacked himself on the forehead. "Callyson—Cally's son! Sharabet—Shar's Bette! Of course! Aunt Dorath made Uncle Drone swear he wouldn't tell me my father was an adventurer, but Uncle Drone told me all about my father, anyway—only he disguised the truth as bedtime stories."

"So, did he tell you how your father used the spur in the stories?" Sudacar asked.

"He—" Giogi hesitated. He racked his brains trying to remember any mention of a magical item in the Callyson stories. "I don't remember for certain. He told me those stories more than ten years ago. I don't think so, though."

"Well," Sudacar said, "since your father wasn't a magic-user, it's probable the spur gave him the power to fly."

"There's lots of other magic like that, though," Giogi pointed out. "Why steal the spur just to fly?"

"It could also have been responsible for Cole's strength and fighting prowess," Sudacar suggested. "Killing a hydra is no small feat. Neither is chopping and carting the lumber for a bridge meant to span a river as wide as the Starwater."

"That's true," Giogi agreed. "It might help if I could pin its powers down more exactly, though."

"Wait a minute," Sudacar said, stroking his chin. "There is someone you could talk to, someone I know traveled with your father at least once."

"A rogue or a ruffian?" Giogi asked.

"Pardon?"

"According to Aunt Dorath, my father traveled with rogues and ruffians. Aunt Dorath is a little funny that way—"

"Yes, I've always found her amusing," Sudacar admitted grimly. "The person I was thinking of, though, was Lleddew of Selune." The instant Sudacar mentioned Selune, the goddess of the moon, he got a strike on his fishing line.

"Mother Lleddew?" Giogi echoed with astonishment. He'd been expecting Sudacar to name one of the adventurers who'd been at the Fish last night. Lleddew was a high priestess and older than Giogi's Aunt Dorath. The idea of the ancient holy woman tramping about the countryside with Cole was a little hard for the nobleman to accept. "Are you sure?"

Sudacar grinned and nodded as he pulled in his line, playing his catch. "Your family dedicated Spring Hill to Selune, but Lleddew built the temple, the House of the Lady, with the booty from her adventuring days. The trips she made with your father were her last. I've heard her call one of them 'the roofing campaign'—Gotcha!"

Sudacar interrupted his story as he grasped at the gleaming bass on his line and slipped it off his hook. He poked a holding string through its gills, looped the string over a rock, and let the fish drop back in the water to wriggle before suppertime.

Giogi looked upstream toward Spring Hill. Strangers to Immersea often wondered why the Wyvernspurs hadn't built Redstone Castle on Spring Hill. It was the tallest hill on their land; it had the best view of the surrounding countryside, and a natural spring of sweet water gushed from its peak. The family's founder, Paton Wyvernspur, had dedicated Spring Hill to the goddess Selûne, according to legend, at the request of the goddess herself. None of his descendants was ever so foolish as to try to take it back.

These days, the spring's water poured from Selûne's temple, tumbled down the hill in a series of enchanting cascades, and ultimately became the Immer Stream. There was a road approaching Spring Hill from the north, which wound up the hill to the temple, but the hike alongside the water was far more interesting. The sun was getting low, but Giogi figured he had just enough time to make the climb and speak to Mother Lleddew before dark.

Sudacar followed Giogi's gaze and guessed his intentions. "Could be a tricky climb in this weather," he warned. "Maybe you should take the road instead."

"It's so far out of the way to reach the road," Giogi argued. "Besides, I've climbed the stream path often enough as a boy."

Sudacar shrugged. "I hope you find what you need to know," he said as he cast his line out again.

"Thanks." Giogi turned and began striding to the west.

At first, the going was not too difficult. The ground was level, and the muddy banks were frozen enough to hold his weight but rough enough to offer traction for walking. Ahead of him, the westering sun was breaking through the canopy of clouds. The red rays of the last light of day made the crystalline sleet at his feet shimmer like rubies.

Giogi had to slow down once he reached the lowest cascade of water at the base of Spring Hill. The red light had subsided to indigo; the marshy fields ended and thick woods began, and his path begin to climb a steep slope, over large rocks and boulders slick with ice. Giogi tucked his mittens in his pockets to keep them dry as he scrabbled for handholds to keep his balance.

A third of the way from the top of the hill, the stream crossed the road that wound around the hill to the temple. A simple but sturdy stone bridge spanned the water, high enough to allow someone moving up the stream to walk beneath it.

By the time Giogi reached the bridge, it would have been easier and safer—and possibly faster—to climb the banks and take the road. Yet the nobleman couldn't bring himself to abandon his original course, even though he was cold and tired and getting a little hungry. When he was a boy, other children called the cascades Selune's Stair, and they said that if a person climbed to the top of them, he or she was supposed to get his or her heart's desire. Of course, one was supposed to climb them in the water by moonlight, but Giogi figured Selune would make allowances considering the season and weather.

A tiny, niggling voice in his head told him he was wasting his time and energy playing silly games. The voice sounded suspiciously like Aunt Dorath, so Giogi ignored it and continued climbing, leaving the road behind.

So far, he'd been pretty impressed with himself. His skill at scrabbling up the slope and leaping from one rock to another had not deteriorated with maturity. He might not have looked quite as agile as a mountain goat, but he felt it—until he reached the final cascade.

The last cascade was larger and steeper than the rest, and at its base was a wide pool. More mist hung in the air, so the rocks were damper there. Giogi leaped between two large boulders in the twilight, hit a slick spot, and went sprawling on a ledge that hung out over the pool.

He was bruised but otherwise unharmed. The niggling Aunt Dorath-like voice inside his head said, "I told you so," and Giogi began to think he would be lucky if he could reach the top before the light failed and he fell in the drink.

The sky at that moment grew very, very dark. Giogi hesitated. Maybe it's just a darker than average storm cloud over the setting sun, he hoped. He waited on the ledge for a minute, then another, for light to return. The forest around him remained dark.

Giogi realized he'd miscalculated. The sun had set already, and twilight in the dense woods had been very short. The moon would be full tonight, though, he remembered. It should rise soon, now that the sun has set, he reassured himself.

In the meantime, the nobleman couldn't help feeling there was something malicious about the darkness. It was filled with rustling and twig-snapping, which he could hear uncomfortably well over the rush of the cascade. Unwilling to wait for Selune's light, Giogi crawled toward the cascade and began climbing the rocks by feel.

Something scaly brushed against Giogi's hand, and he pulled it back with a jerk, lost his balance, and tumbled sideways, landing with a splash in the pool of water below.

Giogi surfaced immediately, sputtering water and soaked to the skin. The water was only three feet deep, but that was more than enough to submerge his clodders, and the young noble could feel icy water creeping down his stockings.

A beam of moonlight broke through the clouds in the east, illuminating the pool around him. Giogi stifled a shriek and began to back away. In the hip-high water all around him bobbed the bloated corpses of men.

As he stepped backward, one of the corpses in front of him sprang to life, lunging out of the water at him like a trout striking at a lure. Rows of needle-sharp teeth gnashed inches from his face. Giogi shrieked without inhibition, terrified.

He recognized the creatures from Uncle Drone's books. They weren't just corpses, but lacedons, undead monsters that preyed on the flesh of the drowned. Giogi took another step backward, but the lacedons had him surrounded. The nobleman had just enough presence of mind to draw his foil.

A second lacedon breached directly in front of him with its hands raised over its head. Giogi could smell the fetid, mossy scent of the creature's breath as it brought its decayed face close to his own. Then the monster's sharp, algae-covered fingernails struck at his forehead. Giogi jabbed his weapon into the creature's flesh, but the lacedon wriggled itself free and swam off.

The remaining lacedons swam slowly around him, thumping up against his legs, trying to knock him off balance, and occasionally breaking the surface to leer and gnash and slash at his face. They're playing with their food, Giogi thought, fighting back his nausea.

Blood dripping from his wounded brow obscured his vision in one eye and splashed into the water—spurring the undead into a frenzy. Giogi screamed again and stabbed at the hideous beings, trying to clear a path to the shore. It was hard to lunge into the water accurately, though, and there were too many of them to concentrate on one direction at once, without risking attack in the rear.

One of the lacedons toward the back of the pack reared up and began walking forward, so Giogi had a better view of its scaly body, water-rotted face, and bulging, yellow eyes. Another lacedon adopted an erect stance, and another and another, until all the corpses advanced on him like soldiers.

The noble turned in the frigid water, unable to decide on a direction to run. He caught sight of the glimmering gemstone in the top of his boot. The light of the finder's stone pulsed in the darkness, even beneath the water.

Giogi drew the finder's stone out, hoping the light it would cast might frighten off the monsters, or at least hurt their eyes. He tried to recall the bit of rhyme he knew as a child: Vampires fear the morning's lights, something, something, something, and wights.

The finder's stone cast a bright beam to the shoreline, but its light had no effect on the undead monsters' behavior.

The undead began gurgling like the drowned men they were. From the way they raised their claws in unison, Giogi guessed they were making some sort of battle cry. They all leered at him with their fanged mouths. I'm finished, the nobleman thought.

From the top of the cascade behind Giogi came a great roar. Before Giogi's eyes, the lacedons' bodies ignited into cool, blue flames. The corpses slumped back into the pool. The water in the stream sparkled with the blue fire still consuming the undead. The pool turned murky with the disintegrated bodies. Then the murkiness washed downstream, and the pool's water was clear again.

Giogi saw that only two monsters remained in the water with him, both to his left. As the young noble splashed in the direction of the right-hand bank, praying the creatures would be unable to follow him on land, a dark, hulking shape plunged from the top of the cascade, over his head, and into the pool beyond. Giogi threw himself out of the water and landed with a thud on the rocky shore, knocking all the air out of himself.

More splashing and a second roar came from the pool behind him. It took a moment before Giogi could summon the energy to roll over to see what had joined the lacedons in the water.

The headless body of a lacedon floated past the near shore. The second lacedon lay on the opposite bank, pinned beneath the paws of a huge black bear. The monster struggled feebly before the bear ripped it, throat to belly, with a single swipe of its paw.

"Sweet Selune," Giogioni whispered.

The bear looked up at him when he spoke. Giogi froze. He'd never seen a bear so large in all of Cormyr. The creature's coat was as dark as the night, except for two silvery gray, crescent-shaped patches, one on its underbelly, the other on its forehead.

The bear stared at the nobleman for a moment with its head tilted to the side. It snuffled, and great clouds of steam rose from the bear's nostrils. Then it turned and bounded into the darkness of the woods.

Giogi pulled himself up the last cascade and left the dark woods behind him. Atop Spring Hill, a moonlit meadow surrounded the temple. Giogi collapsed on the grass beside the water, shivering and gasping for breath. His head was on fire, but the rest of him was freezing.

In all his years in Immersea, he'd never been attacked by undead. What were lacedons doing in a stream sacred to Selune? Did Mother Lleddew know about them? Giogi wondered. Is it possible she's getting too old to defend the hill from evil?

In the east, the sleet-filled clouds began to break up, as if evaporated by the full moon's light. Moonbeams shimmered across the Wyvernwater, along the Immer Stream, and up Selune's Stair. The moonbeams continued past Giogi, turning the stream, which meandered through the meadow, into a silver ribbon.

Giogi pulled himself to his feet and followed the stream to the temple, water squelching in his boots with his every step. Silvery, moonlit water flowed from inside the temple and down a channel cut into its steps. Giogi climbed the steps beside the channel and entered the House of the Lady.

The House of the Lady, the temple Mother Lleddew had built to Selune, was really not a house, but an open-air shrine. A circle of white stone pillars rose from the temple's floor and supported the domed roof. There were no walls. The rising moon's light shone past the pillars and silvered the spring-fed pool bubbling in the center of the temple.

A slender young girl in an acolyte's robes sat beside the pool, gazing into the spring's depths. The ends of her long tresses trailed along the surface of the water. By some trick of the light, her hair appeared as silver as the water, so it seemed that water flowed from her hair into the pool.

Giogi rang the silver bell hanging from one of the pillars beside the water channel.

The girl looked up without surprise. She had dark skin, a lovely smile, and radiant eyes. She was very pretty, but seemed far too young for her calling. She couldn't have been more than sixteen. "Blessings of the full moon," she greeted Giogi.

"Blessings of the full moon," he responded. "I'm looking for Mother Lleddew."

"Are you sure you're not looking for your heart's desire?" the girl asked with a grin.

"What?" Giogi replied with confusion.

"You did just climb Selune's Stair by the full moon," the girl pointed out.

"Well, yes, I did," Giogi admitted. "All I really wanted, though, was to see Mother Lleddew."

"She's on a night-stalk," the girl said. "I'm here to watch over the temple until she returns."

Giogi sighed with frustration. A night-stalk was a sacred ritual practiced by devout worshipers of Selune. Lleddew would be walking in solitary communion with her goddess until the moon set. Suddenly Giogi remembered the lacedon attack. "Look, I don't mean to alarm you, but there were evil things out in the woods tonight. You shouldn't be alone here, and Mother Lleddew shouldn't be walking alone out there."

The girl smiled with amusement as she stood and drifted toward him. She shimmered like a moonbeam when she moved, and her hair glittered like a cascade of water. "You are the one in danger, Giogioni," she said earnestly. "You can speak with Mother Lleddew tomorrow, after noon. For now, though, I think I'd better send you home."

"I can't leave you alone here," the nobleman argued.

"Kneel," the girl directed him, "so I can have a look at that cut on your head."

Giogi obeyed, curious to see if so young an acolyte really had power to heal his wound.

The girl bent over Giogi and kissed his forehead.

The fire in his head flared momentarily, then subsided completely. Giogi swayed dizzily, then looked up, relieved of all discomfort. "That was wonder—" The noble halted in midsentence. His head spun around in confusion and dripped water all about the Calimshan carpeting.

He knelt in his own bedroom before a roaring fire.

"I must be dreaming," said Giogi, "or hallucinating because of my head wound."

The nobleman pinched and shook himself, but he didn't wake to find himself dying of exposure on the side of Spring Hill. He was still in his own bedroom. The bedclothes held the family coat of arms, a green wyvern on a yellow field. The portrait over the fireplace was of his mother and father. The indigo seashells he'd brought from Westgate lay strewn about the dresser. "It must be my room," he said.

Still confused, he muttered to himself as he stripped off his soaked clothing. "First I was there, and now I'm here. She kissed me, and I appeared here. I didn't know acolytes could do that, but if she wasn't an acolyte, what was she doing in the temple in an acolyte's gown, telling me when I could see Mother Lleddew? And how did she know my name?"

Giogi slid into bed beneath the covers. He lay there wondering if he hadn't just dreamed all about Spring Hill, Selune's Stair, the lacedons, the crescent-marked bear, and the girl acolyte. When the chill had worn off his flesh, he slid out of bed again and padded over to the pile of wet clothing.

Giogi shook his head as he pulled a robe on. He slipped from his bedroom, tiptoed down the hall to the red room, and knocked softly on the door. He had to share his story with someone.

"Mistress Cat?" he whispered. When no one answered, he knocked again.

"Whuzzah? Come in," a sleepy voice called out.

Giogi opened the door.

The red room was well furnished, but Thomas kept it empty of personal items, like a room at an inn. The red velvet hangings and the oaken bed, dresser, chair, and chest were all new and sturdy—not an heirloom in the lot. The guest room belonged to no one, which is how it felt to those who stayed in it.

By the light from the lamp flickering on the dresser, Giogi could see Cat curled up in one corner of the bed, the blankets all wrapped tightly around her. Her coppery hair was strewn over the pillows. Her robes lay draped over the chair before the fireside.

Cat sat up in the bed, looking drowsy but lovely. "I asked Thomas to wake me when you returned," she said, pushing her hair out of her face.

"Um, he doesn't know I'm back yet. I fell in the Immer Stream and a bear saved me from lacedons, and then this lovely girl kissed me and teleported me here."

Tying a sheet around her body, Cat slid out from under the covers and walked to the doorway, where Giogi stood. She put a hand to his forehead, her brow knit with concern. "You don't have a fever," she said after a moment.

"I'm fine, really. You know, your hand is so nice and warm."

Cat smiled and said, "Perhaps you ought to lie down, anyway." She took Giogi by the arm and steered him back to his own room.

Giogi, babbling on, let himself be led. "You know, the guardian said that I'd been kissed by Selune. I think she's just done it again, Selune that is, through one of her priestesses. You see, the kiss cured the scratch the lacedons gave me, which was nice, the kiss, not the cut, I mean. It also brought me home, though, which was strange but nice, too."

"Here we go," Cat said, steering him into his own room.

"But still, it's rather disturbing to be kissed by Selune," Giogi said with a sigh, "since it is one of those things the guardian is always making a fuss about. I know I'm going to dream tonight about all those things—death cry of prey, and so on. Aunt Dorath says she just ignored the dreams, but I don't see how she could," Giogi said with annoyed disbelief.

"Lie down, Master Giogioni," Cat ordered, pressing him down on the bed. "You can rest and talk." As he lay back on his bed, Cat fluffed up his pillows and propped them behind him.

"Did you find anyone who knew about the spur?" Cat asked lightly, seating herself at the foot of the bed.

"Well, Aunt Dorath knows something, but she won't tell me what. She's being absurdly stubborn. I get the idea she wants to carry her secret to the grave. I talked with Sudacar. He didn't know about the spur, but he knew a lot about my father." Giogi's eyes shone when he asked the mage, "Did you know my father was a hero? Not just an adventurer, but a real hero? I went on a mission for the crown, but it's not really the same as adventuring. It must be interesting being an adventurer."

"Why don't you try it and find out?" Cat asked with a smile.

"Oh, I couldn't. It's just not done. Aunt Dorath would have kittens," the nobleman explained.

"But your father did it," Cat pointed out.

"He must have been very brave," Giogi said, shaking his head slowly as if to deny he had that much courage.

"To go out into the wilderness or to defy your Aunt Dorath?" Cat asked with a chuckle.

Giogi laughed, too. "Both," he said.

"What could your aunt do?" Cat asked. "Cut off your money?"

"No. I have my own money," Giogi explained. "Aunt Dorath is family, though. I can't just ignore her."

"But if you were off adventuring, she couldn't bother you," Cat said slyly.

"But she would pounce on me whenever I returned to Immersea," Giogi retorted.

"Then don't ever return," Cat suggested.

"Never return?" Giogi said with shock. "Immersea's my home. I couldn't stay away." Giogi's face fell in disappointment as he realized he'd just talked himself out of a dream. He justified his inaction further by saying, "Besides, I wouldn't know how I should go about adventuring. Not the first thing. Do you have to register for it or something?"

Cat laughed. Brushing her hand through her hair, she slid up the bed so that she sat much closer to Giogi. "First thing you should do is try to look the part. Hold still," she ordered.

The mage reached her hand behind Giogi's ear, and Giogi felt a pinch at his earlobe. When Cat took her hand away, Giogi reached up to rub his earlobe. Attached to his ear was one of Cat's small hoop earrings. He tried to pull it off.

"Ow!" he whined.

"You can't just yank it off," Cat warned. "It's pierced through. You have to slide it out."

"You put a hole in my ear!" he said, disbelieving, touching the maimed lobe delicately.

"Don't be such a baby," Cat chided. "If you want, you can take the earring out, and the hole will heal over."

Giogi sniffed. "How do I look?"

Cat leaned back and eyed him critically. "Like a merchant. You need something else." She took a lock of Giogi's brown hair and plaited it, fastening it together with some green beads she took off a chain hanging about her neck.

"Well?"

"Not quite right," Cat said. "You look like a sailor."

From the open doorway came a polite cough. Giogi looked up

in surprise.

"Oh, Thomas. I took a dive in the Immer Stream, I'm afraid. Could you see to those wet things, please?"

Thomas slipped into the room and began gathering up Giogi's dripping clothes, surveying the damage to each article. He made a special point to keep his eyes averted from the bed.

Last year, when his master's aunt had tried her best to match Giogi with Minda Lluth, Thomas had not approved. The lady had been far too frivolous, but at least she had been a lady. He wasn't sure where he would classify this Cat person, but he knew ladies did not sit on gentleman's beds, wrapped in nothing but bed sheets.

"I'm afraid these boots may be beyond cleaning, sir," Thomas reported, trying to sound regretful about it.

"Oh, no. We can't lose the boots," Cat said with mock alarm. She jumped from the bed and took the clodders from Thomas. She set them down before the fireplace and whispered an incantation. A small whirlwind of steam began to rise from inside each boot and danced up the flue. After a minute, the steam dissipated. Cat brought them to Giogi's bedside. "There you are, Master Giogioni. As good as new."

"I say. What a neat trick. Wasn't that a neat trick, Thomas?"

"Most entertaining, sir," Thomas replied coolly, holding the other soaked articles. "I've been keeping dinner warm. Will you be down to dine shortly, sir, or shall I bring up trays?"

Something in Thomas's tone warned Giogi that it would be unwise to choose the more amusing course. "We will be down as soon as we've dressed," the nobleman replied, trying to sound cool and undaunted by his servant's disapproval.

"Very good, sir." Thomas bowed and exited.

"Trays would have been just fine with me," Cat said.

"Perhaps, but not with Thomas. Dinner tends to be formal when we have guests. We'll have to do him proud and dress to the nines, or he'll be—disappointed."

Cat looked down at the carpeting. "I washed out my robes, but they're still wet. I'm afraid they didn't get too clean in any case."

Giogi struck his forehead with the palm of his hand. "Oh, of course. Forgive me. I should have thought of it before. We'll dig something up from the chest in the lilac room."

Giogi picked up a lamp and led his guest out into the hall. He opened the door to the lilac room.

"How lovely," the mage whispered, stepping inside. She ran her fingers along the delicate silk wall hangings, the crepe bed curtains, the intricately carved dressing table, and the mother-of-pearl jewelry box. "This was your mother's room, wasn't it?" she whispered.

"Yes. Do you like it?" Giogi asked hopefully.

"I've never seen any place so lovely," Cat said softly.

"Thomas thought you might be more comfortable in the red room for some reason. Shall I tell him to light a fire and turn down this bed for you, instead?" Giogi offered.

"Oh, you needn't bother him about it. I can do that myself," Cat insisted.

"All right, then. There are scads of pretty things in that chest there. Several years out of fashion, I'm afraid."

"I'm sure it's all perfect," Cat said, smiling gratefully at the young nobleman.

"I'll leave you to it, then," Giogi said, backing out of the room.

He returned to his own room to dress. Pulling on his breeches, he caught sight of his bare-chested reflection in the leaded window glass. The nobleman posed menacingly, half shutting his eyes, trying to imagine campfires burning instead of a cozy fireplace, and nervous horses staked to ropes instead of comfortable chairs. At length he grimaced and turned away.

"I do look like a sailor," he said with a sigh. He tugged the window drapes closed to avoid catching another glimpse of his scrawny, unheroic figure.

Had Giogi looked out the window instead of at his reflection, he would have seen two furtive figures slipping into his carriage house. The young noble's mind was on his wardrobe, though, and far from the machinations of his relatives.

♣ 12 ♣

The Ass's Pocket

Olive stamped her hoof and cursed Cat for the twentieth time. Why do mages always have to be so damned efficient? she wondered. As if it's not bad enough she's going to betray good ol' Giogi, she's got to go and leave me locked in the carriage house so I can't get out to stop her. I knew that woman was trouble from the moment I set eyes on her.

With some effort,Olive had gotten her burro mouth around the door handle and turned it, but found that Cat had taken the precaution of sliding the bolt on the outside of the door. Ordinarily, given sufficient time, Olive could have worked the bolt over with a wire or something, but hooves severely limited her dexterity. I'd give a small fortune for a thumb, she thought, rattling the door handle with her teeth.

The burro paced the carriage house like a nervous cat. I may never make Giogi understand I'm not a burro. I've got to get out of here and find someone a little brighter than he and powerful enough to change me back into a halfling. Then I have to get back here and warn Giogi that Flattery is one of his relatives, as well as a murdering lunatic, and that Cat is really a viper.

Olive made a mental list of the few halfling adventurers in town who might be trusted with the secret of her awful and embarrassing transformation, and began thinking up ways to communicate with them. She found that with some effort she could scratch her own name in the dirt with a forehoof.

Now, if I could just get out of this carriage house, corner one of my people, and make them hold still for an hour while I demonstrate my abilities, I'm all set, Olive thought.

After an hour of planning, though, she grew tired of anticipating her escape and the heroics that would follow. Each version she imagined ended in a spine-tingling tale of derring-do and last-minute rescues, but all ignored the problem of getting out of the carriage house.

With nothing better to do, she began exploring the carriage

house more fully. The last rays of the setting sun broke through the clouds and streamed through the windows, so there was enough light for her to make out her surroundings.

On the other side of the buggy was quite an organized assortment of adventuring gear. Not the kind of stuff one would expect to find in the carriage house of a man-about-town, Olive mused. This was where all the things that Giogi loaded on me this morning came from.

Everything Olive had carted into the catacombs was stashed neatly in a long line of open chests and crates, which also held sacks and backpacks, tents, blankets, saddlebags, chains, knives and whetstones, camp dishes, a beat-up shield, a Talis deck, dice, a backgammon board, mirrors, snares, nets, magnifying glasses, a few bottles of wine, and even lockpicks. In the loft overhead Olive could spy a few more chests, but she was unable to navigate the ladder to the loft. Gardening tools hung from the back wall, beside varying sizes of tack and saddles.

The halfling studied everything. Most of the equipment was old and worn, though well maintained. In the end, however, her interest in the carriage house's trove waned. A burro had limited options with human tools.

I'm going to die of boredom, Olive thought, walking back into her stall. Cat had left Nameless's portrait leaning against the wall, presumably to prevent a repeat of Flattery's flameflinging at their next rendezvous. The sun had set, but in the gray twilight within the building Olive could see the splotch of black paint on the portrait's back, which blotted out the bard's given name. The paint had begun peeling from the heat of Flattery's outburst.

Let's have a closer look, shall we? Olive thought. She brushed against the back of the canvas with her muzzle, and paint flaked away. She had to step back to focus both her eyes.

Nameless, you aren't nameless anymore, she thought excitedly. Your name is . . . Finder? Finder Wyvernspur. That's a peculiar sort of name. Sounds like a—like the finder's stone!

Could the stone have been the Nameless Bard's? Olive wondered. Is that why Elminster gave it to Alias? Is it only coincidence that it's fallen into the hands of another Wyvernspur?

Olive's nostrils twitched at the smell of the charred painting. Was Flattery's violent reaction to the painting merely a reflection of his hatred for his entire family? No, Olive realized. Flattery's first words upon flaming the portrait were "curse him." His anger had been directed most specifically at Finder. Finder's been in magical exile for nearly two hundred years, though. How could Flattery have recognized him? Has Flattery lived that long and remained as young as he looks by using magic?

Well, I'm never going to answer all these questions by just thinking about them, Olive sighed. I need to get out of here.

She left the stall to stand next to the outside door; she planned to try to slip out the next time someone opened it. I have to be ready to spring into action. I have to be as vigilant as a spider in a web, able to strike with the speed of a snake, as fierce and as wild as a panther, she thought.

As she waited for her chance, Olive fell asleep on her feet.

Voices out in the garden woke her. Darkness had fallen completely. Olive stiffened with alertness. The carriage house door opened a crack. Olive waited for her chance.

"All clear," a male voice whispered.

The door opened farther, but it was blocked by two bodies. A man and a woman slipped in quickly and closed the door behind them. I could get that door open with my teeth if they would just move away from it, Olive thought.

"Steele, this is crazy," the woman hissed. Olive recognized Julia's voice. The man unshuttered his lantern, and its glow illuminated Julia's lovely features. She looked less haughty at the moment. Her face was drawn with exhaustion, and her eyes were glazed with confusion.

The halfling stepped back into the shadow of the ruined buggy. Olive wouldn't put it past the little witch to exact revenge on the burro for foiling her plan to drug Giogi.

"Sister, dear," the man hissed, "would you stop whining and try to show some spine?"

Interesting advice, Olive thought, from a man who tortures kobolds and nearly had his own spine crushed in one of their traps.

Steele held his lantern up to survey the interior of the carriage house.

There's a simple way, Olive realized, to tell Steele apart from Frefford, Nameless, and Flattery, aside from his age and the birthmark by his lip. Frefford had a sympathetic, pleasant smile, which would be impossible for the others to imitate.

Nameless's years of exile and subsequent tortures had taken a lot out of him, so he generally stared into space with a stern, thoughtful look—void of haughtiness, unlike Steele's face.

Steele's demeanor most resembled Flattery's. They had the same cold, calculating look, and, Olive suspected, the same icy laugh. Except for that moment when he'd been burning down the barn—and had resembled a mad dog—Flattery's coolness seemed imperturbable. Steele, on the other hand, was unable to hide a desperation that lay just beneath the surface. And, while Olive doubted he was half as powerful as the mage Flattery, Steele managed to look twice as arrogant.

"You still haven't told me why, in the worst possible weather, we've come all the way out here from Redstone just to sneak into this awful barn," Julia said, not bothering to hide her annoyance.

"It's a carriage house, not a barn," Steel corrected, "and we're here because it's unthinkable that our weak-willed, idiot Cousin Giogi should have the spur. It should be in the hands of someone who knows how to wield power. Someone who knows how to make the best use of it. Someone of strength and valor."

Olive recalled how Alias had once called Nameless a man with overweening vanity. No doubt it runs in the family, the halfling thought. Compared to Steele and Flattery, though, Nameless is downright modest.

"Steele, would you get to the point," Julia snapped.

"You said Giogi had a burro," Steele said.

"Yes," Julia replied. "A vicious little creature that I would rather not run into again." She looked around the interior of the carriage house nervously.

The feeling is mutual, I'm sure, Olive thought.

"I need to find that burro," Steele said.

Olive backed deeper into the shadows. She didn't especially want to be found by a known torturer of kobolds. If only Julia would move away from that door, Olive thought.

"What's so special about the burro?" Julia asked, leaning wearily against the door.

"It cost me a small fortune," Steele told her, "but I paid the priest at the church of Waukeen to perform a divination for me. I asked where the spur was. He told me: 'In the little ass's pocket.' "

"If it's in Giogi's pocket, why are we out here?" Julia complained.

"It's not in Giogi's pocket," Steele replied with exasperation. "It's in the little ass's pocket." Very slowly, as if talking to a child, he explained to his sister, "A burro is a little ass."

Wherever I go, Olive whined silently, *people are always blaming me when something goes missing. It's not fair. I've never even laid eyes on this stupid spur. Besides—*

"Asses don't have pockets," Julia snapped.

Took the words right out of my mouth, Olive thought.

"Obviously it's some sort of riddle," Steele said. Feigning patience, Steele continued to explain to Julia in a slow, steady voice, "The spur could be in the burro's saddlebags, or maybe Giogi made it a little jacket—that's the sort of fool thing he's always doing. Maybe the spur is inside the burro. Then I'll have to skin it."

Olive's heart thudded in her chest as she looked around for some place safer to hide than the shadows. *This isn't fair,* she thought again. *I haven't got the spur in my pocket. Unless— unless it's in Jade's magic purse,* she realized.

Steele stepped into the stall that had been Olive's. "Waukeen's wits," he snarled, "what a mess."

"What is it?" Julia asked, too nervous to stray from her post by the door.

"Looks like there's been a fire in here," Steele said. "Maybe Giogi had an accident with a lamp."

"Look at his carriage," Julia said. "He told Aunt Dorath last night that there was nothing wrong with it."

Steele stepped out of the burro's stall. "Something snapped the wheel in two. I've never seen a break like that before." He shook his head and turned to continue his search. "Maybe he keeps the burro with the mare," Steele muttered. He opened the door to Daisyeye's stall.

Olive's stomach suddenly felt very queasy. *Lady of Luck, don't let it be the oats,* she prayed silently.

Daisyeye nickered.

"Easy, girl," Steele whispered, handing the horse a handful of oats. "You have any company in here? No."

Olive held her breath and tried to keep herself from lowing in pain. Unable to double over, her first instinct was to lie down. *You can't do that, Olive-girl!* she berated herself, *that's* the worst thing you can do. You need to walk around. Fear of discovery by the spur hunters, though, kept Olive frozen in place.

"Aren't you a beauty," Steele said to Daisyeye. "Giogi always has the best horses," he bemoaned, "and then names them all the same idiot name."

"Maybe the burro's out in the garden," Julia suggested.

"In weather like this?" Steele shook his head. "Giogi's too soft-hearted to leave an animal out in the cold and wet."

"Maybe he rented it or boards it out."

"I checked all the other stables in town. I found four mules, but no asses anywhere. No, it has to be here somewhere. Do you think he was stupid enough to leave it tied to his carriage?"

He's going to search this side of the carriage house! Olive thought with panic. She hugged herself nervously in the darkness. I'll never be able to fend off both of them. What should I do? Think, Olive-girl, she ordered herself, massaging her temples with her fingers.

Olive's eyes widened with the sudden realization of what she was doing. She brought her fingers down in front of her and wiggled them in disbelief. I have fingers! Arms! I have arms! Olive looked down at her body. She was a halfling once again. Thank Tymora! she thought.

Steele's lantern light began to creep around to the back of the buggy. Olive slipped as quietly as she could toward the ladder to the loft. She tested the first step gingerly. It felt quite sturdy.

She scampered up the ladder, rolled into the loft, and nearly choked herself to death.

Upon her transformation back to a halfling, her halter had slipped around her neck. A strap of the leather caught on the top of the ladder as she dove over the top. Olive rolled back and extricated herself quickly from the leather binding, but not before she'd gagged out loud.

"What was that?" Julia demanded as a small bit of hay drifted down in the lantern light.

"A cat or an owl or something," Steele insisted. He stood beneath the ladder and held his lamp over his head, looking into the loft.

"Steele," Julia said with the tone of a woman who would put up with no more nonsense, "burro's cannot climb ladders."

She's right, Steele, Olive thought. Better listen to her.

"You didn't even know what a burro was until this morning," Steele pointed out. "How would you know?"

"It walks around on four feet, Steele. For heaven's sake, be reasonable." She slapped her arms at her sides and snapped, "I don't know why I've put up with this madness of yours. I agreed to help you sneak the spur from the crypt," Julia said, desperately trying to convince her brother of her loyalty. "It's not my fault the door opened twelve days early and someone else stole the spur."

"We only have Drone's word for that," Steele said.

"Why would Uncle Drone lie about that?" Julia asked with disbelief.

"Think, Julia. Giogi is away for three seasons, supposedly on a mysterious mission for the crown. He comes back late one evening. The crypt alarm goes off the next morning."

"You think Giogi was using the spur on his trip?" Julia asked.

"Precisely," Steele said. "Uncle Drone was covering for him, just like he covered for Cole. Drone must have forgotten to turn off the magical alarm so Giogi could return the spur when he got back from his trip. Uncle Drone told us he couldn't see who the thief was—because he didn't want to give Giogi away." Steele continued by digging through the chests of adventuring equipment and looking in every tiny nook of the carriage house.

"But if Giogi went into the crypt to return the spur," Julia objected, "why was it missing?"

Steele shrugged. "Giogi changed his mind at the last moment. Not realizing the alarm had alerted everyone at Redstone, he thought it didn't matter if he kept the spur or not."

"But Giogi went into the catacombs looking for the thief," Julia pointed out.

"Only to keep up the appearance of innocence," Steele said.

"Why would Drone say the thief was locked in the catacombs?"

"To stall for time, so I didn't have a divination done sooner. I'm on to their game now. Without Uncle Drone, Giogi is no match for me." Steele thumped his fist on the buggy. It wobbled a little on its three good wheels. "There's no burro in here," he growled at last. "Where else could it be?"

"Giogi could have left it with a friend," Julia suggested. "Shaver Cormaeril keeps a private stable. It could be there."

"That's a possibility. Let's go." Steele returned to the doorway.

"Where?"

"To the Cormaeril estate, of course."

"Steele, it's dark and cold and slicker than oil out there. Couldn't we just head home and check in the morning?"

"No. It will be easier in the dark, and I need you to keep watch," he said, shuttering his lantern. He pushed open the door.

"Steele, I want to go home," Julia said with an iron determination.

"Fine," her brother snapped. He paused, silhouetted by the moonlight shining in the doorway. "Go home. You're useless, anyway." Steele disappeared into the darkness.

Julia stood in the open doorway, and Olive thought she heard the noblewoman sob. After a few moments, though, Julia fled the carriage house without bothering to close the door. Olive heard Julia whisper, "Steele, wait up."

Still in the loft, Olive rolled over and sighed with relief. She stretched out on the straw, wriggling her fingers and toes in the hay. She was once again the lovely, talented halfling she'd been born and bred to be. Even better, the queasiness had left her. It wasn't the oats, after all, she realized. Probably an effect of the transformation.

She was still wearing the clothing she'd worn the night before. She patted down her vest pockets. Jade's magical purse was still there. "I am an ass," Olive whispered with a chuckle, "for not having figured it out before." Who else, she thought, would have been so bold and cunning as to steal the Wyvernspur's prize heirloom out from under their noses? Who else could have gotten past the guardian? Only my protege, Jade.

Olive's pride decayed within moments. Jade would never steal anything again. The halfling's stomach cramped up again, this time with renewed anguish over Jade's death. She curled into a ball with her fists clenched, trying to fight back her misery.

It was no use. The emotion surged through her and took control. Olive wept, something she hadn't done since her mother had died. She lay sobbing in the straw until she was weak with the effort and had given herself a headache.

She lay there a while longer feeling empty inside. Finally her determination to avenge Jade's death returned. Flattery will pay, Olive thought. He may think he's tough, slapping Cat around and murdering my Jade, but he's about to learn otherwise.

Once I return the spur to Giogi, we'll find out what its secret powers are and use them against Flattery, she thought.

Olive sat up and wiped the residue of the tears from her face. She sniffed, looked at her sleeve, and realized that the dirt and grime she'd accumulated as a burro remained with her. If I'm going to enlist Giogi's help, though, she thought, I need to present a more formidable appearance. I need a bath, clean clothes, a decent night's sleep, and time to think up a plan. I'll contact Giogi in the morning, she decided.

Olive stood, brushed the straw off her clothing, and climbed down from the loft. In another minute, she was outside Giogi's front gate and skating her way along the ice-covered roads, back to her room at Maela's boarding house.

*　*　*　*　*

Giogi stood at the bottom of the staircase, watching Cat descend. He was sure there wasn't a more beautiful woman in all of Cormyr. She wore a low-cut gown of lavender satin covered with golden lace. Her long hair was fastened high on her head with a matching golden lace net.

"Is this all right?" Cat asked, halting two steps above him.

"I don't think I'd ever seen mother wear that," Giogi said, trying hard to avoid staring at the dress's decolletage. I didn't know she had anything so, um—"

"Revealing?" Cat suggested, crossing her hands coyly over the gown's neckline, which was nowhere near her neck.

"Small," Giogi said, recovering his wits. "My mother was not as slender as you." He offered Cat his arm.

"Not while she was your mother, perhaps," Cat replied, laying her fingertips on his sleeve and moving down beside him, "but as a girl, she must have been. I found this at the very bottom of the chest. It might have been something she wore when she came out."

"Oh, she was never a debutante," Giogi explained as he escorted the mage through the main hall. "Her father, Shar of Suzail, was a carpenter. He made furniture, of course, but he also supervised the timberwork of all the bridges in Cormyr, and the locks at Wheloon, and they're all still standing. He made a lot of money, but, according to father, he was very humble. King Rhigaerd II, Azoun's father, offered him a peerage for his work, but he turned it down. He said he couldn't do both—work and be a lord. Old Shar begged Father to rescue his daughter, though, when she was kidnapped by an evil mage. That's how my parents met."

"Your mother would have been presented to court, though, when she married your father."

"Yes, I guess she must have."

"Perhaps she wore this then. I didn't want to borrow anything too valuable, but this one fit so well. I did pick out something especially nice for you."

"Pardon?" Giogi asked.

Cat halted and held Giogi back from the dining room door. "Here," she said, pulling something out of her sleeve. "I found it in the jewelry box." Cat held out a platinum headpiece and latched it about Giogi's forehead. "There. That's just right. It gives you the look of nobility."

"It feels funny," Giogi said, shifting it about on his head.

Cat laughed. "You'll get used to it," she said, steering him toward the dining room door.

Giogi turned the handle and led the enchantress in to dinner.

The nobleman was heartened to see that their fancy attire had pacified Thomas considerably. The manservant dropped his earlier reserve and served dinner with considerable courtesy. Giogi caught the servant smiling at him once and sneaking appreciative glances at Cat often.

Thomas wished his master had removed the rakish jewelry in his ear and hair, but the headdress actually pleased the servant. He decided it gave Giogi a commanding air—something he'd always lacked. As for the woman, though her earlier slip in decorum marked her of "lower" birth, her speech revealed a certain amount of education.

He could easily see that his master's interest extended beyond the woman's ability as a spell-caster. It would be impossible not to do so. The woman's attractiveness startled Thomas each time he looked at her.

Ever alert to the dangers that beautiful women presented to a man of his master's fortunes, Thomas considered carefully what course he should take to ensure that Giogioni did not en-tangle himself with this woman on a personal level. Such a situation, he decided as he served the soup, could only lead to scandal.

The servant considered letting news of the woman's presence leak to Dorath, but he dismissed that idea almost immediately. Giogi's aunt would take too heavy-handed an approach, the kind that drove couples closer together. Similarly, Thomas realized while presenting the roast duck, a cautionary word of his own to the young nobleman could backfire drastically.

By the time he cleared the dinner plates and served the apples and cheese, Thomas felt the need to consult with someone who not only cared for Giogi, but who understood the subtlety of the situation, someone who could also keep an eye on Cat and make sure she wasn't using her magic to influence him. The servant realized that he would have to wait until later for such a consultation, after Giogi had retired.

"So," Cat began after Thomas had retreated to Servant Land for the final time, "this man you went to see, Sudacar, couldn't tell you how your father used the spur?"

"No, but we think my father could use it to fly."

"It must have more power than that," Cat said after sipping her brandy, "or Flattery wouldn't have sent me after it. He can already fly."

"Well, Sudacar suggested I speak with Mother Lleddew. She adventured with my father once, so she may know something more."

"Who is Mother Lleddew?" Cat asked.

"The high priestess of the House of the Lady. That's our temple to Selune. I hiked all the way up there tonight, by the Immer Stream path. It got dark, and I fell in the stream. I told you that already."

"That's when you were attacked by the lacedons but were saved by the bear," Cat said, remembering.

"Yes. One of them scratched me right across my face—the lacedons, not the bear. Then, when I got to the temple, there was a girl." Giogi knit his brow. "I didn't think about it at the time, but that girl did look like the Cledwyll statue, except much younger. Since the guardian said I'd been kissed by Selune, I sort of associated this girl with Selune, since she healed me with a kiss, and then—poof!—I was home. Oh, but first she

told me Mother Lleddew wasn't there, and that I should try tomorrow. It was all very strange after the fight with the undead. Do you think I imagined it all?"

"Well, . . ." Cat hesitated and looked down at her lap, then
she looked up again. "Do you know what adventurers mean
when they say someone was kissed by Selune, Master
Giogioni?"

"Well, Selune is the goddess of the moon, so I thought it
meant I was born under a full moon or something. Sort of like
being born under a lucky star."

Cat shook her head. "Sometimes it's used to describe a person
who goes a little mad. Usually, though, it means a person
cursed with lycanthropy."

Giogi paled. "You mean like werewolves?"

Cat nodded. "Or wererats or tigers or bears."

"Wererats or tigers or bears? Do you think that's why I have
those awful dreams about hunting things?"

"Have you ever noticed if they're stronger when the moon is
full?"

Giogi thought for a moment, then shook his head. "I've never
really kept track. No, it's too preposterous. I'd know if I was a
lycanthrope. I'll admit that sometimes I get in late after imbib-
ing a little too much grape and things are pretty foggy the next
morning, but I've never come home in torn clothes covered
with blood. And tonight's a full moon, isn't it? I haven't shaved
since this morning, but I'm not looking any hairier than usual,
am I?"

"Sometimes such curses don't show up until a person
reaches a certain age. Twenty, usually."

"I'm twenty-three."

"Sometimes twenty-five or thirty."

"Then what about Aunt Dorath? She has the same dreams."

"She does?"

"Well, she did. She said I had to ignore them."

"I don't think that's a good idea," Cat said. "Our dreams
tell us important things about ourselves, and sometimes the
gods talk to us in them. Do you plan to go back to this Mother
Lleddew to find out more about your father and the
spur?"

"Yes, the girl in the temple said to try again tomorrow afternoon," Giogi explained.

"May I come with you?"

"I think it would be safer if you stayed here, so we don't run the risk of Flattery spotting you."

Cat looked down at her lap again. "I can't hide in your home forever, Master Giogioni," she whispered.

Giogi was suddenly aware of the pounding of his heart. He wanted to say that he wished she could, but he bit back those words. "Just a little while longer," he assured her. "When we've found the spur and locked it safely away again, Flattery will give up and go home. If not, well, I'll get Sudacar's advice. He's the king's man. He's supposed to preserve the peace. He'll know what to do."

Cat looked up and smiled weakly, but Giogi was afraid he hadn't reassured her.

"Do you think that if your uncle did know more about the thief, he might have written it down somewhere?" she asked.

"Of course!" Giogi said, smacking his head. "He kept a journal. I don't know why I didn't think of it before. He kept it in his lab."

"Perhaps, if you don't think it's too personal, you could let me help out by reading through it, to save you time while you visit Selune's temple. Maybe, too, you could ask Mother Lleddew to perform a divination for you."

"Steele was supposed to be getting that done this afternoon. He may already have learned something. I'll ask him. The list of things I have to do is getting pretty long, isn't it? I know it's not very late, but I've had a long day, and I should be getting to bed so I can get an early start tomorrow. Would you think me a terrible host if I left you on your own?" Giogi asked.

"Of course not," Cat said. "I'm tired as well."

Giogi escorted the mage from the candlelit dining room to the hallway. He felt very odd following her up the stairs. While he'd offered her his protection without hesitation, no other woman except his mother had ever stayed in his house before.

Cat halted by his bedroom door and turned to face him.

Giogi, feeling very awkward, stopped short and clasped his hands nervously behind his back. "So, you prefer to stay in the lilac room, then?" he asked.

"Yes. It's too lovely to resist."

"I'll let Thomas know in the morning."

Cat stepped closer and stood on tiptoe to brush her lips against his. "Good night, Master Giogioni. Sweet dreams," she whispered.

Giogi blinked hard. "Good night," he replied weakly.

Cat turned and walked down the hall to the lilac room. She let herself in and closed the door behind her without looking back. Giogi stood in place for several moments. With a sigh, he entered his own room.

It wasn't until Giogi had finished undressing that he remembered that he meant to stop in at the Fish to look for Olive Ruskettle and ask her about Alias of Westgate. "Bother," he muttered, "I'm just too tired. It'll wait until tomorrow," he decided, sliding between the sheets.

As exhausted as he was, the nobleman lay awake for a long time, afraid to fall asleep and dream. If only Cat's wish of sweet dreams for him could come true, he wouldn't feel so anxious.

He thought he heard Cat crying once, and he hovered on the edge of the bed for several minutes, debating whether he should leave her to her privacy or go in and try to comfort her. The crying subsided before he'd made up his mind. Part of him was relieved, since offering comfort to a lady in the middle of the night could be misinterpreted, but part of him was disappointed he'd missed his opportunity to show he cared. He got back into bed feeling agitated and unhappy. He sat propped up against the headboard, listening for any further sounds from the lilac room.

Finally, unable to resist the silence and his fatigue, he drifted off, still sitting up. As the guardian had threatened, the dream came.

As usual, he soared over the meadow. The field was different tonight, though. It was the meadow atop Spring Hill, and the House of the Lady stood in the center. A great black bear stood on the temple stairs. The young girl acolyte ran through the meadow. Giogi had no control over the dream. His flight was quick and smooth, and the girl didn't stand a chance. She dodged and darted like a rabbit, but, in the end, Giogi dropped down on her with his rending claws. She shrieked with the death cry of all the other prey in his dreams.

Giogi started awake. He was drenched with sweat but very, very grateful he'd missed the end of the dream.

Then he realized he still heard the shriek. It came from Cat's room.

❧ 13 ❧

Olive's Investigation

Giogi leaped out of bed, burst from his room, and dashed down the dark corridor to the door of the lilac room. Before he got there, the shrieking had stopped. Bursting into a lady's room could prove awkward, but the silence coming from the room seemed even more ominous to Giogi. He flung open the door without knocking.

Cat had lit a fire in the fireplace, but a few glowing embers were all that remained. Dressed only in his nightshirt, Giogi shivered with cold. Moonlight streaming through the windows silhouetted everything in the room. The mage, looking pale and shaken, sat up in her bed.

"Are you all right? What's wrong?" Giogi asked.

"There was someone in here!" Cat gasped. "He tried to smother me with a pillow!"

"Where did he go?"

"Through the wall!" Cat cried, pointing to a spot next to the fireplace. "Like a ghost!" The woman's cool, analytical manner had crumbled. She sounded terror-stricken.

Giogi turned up the wick in the lamp on the dressing table, and lit it with a bit of burning straw from the fireplace. He drew aside a silk wall hanging, but there was nothing behind it but wall. He tapped it. It sounded solid.

"I've never heard of a ghost in this room before," Giogi said. "What did he look like?"

"Like Flattery," Cat said with a sob. "But that's impossible."

"Is it?" Giogi asked, uncertain.

"If Flattery were trying to kill me, he wouldn't leave the job half-finished," Cat insisted. "He wouldn't have needed a pillow, either."

Giogi positioned himself prudently at the foot of Cat's bed. She now wore one of his mother's nightgowns, and though it was a prim flannel thing, it was, after all, only a nightgown. "Are you all right?" he asked.

Cat lowered her head and nodded. Her long, loose hair veiled her face, but from the way her shoulders shook, Giogi could tell she was crying.

Damn propriety! the nobleman thought as he rushed to her side. "It's all right," he insisted, sitting beside her on the bed and wrapping his arms around her. "Everything's going to be fine."

Cat laid her head against Giogi's chest and hugged him close. It was a full minute before her sobbing subsided. Then she sniffed and pulled gently away from his arms. "I'm sorry to be such a coward, but I've cast all the magic I can for the day. I'm helpless until I've slept and studied." Her voice quivered, and Giogi was afraid she would go to pieces again.

"Anyone would be upset by what you've just been through," Giogi replied. He stood up. "I think you should wait here," he said.

"Where are you going?" Cat asked with alarm, grabbing at his arm but stopping herself.

"I'm going to get Thomas and search the house," Giogi said. He lit a second lamp and carried it with him out into the hallway. Halfway down the stairs, he met Thomas hurrying up in the darkness.

"Sir! I thought I heard a scream! Is something wrong?" the servant asked.

"Yes, Thomas," Giogi explained. "Someone attacked Mistress Cat in her room. We may have a burglar or worse."

"In the red room, sir? Are you sure?" Thomas asked.

"No. Someone in the lilac room. Mistress Cat preferred it to the red room, just as I thought she might, so I invited her to use it instead. Someone tried to smother her, but fled when she screamed. She says her attacker went through the wall, but she may have been confused or the attacker capable of magic. In any case, we ought to search the house."

Thomas nodded and moved up the stairs toward Giogi. "Perhaps we should start in the lady's room," the servant suggested.

"I was just in there, Thomas. I told you, the intruder fled when Mistress Cat screamed."

"There may be, um, footprints, or some other evidence, sir," Thomas offered.

"Hmmm. You're right," Giogi agreed. He turned around and marched back to the lilac room with Thomas right behind him. The door stood open. Cat had risen from the bed and wrapped herself in a robe. She stood staring out the window at the grounds below.

Giogi knocked on the door frame to announce his presence. The mage whirled around, brandishing a small crystal dagger.

"It's just me, with Thomas," Giogi said.

Cat gave a relieved sigh. She crossed the room to stand at Giogi's side and lean against him.

Thomas nodded politely to Cat before entering the room. "Perhaps I could use that lamp, sir," he suggested.

Giogi handed him the light. As the nobleman stood beside Cat, watching his servant investigate the windows, something brushed against his legs. Giogi let out a cry and jumped aside.

A large black-and-white cat looked up at him and meowed with annoyance.

"Spot! Thomas, it's Spot." Giogi said, picking up the large tom-cat and brushing its face fur. The cat began purring immediately.

"Is it possible, Mistress Cat," Thomas asked with an exaggerated patience, "that Spot tried lying on your face and you mistook him for a smothering pillow? When you screamed, he would have jumped away. His shadow in the moonlight could have been mistaken for a larger figure. When he landed, he would have disappeared from your sight and perhaps slunk beneath a piece of furniture."

"It was not a cat," Cat insisted.

"Someone must have sneaked in somehow, Thomas," Giogi said.

"I will check all the doors and windows, sir, though it is also possible that someone broke in magically, in which case, they would undoubtedly have left by that way as well."

"Well, Thomas, we'd better have a look around, just in case."

Master and servant went through every room in the house but turned up no forced or broken windows or doors, nor any house-breakers. Giogi dismissed Thomas and trudged back upstairs to the lilac room.

"Nothing," he reported to Cat. "Is it possible Flattery might have sent someone else to do his dirty work, someone less competent than he would be?"

Cat paled. "I don't know," she whispered. "Perhaps."

"I think, just to be safe, you had better sleep in my bed. I'll stay in here."

Cat nodded. Giogi escorted her to his room. He checked behind all the curtains and wall hangings and under the bed. "All clear," he said.

"I don't know if I can sleep," Cat said.

"You must try. I'll be right next door if you need me." Feeling a little more confident, Giogi bent over and kissed Cat on the forehead before he turned and left the room.

Back in the lilac room, Giogi sat on the edge of the bed, wondering if Thomas could be right about Cat mistaking Spot as her attacker. The nobleman certainly hoped so, for the lady's sake. But suppose Thomas had been wrong. Who but Flattery would want to harm the mage? Cat felt sure that Flattery wouldn't have failed if he meant to kill her, but suppose the wizard had meant his attack as a warning? Suppose Flattery were trying to frighten Cat into returning to his side?

I have to find some way to protect her from him, Giogi thought with determination. He lay in bed debating whether or not to tell Sudacar about Cat and Flattery. Before he came to a decision, though, he fell asleep. Despite the nobleman's anxieties, no more screams or dreams disturbed his rest.

* * * * *

Maela's boarding house, where Olive had taken a room for the winter, catered to an exclusive clientele. While Maela's rates were reasonable, and her home clean and comfortable, not everyone would consider crossing her doorstep. Maela was a halfling, and she kept a halfling-sized townhouse in the heart of Immersea.

Olive could have stayed at a room in the Five Fine Fish. The Fish was at the center of Immersea night life and where Jade had chosen to stay. The attractions of the Fish could not compete with the comfort of living at Maela's, though. At Maela's, a halfling didn't need to scramble onto the furniture or use her hands to scale the staircases or stand on tiptoes to see out the windows or climb upon chairs to slide door bolts shut. Maela's low ceilings were enough to make Olive feel safe and cozy. The nicest thing about Maela's house was its larder, which Maela kept well stocked and unlocked.

Olive's first action upon returning home to Maela's the night before had been to visit that larder. The remainders of that raid lay on a plate on the dressing table in Olive's bedroom. Olive popped another piece of ham into her mouth and licked her fingertips clean before turning back to the mirror at her vanity table.

Last night she'd soaked and scrubbed at her hands and feet for half and hour before she was satisfied they revealed no trace of the catacomb muck she'd been through the day before. Upon waking this morning, she'd inspected her best gown carefully, stitched up a tear in the lace, and rubbed away a spot of extra spicy mustard before she slipped it over her head. Now she brushed her auburn hair until it gleamed and every stray bit of straw had been removed.

With a disgusted crinkle of her nose, the halfling rummaged through the pile of dirty, smelly clothing at the foot of her bed until she had fished out her quilted vest. Holding the vest on her lap, she turned out an inner pocket and unclasped the pin fastened there for security.

The pin, a miniature harp and crescent moon, had been a gift from the Nameless Bard—Finder Wyvernspur, Olive reminded herself. Tossing the vest aside, she reached for the jar of silver polish she'd borrowed from the larder. She removed every trace of tarnish from the jewelry and buffed it to a brilliant luster. Finally, taking a deep breath, Olive pinned it to her dress, right over her heart.

She had never actually displayed the Harper's symbol before, which some people would have found remarkable, considering the potential for exploitation the pin presented her. Though little was known of the Harpers, rumors regarding their power and good works were widespread enough that their symbol of membership could gain a person instant respect—though not necessarily safety.

Olive understood, however, that possession of the symbol alone did not make her a Harper, even if another Harper, Nameless, had given it to her. Nameless was a renegade, after all. Olive was shrewd enough to realize that another Harper might not look favorably on someone impersonating one of their number, and the farther north she traveled, the greater the likelihood that she would run into a real Harper. So, even though it lent credence to her claim of bardhood—since most Harpers were either bards or rangers—common sense outweighed ego and she had always kept it hidden.

Until now. This is an emergency, Olive thought, and no snooty, goody-goody Harper is going to keep me from seeing justice done. Besides, I'm only planning on doing what a real Harper should be doing—eliminating a menace.

Years of dealing with human prejudices had left Olive unwilling to leave justice in the hands of authorities. She doubted that any of them, even Harpers, ever felt any concern for people like her and Jade. She couldn't trust them to believe her story about Flattery or do anything about him.

She knew Giogi Wyvernspur was different, though. She would take Giogi into her confidence. Giogi, she figured, will be flattered if he thinks I'm a Harper, and it would never occur to him to check into my credentials. As far as he knows, I'm a bard of some renown, and Cat's already prejudiced him against Flattery. It won't be hard to convince him of the truth.

Besides, how can he deny assistance to the woman who restored the wyvern's spur to his family? Olive thought, tossing her hair and watching it shimmer in the mirror. The halfling couldn't help but realize that once Flattery was dealt with, the gratitude of a Cormyrian noble, even one as minor as Giogi, could be extremely useful.

I won't need to explain to Giogi all the details of how I recovered his family's heirloom, of course; he can assume I'm just extraordinarily clever, which is fairly close to the truth.

"Time to arm myself for battle," Olive muttered. One at a time, over her bed, the halfling emptied the pockets of each item of her wardrobe that she'd worn the evening before. She had pockets in her pants, pockets in her tunic, pockets in her vest, pockets in her cloak, and pockets in her belt. Soon a pile of debris collected on the bedspread.

A job long overdue, she thought, appalled by all the clutter she found. Some of it was organized—capital and basic equipment—but most of it was junk she'd been unable to part with because she'd convinced herself that eventually it would prove useful.

Her own purse held plenty of coins: ten platinum tri-crowns, thirty-two gold lions, plus change—sixteen silver and twelve copper coins. Much more lay stashed beneath the floorboards of her rented room. A smaller sack contained twenty glass "rubies" for emergencies and four real rubies for real emergencies. She set both sack and purse aside.

Her lockpicks and wires were nestled neatly in their leather case, though in the corner of the case, wrapped in rags, were twenty-some unsorted picks—some she'd found in her travels; others were broken tools she'd been meaning to replace. More than fifty odd-sized keys jangled from her iron key ring. A few were made to open more than their share of locks; others were rendered useless by distance from, or destruction of, the locks they'd once fit. A spool of sturdy string, a penknife, and a flint with striker completed her "absolutely necessary" pile.

Olive made a separate pile of four more balls of sturdy string, two corks, a fishhook and sinker, hair ties and fasteners, a comb, chalk, three empty glass vials—one missing a stopper—six mismatched buttons, a bag of raisins, two dirty handkerchiefs, a candle, a stick of charcoal, spectacle frames without the spectacles, a yarting thumb pick she'd been searching for all week, last week's shopping list, nut shells, peas, and enough biscuit crumbs to keep a pigeon happy for a month. It was mostly stuff she would throw out—eventually.

"And last but not least," Olive said, pulling Jade's magical pouch out of her vest and untying the strings, "the wyvern's spur," she announced, dumping the contents of the miniature bag of holding on her bed.

"She's as bad as me," the halfling said, astonished by the assortment and number of things that tumbled from the enchanted leather sack. Two handfuls of coins—mostly copper and silver—a purple silk scarf, a brass shot glass, a minty-smelling potion in a crystal vial, a very nice pearl necklace, six keys, a silver spoon, a pair of gloves, a ball of string, a button hook, some regular dice, some loaded dice, a yard of lace, an apple, some chunks of cured, dried meat, and several pieces of hard candy covered in lint.

"Yech," Olive muttered. She shook the pouch some more, but nothing else fell out. "Damn!" she said. "Where is it?"

Olive sat on the bed and picked through the debris. "It has to be here," she insisted. "I'm the only ass in Immersea. Steele said so." Face it, Olive-girl, she told herself, trying to overcome her disappointment at not finding the spur. Steele must have been wrong, as usual.

But Jade being the thief had made so much sense. If the guardian accepted her as a daughter of Finder, the Nameless Bard, Jade could have entered the crypt. Flattery had told Cat that twice his magic had failed to detect the spur. Jade, just like Alias, had been proofed against magical detection and scrying. Jade would have thwarted Flattery's attempts at magical detection.

Then a more unsettling thought occurred to Olive. Suppose Jade did steal the spur and it was on her when Flattery disintegrated her? Wouldn't that be ironic?

But, then, would Steele's divination reveal that the spur was in the little ass's pocket? Could Steele's god have lied to him? Or was there another little ass that Steele had missed somewhere? Giogi might be considered a bit of an ass, but he was far from little; he was taller than Jade had been. Cat was an ass for sticking with Flattery, but if she had the spur, she'd have turned it over to the evil wizard. There could be other Wyvernspurs who were fools, or, for that matter, any one of them could have secretly wed some fool to steal the spur for them, as Flattery had.

Olive wondered idly, Had Flattery really married Cat just to make her a Wyvernspur, or was he just trying to bind her to him? Even if the evil wizard hadn't any idea that Cat was already a Wyvernspur, he still didn't need to marry her to get past the guardian. He could have gone in the crypt himself. Why hadn't he? What had he been afraid of?

Olive wished Finder were there now. If Flattery hated him so much, there was a good chance Finder knew Flattery and could tell her something useful about the evil mage. Finder was far off in Shadowdale, though. This time of year it would take more than a month to ride up to Shadowdale and back. Olive and Giogi needed each other's help now. Even if they didn't have the spur, they still had Cat to use against her master.

The problem is how to convince Cat that Flattery can't do anything to her and that he has nothing to offer her. The first part's easy enough, the halfling thought. Just use the old amulet of protection scam.

Olive looked down at the junk lying on her bed. What do we have here that's uglier than a monkey's paw? she pondered. She scooped up the chunks of cured meat from Jade's purse and tied them tightly in Jade's silk scarf. That'll do for now, she thought, scooping all of Jade's things along with the homemade "amulet of protection" back into Jade's magic pouch.

Olive sighed. The sun had risen. It was time to join forces

with Giogioni Wyvernspur—right after a light breakfast.

*   *   *   *   *

About an hour after Olive had gone down to eat at Maela's, back at Giogi's townhouse, the Wyvernspur noble knocked softly on the door to his own room.

"Come in," Cat called sleepily.

Giogi peeked in the doorway. "Just need to get some clothes," he said.

"Fine," Cat mumbled, pulling up the thick down comforter to her chest and rolling over.

Giogi crossed the room and removed an ensemble from his winter clothes chest. He was searching for matching stockings when there was a soft knock on the door. Giogi shot a quick glance from his search to see Thomas entering with his morning tea tray. The servant crossed to the bed and set the tray on the nightstand by his master's bed, as had been his custom every morning for years. Giogi returned to pawing through the chest.

"I say, Thomas," Giogi said, examining a worn patch in the heel of a stocking, "I'm going to need some more warm footgear. And this one will need darning." Giogi held the stocking out in Thomas's direction, his head still buried in his clothing chest. When several seconds passed without Thomas taking the piece, Giogi looked up. "I say, Thomas . . ." he began, but Thomas was not present.

From the bed, Cat giggled. "He took one look at me and bolted," she explained as she sat up in bed and pushed her hair out of her eyes.

"Why would he do . . . Oh, I say! He couldn't have thought . . . Oh, dear. I'd better go have a word with him."

"Why?" Cat asked, now grinning from ear to ear.

"Well, to clear your honor, for starters," Giogi replied, amazed that she didn't understand.

Cat laughed. "What about your honor?" she asked.

"Well, um . . ." Giogi flushed. "I'll be back," he said, hurrying after his manservant.

Giogi had to track Thomas all the way down to the kitchen. The manservant was polishing tableware with the furious gusto of a man who expected a finicky demon to dine with them.

"I say, Thomas," Giogi began, "I think we need to have a chat."

"That won't be necessary, sir," Thomas responded quickly and primly. "If you shan't be requiring my services as a gentleman's gentleman, two weeks notice will be more than sufficient for me to find myself other employment. Master Cormaeril has already given me to understand he could use the services of someone like myself."

"Shaver Cormaeril's been trying to pinch my servants? By Selune! Some friend. I ought to skin him alive. Now, see here, Thomas, Mistress Cat spent the night in my bed," Giogi explained, then added hastily, "and I spent the night in her bed. That is, I spent the night in the lilac room, in case whoever attacked her returned."

"I see, sir," Thomas replied. His tone had become less formal, though not exactly apologetic. He did, however, put aside the polishing and look at his master.

"My relationship with Mistress Cat is completely professional," Giogi added.

"Yes, sir." Thomas said.

"Naturally, I am not blind to the fact that she is an incredibly beautiful woman, but my intentions where she is concerned are completely honorable." The young noble began to pace the kitchen as he spoke.

"Of course, sir," Thomas said, though he suspected that perhaps Cat's intentions might not be as pure as his master's.

"So let's have no more of this nonsense about giving notice or that scurrilous cove, Shaver Cormaeril."

"No, sir," Thomas agreed.

"You know, Thomas," Giogi confided, "I have noticed that Mistress Cat does seem a little taken with me."

"I do not imagine, however, that your Aunt Dorath would feel the same way about her, sir."

"Well, dash it, Thomas," Giogi replied hotly, "I can't spend the rest of my life trying to please Aunt Dorath, can I?" With that, he spun around and marched out of the kitchen.

Thomas gulped nervously. He suddenly realized that the situation was much more serious than before.

Late last night, after the unpleasantness in the lilac room, Thomas had consulted with his advisor about Giogi and his "professional" relationship with the mage Cat. Thomas had laid out his concerns, but his advisor had assured him there was nothing to worry about. The servant wondered what his advisor would say if he'd just heard Giogi's declaration.

A staccato knock at the front door forced Thomas to focus on his more conventional duties. Slipping off his apron, he hurried out to the front hall, and, regathering his composure, opened the door.

A very small figure dressed in a fur-trimmed cape stood on the stoop. At first, Thomas assumed it was a young child, noble-born he would have guessed, based on the cape and the well-groomed russet hair flowing from beneath the hood.

The figure looked up at him with a very grim expression, and Thomas could see that it was no child, but an adult female halfling. "I must speak with Giogioni Wyvernspur," the halfling declared. She slipped past Thomas's legs and through the doorway.

"Master Giogioni has not yet dressed or had breakfast," Thomas argued, still holding the door open, hoping the little creature would take the hint and leave.

"I can wait," Olive said. "Thomas, isn't it?" she asked, pulling off her gloves.

"Yes," the servant admitted.

"Is the mage known as Cat still here?" the halfling interrogated the servant.

"Uh, yes," Thomas said, closing the front door in surprise. It was a little startling to be confronted with someone who seemed to know the household's goings-on.

"Time may be of the essence. Would you be so good as to tell your master that Olive Ruskettle requests an interview with him?" Olive said, swinging her cape from her shoulders and holding it and her gloves out in Thomas's general direction.

"Of course," Thomas said, accepting the halfling woman's items. Trying to regain some marginal control of the situation, he suggested, "Perhaps you would care to wait in the parlor."

"That will be fine," Olive replied.

Thomas ushered the halfling into the next room, where she sat on a low footstool. Her posture, so perfectly straight and still, reminded Thomas of Giogi's Aunt Dorath, and her tone and demeanor were so solemn that Thomas grew more than concerned; he became alarmed.

This Olive Ruskettle was nothing like any of the halflings

KATE NOVAK and JEFF GRUBB

Thomas had ever met before. What sort of awful business could she possibly have with my master? he wondered as he hurried from the parlor.

Without rising, Olive surveyed the plush room around her. The boy has money, all right, she decided. And taste, too, she added upon catching sight of a marble statue of Selune. I do believe that's an original Cledwyll. Overly endowed and scantily clad. Yes, definitely a Cledwyll. How extraordinary.

Olive looked down at her dress. The pin was still firmly in place, as was her determination. She had to throw herself into this role, she thought. How does one play a Harper? Should she act certain and serious, like all the archetypal, snooty paladins she'd known as a child, or did she dare model herself after the Saurial paladin Dragonbait, who'd befriended Alias, and add a touch of concern and self-effacing humor?

What would Dragonbait do in this situation? she wondered. Probably track Flattery down and run him through with a sword, she answered sternly.

All right, but what would he do if he were me? He wouldn't say much, she thought, allowing herself a slight grin. Dragonbait was mute, which was part of his charm and mystique, Olive realized. He didn't babble. Try not to babble, Olive-girl, she ordered herself. Get to the point.

Then again, it might not be a good idea to fire on Giogi suddenly. Might spook him. Try a little polite conversation first. Hello. So sorry to hear about good old Drone. How's the rest of your family? Then let Giogi know his houseguest is married to a murdering dog who happens to be a relative.

Giogioni did not keep Olive waiting long, and the genuine smile he wore as he entered the parlor did a lot to bolster Olive's confidence.

"Mistress Ruskettle, what an honor! I'd heard you were in Immersea," the young man said.

"I'm so pleased you remember me, Master Giogioni. Our last meeting, at your cousin's wedding, was so brief," Olive replied, holding out her hand.

Giogioni took the tiny fingers in his own and bowed low over the halfling's hand. He released her and stepped back. "It would be impossible to forget a songstress with your talent, and, of course, the day was, um, memorable for other reasons."

"Yes," Olive said, nodding. "There was that unfortunate at-

🦅 176 🦅

tack on your life."

"Well, Sage Dimswart did explain that your friend, Alias, was under a curse. I don't blame her."

"That's very civil of you, Master Giogioni. I'm pleased to say that we did manage to find a cure for Alias."

"Oh, that's marvelous," Giogi said, seating himself across from the bard. "Tell me, is she in Immersea as well?" he asked, testing his theory that Alias had stolen the spur.

Olive shook her head. "No. She's wintering in Shadowdale."

"Oh." Giogi's brow furrowed for a moment, but he recovered from his disappointment quickly.

Olive went on to a new topic. "I heard that your grandfather's cousin, Drone Wyvernspur, has passed on. May I extend my condolences," she said. "I understand you were very close to him."

"Thank you," Giogi replied. He looked away from Olive and stared into the flames in the fireplace. Olive could see moisture sparkling in his eyes. After a few moments, the nobleman turned to face his guest once again. "It came as quite a shock. He was more than a cousin to me. He and my Aunt Dorath raised me after both my parents died. I always called him Uncle Drone. He was a little absentminded but always very kind."

"Your family is in the midst of another tragedy as well, I understand," Olive commented.

"An heirloom is missing, which, according to legend, is supposed to ensure that our line never dies out. The family's a bit on edge, what with its disappearance and Drone's death. You know, Mistress Ruskettle, it's really most extraordinary that you should have come to visit me this morning. You see, I was planning to come speak with you about the spur."

Olive managed to hide her surprise. There would be time enough to find out what Giogi thought she knew.

"Perhaps my coming isn't as extraordinary as you might think," the halfling said with a knowing smile. She raised her right hand to the Harper's pin and fiddled with it, seemingly absentmindedly. Then she let her hand rest back in her lap. "Perhaps you are already aware, Master Giogioni, that the wyvern's spur has attracted the attention of a certain powerful and dangerous wizard."

Giogi gulped. "You mean Flattery?" he squeaked.

KATE NOVAK and JEFF GRUBB

"Precisely," Olive replied, leaning forward in her chair. Without realizing it, Giogi leaned forward in response.

"Perhaps it's time I got to the point, Master Giogioni. This Flattery murdered my partner, and my organization cannot let his crime go unpunished."

"Your organization—excuse me, but I couldn't help noticing; that is a Harper's pin you're wearing, isn't it?"

"Yes, Master Giogioni, it is."

"I hadn't realized . . . You weren't wearing one at Freffie's wedding last spring."

Olive sighed and smiled. "Those were less fateful days."

The door to the parlor opened, and Cat breezed in. She wore a cream-colored morning dress replete with pink ribbon-roses and white beadwork ferns. She wore her copper-colored hair in an elaborate five-strand Sembian braid that hung halfway down her back.

She slipped behind Giogi and took up the braided lock of his hair. It was obvious from her behavior that she did not notice the halfling visitor on the footstool across from Giogi's chair. She held out three small green beads. "I found these in my bed," she said with a smile, then began sliding them into the nobleman's hair.

Giogi colored visibly. He rose and turned Cat to face Olive. "We have company, my dear. Mistress Ruskettle, may I present to you—"

"Cat the mage, apprentice to the wizard Flattery," Olive finished for him, her tone chill.

Cat was taken aback at discovering that her flirtation not only had an audience, but one who knew too much about her. Nervously she slipped one of her hands into Giogi's.

"Um, well, she's decided to leave Flattery," Giogi reported. "She's here under my protection."

"A wise decision, Mistress Cat," the halfling said, nodding sagely. "And not a moment too soon," she added.

Even as she spoke, Olive realized she would have to handle Cat without any help from Giogi. From what the mage had just said to the nobleman, it was obvious that he had offered Cat more than his protection. He's not likely to welcome any suggestions that the woman might betray him, Olive thought. Human men are funny that way. It's a pity I can't let him know that I'm sure of her disloyalty because I eavesdropped on her in his carriage house.

"Cat," Giogi said, finishing the introductions smoothly, "this is the bard, Olive Ruskettle. We were just discussing Flattery when you came in."

Cat made a curtsy to Olive, not oblivious to the fact that Giogi had chosen to present her to Olive and not the other way around.

"It seems," Giogi gulped, "that Flattery killed Mistress Ruskettle's partner," Giogi explained to the mage.

Cat did not look surprised in the least. She merely blinked once and asked, "Why?"

Olive was struck by an inspiration. She smiled knowingly. "An interesting question, Mistress Cat," she said. "One that I suddenly realize you might be able to answer better than I."

"Me?" Cat paled, no longer so collected.

"You," Olive replied. "My story is a little complicated," the halfling said. "Please, won't you both sit down?"

Giogi sat on the sofa and drew Cat down beside him, still holding her hand in his own. She looked as though she needed his strength.

Maybe this will bring you to your senses, Cat, Olive thought. Perhaps we can make you more afraid of going back to Flattery than of leaving him.

"You have no doubt noticed, Master Giogioni," the halfling began, "that Mistress Cat bears a strong resemblance to Alias of Westgate."

"Well, actually, yes, I have," Giogi said, "but Cat said—"

"She's never met anyone named Alias," Olive supplied. "That she is from Ordulin. Mistress Cat comes from a branch of Alias's family separated by . . . hard times. Yet her relatives all show a striking family resemblance to one another, much like in the Wyvernspur family. In addition, all of the women in Alias's clan inherit an unusual marking on their right arm. It appears overnight without explanation, and cannot be dispelled magically."

Cat touched her right sleeve with her left hand. Giogi looked at her questioningly, and the mage nodded her head.

Olive continued her story. "My partner, Jade, was also a member of this family. She, too, resembled Alias of Westgate, as well as you, Mistress Cat. At any rate, two nights ago, we sighted Flattery in the streets of Immersea. We followed him, as we were aware that he had unscrupulous reasons for visiting your town.

"Jade has been specially trained in picking pockets—in the line of duty, you understand," the halfling explained. "We thought it likely that Flattery had stolen the wyvern's spur, so Jade closed in on him to investigate the contents of his pockets. Jade liberated an unusual item from the wizard right off: a crystal as big as my fist and as dark as a new moon. I know, because she held it up for me to see before she continued stalking Flattery."

Olive took a deep breath. "Jade was just reaching for Flattery's pocket again when he turned around. He seemed to mistake Jade for someone he knew. He cried out, and I quote, 'So, you treacherous witch, you've escaped, and now you try to steal what you have not earned.' Then he . . . he killed my partner—disintegrated her with a vile magic spell."

Olive paused. She did not need to feign grief and rage; they came naturally. Giogi was rapt with the bard's tale. His mouth hung slightly open, and his eyes were wide. The cool and rational Cat clutched Giogi's hand tightly, and her gaze seemed to bore holes into Olive.

It was some moments before the halfling could bring herself to finish, and when she did, her voice was no longer as steady as it had been. "I think Flattery mistook my partner for you, Mistress Cat," she explained. "The question I have for you is: Is it possible your former master would kill you if he thought you were trying to steal something from him?"

Cat turned even paler. She nodded wordlessly.

Olive nodded at her admission. "After seeing Jade murdered, I'm afraid I lost my head," Olive said. "I screamed, and Flattery spotted me, got a good look at me. I managed to escape his pursuit with some magic of my own, but I was witness to his crime, and he has no love for Harpers."

Olive gave a shuddering sigh. "If I were farther north, I would have greater resources to draw upon to bring him to justice—companions with discretion. As it stands now, I am alone and far from home. I could use your help."

"I'm honored that you would come to me, Mistress Ruskettle," Giogi said, feeling a little astounded. "I will do all I can to help. But why did you come to me? Surely, in all of Immersea, you could find more powerful allies than myself."

"But not as discrete, I fear, and I thought you would wish to keep this in the family. Of course, I might have gone to your Cousin Frefford, but he has a young wife and new baby, and this may be a hazardous mission. As for your Cousin Steele, he is, I'm afraid, unsuitable."

"I'm sorry. I don't quite follow you," Giogi said, "about keeping it in the family."

"As Flattery is one of your own, I thought you might wish to bring him to justice, to help avoid a scandal, as it were."

"Flattery is . . . You don't mean to say that he's a Wyvernspur?" Giogi gasped.

"Yes. You didn't know? I thought Mistress Cat would have explained that," Olive said, though of course, she'd thought no such thing and would have been surprised to learn that Cat had told Giogi anything useful about her master.

Giogi turned to the mage beside him and waited silently for a denial, an explanation, an excuse. Anything.

Cat looked down at her hands. "I didn't know for certain. I just began to suspect it yesterday. He looks just like your cousins, Steele and Frefford. I was afraid that if you realized he was a relative, you might not take my side against him and let me remain in your protection."

Not very good at making up lies, are you? Olive thought.

Giogi looked wounded. "How could you even think such a thing?" he asked.

"You're always talking about how important your family is to you," Cat whispered. " 'Wyvernspurs look out for one another,' you said."

"But, you're family, too," Giogi protested.

"Suppose I weren't," Cat said.

"But you are," the nobleman insisted. "The guardian let you past, so you must be."

And I'm willing to bet, Olive thought, that that's not just because of your marriage to Flattery.

"But suppose I weren't in your family?" Cat insisted.

"It would make no difference," Giogi replied coldly, offended that Cat did not think more highly of his honor. "I'm not the sort of man who leaves young women in the hands of murdering wizards."

Cat looked down at her lap, unable to explain her anxiety. Giogi sat stiffly beside her, no longer holding her hand.

You've made a miscalculation, woman. Olive chided Cat mentally. You knew you couldn't tell Giogi that he's fallen in love with another man's wife. He might have accepted your not confiding in him, but, by suggesting he might turn you out, you've wounded his pride.

He's not suspicious of her, but at least she's on the defensive, Olive thought triumphantly.

"Anyway, you are a member of the family," Giogi insisted as if reminding himself he still had a duty toward her. "As a Wyvernspur himself, Flattery must have a record of the missing branches of our family tree. That's how he knew it would be safe to send you in after the spur."

Olive nodded, then caught herself. She wasn't supposed to know Cat had been in the crypt. "Do you mean to say Flattery had Mistress Cat steal the spur?" she asked, acting surprised.

Giogi flushed, realizing he'd just betrayed Cat. "Well, yes and no."

"My former master sent me after the spur, but it was gone when I got there," Cat explained hurriedly. "You see, their family crypt has a secret door, which opens—"

"Every fifty years," Olive concluded with a dismissive wave of her hand. "Yes, we know about that as well. What I don't understand is why Flattery sent you after the spur."

The question that had plagued Olive occurred to Giogi in a flash. "Yes! If Flattery is a Wyvernspur, why didn't he just go after the spur himself?" Giogi asked.

"If we knew the answer to that question, Master Giogioni," Olive announced, "we might just know how to defeat Flattery."

❧ 14 ❧

Breakfast Talk

Thomas knocked and entered the parlor. "Breakfast is ready, sir. Shall I set an extra place for Mistress Ruskettle?"

"Oh," Giogi said, turning from Thomas to Olive. "Would you do us the honor of joining us?" he asked.

"That would be most convenient," Olive replied. "We have much to discuss." Another breakfast couldn't hurt, she thought. It'll be different, at any rate, from eating all that hay and grain he's fed me.

"Yes, Thomas. Three for breakfast," Giogi replied. The nobleman stood and offered Cat his hand. After the mage rose to her feet, however, Giogi ushered her ahead and waited for Olive to rise. He could hardly offer the halfling his arm, as she didn't stand any higher than his hip, but he walked beside her to the dining room.

As Olive and Giogi followed Cat to breakfast, the halfling could sense Cat's displeasure. Again she reminded Olive of the sorceress Cassana. Cassana never could stand any competition, no matter how small.

Thomas set out a high chair for Olive at Giogi's right hand, leaving an ordinary chair for Cat on his master's left. The servant was heartened to see that the unusually serious halfling had an appetite comparable to all the other halflings he had ever known. Her conversation topics, however, were most disturbing.

Giogioni listened with unusual attentiveness to his new guest. It seemed to Thomas that his master was disturbed as well, though not completely by the halfling's talk. The servant couldn't help but notice that Giogi's attitude toward the mage had turned considerably cooler.

Thomas wished he'd had the opportunity to put an ear to the parlor door so he could know what had happened between them.

"We will need the help of others of talent and power," Olive explained as she reached for two breakfast rolls and smeared a tablespoon of butter on each. "I will leave it to you to choose persons you feel you can trust with the knowledge of Flattery." Olive bit off half a roll.

Giogi thought for a moment. "I was going to visit Mother Lleddew today. I don't know how I will be received exactly, but I'm sure I can trust her with a family secret. She once was a companion of my father."

"Mother Lleddew," Olive muttered through a full mouth. She chewed rapidly and swallowed. "Mother Lleddew," she repeated. "Priestess of Selune, isn't she? Has quite a reputation. If you're willing to trust her, I'm sure she'll be most useful."

"There is something else you might consider, Master Giogioni," Olive said, dabbing a stream of butter from her chin. "It may be unseemly to bring it up so soon after your uncle's demise, but did he possess any magical items we could use?"

"I don't know," Giogi admitted. "I was going to search through his lab for his journal this morning. I wouldn't really know what to look for, though, when it comes to magical items."

"Mistress Cat would be able to aid you in that respect, surely," Olive said as she plopped five sugar cubes into her tea.

"I had hoped to keep her hidden from Flattery's sight," Giogi explained without looking in Cat's direction.

The enchantress, who had remained silent until now, reminded her protector, "It may be too late for that." Then she looked into her lap to avoid Giogi's eyes.

Olive looked up in surprise. Are we to get a confession now? she wondered, thinking that Cat was about to admit to having contacted Flattery the day before.

"Oh, yes. I'd forgotten," Giogi said, his forehead furrowed.

"Forgotten what?" Olive asked.

"Late last night, someone broke in and attacked Mistress Cat. Fortunately, she managed to raise an alarm, and her attacker fled."

"I thought it was my master, Flattery," Cat explained, still not looking up. "It looked like him in the moonlight, but I don't think Flattery would have tried to smother me in my bed."

"No. I can't see the wizard who disintegrated Jade relying on down pillows," Olive agreed.

There was a clatter of silverware on oak at the far end of the table. All three diners looked up suddenly at the noise. Giogi's manservant was looking at the halfling, temporarily oblivious to the disturbance he'd just created by dropping a pile of flatware on the table.

"Thomas, is something wrong?" Giogi asked.

"Excuse me, Mistress Ruskettle," the servant said, looking pale and stricken, "but did I hear you just say someone had been . . . disintegrated . . . by this Flattery person?"

Olive held her ham-laden fork suspended in midair. "Yes, Thomas," she answered. "My partner, Jade More. Two nights ago. Why?"

"Forgive my interruption, sir," Thomas addressed Giogi, "but, um, I understand from the servants up in Redstone that nothing was found of your Uncle Drone, save a pile of ash, his robes, and hat."

Giogi tapped his forehead with the flat of his palm. "Sweet Selune. You're right. It looks as if this Flattery could be responsible for the death of my Uncle Drone as well. Good thought, Thomas." Thomas did not hear the compliment however. He'd bolted for the kitchen.

"Why should Flattery kill your Uncle Drone?" Cat asked.

"I would think it's obvious," Olive answered her. "Flattery sends you in after the spur. You don't come back right away. He must presume you're in trouble. Remember, later that evening, when he mistook my partner for you, he said, 'you've escaped, and now you try to steal what you have not earned.' He may have assumed you'd been captured by Drone—"

"That's possible," Cat admitted, softly. "Flattery told me he would not be able to watch me with his scrying crystal because the catacombs and crypt were proofed against magical eyes."

"Uncle Drone had them shielded from magical sight from all but himself," Giogi added, "and even he had trouble looking into the crypt after the robbery."

Not that either of them would have been able to spot Cat, Olive thought to herself. Like Alias and Jade, Cat must be proofed against magical detection and scrying. It seems, though, that Flattery has never told her. He wouldn't want her to think she could hide from him.

"Mistress Ruskettle, you were saying," Giogi prompted Olive out of her reverie.

"Anyway," Olive continued aloud, "when Flattery sees Jade later that evening, he assumes you've escaped, and, thinking you have just picked his pocket, he believes you have betrayed him and he slays Jade, mistaking her for you. Like the witness to Jade's murder, namely myself, who he did try to kill, Drone is a loose end. Drone may have interrogated you and learned all about him. Also, Flattery would not have given up his quest for the spur. Drone might have taken the spur from you and have it in his lab, where it would be easy to get. If the spur was still safe in the crypt, Flattery could have stolen Drone's key before killing him."

"But I never had the spur, never even saw it. It wasn't in the crypt when I got there," Cat protested, some of her old spirit returning to her voice. "Someone else had stolen it."

"Ah," Olive said, "but Flattery couldn't see into the crypt, so he couldn't know that, unless he looked for himself. Later in the day, after he'd already destroyed Drone, Flattery would have discovered that someone had been successful at stealing the spur."

"Yes," Giogi said guiltily. "It does seem to have gotten out."

Cat, Olive noticed, stirred uncomfortably in her seat. As well she should, since she was the culprit, the halfling thought.

"And somehow," Olive said, pointing a spoonful of eggs at Cat, "Flattery's found out you're still alive and at large."

"I told you he has a scrying ball," Cat said.

"If he thought you were dead, he wouldn't have been scrying for you," Olive pointed out. She hoped Cat would realize that if she hadn't been stupid enough to contact Flattery yesterday, he'd probably be pretty much in the dark. Too bad the mage hadn't known that Flattery can't scry for her at all. At least we can use that to our advantage, Olive thought.

"In any event, Flattery discovers you're still alive," Olive continued, explaining to Cat, "and learns that you've taken refuge here. It may look to him as if you've got the spur, and you're negotiating to return it to Master Giogioni. So he sends a flunkie after you. I presume he has flunkies?" Olive asked.

Cat nodded. She looked very confused, though, and Olive could tell she'd planted the seed of doubt in the woman's head.

"Master Giogioni, I believe it is probably safer for Mistress Cat to remain with us wherever we go," Olive concluded. "We will no doubt profit from her expertise as well."

"You asked yesterday if you could come with me," Giogi said to Cat. "I guess you'll get your chance. Thomas!" the young noble called out, ringing a small silver bell beside his plate.

Thomas, looking pale, appeared at the doorway to Servant Land. "Yes, sir?" he asked.

"After breakfast, the ladies and I will be riding up to Redstone and then to the Temple of Selune. Would you please harness Daisyeye to the buggy?"

"Yes, sir," Thomas said, fading back through the doorway.

Olive downed her breakfast with relish, except the oatmeal. She didn't quite have the stomach for that. The two humans poked their food around their plates in silence, though. Olive could understand Cat not being very hungry. She'd just lost her place in the sun. Giogi's loss of appetite worried Olive more. She needed him to be alert and enthusiastic.

Olive was just finishing her third pot of tea when Thomas, looking distraught as well as pale, returned to the dining room. "It appears we've had some vandalism in the carriage house, sir," he informed Giogi in a tight, level voice.

"The deuce you say," Giogi replied, rising with alarm. "Not the animals?"

"Daisyeye appears to be unaffected. The buggy is damaged, though, sir, and it appears someone started a fire but extinguished it before it did much damage."

"What about Birdie?"

"Birdie, sir?"

"The burro. I named it Birdie. Did it have another name already?"

"Uh . . ." Thomas looked like a man whose ordered life had been disrupted by a visit to another plane. "What burro, sir?" he asked with confusion.

"The one I took into the catacombs yesterday."

"Oh, yes. You mentioned a burro, I recall. Did you rent the burro from a local stable, sir?"

"Did I—? I thought you bought the burro for me, Thomas," Giogi replied.

"I, sir? No, sir. Why would I buy a burro for you, sir?"

"Look here, Thomas. If you didn't buy the burro, what was it doing in my garden the night before last eating my roses?" Giogi demanded.

"It's only Ches, sir. Barely spring. There aren't any roses in bloom yet," Thomas pointed out.

"Eating my roses was only a figure of speech, Thomas," Giogi said sternly. Then he sighed. "Please, send down to Dzulas's Stables for a carriage and four while I go search for the burro. Perhaps you ladies would care to wait in the parlor while we get this straightened out," Giogi suggested.

"Poor little Birdie," the nobleman murmured as he followed Thomas from the room. "She must be scared out of her mind."

Cat rose from her chair. "If you would excuse me, Mistress Ruskettle," she said, "I should take advantage of this delay to study my spells further. If we are going to a wizard's tower—"

"Sit back down, if you please, Mistress Cat," Olive interrupted. "I need to speak with you."

Cat hesitated for a moment, but she seemed to think better of offending this strange halfling that Giogioni held in such high regard. She returned to her chair.

"As I understand scrying crystals, the distance between the observer and subject is no obstacle, correct?"

"Essentially," Cat said with a nod.

"But the knowledge the viewer has of the subject makes a big difference, doesn't it?"

"Yes."

"Persons not known are actually very difficult to locate, and the time they can be spied upon is much reduced, right?"

Cat nodded curtly. "You seem well versed on the topic, Mistress Ruskettle. I do not think you need my advice on the matter."

"No, I don't. I needed to be sure you were well versed on the topic. Based on what we have just established, who is in the most danger of being scried by your master?" Olive asked.

Cat took a deep breath. "Myself," she said at last.

"Exactly. So you are the one we need to protect the most. If he can't spy on you, he is unlikely to discover the doings of Master Giogioni and myself. I have something for you."

Olive reached into the pocket of her skirt and drew out Jade's magic pouch. She undid the laces and felt around inside for the "amulet." Stern-faced, Olive drew it out. She laid the object, still tied up in the purple silk scarf, on the table between herself and the mage, as if presenting an ancient artifact.

"What is it?" Cat asked, reaching over for it.

"An amulet to protect against detection and scrying. A very powerful one."

Cat began unknotting the scarf.

"No! Don't unwrap it!" Olive warned. "The magic is so strong, it must remain covered. The last person that tried to look at it went blind and mad. Just keep it with you at all times."

"That's very generous of you, Mistress Ruskettle," Cat said with surprise, slipping the amulet into her skirt pocket.

"Well, yes. It's just a loan until we complete this mission. Try not to lose it. Elminster would never forgive me."

"Who is Elminster?" Cat asked.

Olive's eyebrows shot up. "Elminster. The Elminster. Elminster, the sage. I hadn't realized people from Ordulin were so isolated. Elminster is . . . Ask anyone. I have another question for you. You were going after the spur for Flattery. What was Flattery going to give you in return for the spur?"

"Nothing," Cat replied, a little too quickly, Olive thought.

"He said to Jade before he killed her, 'Now you try to steal what you have not earned.' Was he paying you for the job?"

"No. He was my master. I did as he bade me without expectation of any reward. That is the normal way with apprentices and masters."

"You're a little old to be an apprentice. Why else does one mage work for another? Has he promised to teach you some special spells or offered you a particular magic item?"

"What does it matter now that I've left him?" Cat asked archly.

"Well, when we defeat him, his estate is up for grabs, so to speak. If there was something particular you were interested in, it would be yours as far as I'm concerned. Providing, of course, that Flattery still has the item."

"What do you mean?" Cat asked with confusion.

"Well, there was that crystal I mentioned, the one as big as my fist and as dark as a new moon, the one Jade lifted from Flattery's pocket. I'm afraid that's something you'll have to forget," the halfling said. "Jade was holding it when Flattery disintegrated her. Whatever it was, gem or magic, it's destroyed. Of course, that also means he can't use it against us."

"Well, that's very interesting, Mistress Ruskettle," Cat said, trying to appear aloof, "but my master—Flattery, I mean—had many unusual items. One more or less could hardly matter to his power." The woman fidgeted.

"Except the spur," Olive countered, "or he wouldn't be so anxious to get it. I wasn't talking about Flattery's power, though. I was discussing why you became his servant in the first place. I thought this crystal might have had something to do with it, since, when he mistook Jade for you and killed her, Flattery accused her of trying to steal what she had not earned."

"I don't know what Flattery meant. I'm sorry. I really must go study my spells," the mage said, rising from the table. "Please ask Thomas to call for me when the carriage arrives."

Olive sighed as Cat hurried from the room. Most people would have given you enough rope to hang yourself, girl, the halfling thought. I'm just trying to take a few lengths away as a favor to you—and so Giogi and I aren't caught in the noose with you.

Thomas re-entered the dining room with a tray to clear the table. "Excuse me, ma'am. I thought you were finished—"

"Oh, I am, Thomas. Don't mind me," Olive said, waving her hands over the table to indicate he was welcome to continue with his duties. "You've sent for the carriage, Thomas?" she asked.

"Yes, ma'am."

"How long will it take, do you think?"

"That all depends on how soon Mister Dzulas is willing to rent a carriage today," the servant explained as he began scraping food scraps into a bowl. "The roads are still very icy this morning, and Mister Dzulas is very attached to his animals and equipment. He'll wait until the sun has had a chance to warm the streets some more. Less than an hour, I'd say."

Olive nodded as Thomas stacked the saucers on top of the dishes. "Last night, Thomas, did Mistress Cat's attacker enter her room directly, do you know, or come in from another part of the house and have to search for her?"

"No one else saw this attacker but Mistress Cat," Thomas said, stressing the word "saw" in such a way that he cast doubt on the existence of the attacker.

"You think she invented it?" Olive asked with a delighted, conspiratorial smile meant to encourage the servant to speak.

Thomas was not so easily drawn out, though. "I would not suggest that, ma'am, only that the . . . lady may have been mistaken."

"She imagined it, then?" Olive asked.

"She may have had a nightmare," Thomas suggested, "or the cat may have disturbed her in her sleep, and she awoke not exactly sure what was in the room with her."

"Hmm. She does seem the nervous type," Olive commented. More to herself, she mused, "You have to be very careful trying to convince someone like that to do the right thing, you know."

Surprisingly this last remark drew more of a response from Thomas. "I was just thinking that same thought earlier this very morning, ma'am," the servant agreed. "The more you try to warn some people, the stubborner they become, and there are some people who will deliberately do something the moment someone forbids them to, even if they wouldn't have dreamed of doing it ordinarily."

"The old forbidden fruit," Olive said.

"Precisely, ma'am."

"I'll be in the parlor, Thomas," Olive said, climbing down from her high chair.

"Very good, ma'am."

Olive left the dining room through the doors to the main hall, closing them behind her. She crossed to the parlor, opened the door, and closed it again loudly, but remained in the hall.

She then hiked up her gown and shot up the stairs.

Six closed doors lined the upper hallway. Five keyholes later, the halfling discovered which was the enchantress's room. It was a large, comfortable bedroom decorated in hues of lavender.

One of the windows was open, and, as Olive watched through the keyhole, a large, familiar raven flew in through the window. Another quick arrival, noted the halfling. *Where is this man hiding when he isn't terrorizing people?*

Cat stood in the center of the room, her head bowed but her body obviously tensed, while her master transformed into a human.

"Well, Catling?" Flattery asked.

"Someone tried to kill me last night," the mage said with annoyance in her voice. She looked up at Flattery.

"Really? So?" the wizard asked without concern.

"I thought it was you," she said, glaring at her master.

Flattery sat on the bed and swung his wet boots onto the coverlet. "You wouldn't be breathing now if it had been me."

"Unless you meant it as a warning."

"Do you need warning, Catling?"

"I'm doing all I can," the woman insisted. "I want the memory crystal."

"You'll get it just as soon as I have the spur," Flattery said off-handedly, stifling a yawn.

"I want to see it," Cat insisted.

"I haven't brought it with me," Flattery retorted. His eyes narrowed into angry slits.

"You're sure you have it?" Cat demanded.

Flattery bounced from the bed and leaped at Cat, grabbing her by the throat with one hand in a fluid motion. His face was dark with anger. "I don't think I care for your tone, woman."

"Did you murder Drone Wyvernspur?" Cat gasped, trying to keep her face passive.

"Who told you that?" Flattery asked, his brow furrowed with curiosity.

"Giogi thinks you did," Cat answered in a tight whisper.

"And who gave him that idea?" Flattery demanded, shaking the mage by her neck.

"His servant, Thomas," Cat gasped.

The wizard released the woman. Cat slumped back, raising one of her delicate hands to her neck.

"A servant. And how could he know?" Flattery mused.

"You did murder Drone, then," Cat stated.

"Not exactly," Flattery said with a grin. "Something less handsome than I and much less lively did it. Unfortunately, that agent did not return to report its success or whether it found anything in the wizard's tower. Undead can be so unreliable."

"How many other people have you killed?" Cat asked, aghast.

Flattery's face clouded again. "Don't ask stupid questions, or I could become a widower."

"You haven't made yourself a husband yet," Cat shot back. "You've never even kissed me."

"Is that still bothering you, Catling? Come here." Flattery pulled the mage roughly toward him. His embrace might have snapped her back had it been any tighter. He forced his mouth down on her own.

Unable to risk a scream, Cat struggled silently to break away, but Flattery dug his nails into her back. The woman went limp. Flattery pushed her away and held her at arm's length by her shoulders.

"You want the stupidest things," he spat, obviously annoyed that she hadn't continued to put up a fight. "Get me the spur, and I'll deliver. Now, what progress has Giogioni made?"

"None," Cat answered weakly, looking away.

"None!" Flattery growled, cuffing Cat's ear. "I knew you were wasting your time."

"I still think Giogi will be the one to find it, even though he doesn't seem very interested in it. According to his Uncle Drone, the spur is his destiny."

"What?" Flattery looked surprised.

"That's what the message his uncle left him said. Giogi's father used to use the spur, and Giogi is the only one the guardian talks to. He's going to the Temple of Selune this afternoon to speak with a priestess who knew his father."

"LLeddew," Flattery muttered with annoyance.

"Yes. He tried to see her last night, but she wasn't—" Cat gasped as realization sunk in. "You sent those lacedons after him," she accused him. "Why?" she asked with exasperation. "He can't find the spur if he's dead."

"Lleddew can't help him find the spur," Flattery stated. "He doesn't need to see her. Convince him of that."

"Are you afraid of this Mother Lleddew?" Cat asked with uncharacteristic courage.

Flattery went livid again. His hands shot out, and he pushed Cat backward and onto the floor. "I'm not afraid of any woman. You would do well to remember that. If you value this noble's chances for finding the spur, you will keep him away from Lleddew and the Temple of Selune. I will see him dead before I see him with Lleddew."

"But he was going to have her do a divination for him as well," Cat protested meekly.

"His Cousin Steele already had one done by the church of Waukeen. The message was gibberish. The gods have no more idea who stole the spur or where it is now than my sources in the Abyss."

"How do you know what the church of Waukeen told Steele?" Cat asked, picking herself up from the floor.

"Waukeen's priests are more interested in large donations than in protecting their worshiper's confidentiality. I have ruled out Steele and his sister as suspects in any event. Drone is the most likely candidate for the original theft, since he had chief responsibility for the spur's security. If Drone wanted Giogioni to have it, he would have provided a way for him to find it. The little fool hasn't figured it out yet, that's all."

"Suppose one of the other members of the family stole it?"

"If Frefford had it, he would have used it by now."

"But Dorath would have kept it hidden if she took it."

"Dorath does not have a key to the crypt, and she is too old and feeble to have made it through the catacombs."

"What about other lines of the family?" Cat asked.

"There are no other lines," Flattery said. "Only Gerrin Wyvernspur's heirs and my father's."

"Who was your father? And are you sure you're an only child?"

Flattery laughed unpleasantly. "One of me was all his ego could handle and more than the Realms would accept."

"Giogi thinks I must be from a missing line, since I got past the guardian," Cat said quietly.

The wizard snorted. "The guardian let you pass because you are Wyvernspur by marriage, not by blood. Keep Giogioni fixed on Drone and where the old man might have hidden the thing," Flattery ordered, "not some mythical family member."

"We're going to visit Drone's lab and search for his journal as soon as the servant arranges a carriage," Cat said.

"Good. Remember, Drone was no fool. Be sure you check for ordinary and magical traps before you touch anything. Have Giogioni handle everything first."

"Use him the way you use me," Cat said sarcastically.

Flattery was oblivious to Cat's bitter tone. "Precisely. You are learning something after all. Has it occurred to you that, perhaps, Giogioni is using you as well?"

"He's not that sort of person."

"No? Perhaps he already has the spur and is still trying to figure out how to use it."

"He would have told me," Cat insisted.

"Not if he doesn't trust you."

"If he didn't trust me, why would he let me stay here?" Cat snarled.

Flattery shrugged and smirked. "For a treacherous witch, you can be very easy on the eye," he said with a grin. "Surely he's made you an offer."

Cat brought her hand up to slap Flattery's face, but he grabbed her wrist effortlessly and twisted her arm behind her back. "He has, hasn't he? I suppose this means I'll have to avenge my honor on the little fop," the wizard declared, half taunting, half serious. "After he finds the spur for me," he added with a grin.

Olive heard footfalls on the stairs. She drew back from the keyhole and pressed herself flat behind a linen chest. Peeking around the furniture's corner, Olive spied Thomas at the top of the stairs, carrying a tray laden with covered dishes. He turned down the hallway in the opposite direction. His pace was brisk and nervous. He let himself into a room at the far end of the hallway and closed the door behind him. Olive could hear him climbing more stairs.

The halfling was torn between following the servant and catching the end of Cat's conversation with Flattery. She was denied the opportunity to do either, though. There were more footfalls on the lower stair, this time accompanied by whistling. Giogi's rhythmless whistling.

Olive scrunched up tighter behind the linen chest. Giogi strode down the hall toward Cat's room. He was carrying a fur-lined cape, fur-lined boots, and a fur muff. He stopped in front of Cat's door and knocked sharply.

Cat called out, "Come in."

Giogi opened the door. "It's cold in here," he noted stiffly.

"I was looking out the window. Did you find Birdie?"

"No," Giogi replied curtly.

"Perhaps she'll come home by evening. You treated her well," Cat said gently.

Giogi shrugged without comment. He laid the furs on the bed. "It's colder today than it was yesterday, so I brought these for you to wear. I'll let you get back to your studying," he said, backing out of the room and closing the door behind him. His manner was as cold as the room.

So, the kind-hearted Wyvernspur can snub people, too, when his pride is wounded, Olive thought.

Giogi went down the hall to the room beside Cat's. He entered the room, leaving the door open behind him. Olive could see him rummaging through a chest at the foot of the bed.

It would be a bad thing to be discovered up here, Olive realized. Time to return to the parlor while I have the chance.

The halfling slipped past Giogi's open door and hurried down the stairs, though not without regret. I should have taken a peek to see who or what Thomas was feeding in the attic, she thought as she let herself into the parlor and closed the door very softly behind her. My nerves aren't what they once were.

She paced about the room. In my younger days, I'd have cased every room in this house and stolen three resalable things before breakfast, she chided herself. Being prosperous takes all the fun out of life. Now all I do is eavesdrop and worry that I'm going to be discovered. That's the problem with respectability—you always worry about losing it. Paladins must be nervous wrecks, she thought with an amused snort.

A bowl of dried fruit and nuts drew her attention. Food. That will help steady me. Olive lifted the bowl from the coffee table and carried it over to the fireside with the footstool. She cracked some nuts and picked out the meats, stacking the shells and meats in piles to represent good and bad as she weighed Cat's recent actions.

She contacted Flattery again, which was bad, the halfling thought, dropping a shell to her left. Probably stupid, too, Olive added, starting a pile with dried apricots for stupid actions.

Dropping a nut meat into a pile at her right, Olive thought, She did show more spine and grill him for more information, which was good. She gave away our day's itinerary, which was bad. She didn't say a word about Jade or me. That was good, unless she's playing both sides against the middle. Olive dropped another apricot in the stupid pile.

She could be thinking of me as our ace in the hole. Maybe she's superstitious about halfling luck. Olive started a pile for Cat's smart decisions with dried figs.

She didn't tell Flattery we were planning to come after him. Good and smart. Is she hoping we'll kill him for her? Is she planning on lending a hand when the time comes? In the short run, is she going to do as Flattery bids and use Giogi to test for traps in Drone's lab, and will she try to convince us not to visit the Temple of Selune?

Olive looked down at the piles of food. "She's one mixed-up mage," the halfling muttered. She tossed the nut shells into the fire and watched them burn while she munched on her remaining piles.

There was a knock on the door, and Thomas came in, carrying her cloak and gloves. "The carriage has arrived, ma'am," he announced.

Olive laid the fruit-and-nut bowl aside and accepted Thomas's help with her cloak, then joined Giogi and Cat in the front hall. The door stood open. Every bush and tree branch glittered in the sunlight and dropped globs of water and shards of glassy ice to the ground beneath it. A white carriage with four white horses stood waiting outside the front gate.

Giogi escorted the two women out and handed them into the carriage. As he checked the horses' tack and harnesses, Olive settled beside Cat and whispered, "Have you got it on you?"

Wordlessly Cat drew the silk-wrapped amulet halfway out of her pocket and slipped it back out of sight.

"Smart girl. Have a fig," the halfling offered.

"All set?" Giogi asked as he hopped up in the driver's seat.

We may never be that, Olive thought, but she called out that they were.

Giogi clucked at the horses, and the carriage moved forward. None of the party noticed the sleeve of a robe clear the frost from the attic window or a pair of piercing blue eyes watching them move out of the courtyard and onto the street.

❧ 15 ❧

Drone's Lab

Giogi drove the carriage through the heart of town and then south into the countryside. Since the nobleman sat outside the carriage, making normal conversation with him impossible, and Cat sat looking out the window, lost in her own thoughts, Olive napped for the length of the half-hour trip. Cat nudged her awake as they drove through the front gate of Castle Redstone.

The Wyvernspurs' ancestral home was an imposing edifice, but Olive always thought castles ostentatious, and red sandstone buildings made her think of rust. She could see why Giogi chose to live in a townhouse in Immersea. Even Cat shuddered when she saw the castle.

A servant ushered them into the parlor, where Gaylyn lay knitting, alone on the couch. "Giogi, you've brought company. How wonderful," the young woman said, peering intently at Olive and Cat. "Don't I know you? Olive Ruskettle the bard, isn't it? What a delightful surprise. Everyone was so pleased with your performance at the wedding reception. We were disappointed that you had to leave early. Aren't you Alias?" she asked Cat.

"She's, um, a relative of Alias's," Giogi explained. "Gaylyn, allow me to present Cat of Ordulin, a mage. Mistress Cat, this is my Cousin Frefford's wife, Gaylyn."

Cat curtsied and whispered a hello.

"You'll excuse me for not rising, I hope."

"Of course," Olive replied. "We've all heard your good news. How is your little girl, Lady Gaylyn?"

"If I ever see her again, I'll let you know," Gaylyn said, laughing. "Amberlee's Great-grandauntie Dorath stole her away the moment she was born and has spent all her time since then doting on the child. Actually, you've just missed her. Aunt Dorath brought her down here for breakfast, and when Amberlee was finished, her Aunt Dorath took her away to sleep in the nursery so I could entertain without waking her," Gaylyn explained.

"Please, sit down," the new mother encouraged them. "You must be freezing from your ride. There's a pot of tea over there," Gaylyn said, pointing to a silver tea set desperately in need of polishing. "Giogi, since we ladies outnumber you, you may do the honors."

Giogi filled and handed out teacups. Gaylyn passed a plate of cookies around. "It's lucky you're here, actually. Freffie has been so busy looking for someone who might be a lost member of the family. He spent all night questioning people at the inns—merchants, mercenaries, adventurers, farmers, fishermen, and now he has to deliver some packages for the memorial service tonight for Uncle Drone. He's up in the tower."

She fixed Giogi with the bright green eyes that had ensnared his cousin. "You wouldn't mind running the packages up to the Temple of Selune for him, would you, so I could get a little more of his attention?"

"Of course," Giogi agreed. "I was going there later, anyway. But I thought Julia was handling the arrangements for the memorial service."

"She was, but she twisted her ankle while walking in the ice last night, so she's out of commission. Aunt Dorath was beside herself, claiming how the curse had found another victim."

"That must have put her in a foul mood. Julia, I mean."

Gaylyn laughed. "Silly boy. It's been the luckiest break she's had all year. There's nothing like an ankle injury. No one can say you're malingering, because its so gruesome-looking, but you can cover it up with your petticoat and still look marvelous for all the suitors who come to wait on you hand and foot."

"Julia has suitors?" Giogi asked with mild surprise.

"Well, only one, but that's all she wants. She's in heaven right now. Sudacar couldn't have found a better excuse to fuss over her unless she'd been kidnapped by a dragon."

"Samtavan Sudacar is Julia's suitor?" Giogi asked, astonished.

"Who else? Sudacar is so commanding. Of course, Steele isn't keen on it, because Sudacar doesn't come from forty generations of nobility and isn't rich. Just between you and me—I shouldn't be saying this to outsiders," she whispered to Olive and Cat, "but Steele is acting like an old poop. He just wants to keep Julia under his thumb, because he'll never get a nice girl to do things for him if he doesn't sweeten himself up."

She has Steele's number, all right, Olive thought.

Giogi tried to imagine Sudacar fussing over Julia, and Julia being pleased about it. No one has that much imagination, he thought and shook his head. "Gaylyn, I'm afraid we've really come on business," he said.

"I know," Gaylyn said with a sigh. "I was just pretending otherwise. I know it's awful about the spur and Uncle Drone, but it's hard for me to be gloomy, what with Amberlee and all. Uncle Drone wouldn't mind. You know, right after Uncle Drone died, I dreamt of his spirit while I was sleeping with little Amberlee lying beside me. In my dream, Uncle Drone appeared by my bed and bent over the baby. He tickled her under her chin and made funny faces at her. Then he disappeared. I know it was his spirit, because he was dead by then, but not even being dead stopped him from playing with his new niece."

Olive smiled at the young woman's fanciful notion.

"That sounds like Uncle Drone's spirit," Giogi agreed. "Gaylyn, we need to look over things in Uncle Drone's lab. I was hoping he might have written something in his journal about the theft of the spur. We'll be looking through his magic, too, in case there's something there we can use."

"Oh, dear. It's a good idea, but Aunt Dorath has forbidden it. Steele wanted to do it yesterday. She told him it was too dangerous and sent him off on other duties. She's probably right, you know."

"Yes. That's why I brought Mistress Cat and Mistress Olive along as advisors."

"Well, in that case." Gaylyn stopped for a moment, tilting her head like a child considering some mischief. "You might want to sneak up the back stairs, so you don't disturb Aunt Dorath in the nursery. I kept a catalog for Drone. It's a lovely pink book with pressed flowers on the cover, and it's on his desk."

"You cataloged his magic?" Cat asked. "Have you studied magic?"

"Oh, no," Gaylyn said, laughing again. "My father was a sage, though. I used to catalog all his things for him. When I helped Uncle Drone, he was always around to keep me from anything chancy. You will be careful, won't you, Mistress Cat?"

Cat nodded.

"You know, you really are much prettier than your relative,"

Gaylyn complimented the mage. "I like the way you've done your hair."

Cat flushed and bowed her head.

"We should get started," Giogi muttered, obviously annoyed with Gaylyn's admiration of the mage.

Apparently, Olive realized, it's going to be a long time before he forgives Cat for suggesting he would abandon her.

They took their leave of Gaylyn and left the parlor. Giogi led them through a maze of hallways and stairways. They headed in every conceivable direction, including up and down.

"Are you sure we aren't lost?" Olive asked.

"Oh, no," Giogi said. "After my mother died, I lived here at Redstone. There are simpler routes, but I thought, as long as we're avoiding disturbing Aunt Dorath, we may as well try avoiding disturbing Steele, too."

"Why did you move back to town?" Olive asked.

"Well, town is so much more interesting than the country. The inns and the adventurers passing through and—"

"And not needing to avoid disturbing Aunt Dorath," Cat suggested with a smile.

"Aunt Dorath isn't that bad," Giogi snapped at the mage.

Olive groaned inwardly. Loyalty to your family is fine, Giogi, my boy, she thought, but you don't want to get tetchy with our mage just before you start going through your uncle's magic.

Anxious to stem any flood of bad feeling, and remembering something Giogi had said to his burro, Birdie, about his family interfering in his life, Olive volunteered an observation of her own. "Everyone needs to make his own life for himself, though," she said aloud. "Cyrrollalee knows, I loved my mother, but she never understood why I chose music over merchandising, so I hit the road. The people who love us the most have more trouble accepting that we're different from them than strangers do."

"That's true," Giogi agreed as he opened a rusty door. Olive noticed that, despite the rust, the hinges were well oiled. A cool, dry darkness lay beyond the door.

Giogi drew the finder's stone from his boot and held it out in front of him. It illuminated a long, low tunnel. Giogi and Cat were both forced to stoop to get through, though Olive could walk upright. The tunnel ran into a round room no more than ten feet in diameter but several stories high, more like a chimney than a room. Centered in the room was a steep, tightly spiraled iron staircase rising into the blackness above.

Loviatar's Lackeys, Olive groaned inwardly. What possesses humans to construct such torture devices? "You two go on ahead. I'll catch up," she said.

"We can't leave you behind," Giogi objected. "It's too dark."

"Not for me," Olive said, massaging a calf muscle. "I can see just fine in the dark."

"You can? How extraordinary," Giogi commented. "But are you sure you'll be all right?"

"I'll be fine."

"Very well. It's just at the top of the stairs."

With his long legs, Giogi clambered up the stairs two at a time. His boots sounded against the steps like a gong. Cat followed, taking one step at a time, but her feet moved quickly enough to keep up with the nobleman. Her boots tapped a noise like a cobbler's hammer.

Olive waited until they were too far ahead to look back and witness the undignified methods a halfling had to resort to, to climb human stairs. With a sigh, she hiked her skirt up over her arm and began scaling the tower stairs, using both her hands and feet.

Olive climbed for a few minutes, then looked up. The light from Giogi's finder's stone had vanished. Presumably he and Cat had reached the top and turned some corner. But the stairs still reverberated under her hands with someone's tread. Olive looked down.

A lamp glowed far below her. Who could that be? Olive wondered. Her dark vision had never been as reliable as that of other halflings, so she was unable to make out any details of a face or even clothing from a distance. She could rule out Gaylyn and Julia. It was unlikely to be Aunt Dorath. It has to be a servant, Steele, or Frefford, Olive concluded, unless the Wyvernspurs keep some monstrous guardian here, too. She began climbing more quickly.

At the top of the stairs was another rusty door, which Giogi had left standing open. Olive stepped through it and into Drone's lab. She closed the door quietly behind her. There was a key in the lock, so she turned it. Whoever's down there can knock if he wants to join us, she thought.

Olive had seen the labs of more than a few powerful wizards

in her travels. They all shared one thing in common: clutter of mythic proportions. Telescopes and astrolabes stood in front of every window, even though the view at every window was blocked on the inside by potted herbs and on the outside by kudzu vine. On a large bench, a maze of alchemic equipment distilled the life out of a blackened muck. There was no bowl catching the final product—a green ichor that had burrowed a hole an inch deep into the bench's granite surface. Notebooks full of internal anatomical charts of squirrels and rabbits and mice and rats and birds and fish covered pans containing the models from which the studies were drawn—all with their heads chewed away. Baskets of rock were stacked beside a kiln. Jars full of dead frogs and snakes and live caterpillars and ants and crickets and vials of potions filled an entire bookcase. There was no telling what was in the locked cabinets. Saucers of water and bones and dried cheese and curdled milk lay beside a desk.

The finishing touch, of course, was the paper—paper littered every available flat surface. Stacks of tomes and notes and letters lay on the desk and improvised tables of old crates and sawhorses covered with planks. Folded paper animals roamed the mountains of paper. Charts pasted to the walls overlapped other charts pasted to the walls. Finally, a crisis in housing had occurred, and the paper stacks had migrated to the floors beside walls and beneath tables. To Olive's astonishment, nothing littered the ceiling.

Drone's lab was more spacious than most, about forty feet in diameter, and it took the halfling a minute to thread her way through the maze of equipment and junk before she found her companions. Giogi and Cat stood beside a desk, speaking to Frefford Wyvernspur. Giogi's cousin held a silver urn, a sheet of paper, and a floor brush.

Freffie was saying, "I think you're right. There is evidence that it might not have been something he summoned himself. A window pane was broken. Nothing out of the ordinary with that, considering Drone, but all the kudzu vine from the roof to the window was blighted and withered. Those piles of papers by his desk were scattered across the floor."

"Any other signs of a struggle?" asked Cat.

Frefford gave a shrug, "With this mess, who could tell? I'd really better start heading down. Aunt Dorath is standing at the foot of the outer stairs, waiting for me. If I take too long, she's liable to send a division of the purple dragoons up.

"It was so kind of you to offer Giogi your aid," Frefford said as he bowed over Cat's hand, "in bringing Steele down from the mausoleum."

"It was nothing," Cat muttered.

"I hope you've shown her your appreciation, Giogi," Frefford said, his eyes still fixed on the beautiful mage.

"Yes," Giogi replied flatly.

"Well, then," Frefford said, not noticing his cousin's frown, "I'll have the things to take to the temple piled in your carriage before you leave. Be careful up here."

Frefford turned and left the tower room by a second door, which led to a wider, windowed staircase running along the outside of the tower.

Olive popped out from behind a large brass gong. "I take it your cousin was only up here to collect the last of your uncle's remains," she said.

"Yes. There wasn't very much to collect, though," Giogi said.

"No. There wasn't much of Jade, either," Olive said. "I went back to look for her ashes, but the rain had washed them away."

Cat said nothing but flipped open a book on the desk. It was the pink catalog Gaylyn had kept for Drone. Inside were lines and lines of small, neat handwriting. Cat lifted a few scrolls and manuscripts off a pile beneath the desk and compared each one to a list in the book. "Your cousin's wife has done a remarkable job. There is some organization to this whole mess. Only a small minority of these papers are actually magic, however. It will still take some time to separate the gold from the dross."

"Can't you just cast a detect magic and find the most useful things?" Olive asked.

Cat's face broke into a grin. "Good thinking, Mistress Ruskettle. I will cast the spell while you collect everything that glows. Look sharp, we do not want to miss anything," the mage warned.

"I'm ready," Olive declared.

Cat walked to the outer doorway and turned to face the room. Holding her hands clasped behind her back, she closed her eyes and began a whispering chant.

Olive tensed with excitement, her eyes wide.

Blue light flared all around her—light so bright that Olive instinctively closed her eyes and raised her hands up to cover them. She tried squinting and peeking through her fingers. So much light flooded the room that it was like being underwater.

"Do you have everything, Mistress Ruskettle?" Cat's voice asked mockingly through the azure radiance.

"Very funny," Olive said with a sniff, "You've had your little joke. Now, if you don't mind—"

The light dimmed and faded.

"I thought you said only a few things here were magic," Giogi said testily, trying to rub the spots from his eyes.

Cat shook her head. "No, I said a minority of these papers were magic. There are still many, many papers, and the room itself has enchantments cast on it, as do many of the items."

"I see. Well, you'd better start sorting through the magic," Giogi said. "That's what we brought you for," he added. Then he turned sharply away from the mage.

Olive saw Cat look down at the floor as if she'd been slapped by Flattery. The mage returned to Drone's desk.

"Mistress Ruskettle, you and I can start looking for clues Uncle Drone might have left about who the thief was," Giogi said more enthusiastically.

Olive nodded wordlessly, wishing she could shake Giogi and explain to him that it was imperative he win the mage's loyalty—something he wasn't going to do by treating her like a dust rag. With a sigh, the halfling began studying the papers piled on the floor.

The nobleman drifted toward the stone table holding the alchemy setup and sniffed at the air. He thought of all the time he used to spend in the room when he was little—begging his Uncle Drone to teach him magic. The wizard had always told him he should concentrate on his other talents. Giogi had never figured out what other talents he had, though.

Olive perused a letter dated nearly thirty years before. It was signed by King Azoun's father, Rhigaerd II. Wax imprinted with the royal seal was still affixed to the letter. The halfling looked up at Giogi and Cat. Giogi was sifting through the papers on the stone table, and the mage had her nose buried in Gaylyn's catalog. Olive slid the document into her skirt pocket.

"Here's Uncle Drone's journal," Giogi said, "propped under this alcohol burner."

Olive, her eyes still fixed on Cat, saw the mage's head snap up in alarm as she heard the sound of the book's leather cover sliding along the stone tabletop. The mage wheeled in place as Giogi said, "Ick. What's this yellow powder all over it?"

"Giogi! No!" Cat cried, throwing herself at the nobleman just as he flipped open the journal's cover.

Olive instinctively threw herself in the opposite direction. An explosion thundered through the room, pressing the halfling to the floor like a great hand. Papers gushed up and fluttered back down. Glass alembics and vials from the alchemy set smashed into the far wall and slid to the floor, their contents streamed out in greasy rivulets.

"Giogi?" Olive whispered into the smoke.

"Did I do that?" Giogi whispered in reply.

Olive picked herself up off the floor and stumbled across to help Giogi, who lay pinned beneath the mage. "Are you all right?" she asked.

"I think so. Cat?"

Cat lay still on top of the nobleman. The back of her cream-colored gown was scorched yellow and brown. Giogi rolled on his side and slid the mage over gently. Her face was very pale.

Damn! Olive thought.

"Cat?" Giogi whispered. "Oh, please, say something."

Cat remained silent and motionless.

"Mistress Ruskettle," Giogi ordered, "run and get Freffie! He's in the room two stories down. Tell him to bring a healing potion. Tell him to hurry!"

Olive tore down the outer stairs. It might be all right, she tried to convince herself. Cat might not be as bad as she looks. She can't die. We need her. Damn that stupid fop!

Giogi cradled the mage's head in his lap. Hot tears streamed down his cheeks. "Cat," he whispered. "Don't die. Please, don't die. I'm so sorry."

"Giogi, you fool," Cat whispered.

"Cat! You're all right!" Giogi cried out.

Cat gulped and swallowed with some effort. "Could've killed yourself, you idiot."

"I'm sorry. I'm really sorry. I won't do it again. Ever. Tell me you're all right."

"Hurt like hell."

"Mistress Ruskettle's gone for help. We'll get you a healing potion. You'll be fine." Giogi bent over and kissed the mage's forehead. "You had me so scared. I'm so happy you're all right."

"I thought you hated me," Cat muttered.

Giogi felt his heart pounding. "You little ass, I could never hate you. I'm crazy about you. I was an absolute fool to be so angry with you and act so mean. I'm so sorry."

"Not a little ass," Cat whispered.

"Yes, you are. You just threw yourself into an exploding book and saved my life," Giogi pointed out.

"Precisely," Cat croaked. "I'm a big ass." She smiled weakly.

Giogi laughed and kissed the mage's forehead again.

An out-of-breath Olive burst back into the room with a similarly winded Frefford right behind her.

"Giogi! What happened?" Frefford demanded, puffing.

"I was stupid, as usual. Did you bring a healing potion?"

Freffie handed Giogi a small crystal vial. Giogi uncorked it and held it to Cat's lips. "Drink this," he urged her, helping her lift her head up so she could swallow the potion.

Cat emptied the vial and lay back, licking her lips. " 'S good," she murmured. "Feeling better." The mage closed her eyes as if she'd fallen asleep. Giogi brought her left hand up to his lips and kissed it. Suddenly Cat's eyes snapped open again and she sat up. "I think I'll live," the mage said with surprise.

Giogi breathed a sigh of relief.

"But only because you need someone to remind you not to do anything else that stupid ever again," Cat added sharply, climbing to her feet with Giogi's support.

Olive studied the pair with interest. It was a relief seeing Giogi get over his resentment. More astonishing, though, was Cat acting once again like the mage they'd met in the catacombs—saying what she thought. All in all, that was probably a good sign, the halfling decided.

"Giogi," Frefford said, "why didn't you tell me Mistress Ruskettle was here as well? So pleased to see you again, ma'am."

"Thank you, Your Lordship," Olive replied.

From down the outer staircase came an irate call, "Giogioni Wyvernspur! Just what are you doing up there? Are you trying to blow us all to the seventh heaven, you fool? Come down from that room this instant."

"Aunt Dorath!" Giogi whispered, jumping to his feet. "She

found out I'm here."

The halfling ran to the door to the outer staircase and pushed it shut. "The lock's broken on this side," she whispered.

"I had to break the door down yesterday," Frefford reminded Giogi.

They could hear Dorath stomping up the stone staircase. The sound of her footsteps echoed through the tower. Fortunately, Dorath had several flights to climb.

Cat looked at the door with annoyance. "Seal," she said.

Olive felt the door shudder beneath her shoulder.

"That will buy us a few minutes," the mage said.

"What for?" Frefford asked.

Cat turned to Giogi and put her hands on his arms. "Giogi, we still need to search this room for clues about the spur and magic we can use. You must leave with your cousin and Mistress Ruskettle. Your aunt doesn't know I'm here. Lead her away so I can search the room. Go to the temple. You need to speak to Mother Lleddew. I will join you back at your townhouse when I'm finished here."

Suddenly suspicious again of the mage's motives, Olive suggested, "Maybe I should stay and help Mistress Cat."

"I can manage on my own," Cat insisted. She crossed the room to the small shelf of potions. She studied the vials for a moment, checked in the pink notebook, then selected two potions, one a slate gray, the other a glittering gold.

"What are those for?" Giogi asked, following behind her.

"You and Mistress Ruskettle." Cat pressed the golden vial into Giogi's hands. "If you have any more trouble—lacedons, bears, anything—drink this," she said.

"What will it do?" Giogi asked.

"It will make you powerful. Now do me a favor. Move the journal to your uncle's desk so I can study it."

"Is it safe to touch now?"

Cat nodded like a mother encouraging her child to mount a pony. Giogi lugged the heavy wood-bound tome from the stone table to the desk while Cat joined Olive, who stood next to the door.

The mage knelt beside the halfling and addressed her so quietly that her words could not be heard by the men. "Please, Mistress Ruskettle. You've already made me safe with your amulet. Go with Giogioni. He needs your protection more than I.

Flattery commands many undead. This potion will help if you are attacked by any." She handed Olive the slate-gray potion.

Olive took the vial uncertainly, not sure what to make of Cat's behavior. *She's encouraging Giogi to do just the thing Flattery warned her against, but she isn't joining us in the activity. So she's still avoiding a direct confrontation with the wizard—a confrontation that would reveal exactly where her loyalties lie. Am I going to regret giving her a free rein with Drone's lab? She could find something about the spur, or even find the spur itself and take it right to Flattery.*

"Please, look out for him?" Cat pleaded in a whisper.

Olive wanted to say, *Me? Woman, I'm no hero, just a halfling that knows more than is good for the both of us.* Instead, she pocketed the vial and nodded grimly. "Don't worry," she said.

The door handle rattled and shook, and someone began thumping on the door.

"Giogi," Frefford whispered to his cousin, "I'm not sure that this is such a good idea."

"Freffie, it'll be just fine," Giogi whispered back. "Do me a favor and lend Cat a horse to ride home—I'll have Thomas return it right away."

"Giogi, she's not staying at your house, is she?"

"It's more complicated than that," Giogi tried to explain.

"She is. You devil," Frefford said with a grin.

"Freffie, it's not like that."

"No? You know you'll take as much heat for being innocent as for being guilty if Aunt Dorath finds out."

The pounding on the door stopped, and a voice that could wake the dead shouted from the other side, "Giogioni Wyvernspur, you open that door right now!"

"Just a minute, Aunt Dorath. I'm, um, trapped under a—a gong," Giogi called out, banging on the brass gong beside the desk.

Cat stepped away from the door and crept to Giogi's side. "I have to hide now," she said. "Good luck. Take care." She took another potion vial from the shelf and unstoppered it. After taking only a little sip, she restoppered and pocketed the rest of the potion. In a moment, she vanished before their eyes.

"Frefford, are you in there with your cousin?" called the voice of doom.

"Yes, Aunt Dorath."

"Open this door immediately."

Frefford strode over to the door and yanked on the handle. "It seems to be stuck, Aunt Dorath. I must have bent a hinge when I broke it down before."

"Keep pulling at it," Aunt Dorath demanded. "Giogi, you get out from under that gong and give Frefford a hand."

"Yes, Aunt Dorath," Giogi called out, giving the gong another bang. He felt something brush against his lips. "Cat?" he whispered. The invisible mage kissed him again, on his ear.

"Behave yourself," he whispered.

"I am behaving," Cat whispered back.

"Yes. Badly," he replied, although he was unable to keep the grin from his lips.

The spell that Cat had cast to hold the door shut wore off suddenly, with an almost tangible *crack*. Unprepared, Frefford bashed the door into his head, and Aunt Dorath came tumbling into the room.

Giogi rushed forward to help the elderly woman to her feet.

Dorath rose on her own and shook off her nephew with a look of displeasure. "Gaylyn told me you were up here. You've frightened her half to death. I demand to know what you've been doing!"

"I came up to look at Uncle Drone's journal," Giogi explained. "I thought he might have something to say about the spur in it, but it was—"

"Firetrapped, you fool!" Dorath interrupted. "How many times has your uncle told you not to touch things in his lab? You almost didn't live to see your tenth year because of that incident with the bottled efreet, or have you forgotten?"

"No, Aunt Dorath. I had not. I thought it was worth the risk if it helped us find the spur."

"If your uncle knew anything about the spur, don't you think he would have told me?" Aunt Dorath snapped.

Giogi bit his tongue.

"That book and this room are off-limits to you for good reason. Isn't it bad enough that one of those spells killed your uncle?"

"But, I thought—" Giogi began, but, catching sight of Frefford, who stood behind Aunt Dorath, shaking his head warningly, he let his words trail off. Obviously Frefford hadn't wanted to worry the older lady with his theory that something had broken in.

"I'm sorry, Aunt Dorath," Giogi said simply. "I shan't do it again."

"And who is this?" Dorath asked, finally noticing Olive standing very quietly to one side.

Frefford stepped forward. "Surely, Aunt Dorath, you must remember Olive Ruskettle—the bard that sang at my wedding reception."

Dorath squinted at the halfling. "You're the one with the companion who tried to kill Giogi."

"Um, yes," Olive admitted, "but we stopped her in time if you'll remember."

"Oh, I remember. I just don't know why you bothered. Giogi is determined not to see out his first quarter-century. However did you get involved in this harebrained scheme?" Dorath asked Olive.

Olive picked her words carefully. "I came along as an advisor. I have some experience with magic. Unfortunately, I was not quick enough to prevent your nephew from setting off the firetrap. I am so sorry that we alarmed you. I think perhaps you are right. This room is beyond my expertise, as well as that of your nephew's. We should all leave immediately."

Pacified some by the halfling's agreeableness, Dorath grew calmer. "Perhaps, Mistress Ruskettle, since you are here, you and my nephew would care to join us for lunch. I know Gaylyn would be glad for the company. Confinement has been so tedious for her. She's such a high-spirited young woman. Giogi will be glad to make some time in his castle-destroying schedule, won't you?"

"What are you having?" Giogi asked.

Aunt Dorath shot the young nobleman an angry look.

"Glad to stay," Giogi quickly amended.

"Then after lunch you can take some packages up to the House of the Lady, for the memorial service tonight. Frefford can then devote some time to Gaylyn."

"I'd be happy to oblige," Giogi said.

"It's just like your Uncle Drone to leave a note behind that we use Selune's temple for his memorial service," Dorath said as she began descending the stairs. "He knew how much I hate traveling up that hill."

Olive and the gentlemen followed the elderly woman down

the outside staircase. Olive shot a look back into the room, but, of course, she saw no one within, only the massive clutter. With the excitement of the last few minutes, and her state of confusion and indecision about Cat, and, of course, her anticipation of lunch, the halfling completely forgot the unseen figure that had followed them up the tower's inner staircase.

❧ 16 ❧
The House of the Lady

The cook at Redstone lacked Thomas's talents with sauces and seasonings, but Gaylyn's company added considerable cheer to the lunch. She was shrewd enough not to ask about Cat in front of Aunt Dorath, but she regaled them with funny stories of the naughty things she did as a child. Olive got the impression the lady would turn out to be a pretty permissive parent.

Steele never showed up for the meal, which also added to everyone's lightheartedness. Sudacar did show, and, giving Giogi one of his sly winks, seated himself beside Julia and attended to her every word.

Giogi and Olive both felt very strange watching Julia's behavior in Sudacar's presence. She'd become the model of a sweet, modest young lady in the Lord of Immersea's presence. Giogi's feeling of family loyalty struggled with his urge to warn Sudacar of Julia's natural viciousness. Olive, for her part, was reminded of Cat, who kept her sardonic nature around Giogi in check to keep his favor, and around Flattery to keep her head from being staved in.

Near the end of the meal, Gaylyn excused herself to check on the baby, and Aunt Dorath went with her. In his aunt's absence, Giogi asked Olive to tell them all about her travels last season with Alias of Westgate, and Frefford insisted. So the halfling complied, without actually mentioning the secret of Alias's— and Jade's and Cat's—origins. She made a point of mentioning the help they had from the Nameless Bard, but none of the Wyvernspurs seemed to have heard of their black sheep ancestor.

As she spoke, Olive grew aware that Lord Sudacar was studying her more intensely than he ever had when she had told the same story in the Five Fine Fish. Then she remembered that she still wore the device of the Harpers. The king's man did not interrupt her, however, nor question her about the pin.

KATE NOVAK and JEFF GRUBB

Her story carried them to the end of the meal, and when Giogi announced that they must be going, Olive sighed inwardly in relief to be escaping Sudacar's stare. In the tavern he seemed just a retired adventurer, but here he represented the law of the land, and Olive was always uncomfortable with laws.

The sky was still clear and bright, and the sun still high in the sky, when Olive and Giogi climbed into their rented carriage. Olive sat beside Giogi on the driver's seat, partly to keep him company and partly to avoid the crush of food boxes they'd been volunteered to take up to the temple for that evening's memorial service. Dorath apparently expected a big turnout and didn't want to be caught short.

"I've spent all winter here in Immersea," Olive said as they pulled away from the castle, "but I've yet to visit this temple. People tell me it's very impressive. I've never met Mother Lleddew, either. She's a bit of a recluse, I understand. What's she like?"

"I don't know exactly," Giogi said. "I haven't seen her since I was a boy. My parents took me up to the temple a few times to have tea with her. After my parents died, Uncle Drone only took me up there to watch eclipses, and then there were so many people there that I never really got to see much of her. When I got sick or hurt, Aunt Dorath took me to the shrine of Chauntea. I think Aunt Dorath disapproves of Selune, but I don't know why.

"Anyway, from what I remember, Mother Lleddew was a big woman, older than Aunt Dorath, with shaggy black hair and funny brown eyes. Her temple is all open, just pillars and a floor and a roof. I never figured out where she lived. When we came for tea, my parents and I, it was more like a picnic. We'd sit in the surrounding meadow beside a little fire. Mother Lleddew would serve berries and fresh herb teas.

"There's a silver bell you ring, and she shows up. Mischievous kids used to sneak up the hill, ring the bell, and run off, watching from the woods, but she always seemed to know when it was a practical joke, and never showed up."

"Any of those mischievous kids used to live at Redstone?" Olive asked.

Giogi grinned. "Some of them. According to Sudacar, Lleddew adventured with my father, but she never travels anymore. Frefford said he tried to get her to go down to Suzail to officiate at his wedding, but she wouldn't leave the temple."

"There was a priestess of Selune at the wedding, though," Olive recalled.

Giogi nodded. "She was someone from Suzail. Couldn't have a Wyvernspur wedding without Selune's blessing. Paton Wyvernspur—our family's founder—was said to be favored by her."

They reached the intersection of the two main roads that ran through Immersea. Giogi steered the horses west and had to slow the carriage for the tradesmen, teamsters, and fishmongers who crowded the streets.

"Mistress Ruskettle, could I ask your advice on something?" the noble asked.

"Never play dice with anyone named High-Roll," Olive said.

"Pardon?"

"Just a little joke. Sorry. Of course, Master Giogioni. Please feel free to confide in me at any time."

"Well, if you had someone who was a friend, not someone you knew really well but someone you thought was a capital fellow, and he became involved with someone else who you thought might not be so capital but who was a member of your family, for instance, do you think you would tell the capital fellow?"

"No," Olive replied at once.

"No?" Giogi asked.

"No," Olive repeated.

"But, I mean, maybe he would want to know. I would want to know."

"No, you wouldn't," Olive said, thinking of Cat and Flattery.

"Yes, I would."

"No, you wouldn't. Believe me. As for telling Samtavan Sudacar that you think your Cousin Julia is a schemer, I think you should butt out."

Giogi stared at Olive as if she'd just sprouted wings. "How did you know? What are you? Some kind of mind reader?"

Olive laughed. "No, just a student of human nature. Men never want to hear anything bad about women they think they're in love with. Period. Besides, Sudacar seems to be a good influence on her."

"You don't know, though—Steele wants to find the spur first so that he can keep it for himself, and Julia's already done something that wasn't very nice to help him."

"Does Steele have anything to hold over her?" Olive asked, already knowing the answer.

"Just his bullying," Giogi said.

"What about money?" Olive suggested. "Halfling sons and daughters inherit equally in their parents property, but you Cormyrian nobles have this barbarous practice of cheating your daughters out of their inheritance by marrying them off with a pittance of a dowry."

"Julia's father left her a very large dowry," Giogi objected.

"And she can just hand this dowry over to any husband she chooses?" Olive asked.

"Well, no. As her older brother, Steele would have to approve—" Giogi broke off, finally getting the gist of Olive's argument. "And Steele doesn't care for Sudacar," he recalled aloud. "But Sudacar wouldn't care if Julia had a dowry or not," Giogi insisted. "He's not that kind of man."

"So certain of that, are you?" Olive said, finding it hard to believe that any man would be just as happy with a poor wife as a rich one. Humans had such romantic notions. "That's not the point, though, Master Giogioni," Olive explained. "It would matter to Julia. She'd be too proud to go into a marriage penniless. Most women would be."

"That shouldn't matter if she's really in love," Giogi said.

"Ever been penniless, Master Giogioni?" Olive asked.

"Um, well, no," Giogi admitted.

"Now, some women, myself for instance, know that their worth has nothing to do with money. I don't suspect anyone has ever told that to your Cousin Julia, though. Certainly not her brother."

Giogi considered Olive's words silently for a few minutes. Finally, he said, "You must be awfully wise, Mistress Ruskettle."

"Just experienced," Olive replied.

If only I'd been turned into an ass earlier and had witnessed the theft of the spur, the halfling thought, he'd be proclaiming me Cormyr's greatest sage.

Giogi passed his townhouse and continued west out of town.

"Isn't the town graveyard out this way?" Olive asked.

"Yes, but we turn off before then. The temple road is that one on our left, just up ahead."

Olive's eyes followed the temple road's progress south

through fields of winter wheat, to the base of a high tree-ringed hill, where it began its ascent, winding to the west. Olive squinted in the sunshine at the cleared hilltop. She could just make out a blob of white that might be the temple. One lone cloud, an ominous shade of gray, hung in the sky to the east of the hill's peak—a blot on an otherwise perfect picture.

Giogi turned the carriage off the cobbled main road and onto the muddy temple road. The wheels sank a few inches into the mire, but not so deep that the horses were unable to cope. Once they entered the woods and reached the hill's slope, the going got even slower. The forest around them grew dark. Olive craned her neck to look up at the sky. The lone cloud she'd noticed before was now overhead, visible through the barely budding branches.

A large black bird swooped down from the cloud and disappeared behind the tree line, on their uphill side. Toward the temple.

"What was that?" Olive asked.

"What was what?" Giogi asked.

"There," Olive said, pointing up to the cloud as a second dark shape plummeted earthward. There's another, and another—a flock of somethings."

"I've never seen anything like them before, "Giogi admitted, squinting at the creatures far overhead. "They all seem to be carrying something."

"Maybe Mother Lleddew trains giant crows or bats or something," Olive muttered.

Trees overhanging the road obscured their line of sight until they reached the high stone bridge crossing the Immer Stream. The woods were thinner along the stream bed, and now Olive could make out the pillars and roof of the House of the Lady, above the cascading waters. The hill was entirely shaded by the lone cloud, so that, despite the afternoon sunshine, it was as dark as twilight.

Olive could just make out several shadowy figures surrounding the temple, milling about in the meadow around it.

"Could those be people arriving extra early for the memorial service?" the halfling asked Giogi.

"Maybe," the nobleman replied uncertainly.

Once across the bridge, the road became firmer and the trees thicker, and human and halfling lost sight of the hilltop again. On the hillside above them, something large rustled and snapped through the undergrowth. Olive kept her eyes wide, expecting a deer or bear to come bounding across the road.

Suddenly something heavy dropped onto the carriage roof with a thump.

"What was that?" Giogi cried out.

Olive turned around and stood up on the driver's seat. Something vaguely humanlike was crawling across the carriage roof in their direction. Its sharp fingernails dug into the painted wood, and its long tongue flicked at the air through sharp teeth, like a serpent. The right half of its face had been staved in, and it glared at the halfling through empty eye sockets, which dripped a milky fluid.

With a gasp, Olive dropped down to the seat beside Giogi and grabbed the reins from his hands. She slapped the leather straps hard against the horses' backs, shouting "Eeeee-Yah!"

The horses took off, and the carriage jolted behind them. Giogi let out a surprised yelp. Behind her Olive heard the scrabble of nails trying to gain purchase on the carriage roof and the *thunk* of their unwanted passenger striking the ground.

Her grin of satisfaction was quickly stanched by the sight of three more figures ahead, stumbling out of the forest and onto the road. Two appeared normal, but the third leaned heavily to one side, as if favoring a leg injury.

The halfling smashed the reins down on the horses again, hollering at the top of her lungs, "Giddy, giddy, go!"

The horses plowed through the creatures trying to intercept them. The creatures made no motion to get out of the way. The carriage tilted to one side for a moment as the wheels ran over their bodies, and the boxes within slammed from one side of the carriage to the other.

"Mistress Ruskettle!" Giogi shouted as he turned to stare in horror at the corpses in the road. "You just ran those poor people over!"

"Those weren't poor people, Master Giogioni. Those were dead people. Ghouls, by the looks of them." Olive's initial triumphant glee had turned to fearful concern.

"Ghouls! Last night it was lacedons! Should we try to turn around and go back, do you think?" Giogi asked nervously, studying the road ahead for a wide spot.

"Is the road clear behind us?" Olive asked.

Giogi looked behind them. At least a dozen figures poured onto the road from the way they'd come.

"Um, no," he said, turning around again quickly—horrified by the creatures' twitchy, marionettelike movements.

"Then we keep going up," Olive shouted over the noise of the horses' hooves.

"How can all these evil things dare to tread a hill sacred to Selune?"

"They're probably more afraid of something else than they are of Selune."

"But what?" Giogi asked.

"Flattery would be my first guess. He's a pretty scary guy, and he's partial to the undead. How much farther to the top?"

The young noble's face was pale. "Two more bends, I think. What are we going to do once we reach the top?"

"Ring the bell and hope Mother Lleddew doesn't mistake us for children playing a practical joke. You have the potion Cat gave you?" Olive asked.

"Yes, in my belt. Should I drink it now?"

"Not yet. Hold off until we're sure you need to. Here, take these," Olive ordered, handing the nobleman the reins. "If it's ugly, run over it." Once her hands were free, Olive reached into her shirt pocket and drew out the potion Cat had selected for her.

The carriage rounded the last curve in the hillside road and rumbled to the top of the hill. The clearing at the top was a meadow about twenty-five yards across. The temple took up about a third of that space.

Throngs of disgusting undead creatures shambled about the meadow. More were raining down into the clearing, dropped by giant vultures that looked no more healthy than their cargo. A few of the birds mistimed their drops; as Olive watched, one zombie smashed into the temple's domed roof, rolled off to the ground, and lay unmoving on the temple's granite steps.

The horses tried rearing in their harnesses once, then froze in place, petrified with terror. Giogi slapped the reins again, but the beasts were rooted in place.

About a dozen zombies, moaning pitifully, shambled slowly toward the carriage. They all wore dirty uniforms. They weren't as badly decayed as most zombies, but each sported some gruesome mortal injury—a severed arm, a slit throat. Their corpses had obviously been raided from a battlefield. From the dented, red-plumed helmets of most of the zombies and the tattered and torn black capes of the rest, Olive guessed they'd been Hillsfar and Zhentil Keep forces—victims of their cities' perennial war over the ruins of Yulash.

"Giogi, you need to drink that potion now," Olive said decisively, unstoppering her own vial and quaffing the gray mixture in three gulps. It slid down her throat like a lump of mercury and left a cold feeling in her stomach.

Giogi dropped the reins and pulled out his potion. As he poured it down his throat, Olive stood up on the driver's seat and surveyed the zombies imperiously. The cold in her stomach spread to her heart. She felt a surge of power in her spirit. It was a moment before she recovered sufficiently to issue a command. "Get thee hence, vile creatures," she ordered the undead, waving her hand in the directions of the trees.

The zombies ceased moaning and looked up at the halfling. Then they shuffled a little more quickly in the direction of the carriage.

"Well, that worked real well," Olive muttered, pitching the empty potion bottle at the forehead of the lead zombie. She wondered if Cat had made an honest mistake. At least it wasn't poison, the halfling thought as she scrambled into the carriage through the front window.

Recovering from the first dizzying effect of the golden potion, Giogi shouted, "What now?"

"Draw your weapon and defend yourself," Olive hollered from inside the carriage.

"What are you doing?" the nobleman shouted back, teasing out the peace knot that bound his foil to its sheath.

"Getting ammo," Olive explained. "Gee, its a mess in here."

The lead pair of horses broke down entirely, dropping to their knees as the undead approached. The zombies shambled past them, ignoring their panic-stricken neighing. Instead, the undead surrounded the carriage and began beating on the sides. A few started to climb up it.

Giogi took a deep breath. Suddenly he felt quite clear-headed and calm. All he had to do was stab the foul creatures. What could be simpler? he thought.

He plunged his foil in and out of the throat of a zombie that was trying to climb the step to the driver's seat. When the monster kept coming at him, Giogi stabbed it again. The zombie teetered toward him, but with a swift kick, the nobleman sent it falling backward to knock over two of its fellow creatures.

"How are we going to ring for Mother Lleddew?" the nobleman called to Olive.

"Don't need to. I think she knows," Olive shouted back. "She's at the temple."

Giogi looked over the heads of the zombies. On the temple steps stood a very large woman wearing only a brown shift and sandals. A ring of ghouls, like the first undead that had landed on their coach, surrounded the priestess. She leaned on an oaken staff while the monsters hissed and screeched at her. None of the undead, though, drew close enough to attack her.

Giogi lanced another zombie, then shouted out, "Mother Lleddew!"

The priestess waved Giogi away. "Stay back!" she warned with a bellow that could have carried to the foot of Spring Hill.

The pack of ghouls surrounding the priestess looked in Giogi's direction. They hissed and screeched as they turned toward the carriage. A large carrion bird swooped toward the carriage as well. Giogi could see bones protruding from its withered wings. He ducked just in time, and the vulture crashed into the trees beyond the clearing.

Olive climbed back out of the carriage's front window, laden with two heavy sacks. "Give me a hand up to the roof," she said.

"What about Mother Lleddew?" Giogi asked.

"She's got some protection of her own. The undead aren't bothering her," Olive huffed. She took a swing at an overzealous zombie with one of the sacks and knocked the monster off its perch on the front carriage wheel. "They're coming after younger prey now—namely us. Give me a boost."

Giogi hefted Olive onto the top of the carriage. The halfling pulled the sling out of her garter and grabbed a handful of ammo pilfered from Uncle Drone's memorial feast. She loaded a golden apple into her sling and whipped it around.

"Have some apple sauce!" she yelled, loosing the fruit down on the crowd of zombies. "Go on, get out of here."

The ripe apple caught an undead square in the forehead, and it toppled backward. By the time it hit the ground, two more apples were zinging with halfling accuracy through the ranks of the undead. Those monsters that came close enough to climb the coach were met by Giogi's merciless foil.

The nobleman parried their clawlike hands and stabbed at them fiercely. Their lack of self-preservation appalled him. At the same time, he worried about his own preservation. Just how long will this magic potion last? he wondered as sweat began breaking out on his forehead. Will I be able to tell right away?

Giogi glanced toward the temple, but Mother Lleddew had abandoned her defense of the stairs. She was heading toward the carriage, wading through the crowd of zombies, jostling them as she went. The creatures paid no more attention to her than they did to each other.

"Giogi! Look out!" Olive cried, snapping an apple at a ghoul that had managed to climb up to the driver's seat. The red missile splattered in the middle of the undead's shredded face, but the ghoul kept coming. A hissing snarl escaped its torn lips and the ghoul leaped on Giogi.

In a moment, the creature had Giogi bent backward, its claws securely fastened on the noble's shoulders. A paralyzing coldness crept from the ghoul's fingers, and Giogi felt himself go numb. His foil fell from his unfeeling fingers and clattered to the driver's seat. The ghoul's ruined mouth smiled and opened, displaying a row of fanglike teeth.

Olive ran across the carriage roof and kicked the monster in the head before it managed to sink its teeth into Giogi's throat. The ghoul loosed its grip, but Giogi was unable to move to balance himself, and he toppled from the driver's seat into the zombie horde below.

A collective "Ah!" of undead delight issued from the mouths of nearby zombies. They fell on top of the man and began pummeling him with their corpse-white hands.

Olive screamed and began pelting the zombies below with apples thrown by hand. A few fell back, but more took their place. The halfling was just wondering if it would be worth risking her life to jump down on top of the fray when something grabbed her ankle.

Olive twisted around. The ghoul who had paralyzed Giogioni had not fallen over with the nobleman. Now the monster was dragging Olive toward the edge of the carriage roof.

"Let me go, you ghoul!" Olive shouted, reaching frantically

for the dagger she kept up her sleeve. The ghoul laughed until Olive slashed off its hand at the wrist. She jerked her leg back and gave the undead another kick—sending it into the hordes below. She poked with her dagger at the fingers of the dismembered hand until it fell away from her ankle.

On the ground below, Giogi was wondering if the potion had already worn off. The fists of the zombies rained down on him in a torrent. He could never recall hurting so badly in his life, and the paralyzation was like a nightmare. The worst part, though, was his inability to breathe.

One of the zombies had enough sense left in its undead brain to throttle him. It knelt beside him and gripped his neck in the bony vise of its fingers. The other zombies pulled back and watched their compatriot choke the noble. Dark spots danced in front of Giogi's eyes. Somewhere in the distance, Olive shouted.

Something warm touched Giogi on the face. The warmth spread downward to his torso and then to his arms and legs. In a moment, he felt his muscles relax, and in another, he could move again. He brought a fist up sharply in the face of the zombie who was choking him. The creature fell backward from the sudden assault. The noble kicked and pounded and stabbed at the zombies who tried to close on top him. Strong hands, warm and living, latched about his arm and helped him to his feet.

Mother Lleddew stood beside him. "Get back up on the carriage and take the reins," she ordered, "I'll clear a path for you to turn around."

Looking up, Giogi saw Olive squaring off with a noseless zombie on the driver's seat. Giogi plucked his foil up from the seat. Leaping up the carriage step, he thrust his weapon into the zombie's back. The creature crumpled. Giogi withdrew the foil and pushed the zombie from the carriage. The noble took his place on the driver's seat.

"Better hold on, Mistress Ruskettle," he warned Olive. "We'll be moving soon."

Mother Lleddew moved forward toward the horses, whispering and patting them comfortingly. The ghouls drew back from her. The zombies remained all around both her and the horses, though they did not attack. Slowly the woman spoke into the lead mare's ear, and the horse rose from its knees, pulling its companion to its feet as well.

The priestess placed herself in front of the lead right horse and began muttering loudly. The zombies suddenly noticed her presence and began crushing in on her, trying to drive her under the mass of bodies. Mother Lleddew held up a platinum engraving of Selune's sign and cried out, "Return thou to dust!"

The engraving glowed, and the zombies in the carriage's path ignited with a mystic blue fire. In another moment, they'd crumbled to gray ash.

Mother Lleddew stepped aside and smacked the lead horse's rump. It charged forward. More zombies rushed to fill the gap left by those the priestess had disintegrated, but the horses trampled over them. The priestess grabbed hold of the carriage door as it shot past. The carriage shifted precariously from her weight until she managed to scramble up to the roof.

For a bulky old priestess, she's pretty spry, Olive thought, clutching the back of the driver's seat.

The carriage shot across the meadow toward the temple, the horses trampling undead and the carriage wheels crushing them. Giogi yelled and steered the horses so the carriage made a wide turn back in the direction of the road.

Overhead, the great carrion birds wheeled beneath the shadowy, solitary cloud. "You, halfling," Lleddew called, pulling from her shift pocket a fragile glass vial of clear liquid and tossing it to Olive, "try this."

"Holy water?" Olive guessed.

"Yes. Don't bother with anything on the ground. Get one of the vultures in the air."

"The vultures?"

"Yes. They're undead as well."

A vulture swooped overhead with a ghoul in its claws. Olive shot at it as it banked toward them. The vial of water smashed into the vulture's wing. The bird dropped its cargo as its wing burst into smoke. It crashed to the ground, smashing several zombies beneath it.

"Nice! Got any more?" Olive asked with delight.

Mother Lleddew handed her another vial and Olive loaded it into her sling. The carriage pulled out of the hilltop clearing and into the light cover of the trees.

Olive hit a second undead vulture with a holy water missile. The bony creature broke up in the air and crashed into the temple pillars. It lay still, but in the temple behind it something else moved.

Olive's mouth fell open as she caught sight of what caused the movement. "There's a girl back there!" she gasped.

"Where?" Giogi cried, pulling back on the horse's reins.

"Don't stop!" Mother Lleddew ordered, her wrinkled face tight with panic.

Giogi stood in his seat and looked at the temple. It was the girl he'd spoken with the night before. "We can't leave her!" he objected.

"You must," the priestess insisted. "She's a Shard. It's her duty to protect the temple. Mine is to protect you. Now go!"

Giogi stared at the girl, shimmering still like a moonbeam in the shadow. "But she's just a girl," he said, unable to bring himself to abandon so helpless a creature.

"She just looks like a girl," Lleddew argued, moving forward to take the reins from Giogi. A pair of ghouls dropped onto the carriage roof from an overhead branch. One slammed into Mother Lleddew and succeeded at knocking her to the ground. The other lunged at Olive. Giogi stopped the carriage immediately.

These ghouls stank with an overwhelming odor of rotting meat. The halfling doubled over with nausea, but managed to sidestep the undead attack anyway. Brandishing her dagger, she whirled about to keep the creature in sight. "You really need a bath, pal," she gasped. "Why don't you go jump in the lake?"

To Olive's astonishment, the creature immediately turned from her, hopped off the carriage roof, and headed down the hill.

Realization and recognition flamed in the halfling's mind. "It just obeyed me. A ghast! That was a ghast! I just commanded a ghast!" she cried excitedly. "The potion only works on ghasts!"

Suddenly remembering Mother Lleddew, Olive looked down at the ground. The other ghast had the priestess pinned to the ground with its inhuman strength. Olive scrambled down from the carriage roof and gave the creature a kick, trying not to inhale its odor.

"Get off her, you stupid undead," Olive ordered the ghast.

The ghast stood up and blinked its bloodshot eyes in confusion.

"Go away!" Olive shouted.

The ghast stumbled off into the woods.

"Ugh!" Olive grunted. She bent over the priestess. "Are you all right?" she asked.

Mother Lleddew groaned. Her shift had been slashed in a dozen places, and she was bleeding profusely. Her breath was husky and labored, and the whites of her eyes had gone strangely dark. Olive couldn't tell if these were symptoms of an injury or an effect of the ghast's touch. She tried to pull the large woman to her feet, but Lleddew slumped against the halfling, driving Olive to her knees.

"Damn! Giogi, give me a hand here!" Olive cried.

Oblivious to the undead closing in on the carriage, Giogi stood on the driver's seat, watching with horror the undead surrounding the dark-skinned, silver-haired girl. The girl shone now more like a powerful magic light, and the undead nearest her covered their eyes with their hands.

Olive looked up at the nobleman and noticed with panic the ghouls coming down upon them. "Giogi!" she shrieked.

Huge arms lifted Olive from behind and tossed her onto the top of the coach. Olive looked down to see Mother Lleddew, once again on her feet, facing the pack of ghouls with her arms outstretched. Her whiteless eyes held a manic gleam. The priestess roared a guttural, incoherent cry of rage. Then the ghouls were upon her, toppling her and burying her with their bodies.

Olive shouted Giogi's name again.

The roar, and Olive's shouts, finally attracted the noble's attention from the girl at the temple. He looked down to where Olive pointed frantically just in time to see Lleddew disappear under a torrent of undead.

Like a man awakening from a dream, Giogi whispered, "No, no," and then shook himself to action, screaming, "No!" He leaped down and began stabbing like a madman at the pile of ghouls.

Olive wondered if, by now, it wasn't too late for the priestess when the pile of undead began to shift and grow, like a swelling seed. A huge paw broke through one side of the pile, flinging a pair of ghouls off. Then a second paw shot out, spearing a ghoul clean through the chest with its claws.

A huge black bear waded out of the pile of ghouls, shaking their broken bodies off it like they were hunting dogs. The bear's forehead and chest were marked with silver-haired crescents, and Olive saw Mother Lleddew's manic gleam in the beast's eyes.

The great bear roared, a roar more powerful than the one Lleddew had made a moment before. The remaining ghouls broke away from the pile and fled from the bear.

An eerie keening rose from atop the hill. Giogi looked back at the temple. He could no longer make out the girl who Mother Lleddew had called a Shard. There was nothing but a white fire burning at the heart of the temple. The undead on the hilltop were fleeing into the woods.

The bear fell to all fours and wobbled unsteadily. Its front paws looked as if they'd been caught in a trap, and its massive shoulders slumped. Olive scrambled down from the coach once more and checked the bear's wounds. They were many and deep.

"Get the carriage door," Olive ordered Giogi.

The nobleman obeyed automatically; his attention was fixed on the hilltop. The bright white flames seemed to be dying down, and the noble caught sight again of the Shard, but she seemed to fade with the fire. A thick, glittering fog rolled around her, and she seemed to grow as one with the mist, which drifted out the open sides of the House of the Lady.

Olive looked at the mysterious, growing fog with anxiety. "Hop in, Mother Lleddew," the halfling said. She gave Giogi a sharp nudge. "Get up there and drive," she ordered.

The bear scrabbled into the carriage and collapsed onto the boxes of food. Olive slammed the door and climbed up beside Giogi.

The nobleman turned about and looked over the roof of the carriage. The Shard had vanished. The cloud roiled and bubbled as it descended the hill, and the undead fled before it. Those who were caught in its coils screamed and then collapsed beneath it and were silent.

Suddenly a single lance of white light shot up from the center of the temple, pierced through the roof, and struck the lone dark cloud overhead. As if it were a wounded beast, the cloud shot away from the light striking it. Afternoon sunlight returned to the hill immediately. The fog became milky white and began dissipating in the warm spring sunshine.

"She's gone," Giogi whispered.

With a sigh, Olive took up the reins and slapped the horses into motion. The unevaporated edges of the fog slid beneath the carriage and through the horse's feet. The mist hid the road from their sight, but caused them no harm. Of the undead that had haunted the woods beside the road there was no sign.

From inside the carriage, the bear echoed the Shard's keening with a plaintive wail of its own.

❧ 17 ❧

The Spur

Cat leaned over Drone's journal with her elbows holding the binding open and her head propped up in her hands. Despite the shattered window and broken door, the tower room was a comfortable temperature, as long as she kept her fur-lined cape draped around her shoulders. Isolated from the rest of the family's living quarters, the room was also marvelously quiet, but the mage could not concentrate. The old wizard's crabbed handwriting blurred before her eyes, and her gaze wandered about the room, unable to focus on anything.

Idly she pulled out the amulet of protection from her skirt pocket. She could feel five lumps of varying sizes and shapes wrapped in the silk. Her curiosity prodded at her to peek at just one of the lumps, but with a sudden burst of will, she shoved the amulet back in her pocket. Ignoring Mistress Ruskettle's advice would be like asking Tymora to send me more bad luck, and I've had more than my share of that, Cat thought.

She stared into space and let her mind wander from the duty at hand to the events of the past year. Nothing had gone right for her since the previous summer. She'd awakened on Midsummer Day in a Zhentil Keep alley with no memory of how she'd gotten there, or indeed any memory at all beyond her name and place of birth. The rest of her history had vanished, leaving an irritating void in her head and an uneasy feeling in her heart.

With nowhere to go, she wandered the streets after dark and ran afoul of one of the Keeper press gangs. After the briefest of struggles, she became their prisoner. She foolishly bragged of her magical power, hoping to coerce or frighten the recruiting thugs into letting her go. Instead she'd found herself drafted into an army unit headed for Yulash.

An ugly little spider of a Zhentarim wizard tested her powers. He gave her a slender book, containing only such spells as slave mages could be trusted with. From the tiny size of the book, and the bloodstains on its cover, it was obvious that her masters did not expect her to survive, much less excel at combat.

After five days of forced marching, her unit engaged in its first battle, against a unit of Hillsfar's Red Plumes. The battle was a mutual slaughter—only officers on the sidelines survived. Cat's magic power was quickly spent as the enemy overran her position. Powerless and exhausted, she lay down in hopes of passing for one of the dead and escaping after dark. That was when Flattery had rescued her.

Maybe rescued wasn't the right word, Cat thought. Collected would be more accurate, she decided.

As soon as the army officers had quit for the evening, retiring to their tents and dinners, Flattery's zombies stumbled onto the battlefield and began collecting bodies for Flattery's experiments—and as food for some of his more disgusting undead minions. A particularly mindless zombie, unable to distinguish between the dead and the unconscious—for Cat had fallen asleep—collected her and brought her to its master in his fortress.

Cat remembered how impressed she'd been at her first sight of Flattery as he stood on a parapet overlooking the rolling fields far below. She thought his hawklike features and wolfish smile quite handsome. His capability and power were equally alluring.

But Flattery guarded his power and secrets jealously. He had no apprentices, no familiars, no companions, but surrounded himself with undead servants. He isolated himself from the outside world and everyday life, using his minions to gather everything he needed to work and live. The wizard had erratic fits of temper, which might explain why he chose to work with blindly obedient slaves. On the other hand, working with such slaves might have contributed to his quirkiness.

The wizard could have made Cat a zombie, or fed her to the ghouls, or resold her to the Zhentarim. But he didn't. Instead he took her under his wing—kept her in pleasant surroundings, taught her some new magic, and worked on a spell to help her regain her memory. Cat was not averse to being sheltered and trained, but most especially she wanted her memory back.

A gnawing desire to fill the void in her head grew in her daily.

Regaining her forgotten history was worth everything to her—enduring Flattery's mad temper, living among the undead servants, reconciling herself to the confinement of Flattery's fortress. After all, she told herself, slavery to the Zhentarim could be much worse.

Finally, one evening many months later, Flattery finished the spell creating the dark jewel that held her missing past. He presented it to Cat with a proposal of marriage. Cat had looked at the gem, yearning to hold it. Afraid of Flattery's reaction should she refuse him, she agreed. She'd flattered herself into believing he'd come to prefer her company to the undead, that he found her beautiful, that he wanted to take care of her. After all, she told herself, he was handsome and clever and very powerful—she could do worse.

After the hasty wedding ceremony with the only attendant being a wobbly priest of Mystra, goddess of magic, Flattery had become irrationally angered by her request to have the gem. He demanded she prove her worth before he restored her memory to her. Then he assigned her the task of sneaking through the Immersea catacombs to fetch the wyvern's spur from the Wyvernspur family crypt.

Eager to get her hands on something the wizard truly desired, something she could barter for her memory, Cat didn't think twice about entering the secret door to the catacombs. It felt good to be away from the undead and free of Flattery's nerve-racking presence. She even enjoyed encountering some of the monsters that lived in the catacombs. They were awful, but at least they were alive; you could talk to them and bribe or trick your way around them.

Finding the spur missing came as a crushing blow to all her hopes. Finding her escape blocked hardly seemed to matter. Trapped inside those horrible tunnels, without even the comfort of having succeeded at stealing the spur, she wandered as aimlessly as any monster. As she wandered, Cat began to re-evaluate her last few months. She decided she could have done better.

Then she'd stumbled across Drone's nephew, Giogi. Giogi's offer of protection had been pretty amusing. Even if the nobleman found the spur, he didn't stand a chance against Flattery. She knew that Giogi's Uncle Drone could be a powerful ally, though. Flattery had taken the trouble to warn her how shrewd Drone was and how cleverly he'd warded the crypt against magical entry and scrying. After talking to Giogi, Cat fell upon a plan: In exchange for information on Flattery and his plot to steal the family's heirloom, Cat had hoped to get Drone's help stealing the crystal that held her lost memory.

To Cat, Drone's death had been nearly as big a blow as finding the spur missing from the crypt. Giogi's chances at finding the spur did not look very good to her, but he was her only hope. If Flattery found the spur first, she would have nothing to barter for the memory crystal—until the wizard found some other, possibly even more dangerous or distasteful, way for her to prove her "worth."

Then someone had tried to smother her in her sleep. In the moonlight it had looked like Flattery. Frefford and Steele Wyvernspur both resembled Flattery, but neither of them had any reason to kill her, and she doubted that either of them could walk through walls.

Flattery could have been playing some sick game or testing her loyalty. Or he might have decided to make himself a widower, in some mad fit of anger or jealousy, and then changed his mind.

On top of last night's shock had come Olive Ruskettle's accusations about Flattery killing that Jade person. Giogi seemed to trust Olive completely. At Thomas's mention of the halfling's name, the nobleman had raced down the stairs with positive excitement. No one challenged the halfling's claim to be a bard, even though Cat was pretty sure halflings were not accepted at barding college, but then Cat hadn't known that Harpers accepted halflings into their organization, either.

Then, when confronted with the accusation that he'd been responsible for Drone's death, Flattery not only did not deny it, but joked about it. That had been the final blow. Cat realized she was an absolute fool to trust him.

Finding the spur was no longer enough. She had to find the power to ensure herself against Flattery's power and deceptions. Olive Ruskettle's amulet of protection had been her first lucky break. The halfling convincing Giogi to bring her to Drone's lab had been her second.

Even if Drone's journal did not reveal information on the spur's whereabouts, Cat could loot from it enough magic to guarantee her survival.

And, if Giogi reaches Mother Lleddew in time to learn whatever she knows but which Flattery does not want Giogi to learn, then manages to bring that information back to me, Cat told herself hopefully, I may even have some power over Flattery.

The mage could not deceive herself about Giogi's chances, though. They were very, very small. He's so aimless and ridiculously romantic, she thought. One knock on the head, and he thinks he's been kissing a goddess, for heaven's sake. Even with a potion of superheroism in him, he's not likely to be much of a challenge against Flattery's hordes of undead. Still, I'm obeying Flattery's suggestion to use him to get what I want. Now, if I could only concentrate on the task I've set for myself.

She couldn't, though. The silly fop's face kept appearing in her mind's eye, wearing her earring and hair-beads and that priceless headband. She kept hearing his voice offering her his protection and telling her it was going to be all right and begging her not to die.

He cared about her. For all Cat knew, he was the only person in the Realms who ever had.

She also kept hearing him describe his dreams—the death cry of prey, the taste of warm blood, and the crunch of bone. For no good reason she could think of, the words excited her. In her own dreams, she was always fruitlessly searching dull desertscapes for something. She never knew what the something was. The dreams left her unhappy and anxious. Flattery denied having any dreams. He claimed they were for the guilty. How could such a weak fool as Giogi have such interesting dreams?

Cat looked down again at Drone's journal, but her elbows were in the way. "Damn!" she muttered. The swig of invisibility potion she'd swallowed had worn off already, which meant she'd been staring into space far too long.

Outside the tower she heard the rattle of a carriage. She ran over to a window and looked down. Giogi and Ruskettle were driving away. They'd finished lunch already, servants had loaded the carriage with packages for Drone's memorial service, and the halfling and noble were leaving for Selune's temple.

I've been staring into space far, far too long, Cat thought with a frown.

She flipped through Drone's journal. It was merely a day-to-day diary. There were no spells written within, no formulas for magic potions scribbled in the margins, no treasure maps stuck between its pages. Page after page accounted family squabbles, purchases, meals, and rumors from court. The last entry was dated the twentieth of Ches, yesterday, just before Drone was killed. The full entry read:

> *Giogi arrived at last night's meeting twenty minutes early, as-tonished Dorath. Boy looks fit. Traveling must agree with him. Didn't get a chance to speak to him alone. Thomas went to meet his girl, but she never showed. Taught Spot a new trick. Gaylyn up all night with contractions. Frefford a wreck. Dorath in her glory. Healthy baby girl born after dawn—Amber Leona, named for both the parents' mothers.*
> *Breakfast burned.*

Nothing, Cat thought with a sigh. An ordinary day in an ordinary castle. Arrivals, departures, births, deaths, the love affairs of servants, the muddling of a meal. A boring life.

A peaceful life, some other part of Cat's mind argued.

The mage slammed the journal closed. She surveyed the lab impatiently. Where are his spell books? she wondered. Were they destroyed with their master? Which of the undead that Flattery commands can cast a spell of disintegration?

Cat took up Gaylyn's catalog. What sort of wizard lets his possessions be cataloged in a pink book with pressed flowers on the cover? she thought disdainfully.

Yet, as she stared at the flowers beneath the crystal plate fastened to the catalog binding and thought of Gaylyn, she knew she was envious of the life the Wyvernspurs lived. They got to be happy—she would have to settle for surviving and, with Tymora's luck, regaining her memory.

Cat spent half an hour sorting through the stacks of paper, gathering the most powerful spell scrolls and potions she could find. Dust billowed as she moved piles of documents, but her stack of magic grew steadily.

Then she came upon a stack that was missing a scroll—a scroll that held a disintegrate spell. She double-checked the pink book, but everything else was in place. "How odd," she murmured.

"Don't move," a man whispered harshly in Cat's ear. The point of a dagger pressing lightly against her jugular vein compelled the mage to obey. The dagger's owner stood behind her. "One word, one move," he said, "and you'll be dragon bait, understand? Now hand over the spur."

Cat remained speechless and motionless.

Her attacker shook her by the shoulder. "Did you hear me, witch? I said hand it over."

"You also said don't move and don't speak," Cat pointed out with a mocking tone, "so I'm just a trifle confused."

"You'll be a trifle dead if you keep acting smart, you little ass," the man said. With his dagger still pressed into her flesh, he moved around her so that they stood face to face.

Cat shuddered when first confronted with the man's face—Flattery's face. After a moment, she saw it wasn't Flattery, though. The man was too young, too nervous, and he had a birthmark by his lips. He was Steele, the kobold-torturer.

"Now, give me the spur and don't try anything. My uncle was a wizard, so I know all your foolish conjurer tricks."

"I don't have the spur," Cat objected.

"Don't lie to me. I was at the inner stair door. That halfling freak locked it, but her people aren't the only ones who can pick locks or listen at doors. I was listening. I heard Giogi call you a little ass, and he was right. Only an ass would risk her neck to save that idiot. The divination said the spur was in the little ass's pocket. Now, reach into your pocket very slowly and pull it out and hand it to me."

"I'm afraid you're mistaken, Master Steele. I haven't got the spur. Maybe the divination referred to the little burro that Master Giogi had yesterday. A burro is a small ass, you know. It's missing, though, like the spur, I'm afraid."

"Asses don't have pockets!" Steele shouted angrily. "Now give me everything you've got in yours."

"I have to put these scrolls and this book down to use my hands," Cat said.

In a fury, Steele knocked the book and the scrolls out of Cat's arms.

"Now, that pocket first," the nobleman ordered, pointing to the right-hand side pocket of her dress's skirt.

One at a time Cat pulled out three potion vials she'd removed from Drone's shelves. Steele knocked each one to the ground, where all three smashed to pieces. Cat bit her upper lip angrily but remained silent.

"I want to see you turn the pocket out to prove it's empty," Steele said.

"There's something else in there," Cat replied.

"Give it to me."

"Very well." Cat drew out the last item and held it out for Steele's inspection.

"What is it?" Steele growled.

"Something inflexible, Master Steele," she said, inscribing a circle in the air with the small iron nail she held. At the word "inflexible" the tip of the iron bar sparked and the nail vanished.

Steel tensed to lunge, but he was transfixed by the mage's spell. He stood as still as a statue with his one hand reaching for the magically expired nail, the other still holding the knife. Cat pulled away carefully from the Wyvernspur's blade. Steel remained immobile. Hastily the mage gathered up the scrolls she'd dropped and stuffed them into a sack. She wiped the broken potion vial glass and liquid as thoroughly as she could from the cover of Gaylyn's catalog and left the book on Drone's desk.

Snatching up her fur muff, Cat backed toward the outer stair's door. "Apparently that's one trick you didn't learn from your uncle, hmmm, Master Steele? Mages call it 'hold person,' spell component, a small piece of straight iron."

Cat laughed and was turning toward the door when something heavy cracked across her temple. The blow felt as if a fireball had exploded in her skull and left a fire raging there.

Cat collapsed to her knees as a woman's voice said, "We know the trick 'hold mage,' though. Spell component, a stout stick."

Cat felt a pinprick at her throat.

"This pin's coated with poison. If it breaks your skin, you'll be dead," the woman's voice warned. "Now, release Steele," she demanded.

Despite the agonizing pain in her head, the mage managed to recall the magic word. "Willow," she whispered.

Steele sprang back to life, half falling forward, jabbing at the empty air with his knife. He caught himself and straightened up. "Good work, Julia," he said. "You managed to tear yourself from your peasant lover, I see," he added with a sneer. "You've hobbled up here just in time."

Julia, Steele's sister, Cat remembered. She must be as crazy as he is, the mage thought. Julia drew her poison pin away from Cat's throat, but Cat remained kneeling on the floor. The fire in her skull made any movement too excruciating, and the light in the room was too bright to open her eyes.

"Aunt Dorath's been looking for you everywhere," Julia said anxiously. "She'll check up here any minute now. You are going to catch Nine Hells if she finds you here. You know she's put the room off-limits."

"Nothing will be off-limits to me in a moment," Steele said. He pointed at Cat. "Check her pockets. She's Giogi's little ass. She has the spur."

"What are you talking about?" Julia asked.

"Just do as I say," Steele ordered.

Using the large staff she'd used to club the mage, Julia lowered herself clumsily to one knee. Keeping her poison pin pointed at Cat, Julia ran her hands through the folds of the mage's gown until she came on an item. Julia drew out a silk scarf wrapped around a lumpy bundle—the amulet of protection against scrying and detection.

Through clenched teeth Cat growled, "My amulet."

Slipping her pin into the bodice of her gown, Julia stood and unwrapped the material. "Eeeew," she said, sniffing at the contents of the scarf with disgust. From the five pieces of dried, cured meat she selected the largest chunk. It was the size and shape of a baby zucchini, and uglier than a three-month-old sausage. "Steele! It is!" she cried excitedly. "It's the spur!"

Steele strode forward, but Julia stepped back, pulling out her poison pin and holding it out warningly.

"You can't fool me, Sister, dear. I know you don't have poison on that pin. You're too tender-hearted."

"I do have the sleeping sap you gave me, though, which works just as well for my purposes. I helped you, Steele. Remember what you promised," she demanded.

"Yes, yes. All right. Now give me the spur."

"On your honor as a Wyvernspur, swear it."

Steele huffed. "On my honor as a Wyvernspur, you have my permission to marry any jackass you please. It could be a Calimshan merchant for all I care. Now hand the spur over."

Cat opened her eyes against the stinging light just in time to watch the spur tossed across the room. It looked like a piece of brown, dried meat someone had kept in a knapsack for a few years too long. Steele snatched it from the air. His laughter sounded like Flattery's.

Frefford burst into the room. "What is going on here?" he hissed. "Aunt Dorath said she heard glass breaking."

Gaylyn came in behind her husband. "Julia, you shouldn't have climbed all the way up here with your ankle. It could get worse . . ." Gaylyn's chiding died on her lips and she blanched when she spotted Cat kneeling on the floor.

Frefford looked down at what had upset his wife. "Mistress Cat, are you all right?" he asked, dropping to his knees beside the mage. "What happened?"

"Hit on the head," Cat muttered. Her head throbbed too much to say more, but she rose shakily to her feet with the Wyvernspur lord's assistance.

Gaylyn, aghast, stared at the pin in Julia's hand. "Julia, what have you done?" she gasped.

"Steele's found the spur," Julia said, pointing at her brother as if his discovery would explain everything.

"And now its power will be all mine," Steele declared.

"Steele, it doesn't work that way," Gaylyn insisted, trying to keep her voice calm and steady. "Uncle Drone explained it to me the night before he died. Only one of the guardian's favorites can use the spur safely. Put it down, please."

Cat focused on the spur. It was ugly for an artifact, but its power was already obvious. Blue sparks were shooting from its surface between the fingers of Steele's fist.

"Oh, no," Steele said. "I'm not buying that silly story, Gaylyn, dear. The guardian is a family myth only someone as foolish as Giogi could possibly believe in. I am not letting that idiot get his hands on the spur. I don't care if Drone wanted to give it to him. I found it. It's mine."

Steele held the spur with both hands and raised it above his head. "I can feel its power already," he said. The blue sparks were now bolts of blue light, which flickered down Steele's arm.

Aunt Dorath huffed into the room and pushed past Frefford and his wife. Like a mother who'd found her little child playing with a dagger, Aunt Dorath fixed Steele with a hard glare. "Steele Wyvernspur, you put that thing down this instant," she commanded angrily.

Steele just laughed. His arms began to glow blue, and the light bolts spread down his torso.

"It's happening. The power is mine. I can do anything." Steele jumped up to the shattered window's sill.

"Steele, no!" Julia screamed.

"Watch this, Sister, dear," he said gleefully. He pushed open the broken window's casement and spread his arms wide.

"Fluff-fluff," Cat whispered just as the Wyvernspur leaped from the tower.

Aunt Dorath and Frefford dashed to the window. "He's just floating down!" Frefford gasped.

"What?" Julia cried. "Then it works? The spur works?"

Cat bolted for the door and dashed down the outer staircase. Behind her she could hear Aunt Dorath shout, "Frefford, get down after Steele! Get that cursed thing away from him!"

Cat felt dizzy and sick, but she was not going to let an insane kobold-torturer get away with her prize. Because of her spell, Steele was falling with the resistance of a feather, so it would take him at least a minute to reach the ground.

The mage raced from the manor house and rushed to the corner tower. She stood at the base of the tower as Steele drifted toward her. He was still cackling about the power of the spur and flapping his arms, oblivious to the fact that he was really falling.

When his feet touched the earth and he was finally released from her feather fall spell, he wheeled to face her, his eyes wide with crazed rage. "Die!" he shrieked, swiping in her direction with his hand cramped like an animal claw, although he was not close enough to actually reach her.

Cat sprinkled sand over an imaginary baby in her arms and whispered, "Lullaby, Steele."

The Wyvernspur slid fast asleep, into the slush and mud. Cat pounced on him and tore the spur from his hands.

All this time, she thought, I was expecting some shiny piece of metal, something that can be attached to a boot and used as a prod. What does the spur turn out to be? A disgusting piece of shriveled, mummified—ugh—someone actually slashed it off a wyvern's foot.

A shadow fell across her and the snoozing Steele.

Frefford stood over her, offering a hand to help her up.

"I'm taking this to Giogi," Cat muttered, backing away from

Frefford on her knees.

"Well, now, it would be foolish for me to argue with such a battle-hardened and powerful spell-caster, wouldn't it?" Frefford said, grinning as he looked her up and down.

Cat was suddenly aware of how comical she must appear, with her gown scorched by fire and covered with mud and a lump the size of an egg on the side of her head. Despite herself, she laughed. She held her hand out and let Frefford pull her to her feet.

"I have a horse saddled and waiting in the stable," the nobleman said. "Bronder," he hailed a passing servant, "have Sash bring out Poppy, and be quick about it."

The servant scurried off to the stable.

Cat studied Frefford with amazement. "You really aren't interested in possessing the spur, are you?" she asked.

Frefford shrugged. "You heard Gaylyn. Giogi's the only one who can use it. Aunt Dorath doesn't want him to, but that's really for Giogi to decide, isn't it?"

Cat felt dizzy for a moment and touched the lump on her forehead. Far above them, Dorath shouted down, "Frefford? Did you get it?"

"How's your head?" Frefford asked, ignoring his aunt.

"If it were a horse, I'd have to put it to sleep," Cat groused. "I didn't know I had the spur," she explained. "Someone else gave it to me. I thought it was something else . . ." Her voice trailed off.

"Are you sure you're up to riding?" Frefford asked.

"Yes," Cat insisted. "Why are you being so nice and understanding about this?" she asked.

Frefford grinned. "You could turn out to be a relative someday. We Wyvernspurs stick together, don't you know."

"How did you know—" Cat bit back her words. He didn't know she was a Wyvernspur. He was thinking of her in terms of Giogi. She could feel the blood rushing to her face.

"You're sure you feel up to riding? You look a little flushed," Frefford teased.

"You don't understand," she said. "This is serious. There's a wizard, Flattery. He killed your Uncle Drone. He'll kill Giogi to get the spur from him. He doesn't even want Giogi visiting the Temple of Selune to find out anything about it."

"Once Giogi has the spur, I don't think anyone will be able to take it from him," Frefford said calmly. "It will be a simple matter for him to bring this Flattery to justice. As for the Temple of Selune—Giogi's already there by now. You could join him. Mother Lleddew serves a lovely tea in the open air."

Frefford pointed northwest over the fields. "The temple's on Spring Hill—that big hill there. There's a shortcut to the west side of town if you follow the footpath down the north slope of this hill instead of the road into town," Frefford explained. "The road to the temple comes before the road to the graveyard."

A stableboy, leading a chestnut mare with a black snip, approached Frefford. His Lordship helped the mage into the side-saddle and handed her the reins. "It's a nice day for a ride, but you'd better hurry before Aunt Dorath gets down here," he said and smacked the horse into a trot.

Cat bounced out of the castle's front gate feeling nauseated. She couldn't remember the last time she'd been on a horse. Before she'd been kidnapped in Zhentil Keep, she guessed. Has riding unsettled me this much before? she wondered.

Once outside the castle walls, Cat followed the path that Frefford had recommended. From the hillside, she could look out across most of the Wyvernspur lands. A dark gray cloud loomed over Spring Hill. Huge birds of death circled beneath the cloud.

Vultures in for the kill, Cat thought, her queasy stomach turning to ice.

Fearing she might already be too late, Cat urged her horse into a canter, but the sensation of being unbalanced as the beast sped down the hill was too unpleasant. She slowed the horse to a walk. Her heart was pounding hard, but she still didn't know what she was going to do.

Ruskettle lied about the amulet of protection. Flattery could be watching me this very moment. I could take him the spur, but if Ruskettle did tell the truth about seeing a dark crystal being stolen from Flattery's pocket, he has nothing to offer me—except my miserable life.

If I take the spur to Giogi, though, can he really use it to defeat Flattery? Or, if not, can he at least weaken Flattery enough to give me an opportunity to search for the memory crystal in case Flattery does still have it?

An eerie keening wafted across the fields. Cat looked up at Spring Hill. A brilliant white light flickered at the top. A moment later, a shimmering fog rolled down from the hilltop. Cat kept her eyes on the hilltop, still letting her horse plod along. When she saw the bolt of white light shoot from the hilltop, though, her fear for Giogi outweighed her fear of falling off the horse. She kicked it into a trot, and then into a gallop.

* * * * *

Olive held the brake just enough to keep the carriage from passing out of the shimmering fog, taking advantage of the protection it offered them. Undead lay on either side of the road, unmoving. The fog stopped at the bottom of the hill.

The carriage squelched through the field road. Olive spotted a large brown bear clawing at something out in the tall grass, but she had no desire to investigate any closer. She presumed it was one of Mother Lleddew's chums taking care of an undead creature that had managed to escape the fog.

Olive looked over at Giogi with concern. He was leaning back with his eyes closed. He was pale and bruised and bleeding. "You don't look so good," she said. She tied the reins up, letting the horses set their own pace down the road, and turned to check the nobleman's wounds.

"I don't think I was cut out to be an adventurer," Giogi muttered. "It hurts too much."

Olive laughed. "But you were great," she insisted. She sliced a piece off the bottom of his cape, folded it up, and pressed it against a gash in his neck. "Press on that," she ordered.

Giogi obeyed, but he had to disagree with the halfling's assessment. "I nearly got Mother Lleddew killed."

"She'll be fine. Werebears heal fast, and they're harder to kill than people. Did you know she was a werebear?" Olive asked.

"No, of course not. How can a werebear be a priestess?"

"It's traditional for lycanthropes to worship the moon," Olive said with a shrug. "Even priests need hobbies."

Alerted by the sound of a galloping horse, Olive looked across the fields again. "I think that's Cat," she said, pointing to a just barely mounted rider.

Giogi opened his eyes. "It is. She's riding Poppy." The nobleman reached over and pulled back on the horses' reins, stopping the carriage.

Cat came charging up to them. She pulled back too hard on

Poppy's reins and set the mare rearing on her hind legs. The mage toppled from her saddle and into the muddy field. Giogi leaped from the carriage and rushed to the woman's side.

"Obviously he doesn't hurt as bad as he thought he did," Olive muttered. She climbed down from the driver's seat and scrambled up the carriage door to check on their passenger. Mother Lleddew remained in her bear form. A good sign, Olive knew, since lycanthropes turned human when they died. The bear brushed its nose with a paw. She's just sleeping off the pain, Olive decided.

"I'm fine," Cat moaned as Giogi bent over her. "I just forgot," she said as he helped her to her feet, "that I don't know how to ride."

Giogi grinned until he caught sight of the bruise on her temple. "What happened? Who hit you?" he demanded angrily.

"Your fool Cousin Julia, trying to rescue her fool brother, Steele. I should have let him fall to the base of the tower, but, as you keep saying, we Wyvernspurs have to stick together. Giogi, don't fuss. It was a very soft stick. Here. This is for you," Cat concluded, holding up the spur for Giogi to see.

"You found it!" Giogi shouted. "You clever, clever woman." He picked the mage up by the waist and twirled her around. When he set her back down, he kissed her on the cheek.

"Would you please take it away," Cat asked. "You never told me it was this ugly."

Giogi laughed and took the spur from the mage. "It is, isn't it?" he agreed, holding it up to his face. "Where was it?"

"You'd better ask Mistress Ruskettle," Cat suggested.

Giogi turned around and faced Olive with confusion, holding the spur out for her to see.

Olive looked at the artifact with a bit of confusion of her own. She'd presumed, as Cat had, that the spur would be a metal prod to strap around one's ankle to spur wyverns into the air or something. It took her several moments to recognize the hunk of mummified flesh as one of the pieces of dried meat she'd tied into the bundle she'd given Cat.

The halfling had some explaining to do, she realized. Olive needed time to figure out what to explain first. She looked up into the clear blue sky. "How about you tuck that away, and as soon as we're safe indoors, I'll explain about the spur," she promised. "Flattery could always fly over in the shape of a bird or something."

Giogi looked up nervously. The sky was empty. The lone cloud that had shaded Spring Hill had vanished. He didn't see any birds. Still, he was inclined to take Olive's suggestion. "I'll tie Poppy to the back of the carriage, so you can ride with us," he said to Cat.

"Can't you explain on the way?" Cat asked Olive with pseudo-innocence.

"No," Olive said. "I think I'd better stay in back with Mother Lleddew. She's not well."

"Mother Lleddew? What's wrong with her?" Cat asked anxiously. She peered into the carriage window and pulled back quickly. "Giogi," she whispered, "there's a bear in there."

"Don't worry, dear," Olive said. "She'll sleep it off. If you would be so kind as to open the door for me, we can be off."

Once they were all loaded back on the carriage, Giogi and Cat on the driver's seat, Olive inside with Mother Lleddew, and Poppy clopping along behind, Olive began racking her brain for exactly what she would tell Giogi and Cat. At the same time, she kept an ear on the conversation between the nobleman and the mage.

"I thought it was some sort of metal spur, such as for a horse," Cat said. "It's been sliced off a real wyvern's foot, though, hasn't it?" she asked.

"Yes," Giogi said. "It was a gift from a female wyvern to Paton Wyvernspur for rescuing her children. She sliced it off her dead mate."

Yuck! Olive thought inside the carriage.

"Yick!" Cat exclaimed. "How gruesome."

"Well, yes. Speaking of gruesome, are you sure you're all right? That's a nasty bump you've got there," Giogi said.

"You should talk," the mage laughed. "You're three colors that humans don't generally come in," she said, poking at a large bruise on his cheek. "You're bleeding, too. What happened?"

"We ran into a few undead," Giogi said with a shrug. "Nothing we couldn't handle. The potions you gave us helped a lot, though."

Olive mentally amended: An army of undead that we beat only with help from a werebear and a goddess's powerful minion. And the potions helped only as long as the right type of undead attacked us.

"So, how was your afternoon? Giogi asked the mage.

Cat related the events at Redstone in detail.

Giogi looked astonished by her story. "Is that all?" he asked with mock ennui.

"Is that all?" Cat echoed. "No. One more thing."

"What?"

"I missed you," the mage admitted.

"Really?" Giogi asked, feeling his heart pounding in his chest.

Olive shifted uneasily inside the carriage. Despite the mage having loyally handed the spur over to Giogi, Olive could not trust her. She hadn't leveled with Giogi about being Flattery's wife, but she continued to flirt with him. The halfling had first-hand experience at betraying people. She couldn't help thinking that Cat still had some sort of scheme in mind that required Giogi's cooperation.

❦ 18 ❦

Mother Lleddew's Tale

From the Journal of Giogioni Wyvernspur:

The 21st of Ches, in the year of the Shadows

While it seems like an age ago, it was only the day before yesterday when our family heirloom was stolen, and it was only yesterday that my Uncle Drone died—foully murdered, as I now suspect, by the evil wizard Flattery. The spur has been returned by the remarkable Harper bard, Olive Ruskettle, who has suffered the loss of her partner, Jade More, at Flattery's hand.

Mistress Ruskettle is still uncertain of the details, but she believes Jade removed the spur from our family crypt at the request of my Uncle Drone, convinced as he was that I was destined to use the spur. Jade, Mistress Ruskettle has explained, was a Wyvernspur from the same lost line as the mage Cat, which my Uncle Drone must somehow have known, or he would not have sent Jade in to face the guardian. One other attribute made Jade perfect for the task—apparently she could not be detected magically, which would have kept the spur's location a secret as long as she held on to it.

Mistress Ruskettle claims Cat also possesses this remarkable undetectability, which is why she hid the spur on Cat early this morning, disguised as a magical amulet. Jade gave the spur to Mistress Ruskettle moments before being killed, but it took the bard a day to discover that she was carrying the most sought-after item in Immersea. She has apologized for not trusting me with its location sooner, but she feared that once I knew it was safe I would abandon my quest to learn its power and neglect my responsibility to use it. I cannot deny that she might have been right.

Having fought my way through Flattery's minions to reach Mother Lleddew, I would feel rather foolish now not asking about the spur. I have an uneasy suspicion that I may need her knowledge not only to ensure the spur's safety but my family's safety as well.

Giogi laid his quill down on the desk and put his head in his hands. While he shared Olive Ruskettle's thirst for justice and had no intention of backing down on his promise to do all he could to help her, he felt uncertain that he could really bring himself to use the spur.

There had to be something bad about the artifact if Aunt Dorath believed it to be cursed. Moreover, the fact that a wizard as evil as Flattery desired its power for his own did not bode well concerning the nature of that power. Hopefully Mother Lleddew could shed light on the mystery of the spur—perhaps on Flattery as well—as soon as she recovered from her wounds sufficiently to speak.

* * * * *

Olive sat all alone in the dining room of Giogi's townhouse, wolfing down tea and crumpets. Giogi was in the parlor, scribbling in his journal. Cat was still changing into something clean. And Mother Lleddew, who had shaken off her bear shape before they'd arrived home, was still resting in the guest room.

The halfling leaned back and sighed with satisfaction. After helping Mother Lleddew to her room, Olive had managed to present Giogi with a brilliant explanation for having the spur and for giving it to Cat. It was an explanation that not only concealed her own ignorance of the spur's appearance but convinced Giogi that her motives were completely noble. Cat hadn't seemed too pleased with her story, but it had satisfied Giogi completely.

The door to the hallway opened, and Mother Lleddew stood on the threshold. With her massive frame, thick black hair, taut muscles, and shy eyes, her human appearance was still rather bearlike. She wore only her brown shift and leather sandals, but the dirt had been brushed from them, and as a further concession to society she'd tied her mane of hair back with a ribbon.

Few people could make Giogi's house look small the way she does, Olive thought. The priestess walked stiffly into the room, though—not as spry as she'd been when engaged in combat. It was obvious that, despite the power her were-nature granted her, Mother Lleddew was a very old woman. Her face appeared all the more drawn and haggard for the wrinkles in it, and she twitched from aches and twinges in her muscles. She could heal the injuries she'd received in battle, but she would never recover from the ravages of time.

Alerted by the sound of the priestess's tread, Thomas bustled into the dining room from the kitchen. "Master Giogioni asks that you not wait on his account, Your Grace," the servant said as he pulled out a chair for the priestess.

Mother Lleddew sat and held her hands in her lap until Thomas finished pouring the tea. She dolloped honey into her drink and stirred it very carefully, sneaking a look at Olive, then back at her tea without speaking.

Finally, after a fourth furtive glance, she spoke. "I'm pleased to meet you at last, Olive Ruskettle," she said. Her voice was almost too soft to hear. "Sudacar tells me you sing a song about Selûne."

"Um, yes," Olive answered with surprise. "The Tears of Selune. A friend of mine wrote it."

"The Shard said it's been too long since it was sung in the Realms."

"It's sung other places than the Realms?" Olive asked.

"Other Shards sing it for Selûne."

"Really?" Olive's head swam. The Harpers ban all of Nameless's music for centuries, and the gods listen to it anyway, she thought with amusement. Nameless would be pleased to hear that. Then again, that could be just a little too much for his ego to handle.

"My friend probably wrote that song here in Immersea," the halfling told the priestess. "He was a Wyvernspur, you see."

Mother Lleddew held her teacup with both hands and sipped slowly, keeping her eyes on the drink. She kept glancing at Olive without speaking.

At first, the halfling thought Lleddew just couldn't think of anything to say and wondered if she shouldn't try to carry the conversation herself. It dawned on Olive after a few minutes, though, that Lleddew was a little like Dragonbait, the Saurial paladin. He didn't need words to communicate and could judge people by their silences, too. So Olive just smiled and bit into another biscuit the next time she caught the priestess looking at her.

Giogi came in with Cat on his arm. He was decked out in a tabard bearing his family coat of arms, a green wyvern on a field of yellow, and the small platinum headpiece around his forehead. Cat wore a green silk gown. The gown would not lace tight enough to fit her shapely form, so the mage had wrapped a yellow sash around her waist.

The couple's color coordination did not bode well, to Olive's way of thinking. Giogi was letting himself in for a lot of heartache. She thought of the nobleman's ironic insistence that he would want to know if a woman he was involved with was "not so capital."

The mage looked happy beside the nobleman, but anyone who could take one of Flattery's blows calmly would have to be a superior actress. Olive wondered which had more to do with Cat's returning the spur to Giogi, his kindness and generosity or fear of returning to Flattery.

Giogi bowed very deeply to Mother Lleddew.

"Giogioni, it is good to see you," the priestess said. "I feared once that I might never see you again."

Giogi rose and flushed. "I regret not having come to visit you before," he stammered.

Mother Lleddew looked curiously at Cat, the priestess's head tilted to one side in expectation.

"Allow me to present the mage Cat of Ordulin, Your Grace," Giogi said.

Cat curtsied low and looked up at Mother Lleddew with wide-eyed awe. Olive couldn't help but remember how Alias thought of all priests as fools. Did Cat think differently, or was this a display for Giogi's sake?

The priestess motioned for both young people to be seated. "How is your Aunt Dorath?" Mother Lleddew asked.

"Um, fine," Giogi answered with some surprise. He pulled a chair out for Cat to sit, then seated himself. When he looked up again at the priestess, she still had an expectant look in her eyes, so he continued. "She's seems overjoyed to be a great-grandaunt. She likes taking care of the baby, apparently."

The priestess nodded. "Poor Dorath," she whispered, looking down at her teacup.

"I didn't know you even knew my aunt."

"We were very close once," Mother Lleddew said. "Her mother and I adventured together."

"Great-grandmother Eswip was an adventurer?" Giogi gasped.

"Oh, yes. Perhaps, Master Giogioni, I should start my tale in the middle. The beginning is very interesting, and just as sad, but it is the middle and the end of the tale that Flattery does not wish you to know. He has nearly exhausted his forces of undead trying to keep you from meeting with me. Now that we have overcome those obstacles, I should tell my tale without further delay."

"You know about Flattery?" Giogi asked.

"Not just about him, Giogioni. I know him. I watched him kill your father."

Giogi turned pale and clenched his fists. Cat looked numb.

Somehow, that doesn't surprise me in the least, Olive thought, remembering the scorched portrait in the carriage house, and how Flattery had screamed, "Curse them all!" meaning all Wyvernspurs.

Since no one spoke, Mother Lleddew began the middle of her tale. "When your father first learned he could use the power of the spur," she said, "he announced to me his intention to go adventuring to find a fortune that would finish the temple his grandmother and I had begun. I was too old by then to go tramping about the countryside bashing monsters, but Cole would go whether I joined him or not, and for the love I had for his grandmother, I agreed to accompany him. I thought I would be keeping him from harm." Lleddew chuckled at the irony of her intentions.

"Your father didn't want keeping from harm, though," she said with a grin. "With the spur's power, he was nearly indestructible. We spent a summer season in Gnoll Pass—that was long before His Majesty started building Castle Crag to station the Purple Dragoons. When we finally returned to Immersea, we were carrying enough wealth to embed diamonds in the ceiling of the House of Selune."

"But what was the spur's power?" Giogi asked.

"Dorath would not let Drone tell you even this, would she?"

"Tell me what? Please, tell me," Giogi asked.

"Each generation the guardian chooses a favorite," Mother Lleddew explained. "The favorites can use the spur to shape-shift into the form of a wyvern. A very large wyvern."

"A wyvern. My father could turn into a wyvern. You mean he fought as—as a wyvern?"

"Of course," Cat said to herself. "Wyverns can fly. It's a wyvern's spur."

"But why did Flattery go to so much trouble to keep me from meeting you and learning that?" Giogi asked.

"It is the rest of my story that Flattery did not wish you to hear," Mother Lleddew explained.

"Oh, sorry. Please, continue," Giogi said.

"The next spring, your father went out again, but, having seen him in action, I did not feel a need to accompany him. He could take care of himself. He built himself a reputation throughout Cormyr, though he kept his wyvern form a secret for the most part. He might have traveled further and grown more famous, but he met and married your mother at the end of his second summer season, and he did not like to leave her for long. He only left Immersea to accomplish such services in Cormyr as the crown requested of him.

"Then, one day, fourteen years ago, late in the fall, after your father had returned home from a summer journey, a small tribe of elves passed through Immersea. They were refugees from a settlement in the Border Forest. A terrible wizard had come out of Anauroch, the Great Desert, and stolen their riches, destroyed their city, and enslaved many of their people.

"When these elves saw your father, they went mad with hatred and attacked him. They mistook him for the wizard, you see. Of course, your father's companions restrained them and convinced them after much arguing that he was not this evil image.

"Cole realized, however, that the wizard must be a lost Wyvernspur. The family honor was at stake, so he thought, and he swore he would set things right, vanquish this wizard, and return what had been stolen to the elves. Two of the elves agreed to guide him back to their homeland and lead him to the wizard's fortress.

"Your mother had many horrible premonitions. Just for him to be traveling in the fall and winter was dangerous enough. That he was planning to attack a powerful wizard drove her to distraction. When she could not talk him out of it, she begged me to accompany him.

"There were nine of us, including your father and the elves. We made good time to Shadow Gap and beat the snows. The people of Daggerdale were most inhospitable, so we pressed on quickly through that land as well. At length, we reached the Border Forest and the elven settlement.

"Our elven guides, and indeed all of us, wished we had never seen the remains of the elvish city. Flattery had turned all the enslaved elves into zombies and left them in the city to guard it as an outpost of his desert kingdom.

"The Wyvernspur family resemblance was our greatest asset. Mistaking Cole for their new master, the undead let us pass through the city unharmed. Thus we approached Flattery's fortress unheralded.

"The fortress was only half the size of Immersea, but its walls were twice as high as Suzail's. Only Flattery lived within, waited upon by undead. Cole deceived the zombies at the gate as easily as the ones in the elvish city, so we were able to enter Flattery's stronghold and destroy many of his servants before he was even aware of our presence.

"We cornered the wizard alone, and Cole demanded to know Flattery's father's name. Flattery laughed and declared his father would remain nameless unless Cole agreed to single combat. Cole accepted, engaging the power of the spur to change his shape and taking to the air. The sun had not yet risen, but we could watch the battle in the early dawn light."

When the priestess paused for a moment, Olive took the opportunity to interrupt with a question. "Excuse me, Mother Lleddew. Was that the exact phrase Flattery used—his father would remain nameless?"

Mother Lleddew nodded. "Yes. An odd choice of words, isn't it?" she asked.

Quick on the uptake, Giogi asked, "Mistress Ruskettle, are you thinking of the Nameless Bard you mentioned in your tale about Alias?"

Olive nodded, but waved her hand to defer any more of Giogi's questions. "Let Mother Lleddew continue her story. Sorry for the interruption, Mother Lleddew," she said.

The priestess nodded and launched into a description of the battle between Flattery and Giogi's father. "Flattery first cast a lightning bolt at Cole, but the shot went wide. Then Flattery cast a wall of fire in the air, but Cole easily evaded it. The mage attempted a third spell as Cole swooped down upon him, but it had no effect that any of us could discern. You see, in addition to transforming Cole into a wyvern, the spur made him immune to magic cast against him.

"Cole snatched the wizard from the ground and flew high, stinging and biting Flattery until the wizard ceased his struggling. It looked as if Cole had won, but then . . ."

Mother Lleddew closed her eyes as if she could shut out the sight of what she had already seen. "As Cole flew back toward us, a black cloud drifted toward him, moving against the wind. By the time we noticed its strange movements and shape, it was too late for Cole.

"The cloud was a pack of wraiths, fifteen or twenty in number. They may have been acting on their own, but I believe Flattery summoned them, and in doing so broke the rules of single combat. Whichever is the truth, the wraiths fell upon Cole as a single body. Your father shrieked from their icy, life-draining touch and dropped the wizard.

"I invoked Selune to turn the undead away from your father. The wraiths fled, though possibly it was the swift sunrise that sent them away and not I.

"Cole was very weak when he landed, but he began to search for Flattery's body at once. None of us had seen the wizard land.

"Then Cole was challenged from above by a sky-blue dragon. Since his magic could not directly harm Cole, Flattery had taken a shape that could. Cole took to the sky again.

"With all the wounds the wizard had taken in the first combat, and from the awkward way Flattery fought, we did not think he would win. But the wraiths had drained more of Cole's energy than we'd realized. Still, the battle seemed evenly matched, until another set of Flattery's minions interfered.

"Ju-ju zombies, more powerful than most, fired upon Cole with crossbows. Our party's mage cast a fireball at the undead, obliterating them before they could get off a second round.

"It was hard to see the blue dragon against the sky. He dove on Cole, and they fell earthward, tearing one another apart. At the last moment, they parted. Flattery soared off, badly wounded, but Cole crashed to the ground."

Mother Lleddew brushed tears from her eyes with the back of her hand. Giogi tried to swallow the lump in his throat.

The priestess finished her tale.

"Flattery did not return to his city, nor did we find his body. We were sure, though, that if he was not dead, he was so grievously wounded that he had fled for his life.

"Cole was dead. I would have carried his body home myself, on my own back, but he did not change back to human form at death, as a lycanthrope would. We did not know how to change him back and had no way to transport a wyvern's corpse. We had to send for Drone. We waited ten days and nights for him to arrive."

"What did Uncle Drone do?" Giogi asked.

"It was so simple, I was a fool not to have thought of it," Mother Lleddew said, shaking her head, "but it was also ghastly."

"What?" Giogi repeated.

"He sliced off the wyvern's right spur. It transformed back into the mummified spur, and Cole returned to his human form."

Giogi felt a little nauseated. Poor Uncle Drone—having to do such a gruesome thing. Of course, only Uncle Drone could have thought of that.

"I'm not sure that I want to know, but I suppose I ought to," the nobleman said with a glance at Olive. "How did my father make the spur work?"

"I'm not sure. He kept it in his boot, and whenever he needed to change, he would concentrate on it."

"Pardon me, sir," Thomas interrupted, "but you don't have the spur in your boot, do you?"

"Why, yes," Giogi said, patting his right calf, "it's right here beside the finder's stone. Why do you ask?"

"I might recommend that you avoid thinking about wyverns until you step outside. Perhaps, just to be on the safe side, you might want to leave the spur on the table for the duration of the discussion. A transformation in the house might be a trifle uncomfortable."

Giogi slid the spur from his boot and laid it beside his plate. "Good thinking, Thomas," he said. "I'd be the proverbial wyvern in an alchemist shop, eh?"

"Precisely, sir."

Giogi covered the spur with his napkin. The very idea of transforming into something else, even out-of-doors, where there was plenty of room, frightened him. It would be awful, he thought, having wings instead of arms and a horrible stinging tail, loaded with poison, and scales all over one's body. How could Cole have done it?

"Pardon me, Mother Lleddew," Olive asked. "But you said you traveled with Giogi's great-grandmother. She didn't happen to use the spur as well?"

"Yes, she did. That's the beginning of the tale. Lady Eswip's father was Lord Gould the Third. He'd used the spur himself, but he had no son and Lady Eswip proved to be the guardian's favorite. She married her Cousin Bender Wyvernspur, who inherited the family title from his Uncle Gould. They had two sons, Grever and Fortney, and a daughter, Dorath. The guardian didn't care for the boys. She chose Dorath as her favorite."

"Dorath, I take it, did not reciprocate her affection," Olive guessed.

"No," the priestess said, shaking her head. "Eswip died in combat when Dorath was still a young girl. Dorath resented the loss of her mother. Years later, the season Dorath was introduced at court, some haughty fools snubbed her. They called her the beast's daughter. When His Majesty heard about it, he had the idiots banned—Rhigaerd was always sensitive to a pretty girl's tears—but the damage had already been done. No matter that twelve generations of Wyvernspurs before her had won the crown's gratitude protecting Cormyr as wyverns. Dorath perceived the spur's powers as something vulgar and depraved and, of course, the reason her mother had died."

"That's why she didn't want anyone to know about them," Giogi said. "Why the story of the spur passed out of the Wyvernspur family."

"Worse than that," the priestess said, "that's why she never married. She struggled for years to resist the guardian's call to use the spur. It was not easy. She believed the "curse," as she called it, would be passed down to one of her children, like lycanthropy, so she swore to have no children. I could not convince her of her folly. We argued, and she stopped visiting the House of the Lady. She said my advice was tainted because of my were-nature. It must have come as a tremendous blow to her when she learned that the guardian took her Nephew Cole as the next favorite. She blamed the guardian for Cole's death, and Drone for helping the guardian."

KATE NOVAK and JEFF GRUBB

Mother Lleddew rose from the table. "I've told you all I know. I must be getting back to the temple."

"Alone? But won't it be dangerous?" Giogi objected.

"The Shard should have finished clearing away all the undead by now," the priestess said.

"Flattery could return and drop some more from that cloud," Giogi pointed out.

The priestess shook her head. "Flattery will waste no more energy on me. It is you he fears. You have the spur, you can wield its power, and now I have told you that he murdered your father. Now you know that your father would have destroyed Flattery with the spur if the wizard had not cheated in combat."

"So Giogi stands a chance, too," Olive said.

Mother Lleddew nodded. "Remember, though, that Cole was a tried and experienced fighter in the wyvern shape. I would not suggest issuing a challenge without practice."

Giogioni had no comment about fighting Flattery as a wyvern. The idea left him numb.

"I must leave now, Giogioni," Mother Lleddew insisted. "I have a memorial service to prepare for your uncle. Selune smile upon you."

Giogi snapped out of his daze and rose to his feet. He scooped up the spur and escorted the priestess from the room. Thomas followed.

"Well, well," Olive said when the dining room door had closed behind them.

"Mistress Ruskettle," Cat said, with a challenging tone to her voice, "there are still some things I don't quite understand."

"I'll do my best to explain them to you," Olive offered helpfully, secretly praying to Tymora that she could.

"I knew you would," Cat said with just a hint of sassiness. "Well, first, if your partner Jade had the spur, why did she go to the trouble of picking Flattery's pocket to see if he had it?"

"Obviously so I wouldn't suspect she had it," Olive replied. "She had hinted that she had something to tell me, but that someone else had sworn her to secrecy until it was all over. I presume the someone was Drone. I wish she had trusted me with her little family secret. She might still be alive."

Cat drummed her fingers impatiently on the table. She couldn't help feeling that there was something this halfling was keeping from her. Anxious to catch her in some falsehood, Cat launched into her next question. "If I can't be detected magically or scried, how come the divination Steele had done led him straight to my pocket?"

"Oh, but it didn't," Olive explained. "Steele had the divination done yesterday. It told him the spur was in the little ass's pocket. I know, because I was keeping tabs on Steele as well as Flattery. You didn't have the spur yesterday."

"You did," Cat recalled. She remained suspicious of whatever excuse the halfling would make.

"Yes. The divination told Steele the spur was in my pocket." Olive worked her brain overtime. Cat must not suspect she was Birdie. She had to explain why the divination had called her a little ass. "You see, I was—I am," Olive said it more firmly, "Little Ass. It's my code name among the Harpers. Fortunately, Steele doesn't know me or my code name. I presume Waukeen chose not to reveal to him where the spur was, so the divination was as obtuse as possible."

"And what was your partner Jade's code name?" Cat asked disbelievingly. "The Gold Dragon?"

"Silver Spoon," Olive snapped, looking up from the tea set. She reached again into Jade's magic pouch and pulled out the silver spoon she'd noticed that morning. She laid the spoon on the table. "Her trademark," Olive said.

Cat picked up the spoon. "J.W. Jade what?" she asked.

"Wyvernspur, of course. As I told you, she was a Wyvernspur like you, though she went more commonly as Jade More. She liked to keep her true identity a secret." Olive spoke with confidence, but to herself she wondered, What was Jade doing with a silver spoon with her initials on it—was it a gift from Drone?

Cat looked down at the table, a little less certain that the halfling had been lying to her. "Mistress Ruskettle, about that crystal you saw Jade steal from Flattery—the one as dark as a new moon? Are you sure it was destroyed? You didn't tell me that just to be sure I wouldn't go back to Flattery, did you?"

Olive searched Cat's eager face. The mage wanted that crystal badly. She'd asked Flattery about it—called it a memory crystal. "The crystal. That's what Flattery promised you if you helped him, isn't it?" Olive asked.

Cat nodded.

"Let me guess. I'll bet he told you it would restore your

memory," Olive said.

Cat gasped. "How did you know that? There was no way you could know that," she insisted angrily.

Olive wondered if she should just tell Cat the truth—that the mage had no past to remember, that she was only created last year. That would certainly loosen her dependence on Flattery—providing she believed me, Olive thought. No, she decided, this is not a good time to start telling the truth—it's just too unbelievable.

"Answer me, damn it!" Cat demanded.

Olive looked up wearily at the mage. "Jade lost her memory, too. So did Alias. You see, it's something that runs in your side of the family," she explained. "It's the only thing I could think of that would make you desperate enough to take up with someone like Flattery."

"Was the crystal really destroyed?" Cat asked.

"Yes."

Cat looked down at her lap, obviously shaken.

"I know you're not going to like this advice," Olive said, "but maybe you'd be happier if you gave up dredging your past and concentrated on your future."

Cat rose angrily to her feet. There were tears in her eyes. "What makes you think my future is worth concentrating on?" she cried.

Before Olive could answer, the mage had fled the dining room, slamming the door behind her. The halfling sighed. There really wasn't anything more she could do about Cat.

Olive reached for another crumpet, but the crumpet plate was empty. That was too much for her to bear. After all the stress she had been through the past few days, she really needed one more crumpet. She hopped down from her chair and peeked into the kitchen.

Thomas stood at the table with his back to her. Just as she was about to ask if there wasn't maybe another batch of tea cakes baking in the oven, she noticed what it was the servant was doing.

Preparing a tray of tea things. Like the tray of breakfast things. For whom? Olive asked herself. Is there a sick servant in the attic? No, in a household this small, we would have heard about it. Could Thomas have a fugitive relative? the halfling wondered. In Olive's family, fugitive relatives were not uncommon.

Why don't we have a look-see? she decided, creeping behind Giogi's gentleman's gentleman as he left the kitchen and headed upstairs.

*　*　*　*　*

Giogi stood in the back garden, watching Mother Lleddew drive off in his rented carriage back to the House of the Lady. She seemed very nice. She'd been a good friend of his parents. Still, it was a little shocking to learn she was a were-bear.

Not as shocking as the story about his father, though.

He pulled the spur from his boot and turned it over in his hands a few times. Aunt Dorath must be tearing her hair out right now, afraid that I'll use this. Or tearing Frefford's hair out for letting Cat take it to me.

He held the spur out in front of him. Wyvern, he thought, I want to be a wyvern.

He felt no different. He was not shape-shifting.

It's not working. The spur must know I don't really want to be a wyvern. Wyverns are beasts. I don't want to be a beast.

Listen to me, I'm no different than Aunt Dorath. I'll never be an adventurer like Cole. It's just not in me.

He headed toward the kitchen door to go inside, but the thought of going back into the stuffy house was unbearable. The fear of having to face Cat and Mistress Ruskettle and explain that he didn't want to be a wyvern was worse.

I need to groom Daisyeye, he thought.

Whenever he felt really depressed or uncertain, grooming a horse usually helped bring him out of it. He strode to the carriage house and slipped inside.

There was enough light coming through the window to see without lighting the lantern. It took his eyes a moment to adjust, though, from the bright outdoor sunshine. He checked on his buggy first. The rear axle was propped up on a sawhorse so that the broken wheel could be taken out for repairs. The painting that had so startled Birdie was leaning against Daisyeye's stall. Giogi had asked Thomas to leave it there until he decided whether he wanted to restore and reuse the frame.

The nobleman was reaching for the bucket of Daisyeye's brushes when he heard a muffled sob from somewhere overhead.

Hello? he thought. Who's crying in my loft?

As Giogi climbed the ladder, something rustled in the straw. As he reached the top he could see a figure moving into the shadows. He caught a glimpse of yellow silk and gleaming copper and knew who it was immediately. "Cat?" he whispered.

There was a sniff, but the figure did not move out of the shadows. Giogi swung himself into the loft and moved toward the mage. "What's wrong?" he whispered.

"Nothing," Cat answered, keeping her face turned away.

Giogi sat beside her in the hay and turned her gently by the shoulders so that she faced him. Her face was wet and her eyes were red and puffy. "Please, tell me what's wrong?"

"Nothing," the mage insisted. "Nothing worth crying over. I was just being stupid. Wanting stupid things. I've stopped now. See. I didn't mean to. I don't know what got into me. I never cry."

"Yes, you do. You cried last night, when you were frightened," Giogi reminded her.

"Oh." Cat looked down at her hands. "I'd forgotten that. You must think I'm stupid to cry."

"No, I don't. What a thing to say. Everyone cries. It's like that poem: Soldiers have their fears, something, something, something, ladies are entitled to their tears."

Cat burst into fresh sobs. Giogi pulled her to his chest and hugged her gently, whispering, "There, there, my little kittycat." Cat grew calmer.

"What's made you so sad?" Giogi asked.

"You're so nice," Cat said, sniffling.

"I could try to be meaner if it would make you happy," Giogi teased.

"No, you couldn't," Cat argued, looking up at him. "You wouldn't even know where to begin."

"Maybe not," Giogi agreed. "Would it make you cry more if I did something else nice?" he asked.

"Like what?" Cat asked.

Giogi lowered his lips over the mage's and kissed her slowly. Since she didn't start crying again, he kissed her again, longer.

"There. That didn't depress you too badly, now did it?"

"No," the mage admitted. "It wasn't stupid, either."

"Not if you liked it," Giogi said.

"And I can cry if I like, can't I?"

"Of course, but I'd rather see you smile." He began kissing her again, but she turned away and started to cry. "Cat, what is wrong? You have to tell me, darling."

Through her sobs Cat stammered, "Flattery told me crying was stupid, and kissing was stupid, and, and, other things I wanted were stupid. For the longest time, I believed everything he said, but he was lying, wasn't he?"

"Flattery is a vile monster," Giogi said hotly, "and the sooner you forget about him, the better. You won't ever have to see him again."

"You don't understand. He's my master—"

"Rubbish. You don't need a master. I can protect you."

Cat pulled away. "No, Giogi, you can't. You have to let me finish explaining. I have to tell you. He's my master, and I was afraid not to do everything he told me." Cat hesitated, obviously afraid to tell him what she thought he should know.

A cold fear seized Giogi. He swallowed. "Cat, what did you do?" he whispered.

"I married him."

Giogi sat, stunned. Immense relief mingled with acute heartache. He couldn't choose which to focus on first.

"I didn't know about all the people he killed," Cat said.

Giogi took a deep breath and asked, "Did you love him?"

"No."

Giogi breathed out.

"It doesn't matter, though. I consented."

"Of course it matters, and a vow made under duress is not valid."

"He didn't threaten me, Giogi. I was just afraid of him."

"What were you afraid of?"

Cat shrugged. "That he would sell me back as a slave to the Zhentil Keep army or turn me into one of his zombies or feed me to his ghouls."

"Oh, is that all?" Giogi asked, astonished at the horror in which she must have lived under the wizard's rule.

"Yes. I didn't want to die. I'm not afraid of being hit, but I am afraid to die."

"He hit you?" the nobleman shouted, rising to his feet.

Cat cringed, startled by Giogi's anger.

Giogi slammed his fist into an overhead beam. The wizard's villainy had no bounds. Someone had to stop him.

"I'm sorry," Cat whispered.

Giogi looked down at the cowering woman and felt ashamed of having frightened her. He took her hands in his own and brought her to her feet. "Don't be a little ass," he whispered. He kissed her on her forehead. "Come back to the house with me," he said.

Cat let Giogi lead her down the ladder and out of the carriage house. She walked alongside him through the garden, and he held the front door open for her as she entered the house. The couple hurried to the parlor, where it was warm. It was some time before they thought of Olive and wondered where she was.

*   *   *   *   *

This is such a nice house for sneaking around in, Olive thought as she crept down the upstairs hallway after Thomas. Ought to make it a law—every wealthy house should have thick carpeting. She wished Jade were with her so she could share that joke with her.

Olive stood behind the attic door, listening to Thomas tread up the stairs. Third and fifth steps are a might creaky, she noted.

She opened the attic door a crack. The stairs were clear. She slipped into the stairwell and padded up the first two steps, tested the third along the side where there was less stress, climbed it and the next and then froze to listen.

She could hear Thomas's voice, quiet but clear.

"He's found it."

Olive didn't hear a reply.

Thomas asked, "Is it time yet?"

Speak louder, Olive thought.

"But he might use the spur," Thomas said with a touch of alarm.

Olive crept up the next two steps.

"Do you think that's really wise, sir?" Thomas asked.

He is not talking to a relative of his, Olive realized.

Something soft brushed against the halfling's legs and Olive nearly toppled down the stairs. A black-and-white spotted cat looked up at the halfling and meowed loudly. If it isn't one cat, it's another, Olive growled inwardly. She shooed the beast away, and it went scampering up the stairs.

Thomas did not say anything for at least thirty heartbeats, and Olive grew nervous. Some sixth sense warned her it was time to sneak off. She slipped down the stairs. Just as she reached for the door handle, she heard someone above who was not Thomas utter the word, "Secure."

Olive twisted the doorknob, but the door did not open.

The sound of footfalls crossed the attic floor toward the staircase. Olive spun around and looked up the steep staircase. At the top stood a now-too-familiar figure wearing wizard's robes. "Mistress Ruskettle, you can't be thinking of leaving us so soon. I've been so wanting to meet you."

Olive turned back to the door and pounded and kicked on it. "Giogi!" she screamed. "It's Flattery! Help! Giogi!"

"Static," the wizard whispered, pointing an iron nail at the halfling.

Olive felt all her muscles stiffen at once. She stood frozen with her face and clenched fists leaning against the wood.

"Fetch her up, Thomas," the wizard ordered, "and I'll see to her." The wizard clucked once. "So clever but so much trouble. Just like the other woman in my life."

❧ 19 ❧

Wyvern and Wizard

Thomas finished shoveling the ashes out of the fireplace of the lilac room and laid a fresh fire for his master's guest. He picked up his shovel and ash bucket and left the room. As he descended the stairs to the front hall, he heard a commotion in the parlor. It sounded as if someone were looting the room. Setting down his ash bucket and brandishing his shovel like a club, the servant crept to the parlor door and opened it just a crack.

Giogioni stood by the open bookshelves with a book in his hand. Scattered all about him, on the chairs, the ottomans, the sofa, the tea table, and the floor, were most of the bookshelves' contents—manuscripts and bound books of every shape and size. Journals kept by Wyvernspur ancestors, histories written about the family, tomes about magic, and catalogs of monsters, had all been rifled through and discarded in a most unceremonious fashion. As Thomas watched, Giogioni frowned and tossed one book angrily across the room before snatching up another.

The mage Cat sat at the writing desk, reading more carefully through books Giogi had discarded.

Thomas knocked and stepped into the room.

"Ah, Thomas, have you seen Mistress Ruskettle? She might be interested in lending a hand here."

"I believe she had some personal business to attend to, sir," Thomas said. "No doubt she'll return before dinner. Is there something particular I could help you find, sir?" he asked.

"Yes, Thomas," Giogi snapped, "how to turn into a wyvern. I can't believe with all the junk written by and about our family, no one took the trouble to record how it's done. Should I ever find out, I most certainly shall write it down."

"I presume, sir, that you have already tried concentrating on the transformation."

"I have. It was a complete bust."

"I'm so sorry, sir. I was under the impression, however, that your interest was academic and not urgent."

"Yes, well, I've changed my mind. Thomas, haven't we got a trunk of books in the attic?"

"Yes, sir, but they're all poetry and romances, hardly the sort to hold the information you seek."

"You never know. Something might have been slipped between the pages or scribbled in the margins of a particularly favorite adventure. Don't bother yourself. I'll fetch them down myself." He moved toward the door.

Thomas neatly intercepted his master before he left the room. "Actually, sir, if you are really intent on discovering this information, there is a knowledgeable primary source you ought to consult."

"What?"

"Not a what, sir. Who, sir. The she-beast."

"Aunt Dorath. Yes, she might know, but she would never tell me," Giogi said.

"No, sir. I did not mean your aunt. I was referring to the guardian," Thomas explained.

"Oh," Giogi said. A cold, hardness settled in the pit of his stomach.

"According to legend," Thomas reminded him, "the guardian is the spirit of the wyvern Paton Wyvernspur aided. She gave him the spur. It stands to reason that she would have been the one to instruct him as to its use and such."

"He's right," Cat said, looking up from her book.

Giogi set the book he was holding back on a shelf. There was no escaping. It was inevitable. He would have to go to the guardian, speak to her, and listen to her talk about awful things.

"Giogi, do you want me to come with you?" Cat asked.

Giogi looked down at the mage's lovely face. It's not like Aunt Dorath thinks, Giogi told himself. I'm not being seduced by some demon. I'm choosing to do this, for Cat's sake, for the family's sake. Someone must deal with Flattery. If I'm the only one who can use the spur, then I will just have to use it.

"Giogi, do you want me to come with you?" Cat asked again.

"No. I had better go alone. It shouldn't take too long. I'll be back before dinner." His tone was light, as if he were just going down the street to a tavern instead of a haunted crypt. Inside he was fighting down panic.

"You're sure?" Cat asked.

"Yes. I think she'll be more communicative if I'm alone."

Cat stood, kissed Giogi good-bye, and whispered, "Good luck," in his ear.

Giogi smiled at her gratefully. "I'll be taking Daisyeye, Thomas," he said. "I can saddle her myself, but please see that Poppy is returned to Redstone."

"Very good, sir."

A few minutes later, Giogioni led Daisyeye from the carriage house and out the garden gate, mounted her, turned her west, and kicked her into a trot.

The shining sun made the graveyard appear somewhat cheerier than it had the day before, but Giogi's spirit was heavy. *Yesterday all I wanted was to find the spur and return it to the crypt. I get my wish, and now it's not enough. Now I have to find out how the spur works. I have to learn how to turn into a beast.*

Giogi tied Daisyeye to a post and pulled out the key to the mausoleum. *There's no question about it. Flattery has to be vanquished.*

He turned the key in the lock and pushed open the door. *Of course, I could hire some real adventurers to go after Flattery,* he mused, looking into the darkness.

Giogi walked into the mausoleum and pushed the door shut behind him. He locked the door and pulled out the finder's stone to light his way. *Cole hadn't relied on hirelings to take care of Flattery,* he thought as he skipped over the black-and-white tiles to open the secret door in the floor. *The family honor is at stake; the only way to set things right is for the family to take care of it. Freffie and Steele are no match for Flattery's treacheries, and Flattery's already ambushed the only real threat to his power: Uncle Drone.*

As Giogi started down the stairs to the crypt, he thought of Mother Lleddew's story of how Uncle Drone had to slice off part of Cole's wyvern foot so his corpse would transform back into a man's. It was this that disturbed Giogi more than the fact that Cole had died battling the wizard. *Suppose I get stuck as a wyvern while I'm still alive? Suppose I go wyverny and forget about my family and Cat and Daisyeye and fly off to live in the wild?*

Giogi stood at the crypt door with the key in the lock. Aunt Dorath must have been afraid of the same thing, not being able to change back from a beast into a human being. Had that ever happened to Cole while he was alive? Giogi didn't remember his father ever being away from home for very long, and when he returned, he never showed any signs of being wyverny.

As a matter of fact, Cole was like every other father Giogi had ever known, better, actually. Cole took him riding and boating and told him stories and taught him his letters and numbers. He must have been a good husband, too. Giogi didn't remember his parents fighting very much. They gardened together and danced together and played backgammon and read books to one another by the fireside at night. Even separated by fourteen years and surrounded by the cold stone stairwell leading to the crypt, Giogi could feel the warmth of that hearth.

No, he decided, someone like Cole couldn't forget how to be human. Not until death had left him cold.

Will it be the same for me, though?

"I'll never find out by just standing here," the nobleman declared. He turned the key in the lock and pushed open the crypt door.

As soon as he stepped into the crypt, motes of black swirled on the back wall and coalesced into the familiar shape of the shadow wyvern.

"Giogioni, you're back," the guardian whispered.

Giogi strode into the crypt. He stopped before the empty pillar and pulled the spur out of his boot. "I found it," he said, dropping the heirloom onto the velvet cloth. "I need to know how to use it."

"I knew you'd come back to me, my Giogioni," the guardian said.

"You have nothing to do with it. This is an emergency. I don't want to be a wyvern."

The guardian laughed, her shadowy form swaying on the wall. It was a clear, ringing laugh, unlike her spooky, whispery voice. "I wouldn't want to be a human."

"Well, I need to be one anyway. A wyvern."

"You can never be a wyvern, Giogioni. You may take a wyvern's form, but you will always be human. That is essential."

"What do you mean, essential?"

"The spur's blessing guarantees the Wyvernspur line will continue. If Wyvernspurs were to turn from human to wyvern, they would not be able to continue the line as Wyvernspurs. So that which confers power over the spur, Selune's kiss, is not given to those unable to resist changing completely to wyvern."

A touch of relief spread over Giogi. Then his curiosity overcame his anxiety. "Suppose someone not kissed by Selune tries to use it?"

"They would think they had a wyvern's power, though their body would still be human."

"Is that all it takes to be kissed by Selune—being able to resist going completely wyverny?"

"No. You must want to be different."

"I don't want to be different," Giogi objected.

The guardian laughed. "You are so satisfied with yourself, your life, your world?"

Giogi shifted uneasily. He couldn't lie.

"With a wyvern's power and the blessings of the spur you can change yourself, your life, your world."

"So what do I have to do to make it work?" Giogi asked.

"Take up the spur—"

Giogi set the finder's stone down on the pillar and picked up the spur.

"Keep it near your leg."

Giogi slid the spur into his boot.

"Now you must remember your dreams."

"My dreams?" he sputtered. Then he understood. "Oh. Those dreams," he said. The images sprang to his mind. The death cry of prey—the shriek of a rabbit, the squeal of a pig, the bellow of a cow. The taste of warm blood—salty and full of energy. The crunch of bone—surrendering to the strength of his jaw and yielding up its sweet marrow. He felt the blood pounding in his head, and the room seemed to spin and shrink around him. He bent over to avoid hitting his head on the ceiling.

"A very handsome wyvern form, Giogioni," the guardian whispered.

Giogioni looked down at himself nervously. Actually, he had to look back at himself. He was at least thirty feet longer. He was covered with red scales. His arms had become great leathery wings, and his feet were sharp talons. The strangest thing of all, though, was the tail. It swayed gracefully behind him without him thinking about it. He concentrated on controlling it and it froze, poised in the air, until he unconsciously picked a target.

He bent forward and slashed the tail over his head. The stinger at the tip pierced the velvet cloth atop the pillar.

The pillar toppled over, and the finder's stone rolled across the floor of the crypt. The piece of velvet cloth remained caught on the end of the stinger. He pulled it off with a talon and nearly toppled over, trying to balance on one leg.

The guardian laughed. "You need to remember that your body is a weapon. You should practice with it—especially flying. It's not as easy as it looks."

"How do I change back?" Giogi tried to ask, but his words came out as a growl.

The guardian understood him, though. "I suppose you think of whatever humans dream about," she said. She made a yawning sound. "Dull things," she suggested.

Giogi tried to think of what he dreamed about when he wasn't dreaming the wyvern dream. He thought about Cat. Unconsciously he began beating the air with his wings, and he remained a wyvern. He thought of galloping on Daisyeye, but that reminded him too much of chasing prey. Then he thought of Aunt Dorath, knitting by the fireside. The ceiling got farther away. His boots covered his feet. His arms dropped to his sides. He straightened up, no longer needing to balance his tail with the weight of his neck.

He picked the pillar off the floor, and laid the velvet cloth over it. Then he retrieved the finder's stone.

"When will I see you again?" the guardian asked.

Giogi shivered, but it would be rude to say she scared him to death and he didn't like coming into the crypt. "I don't know," he said. "Why?"

"I'll miss you."

"You will? Do you get lonely down here?"

"Sometimes. Not often."

"Why do you stay?"

"This is where my bones are buried. Beside the bones of those I love—my mate, and all your ancestors who took his form, from Paton to Cole."

"Oh," Giogi said, thinking how strange it must be to love so many people dead for so many years. "I'll be back when I'm finished with what I have to do," he promised, "unless I die."

"You'll be back in that case, too," the guardian said solemnly.

Giogi's eyes roamed over the blocks of stone sealing in his ancestors. "You're right. Well, until whichever."

"Until whichever," the guardian agreed.

"Thank you for the advice."

"You're welcome, my Giogioni." The guardian's shadow faded from the walls and left him alone.

For the first time ever, Giogi left the crypt without a feeling of terror.

Outside, the sun was getting low in the sky. Giogi slipped the finder's stone in his boot beside the spur. He untied Daisyeye, slid her reins off her head, and tucked them into one of her saddlebags. "Go home, girl," he said, slapping her on her backside. The mare took off down the hill without looking back.

Giogi watched her race away for a minute. He closed his eyes and imagined a deer springing through the forest. The sensation of pounding blood overwhelmed him more quickly this time. He beat the air with his wings and ran through the graveyard.

A gust of chill wind caught under the leathery canopies and lifted him over the trees. He flapped the wings faster and propelled himself over the edge of the graveyard hillside, catching an updraft. He soared over the valley. In less than a minute, he was circling over Spring Hill. He could make out Mother Lleddew far below, beside the rented carriage full of provisions for Uncle Drone's memorial service.

He resisted the temptation to fly over Redstone. There was no sense in disturbing Aunt Dorath. Besides, he wasn't sure how well he would land, and he knew it wasn't something he should try after dark. He was also growing very hungry. With any luck, Giogi thought, Thomas is roasting a slab of venison or a side of pork. He banked eastward toward the townhouse, his shadow flying far ahead of him and his stomach growling all the way.

* * * * *

Olive stood propped up against the closet wall like a walking stick. "Are you sure you don't want me to tie her up, sir?" the treacherous Thomas had asked the wizard before closing the door and leaving the halfling in the pitch dark.

Flattery had said it wasn't necessary. After that, Thomas had excused himself so he could get started on cleaning out the bedroom fireplaces.

For the longest time there was no sound in the attic but that of the wizard turning pages in a book. Finally, an interminable twenty minutes later, the wizard's spell faded and Olive could move again. She collapsed to the floor. Her legs and arms were all pins and needles from having been stuck in the same position so long. She stumbled against a box on the floor and banged her shin.

"Keep it down in there, Ruskettle," the wizard ordered, "or I shall turn you into a newt."

Only a newt? Olive thought. Is he serious?

Not wanting to find out, Olive kept silent. Very quietly, she began working on the closet lock.

"Put the lockpicks away, Ruskettle," the wizard ordered in a calm, distracted voice, "or I'll firetrap the door."

Olive slipped the picks back into her pocket. He's watching me through the walls, she thought.

Why doesn't Flattery just kill me? she wondered. If Thomas is his agent, then he must know I've been plotting against him. Perhaps he doesn't consider me a serious enough threat. Well, I'll show him. The halfling sat quietly on the floor, thinking of ways to warn the young noble. Tapping coded messages on support beams was supposed to be good. Tying messages to mice had worked in some stories. Neither support beams nor mice seemed to be in ready supply, though.

The stairs creaked, and Thomas returned. "He's gone to speak to the guardian, sir, fifteen minutes ago," the servant reported.

"Excellent," the wizard said. "And Cat?"

"She's offered to return Lord Frefford's horse to Redstone for me. I would imagine she wants another crack at the lab."

"Resourceful girl."

Thomas began collecting the tea things. Olive took advantage of the clattering noise to renew her attack on the closet door lock. The click of the lock was covered by the rattle of the silver tea pot on the tray.

Thomas went back down the stairs.

Olive opened the door just a crack. The black-and-white spotted cat sat right in front of the door jamb, blocking the door. Olive pulled out her spool of string and wrapped a bit of it up into a ball. She tossed the ball so it rolled away from the cat.

The animal watched it travel across the floor and yawned.

How can you ignore a ball of string? Olive thought at the cat. Haven't you got any self-respect? What kind of cat are you, anyway?

"Mystra's minions," the wizard cursed softly.

Olive heard the spell-caster rise and walk toward the closet. He pushed the closet door shut. "Thank you, Spot. Good kitty."

Of course, Olive chided herself, that kind of cat. A wizard's familiar.

"Mistress Ruskettle," Flattery said through the door, "I have tried to be a polite host, but you have tried my patience once too often. Incendiary. There, now I've firetrapped the door."

The wizard's footsteps stomped away. Olive heard him flipping through pages of another book. She sat in the back corner of the closet and fumed. Then she began testing the floorboards. They were nailed solidly. She pulled out her dagger and began working on digging the nails out of the wood.

Olive had just worked out her first nail when she heard Thomas climbing the attic stairs again.

"I think you'll want to see this, sir," the servant said.

"What?"

"At the window."

The wizard stood and pushed open a window. "It's Giogi! He's flying! He's circling overhead. Quickly! The other window!"

Olive heard the two men scurry across the attic and push open a second window. "Mystra's minions," the wizard chuckled. "I'll bet he doesn't know how to land."

Giogi! Olive thought. I have to warn him! I can signal him from the window. She scraped furiously at a second nail.

This will never do. Olive pictured Giogi flying by, with Flattery pointing at him, waiting for the right moment to reduce him to dust.

I have to risk the firetrap! she decided recklessly. With her body pressed against the wall, Olive reached out, turned the handle, and pushed!

The door swung outward silently.

He lied! Olive thought, indignant. She slipped out the door.

The wizard and the servant were looking out a southern window, closer to the stairs than she was. Olive dashed for the north side of the attic. She scrambled up to the window sill and slid out onto the roof.

Behind her she heard Spot hiss.

"Thomas! The halfling! Grab her!" the wizard shouted.

Olive crawled away from the window, deliberately ripping up half a shingle as she went. When Thomas poked his head out the window, the halfling whipped the curved piece of wood at the servant's temple. Before falling back into the attic, Thomas said a word Olive bet he'd never said in Giogi's parlor.

Olive began climbing to the roof's peak. The wizard hung out the window and shouted up to her, "Come back here this instant before you get yourself killed!"

Olive looked up in the sky. A red wyvern circled the house. Wyverns are supposed to be brown and gray, Olive thought. Leave it to Giogi to turn into a red one. The halfling stood and waved in the beast's direction. "Giogi! Help! Flattery's trapped me up here!" she shouted in the chill air.

"Would you stop shouting that!" the wizard in the window hollered. "I am not Flattery!"

Olive looked down at the window. There couldn't possibly be any more Wyvernspurs I don't know about, could there? "If you're not Flattery," she shouted back, "who are you?"

"I'm Drone."

"Drone is dead."

"If I were dead, wouldn't I be buried in the crypt?" the wizard insisted.

"They're holding the memorial service tonight," Olive said.

"They are. Did Dorath fork out a big spread for it?" he asked with interest.

"Giogi!" Olive shouted again, waving more frantically. The wizard was not going to fool her with any more lies.

"See here, Ruskettle," the wizard called out, "I am Drone. You just don't recognize me because I shaved yesterday."

"Aha. I've never met you," Olive said. "You didn't know that. Giogi! Giogi! Help!" she screamed again, waving her dagger.

"You haven't? No, I suppose you haven't. I forgot. I felt like I knew you. Jade talked so much about you."

Olive looked down at the wizard so quickly that she lost her footing and slid three feet down the roof. "What do you mean

Jade talked about me?" she demanded.

"She told me all about you. When she was staying here last week. I like to know about my daughter's friends."

"Your—" Olive regained her balance and stomped her foot angrily. "That's a lie. Jade hasn't got any parents."

"I know. That's why I adopted her," the wizard said.

"You what?"

"I adopted her. We had a little ceremony with a cleric of Mystra. I gave her a silver spoon, a pearl necklace, a yard of lace, all that symbolic rot, and she gave me a pipe, even though I don't smoke—Dorath would never allow it."

"Why?" Olive asked.

"She doesn't like the way it smells. Don't suppose I do, either, but Elminster does it. Don't see why I shouldn't be allowed to, too."

"Not that," Olive snapped, coming down a few more feet toward the wizard. "Why did you adopt Jade?"

"Oh, that. Well, she seemed like a nice girl, and I needed a daughter to steal the spur from the crypt before Steele stole it."

Olive glared at the wizard in confusion. Come to think about it, he looks awfully old to be Flattery. He looks even older than Nameless, for that matter. His hair is all splotched with gray, and his face is awfully wrinkled. His appearance could be an illusion, though.

"That's the same reason Flattery made Cat marry him," Olive noted aloud.

"Cat married Flattery? Oh, that's not good. He's not a nice person. Won't make her an adequate husband at all."

Olive shivered in the cold and watched Giogi soar on an updraft. She didn't really believe Flattery could imitate a doddering old man so well, but she couldn't risk falling into his clutches unless she was absolutely positive. "I've got it!" she cried. She pulled out the letter with the royal seal, which she'd swiped from Drone's lab that morning. "I'll believe you're Drone if you can tell me what this letter says."

"What letter?"

"This letter I got from Drone's lab this morning. It's dated midsummer, thirteen-oh-six. Year of the Temples."

"That's almost thirty years ago," the wizard whined. "How am I supposed to remember a letter that old?"

"Only twenty-seven years," Olive said, "and it's a very important letter. It's from King Rhigaerd."

"Rhigaerd, Azoun's father?"

"That's the one."

"What would Rhigaerd want back then?" the wizard muttered to himself. "Oh! Yes! It's about the spur. Let's see. Rhigaerd said he understood that Dorath wasn't interested in using the spur, but he wanted to know if there wasn't someone else in the family who would give it a go. That's why I told Cole all about it, even though Dorath told me not to. A royal request outweighs a cousin's orders after all, even a cousin like Dorath."

"All right. You're one for one. Here, in the second paragraph, Rhigaerd writes, 'I don't think your colleague has ever gotten over' something. What is it?" Olive demanded, feeling her toes going blue on the chill roof tiles.

"Never gotten over? Never gotten over Dorath's refusal."

"Who'd she turn down?" Olive asked.

"The letter doesn't say."

"Tell me anyway," the halfling insisted.

"Vangerdahast," the old man snapped.

"Really?" Olive asked. "Old Vangy? Azoun's court wizard?"

"Really," the wizard said grimly. "Now, you little pest, would you come down so I can fireball you without setting Giogi's roof on fire?"

*   *   *   *   *

This landing thing could be tricky, Giogi thought as he circled around his townhouse for the fifth time. He was circling closer each time, looking for a clear spot in the garden, when he noticed Olive Ruskettle on the roof, waving at him. He couldn't imagine what the halfling would be doing on his roof, nor could he hear what she was shouting, but it was clear to him that the roof was a very dangerous place for her to be.

Just as Olive began climbing back toward the window, Giogi swooped down, as silent as an owl. The halfling was just beside the window dormer when the Wyvernspur wyvern snatched her up in his talons and swooped away from the roof.

Olive's screech could be heard down at the Five Fine Fish. The sensation of the roof dropping away from her feet, combined with the icy wind slamming into her face, took all the pleasure out of her bird's-eye view of Immersea at sunset. What does he think he's doing? Olive wondered. My fragile body can't take these reckless stunts!

The halfling had once been snatched up by a red dragon, and while she had been terrified that the monster would eat her, at least she could be certain the dragon knew how to land. He's going to land on top of me and smash me to halfling jelly, she thought as Giogi dropped downward rapidly. At the last moment, he veered up suddenly. He was indeed uncertain how to make his touchdown with cargo. On his second approach, though, he dropped Olive over a yew bush just before he smashed into the side of his carriage house.

Olive's teeth chattered from the cold. Ches is too early in the spring for flying, she noted, scrambling out of the bush. Drone and Thomas rushed out of the townhouse's front door as the halfling was brushing herself off.

"Giogi, my boy. Are you all right?" Drone asked.

The wyvern wobbled to its feet, hissing.

"You'll have to change back to human form," Drone said. "I can't understand a word you're saying. Concentrate on turning human. Think about afternoon tea; that's what your father used to do."

The wyvern shape wavered and shrunk until it was Giogi.

"Uncle Drone! You're alive!" the young nobleman shouted.

"Shhh! Not so loud," the wizard whispered. "It's supposed to be a secret."

Thomas tapped Drone on the shoulder. "Excuse me, sir, but perhaps we should go back inside, just in case—"

Drone shot a glance up at the sky. "You're right, Thomas. Come on, everyone."

Drone and Thomas hustled Giogi and Olive back into the townhouse. Drone motioned to the parlor doors, and they all trooped into Giogi's parlor.

Drone shoved some books off the couch and flopped down. "It's nice and warm in here. You should get a fireplace in your attic, Giogi. It's cold up there."

"What were you doing in my attic?" Giogi asked. "We all thought you were dead. Uncle Drone, how could you let us think that? What were you trying to do?"

"Sit down, Giogi," the old wizard said, patting the cushion beside him.

Giogi sat down with a huff. Olive took a seat on the footstool by the fire. Thomas remained standing by the parlor doors and explained that Cat had ridden to Redstone.

"I'm sorry for any grief I caused you," Drone said to Giogi.

"Well, you should be," Giogi said. "I thought Flattery had killed you."

"He tried," Drone said. "Sent a wight to do the job, but I disintegrated it."

"Then you left an extra set of robes and hat over the ashes of the wight, didn't you?" Olive asked.

Drone nodded.

"But why?" Giogi asked.

"I needed to throw my would-be killer off my trail. It was important that you all believe I was dead so Flattery would believe so, too. Then I could work at searching for the spur and trying to discover more about Flattery without having to look over my shoulder for other undead assassins."

"You told Thomas, though," Olive said.

"Well, Thomas is the soul of discretion, and I needed a base of operations and somewhere to sleep."

Giogi let out a groan and hit his forehead with the palm of his hand. "The lilac room! That's why you didn't want me to put Cat in there," Giogi accused Thomas.

"I'm sorry, sir. Your uncle preferred the bed in the lilac room. I did prepare the red room for Mistress Cat, but you never told me you'd held firm on the lilac room."

"Uncle Drone, why did you try to smother Cat?" Giogi asked crossly.

"I didn't try to smother the girl. In the dark, I didn't know she was there. My night vision's not what it was, you know. I fluffed a pillow and dropped it in the bed; the next thing I know, I've got a hysterical woman shrieking in my ear."

"But Cat thought it was Flattery."

"Without the beard, he looks like Flattery in a dark room or an attic," Olive said.

"Without the—Uncle Drone," Giogi exclaimed, "you shaved off your beard."

"I needed a disguise. Makes me look younger, don't you think?"

Giogi bit his tongue.

"Did you really get Mistress Ruskettle's partner, Jade, to steal the spur for you?" Giogi asked.

"Well, no. I gave her my key and asked her to bring it out for me. Wyvernspurs have that right, after all."

"Then why didn't you do it yourself?" Olive asked.

"Well, Dorath would ask me right off if I took it. If I got someone else to do it for me, I could say I didn't without lying. Then, of course, Jade had the most remarkable undetectability. If she held the spur for me, Steele and Dorath wouldn't be able to locate it. Or Flattery, as it turns out. Of course, neither could I. When she didn't rendezvous with Thomas at the Fish the evening after she stole it, I—well, I thought she'd betrayed me, to be honest."

"She was murdered," Olive said coolly.

"Yes," Drone said softly, looking down at his hands. "Thomas told me. I'm very sorry, Ruskettle. I knew how close the two of you were."

Olive looked down at the floor and fought back her tears.

"We owe you a debt of gratitude for returning the spur to us safely," Drone said.

Olive looked up at the wizard, her eyes burning with vengeance. "Get Flattery for me," she demanded.

"Oh, I intend to," Drone assured her.

"As do I," Giogi added.

Olive smiled with a cold satisfaction.

"You didn't think I'd let my daughter's murderer go unpunished, did you?" Drone asked.

"Your daughter?" Giogi asked. "What are you talking about, Uncle Drone?"

"Your uncle adopted Jade," Olive explained. "He didn't know she was already a relative."

"She was?" Drone asked with surprise.

"Yes," Olive said. "She and Cat are related to the Nameless Bard, and Flattery probably is, too. He said to Cole, "My father will remain nameless." I think he was making his idea of a joke. The Nameless Bard was a Wyvernspur named Finder."

"There isn't anyone named Finder in our family tree," Drone said.

"I'll bet if you check your family tree," Olive predicted, "you'll find a name blotted out somewhere. That would be Finder. The Harpers would have gotten your family to wipe out all traces of his name. See, Finder was pretty callous once. He performed this experiment that got some people killed and—well, the Harpers wiped his name from the Realms."

"We shall do more than that to Flattery," Drone said. "I suggest we start planning our strategy over a hot supper."

"There may not be time, sir," Thomas said, his eyes widening with fear.

"Eh?" the wizard queried.

The servant pointed through the townhouse's large parlor windows, which looked south over the Wyvernspur lands and Redstone Castle.

Giogi, Olive, and Drone lined up at the window to look at what had upset Thomas.

In the last ray of sunlight, the cut stone of the castle's west wall shone as red as blood against an indigo sky. The vision's loveliness was marred only by a blot of darkness that drifted above the keep. The blot's lower surface also shone red, but its surface consisted of jutting edges and jagged crevices, like a boulder torn from the earth by some monstrous cataclysm. Only magic could have raised the stone, though. It was so large, it would crush half of Immersea if it fell to the earth. At the top of the massive rock were walls that rose so high that they disappeared into the darkness of the twilight sky.

"What is it?" Giogi gasped.

"Flattery's desert fortress," Drone said grimly. "It appears he did more than reclaim it. He's brought it with him."

❧ 20 ❧

Flattery's Treachery

Very quietly Cat snuck back out of Drone's lab. She had received Lord Frefford's permission to be there, but there was, after all, no reason to disturb Aunt Dorath. Cat crept down the outer staircase, clutching her sack of scrolls.

In the excitement of Steele's leap from the tower and her recovery of the spur, she'd forgotten about the magic she'd so painstakingly collected. She remembered the sack after Giogi had left for the crypt and decided she could fetch it and be back at the townhouse before Giogi returned.

She had to hurry now, or Giogi would worry. It had only taken a moment to retrieve the sack, but getting to Redstone had been another matter. She might have tried galloping Poppy across the fields, but she'd ridden the mare along the roads, keeping her at a walk all the way. She had no intention of riding her back to Giogi's townhouse. Cat felt safer on foot.

The tower's outer stairs brought her down to the second level of the castle. She stood on the balcony overlooking the two curved grand staircases leading to the entrance hall below. To the northwest and northeast stretched hallways leading to the family living quarters.

The memory of how nice Gaylyn had been to her earlier in the morning sprang to Cat's mind. She felt an urge to say hello to the woman. Thinking Frefford's lady might be sitting in the parlor, the mage turned from the staircases and headed down the northwest corridor.

Cat had just reached the parlor door when a shout came from the entrance hall below. Curious, she ran back to the nearest staircase and looked down. Giogi stood in the hallway, calling out for Frefford. From some room below, a tall, burly man with dark but graying hair ran into the hallway in answer to the noble's cries.

"Sudacar!" Giogi gasped, grasping the man's shoulders excitedly. "Thank Waukeen! It's the baby. He's after Amber Leona.

Where is she?"

"She should be in the nursery," Sudacar replied.

Giogi and Sudacar dashed up the staircase opposite the one Cat stood over. Neither man noticed the mage standing on the shadowy balcony. Sudacar led Giogi down a corridor at the other end of the building. With an uneasy, disturbed feeling, Cat hurried after them.

Sudacar opened the door to the baby's nursery with his heart pounding wildly. He sighed with relief. Dorath kept watch over her great-grandniece like a she-dragon over her treasure. Amber lay sleeping in the cradle. Dorath sat in the rocking chair, darning socks. She looked up at the lord of Immersea with disdain, hastily pocketing her wooden darning sock and sweeping her mending into a basket on the floor.

"Is there something I can do for you, Lord Samtavan?" she asked haughtily.

Giogi pushed past Sudacar and strode over to the cradle. He swept the baby up in his arms.

"Giogioni Wyvernspur, just what do you think you're doing, you fool?" Dorath demanded. "You'll wake her up."

As if on cue, Amber began to cry.

Cat peeked into the room from behind Sudacar's broad back.

"Hand me that baby this instant," Dorath insisted, rising to her feet and closing in on Giogi.

Giogi cracked Dorath across the face with the back of his hand, sending her sprawling across the room. Cat gasped. Giogi looked to the door and spotted the mage. "Catling," he said. "How convenient. Come hold this brat, and I'll take us all home."

Amber began bawling louder, and her face turned bright red.

"No," Cat whispered in horror. "That's not Giogi," she said to Sudacar. "It's Flattery. You must stop him."

Sudacar gave a sharp glance at the woman now standing beside him. Her face was familiar somehow. That wasn't a sufficient reason to believe her—he didn't even know who this Flattery was supposed to be—but when it was combined with the display of violence he'd just witnessed, the Lord of Immersea was inclined to take the woman's word for it. "Put the baby down," Sudacar ordered, drawing his sword, "whoever you are."

The would-be Giogi snorted. He dropped the baby in the cradle. Then he whirled on Sudacar with his hands extended, saying, "Flame spears." Cat dodged out of the doorway just before jets of fire shot out from the wizard's fingertips. Caught unprepared, Sudacar took the full brunt of the magic, his face and hands turned red from the heat, and his shirt and hair burst into flame. He collapsed in the doorway with a groan.

Cat threw her cape over his back and head to extinguish the flames. Then she drew the fur back from his head so he could breathe.

"Catling, get in here!" Flattery shouted with Giogi's voice.

Cat dodged out of the doorway again and cowered in the corridor, not wanting to obey, too frightened to run.

"Now, Catling, or I'll hurt the brat," the wizard threatened. Amber gave an especially loud shriek, as if she'd been pinched or worse.

Cat fought back her terror. It's Gaylyn's baby, she told herself. You can't let him hurt Gaylyn's baby.

When Cat appeared in the doorway, Flattery held the baby again. Amber was sobbing and hiccuping at the same time. Flattery sneered at her. It was awful seeing Giogi's face twisted in such a look of hatred, but Cat stepped over Sudacar's body and walked toward her master, holding out her arms to take Gaylyn's screaming infant.

Flattery gave the mage a suspicious glance. "No. Maybe I'd better hold onto her," he said, pulling the baby closer to his chest. "Take that scroll of paper out from my belt and put it in the cradle."

"What is it?" Cat asked, pulling out the scroll.

"My terms, you witch. This is all your fault. If you'd brought me the spur, I wouldn't need to be wasting my time here."

In the corner of the room, Dorath was struggling to her feet. "Give me my Amber!" she screamed.

With a huff of annoyance, Flattery turned toward the old Wyvernspur dame. Cat pointed a finger at the wizard's back and muttered the words, "Soul daggers."

Three shimmering daggers of light shot from her hand and buried themselves in Flattery's back.

The wizard cried out in pain and surprise. He whirled around, his eyes burning with fury. "You want combat, woman? I'll show you combat," he screamed, pulling out a crystal cone. "Death ice!" he growled.

A freezing blast of cold covered the female mage from head to toe. Her skin felt as if it were on fire and her lungs and heart ached as if she'd been stabbed. Unable to breathe, she collapsed to the floor.

Flattery stepped up to her and slammed his foot into her stomach. "I should kill you," he snarled. He kicked her again.

"Stop that!" Dorath screamed, slamming a porcelain water pitcher over the wizard's head.

Flattery spun to face his new challenger. The quarters were too close to cast one of his offensive spells at her. Besides, he was forced to clench his hands tightly around the baby to keep the old woman from pulling her away from him.

Frefford appeared in the doorway. "What in nine hells is going on here?" he asked. "Giogi! What are you doing with Amber?"

"Frefford, stop him!" Dorath hollered.

Flattery released one hand from the baby and grabbed Dorath's wrist. "Silver path, castle keep," he whispered.

Before Lord Frefford's astonished eyes, his cousin, his grandaunt and his daughter vanished.

* * * * *

Giogi stepped back from the parlor window of his townhouse. "I've got to get to Redstone fast!" he said.

"If we're not too late already," Drone muttered. "Thomas, notify the watch," he ordered. "Giogi, take my hand, boy. You, too, Mistress Ruskettle."

This may not be one of the smarter things I've ever done, Olive thought, taking the wizard's left hand while Giogi grasped the right.

"Silver path, home tower," Drone intoned.

Something buzzed in Olive's ear, and her flesh tingled. She involuntarily blinked, and when she opened her eyes, she, the wizard, and Giogi were standing in Drone's lab in Redstone Castle. From a room downstairs came the shriek of an anguished woman.

"Gaylyn!" Giogi cried. He rushed to the door to the outer stair and dashed down. Olive followed closely on his heels.

Three stories down, the door to the nursery stood open. Sudacar lay slumped in the doorway, unconscious. His face and chest were horribly burned, and his hair was scorched to the scalp. Julia knelt over him, pouring a healing potion very carefully down his throat. Her eyes were streaming with tears.

Inside the room, Gaylyn was seated on the rocker, sobbing hysterically. Frefford knelt beside her with his arms around her waist, but he was pale and silent, without the strength to console his wife.

Cat lay in a heap beside the baby's cradle. Her flesh was a deathly white, and her lips and eyelashes were covered with rime. She clutched a cloth sack to her chest.

Giogi stepped over Sudacar's body and rushed to the mage's side. He took up her hand and shuddered at the cold. He pulled the platinum band from his forehead and held its smooth inner surface near her lips. Still cold from the nobleman's flight, the metal dimmed with the tiniest bit of moisture.

"She's alive!" Giogi cried excitedly.

Sudacar stirred in Julia's arms. "Sam," Julia whispered. "Sam, can you hear me?"

From between his cracked lips Sudacar snarled, "Fell for it. Oldest trick in the book, and I fell for it."

Julia unstoppered another potion vial. "Drink some more," she ordered gently, but Sudacar shook his head.

"Girl," he gasped.

"What?" Julia asked.

"Give it to the girl. She's worse off. He hit her hard."

"Here," Olive said, holding out her hand. "I'll handle it."

Julia looked uncertainly down at her lover's fire-ravaged face. "It's the last one in the house," she argued.

Sudacar patted her hand reassuringly. Unwilling but obedient, the noblewoman handed the halfling the vial.

Olive skipped over Sudacar's legs and hurried to Giogi's side. The nobleman held the mage close to his body with his cape wrapped about both of them, trying to warm her.

"She could probably use a swig of this," Olive suggested, handing Giogi the vial.

Giogi accepted it with a weak but grateful smile.

Olive peered in the baby's cradle. There was nothing in it but a scroll. Olive unrolled it and read through it silently.

Drone appeared in the doorway. "I've secured the castle," he said.

"Too late," Olive replied.

"What happened?" the old wizard asked.

"Flattery took the baby," Olive explained, looking up from the scroll.

"Uncle Drone!" Julia cried in surprise. "You're alive!"

Frefford and Gaylyn looked up.

"That pile of ash wasn't you, then?" Frefford asked.

"No, it wasn't," Drone replied as he knelt beside Sudacar. "How did he get in?" the wizard asked the king's man. "What spells did he use?"

"Looked like Giogi," Sudacar explained. "Said the baby was in danger. I led him right up here. Selune, I'm such a fool."

"Shh, Sam," Julia said. "Conserve your strength."

Sudacar shook his head. "Drone needs to know. Dorath was here. He snatched up the baby. Dorath tried to stop him. He hit Dorath. I pulled my sword, and he fried me. The girl missiled him with magic. He froze her with a ray of cold. Kicked her twice for good measure. Dorath hit him, fought like a tiger. I passed out before he disappeared."

"Gaylyn, Julia, and I were in the parlor. We heard Aunt Dorath shouting," Frefford explained. "When I ran in, he was still struggling to keep Aunt Dorath from pulling Amberlee away. I thought it was Giogi, until he blinked out with Amberlee and Aunt Dorath."

Gaylyn looked up plaintively at the wizard. "Oh, Uncle Drone. You'll get my baby back, won't you?" she sobbed.

"It's out of his hands," Olive said.

Sudacar and the Wyvernspurs turned to the bard for an explanation.

"He left a note," she said, rattling the scroll. "It's for Giogi. 'The brat for the spur and my Cat,' " she read. " 'Bring no one else. Cat can lead you to my audience chamber. If you keep her or try to bring anyone else, you seal the child's doom.' "

Strengthened by the healing potion, Cat stirred in Giogi's arms. "Giogi," she whispered, "I'm sorry. I tried to stop him. I really did. I fought him."

"It's all right," Giogi whispered.

"I surprised him, too," she added, her voice very weak. "He didn't believe I would do it."

Giogi looked up at Frefford, unable to say what he must.

"I understand, Giogi," the young lord said. "No one expects

you to trade one life for another."

Giogi kissed Cat gently and untangled himself from the cloak he'd wrapped around both of them. "I'll take him the spur," Giogi said, rising to his feet. "He'll give me Amberlee or . . . I'll kill him." He trembled as he realized that he wanted to do it.

Olive shook her head. He can't go up there alone, she thought, when another idea struck her.

"Jade's sack," she said, pulling out the magical pouch Jade had given her to hold. "If I can fit into Jade's sack, he won't know I'm with you. I can sneak attack him, in case he cheats us—correction, when he cheats us. He hasn't changed from the time he killed your father," she pointed out to Giogi.

"Jade's sack?" Drone asked. "The miniature bag of holding I gave her? Not even you would fit, Ruskettle. Twenty pounds is its limit. Hold on. Wasn't there a potion of healing in it?"

Olive opened the sack and drew out a minty-smelling vial.

"Take that, Giogi," Drone ordered. "You may need to use it."

Olive held out the vial.

"No," Cat said, snatching the vial. She unstoppered it and quaffed the potion in one fluid motion.

Her skin glowed with a trifle more pink, and she rose to her feet on her own, still clutching the cloth sack she'd held while unconscious. "There. I'm better now. I'm going with you," she told Giogi.

"No, you are not," the nobleman retorted. "I'm not letting you near that madman ever again."

"You haven't got a choice," Cat snapped. "If you won't carry me with you, I'll fly up on my own. I won't leave you to face him alone."

"Mistress Cat, you can't go," Gaylyn said softly. "He'll kill you. I won't let you. Not even for my Amberlee." Gaylyn broke down in tears.

"What makes you think I won't kill *him*?" Cat snapped with steely determination.

Now she sounds like Alias, Olive thought grimly.

"Cat," Giogi whispered, "I don't want you to come."

"I know. I don't want you to go, either. Neither of us has any other choice, though, do we?"

"You may as well give in, Master Giogioni," Olive said. "She'll find a way to follow you. You're better off if you look after each other."

Giogi turned away from Cat, struggling to hide his rage. "I'll change in the courtyard," he said as he left the room.

Cat picked her cape off the floor and followed behind him.

"We can watch them from the tower," Drone suggested.

Frefford, Gaylyn, Sudacar, and Julia remained in the nursery, but Olive followed behind the old wizard with interest. The last of the daylight was fading, and the countryside reflected the deep blues of dusk.

Steele was in the tower room, looting through papers, when they got there.

"Steele Wyvernspur, haven't I told you to keep your paws off my toys?" Drone growled.

Steele stood up sharply as if struck by lightning. "Uncle Drone. You're not dead. How?"

"I just keep breathing—in, then out," Drone snapped. "You're just the person I wanted to see, for a change. Saddle up two horses and ride up to the House of the Lady. Fetch back Mother Lleddew. We need her to heal Sudacar, and if our luck goes from bad to worse, we'll need her to bash a few heads, too."

"Mother Lleddew?" Steele whined. "She's an old woman. Sixty at least."

"I'm sixty," Drone snarled. "She's eighty-eight. Get your prejudices straight, boy. Now scat! You'd make an ugly toad."

Steele opened his mouth to retort, then thought better of it. He hurried from the room and down the outer staircase.

Olive opened one of the tower windows and looked at the courtyard. "They're down there now," she told Drone.

"Keep an eye on 'em," Drone ordered, "while I dig out some scrolls. I'll need more power than I usually carry." He began rooting through the scrolls, tossing them about willy-nilly. "Gods, that girl really took the cream of the crop. If I find one good scroll, I'll be lucky. Aha! Perfect! I'm lucky. Has Giogi transformed yet?"

"Not yet," Olive said, putting her eye to one of the telescopes and focusing it on the nobleman and the mage.

* * * * *

Cat ran to catch up to Giogi as he strode out into the center of the courtyard. She touched his arm, but he wouldn't look at her.

"I love you," she said.

Giogi whirled around angrily. "If you loved me, you would stay here as I've asked you."

"Why? So I can die of a broken heart like your mother did?"

"Don't say that," Giogi snapped.

"I'm not the sort of woman who can sit around and wait, Giogi, unless I'm sitting around and waiting with you. Mistress Ruskettle is right, you know. We're better off if we look after each other. Isn't that what Wyvernspurs are supposed to do?"

The anger in Giogi's heart melted away, leaving only a sad feeling that, having just met and fallen in love, they might both die. "We should say good-bye here," he said softly. "We may not get another chance."

Cat laughed unexpectedly. "I've never seen you so grim. Adventurers never say good-bye. They say, 'Til next season.' What we should do is kiss each other good luck."

"We should," he agreed, his heart lightening a little. Giogi pulled Cat close to him, and they wrapped their arms around one another.

*　*　*　*　*

"Has he transformed yet?" Drone asked Olive again, impatiently.

"No," Olive said with a quiet sigh, stepping away from the telescope.

"What is he waiting for?" Drone looked out the window. "Well, can't begrudge them that," he muttered, tucking a scroll into his shirt.

"I don't suppose you have a plan?" Olive asked hopefully.

"As you said, Ruskettle, it's out of my hands."

"Then what is that scroll for?"

"If they're very lucky, I might have an opportunity to interfere. If they're very unlucky . . ." Drone let his words trail off.

"Then what?" Olive asked.

"Then I will have no choice but to interfere."

The halfling and the wizard looked back down on the courtyard. Cat stood alone in the center. She held the finder's stone so that Giogi's flight would not be made in complete darkness.

Giogi had taken wyvern shape and was already aloft. He flew in a low glide toward the mage, snatched her up gently in his talons and spiraled upward, beating his wings heavily. When he'd cleared the towers, he flew away from the castle until he reached the edge of the massive rock that hung over Redstone. He spiraled up again and was lost to view.

*　*　*　*　*

It's as if we fell off the edge of the world and now we're trying to get back on top, Giogi thought as he climbed through the cold spring evening air to reach Flattery's fortress. He was several thousand feet above Immersea. Hundreds of miles to the west the nobleman could see the Storm Horn Mountains as dark purple silhouettes against the twilight sky. The flying rock obstructed his view to the east.

Finally he reached the top. The moon hadn't risen yet, but the finder's stone shone out like a beacon, illuminating the vast desert plain that lay before them. Red boulders were strewn across the red-brown sand. As they drew closer to the center of the plain, Giogi sighted other things scattered in the sand—corpses, thousands of them, arranged in orderly rows. Then the fortress wall appeared in the stone's light and Giogi pulled up to fly above it. Mother Lleddew had not exaggerated; it was twice as high as the wall about Suzail.

He swooped downward once they cleared the fortress wall. Bodies lay within the inner ward, but these were not neatly stacked. They lay in untidy piles. Even in the cold night air, they smelled strongly of decomposition. Giogi found a clear spot of sand, swooped low, and released Cat. He skidded to a stop several yards away.

The enchantress caught up to him by the time he'd shrunk back to his human shape. She handed back the finder's stone.

"Why are all these bodies here?" Giogi whispered, holding the crystal high overhead to get a better view of the inner ward.

"These are food for the ghasts and ghouls," Cat explained.

"And the bodies outside?"

"Held in reserve to be changed to zombies as needed."

Giogi shuddered.

"I wonder where all the undead are," Cat mused. "He can't have used all of them to attack you at Selune's temple. Not all of them will go out in daylight."

"I'd rather not find either kind," Giogi said. "Which way to Flattery?"

"To the keep," Cat said.

Giogi followed the mage as she threaded her way through the piles of carrion. The keep was a second fortress within the first. A turret rose from each corner, and the roof was lined with crenellated parapets. Giogi estimated the main building to be four stories high, but it was hard to tell exactly, because the keep had no windows. A pair of iron doors at ground level stood wide open. Cat reached for his hand, and they entered together.

They stood at one end of a long, wide corridor, bare of any ornamentation. Sconces holding torches lined the walls, but the torches had burned down to stumps. Giogi held the finder's stone above his head again. It sent a beam of light down the full length of the empty corridor. The light struck a second pair of iron doors.

"Dismal place," Giogi muttered as he and Cat walked toward the white doors. "No wall hangings. No furniture."

"Only Flattery and the undead dwell here," Cat explained. "The undead have no joy in decoration."

"What about Flattery?"

"Flattery only delights in power."

"Did you live here?"

Cat nodded.

"How could you stand it?"

"Until yesterday, being in your home, I had no notion of living any better," Cat said. She pushed at one of the doors before them.

The door opened into a great chamber whose ceiling rose to the full height of the keep. At the far end, a pair of braziers flickered red near the base of a dais. Aunt Dorath sat beside one of the braziers. She was not restrained by chain or rope. She looked very frightened, and her hair had gone completely gray.

Atop the dais, on a throne made of human bones, sat the wiz-

ard Flattery, a faint reddish glow surrounded his body. Amberlee lay on a pillow at his feet, inside a shimmering globe two
feet across. On either side of the dais, in the shadows, disfig-
ured shapes milled about and darker shadows flickered with
excitement.

Giogi dropped Cat's hand and strode into the room. Flattery
laid a threatening finger on the globe holding Amberlee.
"Hold," he commanded. Giogi halted.

"Giogioni Wyvernspur, you were wise to come," the wizard said. "You, Catling, will pay for your treachery. As you
can see, Giogioni, your kin are alive. My minions—" He motioned to the flickering shadows on either side of the dais
— "hate them. Especially the brat. You will note I've taken
special precautions to protect her from their life-draining
touch. Unfortunately, your aunt got out of control and I
had no choice but to let one of my ghosts deal with her. You
can hardly object to her damaged condition, considering all
the use you've had of my wife. Come here, Catling," he
ordered.

"The lady is not part of the deal, Flattery," Giogi retorted
hotly. "She's returning with me. You free Amberlee, Aunt
Dorath, and Cat, and I will give you the spur."

Flattery laughed. "You're a fool, Giogioni. Get over here,
witch!" he shouted at the mage. "You've got three seconds before I make this infant wraith food. Don't leave that sack behind. Bring it with you."

Cat picked up the sack of magic she'd tried to leave behind
Giogi. "You're better off without me," she said to Giogi as she
passed him by, hurrying to Flattery's side. Giogi could see her
eyes brimmed with tears.

"No," Giogi whispered.

"Don't waste your breath," Flattery said. "I'm the only one
who can give her what she wants. Isn't that right, Catling?" the
wizard asked, yanking on the mage's hair.

"Yes," Cat whispered, keeping her eyes down.

Flattery pulled at the sack Cat carried. "A little present for
me, Cat? Something by way of an apology, you witch? Looted
from Drone's lab, I take it."

Cat clutched the sack for only a moment, then released it.
The wizard chuckled and tied it to his belt.

"Now, Giogioni, you will give me the spur this minute," Flattery growled, rising to his feet and taking up the sphere holding Amberlee, "or I will feed this brat to a wraith. Then you will give me the spur or your aunt will be next. Or maybe Cat. Try to change your shape, and they will be dead before you can cross the room."

Giogi drew the spur from his boot. "I want to be sure my aunt is well. Send her to my side, and I will give her the spur to take to you."

Flattery snorted. He descended the dais and shoved Dorath with his foot. "Go," he ordered her.

Dorath rose slowly to her feet and crossed the room. The wrinkles on her face had doubled, and she looked very feeble. She stopped before Giogi and raised her hand to stroke his face.

"Don't be a fool," Dorath whispered, mustering as much of her grandaunt tones as she dared. "He can't be trusted. Flee now. Once he has the spur, no spells will affect him. None of us will leave here alive."

"I can't leave you," Giogi said, pressing the spur into her gnarled hands.

"I won't give him this," she hissed.

Giogi pushed his aunt's hand down by her thigh. "Carry it to him like this. When you reach him, think of the dream," he whispered.

"No," Dorath said, her eyes widening with fear.

"Yes. Do as I say," Giogi commanded through clenched teeth.

"I won't become that beast," Aunt Dorath whispered.

"Stop being a foolish old woman," Giogi said. "Be a hero, like your mother. It's our only chance. Amberlee's only chance."

"Stop whispering!" Flattery shouted. "Bring the spur to me, now!"

"Don't keep him waiting, Aunt Dorath," Giogi said. "Do it."

With her jaw still jutting out stubbornly, Dorath turned around. Her gnarled hands trembled with fear. She shuffled toward Flattery, hunched over with age.

Flattery set Amberlee down and strode toward Dorath, holding his hand out impatiently. Horrified, Giogi watched Dorath hold her hand out to the wizard. Flattery snatched the prize she offered.

Sweet Selune, Giogi thought, she was too frightened.

We're all doomed.

Flattery turned his back on her, muttering casually, "Kill them."

Misty black wraiths and corpse-gray wights began closing in on Giogi and Dorath at once.

✿ 21 ✿

The Final Battle

Giogi drew his foil and rushed forward, shouting, "Stay back!" In his left hand the finder's stone flared with a light as bright as day. The undead backed away from the light, snarling and retreating to the back of the audience chamber.

Flattery whirled around suddenly. "What is this?" he shouted. He hurled at Dorath's head the object she'd just handed him. The old woman's shape had already begun to blur and grow, however, and the wooden darning sock bounced off her red wyvern scales and clattered harmlessly to the floor.

Without a second's hesitation Dorath smashed her stinging tail down on the wizard, catching him in the shoulder with its venomous tip. As Flattery crumbled to the ground screaming, Dorath snatched up in her mouth the globe that held Amberlee, and whirled around.

"Run, Aunt Dorath!" Giogi shouted.

The wyvern plodded from the audience chamber as fast as its two birdlike legs could carry it, ducking to clear the door frame.

From the top of the dais Giogi saw Cat pulling out a scroll she'd concealed in the sash she wore. Giogi rushed toward Flattery, but one undead, a dark shadow unafraid of the light, intercepted the nobleman.

Giogi drew back. He still couldn't remember the entire rhyme about the undead, but the line "A shadow's touch saps the strength" came to him in a flash. He could hear Cat chanting, reading from her scroll.

Flattery stumbled to his feet, a bloodstain spreading on his robe. "After the wyvern!" he screamed.

A swarm of wraiths skimmed around the finder's stone's light, heading for the door, but they all bounced backward, repelled by an invisible barrier.

Satisfied that his aunt would make good her escape, the nobleman turned his full attention to the shadow. He lunged at it with his foil, but the weapon did no more damage to the creature than a stick did to air. The shadow closed on Giogi, its hands outstretched, its body traveling up the length of the foil's blade.

Just as the shadow reached the weapon's guard, Giogi heard Cat cry out the word "coffin," and the shadow halted. Giogi stepped back and withdrew his foil from the undead. Cat ran to the nobleman.

Flattery turned toward them. "I taught you to hold undead, Cat. But where did you get the wall of force?" the wizard asked. "A scroll, Cat? You've blocked your own exit. Why don't you lower it and flee?"

"No," Giogi whispered to her. "We need to give Aunt Dorath time to reach Redstone."

"You've bought your miserable relatives a few hours," Flattery replied. "I will have the spur from them once I've dispensed with you. Your Uncle Drone is dead. The old woman may be able to wield the spur, but she is the only one, and she will be too weak to fight me, even if she can resist my magic. If they do not surrender the spur, they all will die."

He doesn't know Uncle Drone is alive, Giogi realized. If I can stall Flattery long enough for Aunt Dorath to reach Redstone, Uncle Drone will come to help.

"Let's see, Catling. Besides holding that undead," Flattery said, motioning to the immobile shadow that had nearly gotten Giogi, "you assaulted me with missiles. You summoned me earlier today with a whispering wind bird. You have more power still. Cast something else at me."

"Why bother? It's obvious you've made yourself invulnerable to my attacks," she said, indicating the reddish glow that outlined his body. "I'll save my attacks for your undead, should any more of them have the courage to brave the light of Giogi's stone."

"I don't think you have any power left," the wizard taunted, "which makes you just a woman." Flattery advanced toward her menacingly.

"A woman under my protection," Giogi said, stepping forward with his foil leveled at the wizard. With the hand that held the finder's stone the nobleman pushed Cat behind him. Without undead to shield him, Giogi wondered, can I run Flattery through before he can cast a spell?

Flattery snorted at Giogi's foil. "So, the men of the clan still learn to use that ridiculous weapon," the wizard said, stepping back and assuming a fencing stance. He snapped his fingers and whispered, "Ward." A foil appeared in his hand.

"Well, Giogioni," Flattery said, saluting with his foil. "Do we fight over the lady's honor? I use the word 'lady' loosely, of course."

Giogi returned the salute with a cold anger. "On guard," he replied, crouching into his stance. Behind him he could hear Cat begin whispering another chant. In his back hand, the finder's stone remained bright.

For the first few minutes, Flattery parried Giogi's attacks without attacking back, taking the measure of his opponent. The wizard's parries were flawless.

"I take it," Flattery said, "that beyond defending that witch, your intention is to avenge the deaths of your father and uncle."

"Naturally," Giogi replied. He beat at his opponent's blade, forcing the wizard into a step backward.

"What kind of fool would fight for a doddering old man, a father who'd abandoned him, and a slut without a memory?" Flattery asked, finally making an attack lunge at Giogi's shoulder. Giogi parried high, but Flattery's motion proved to be a feint for a lower attack at his ribs. Giogi was forced to retreat a step.

Giogi fought down the anger the wizard's words ignited in him. It looked as if he might be sorely outclassed in this battle. It was imperative that he remain levelheaded.

It was true that Uncle Drone was a bit of a duffer, and secretly Giogi had harbored hostility toward Cole for dying and abandoning him, and there was no doubt that Cat had made a very unwise decision allying herself with Flattery. None of those things, however, were as important as the fact that he loved all those people. They were his family.

Giogi was just beginning to understand why he always stood up for them in spite of their failings. They wouldn't be a family without failings. Poor Steele only feels Frefford's rank and my wealth because he's had to live second to them. Julia only wants to be loved. Aunt Dorath only wanted to protect me from her own fears. As for the others, . . .

"My uncle was foully ambushed," Giogi stated. "My father

died defending the family honor. And the lady never loved you; she was terrified of you. Who could blame her?"

Flattery scowled for just a moment, and his blade wavered. Giogi thought, Can't take what he dishes out, eh?

"I wonder," Giogi continued, suddenly feeling more confident and mixing feints in with his attacks, "What kind of man has no respect for the elderly, no loyalty to his family, and prefers the company of undead to a beautiful woman? You know, Flattery, I don't think you're a man at all."

Flattery made a direct attack, low and clumsy, which Giogi parried easily.

"Close to the mark, eh?" the nobleman said with a chill disdain. "My guess would be you're some sort of lich with an illusion spell to mimic the face of a true Wyvernspur."

Flattery pressed at the nobleman's blade, thrust, and lunged. The foil pierced through Giogi's tabard and pricked the skin below his ribs before the nobleman managed to retreat.

Giogi nearly backed into Cat, who was still behind him reciting the words to some involved magic spell. Startled, the mage broke off her chant for a fraction of a second as she retreated to avoid being trampled by the nobleman. Upon recovering her balance, she resumed chanting, even faster than before.

"People say you're nothing but a useless wastrel with delusions of being a warrior," Flattery snarled. "You aren't even competent with the foil. I've drawn first blood already."

"Ah, but at least I have blood you can draw. What have you got, Flattery? If I get lucky and score a hit, will there be blood on my weapon or just some oozing ichor?"

Flattery thrust and lunged again, but Giogi parried and riposted. Flattery retreated slightly.

Both men slowed their attacks. Somewhere in his past Flattery had learned to fence very well, but it was not a skill he'd exercised for some while. He was tired. Giogi, who'd been riding and walking regularly, making his journey home, could last for some time, provided he wasn't dealt a mortal wound—which ultimately Flattery could deliver.

Since Giogi's purpose was to buy time for his Uncle Drone to arrive, not get himself killed, he slowed his attacks as well.

Still chanting, Cat pulled from her sash the special component the spell required. It was wrapped in a piece of paper and still smelled quite strong. She dipped all her fingers into it.

Flattery's attacks began to speed up again, and Giogi renewed his taunting banter.

"So. What happened to all the zombies and ghouls? Did the Shard's mist destroy every last one? Are those undead cowering from the light over there all that's left of your army?"

"Undead are easy to recruit," Flattery growled. "When we've finished with this battle, I shall give you a firsthand demonstration."

Giogi felt Cat very close behind him. While he realized she needed to stay in the circle of light shed by the finder's stone, so the undead did not attack her, he wished she would back away a little more, for both their safety.

She was practically chanting in his ear, words that made no sense at all to him. Her hands reached about his head, and she ran her fingers down his cheeks, smearing them with her spell component. She intoned, "Be as the beast."

Giogi crinkled his nose. The scent of the spell components Cat had used to hold the shadow, garlic and sulfur, lingered on her hands, mingled in with a much stronger and more unpleasant odor—rather like dung. Cat pulled her hands back. "This is the only spell I have left," she whispered in Giogi's ear. "I've saved it for you, my love." Then she stepped back.

Flattery's nose twitched from the smell. "You can give him the strength of a golem, Catling, but it won't improve his fencing. His skill is abysmal."

The wizard's prediction, however, proved wrong. With the muscles in Giogi's arms strengthened, his weapon suddenly felt lighter, and he wielded it with more speed and fluidity. He broke through one of Flattery's parries and stabbed the wizard's chest.

"One-one, Flattery," the nobleman said. His tone was grim. He knew he could not afford to grow cocky. "Hmm," he said, eyeing the tip of his foil as it danced before him. "Blood. Red blood. Liches don't bleed I'm going to have to reevaluate my opinion of you. Let's see. What bleeds and looks human but isn't? Flesh golems or those devilish little homonculi. Are you a golem, Flattery?"

Flattery growled, beat at Giogi's blade, and lunged for his heart. Giogi tried a stop-thrust with only partial success. His foil went harmlessly through the robe of Flattery's sleeve while Flattery's foil pierced Giogi's shoulder blade.

Giogi clenched his teeth against the pain. "Flesh golems don't get angry, but you're awfully tall for a homonculous."

* * * * *

Olive Ruskettle crept down the front hall of Flattery's keep. Once Dorath had returned with Amber, Drone changed into a pegasus, and he and Olive had flown to Flattery's lair. The half-ling had convinced Drone to wait outside to give her time to scout out the territory. If Giogi was still alive, she would get the spur to him, and he could handle Flattery. If it was too late, then Drone was her only way off the rock, and she didn't want him captured or killed.

She arrived at the audience hall in time to catch the last min-ute of Giogi's fencing duel with Flattery. Olive stood in the door-way and watched with interest. The wizard's fury was out of all proportion to the taunts Giogi made. Olive realized that those taunts must have some basis in truth.

The halfling moved to enter the room but found her passage blocked by an unseen barrier. As she ran her hands across the smooth surface, it crumbled at her touch like a dried sand cas-tle or a spell that had reached its maximum duration. Within the passage of a breath, the way was clear to where Giogi mocked the increasingly furious wizard.

Unfortunately, while Flattery did grow careless in his anger, he did not grow careless enough to give Giogi the winning edge.

Then Giogi said, "You're not a Wyvernspur. You're an over-grown homonculous, some wizard's imp who escaped."

Flattery made a running charge at Giogi, missing him com-pletely in his rage. The charge so startled Giogi that he tripped and fell over backward, losing both his foil and the finder's stone.

The wizard loomed over Giogi, with his foil pointed at the no-bleman's throat. Flattery put a foot on Giogi's chest and said, "I will tell you what I told your father in his dying moments, as we fell toward the earth. My father was a Wyvernspur so vile that the Harpers wiped his name from the Realms and ban-ished him to a Limbo."

"Nameless!" Olive cried out with excitement. "I was right! You did mean the Nameless Bard."

Flattery whirled around, with the same look on his face he'd worn the night he'd murdered Jade and Olive had screamed at him. Olive gulped, but she stood her ground.

Giogi took advantage of the wizard's inattention to roll away and rise to his feet.

"You!" Flattery screamed at Olive. "You freed him!"

"Me?" Olive squeaked. "No."

"Don't lie. I've heard you singing his songs. And you're a Harper. Only Harpers knew where his prison was. I'll find him, and with the spur I can destroy him. I can destroy his whole family."

"But why?" Olive asked.

"Why? Look what he did to me!" Flattery demanded.

Olive stared hard at Flattery. "You look all right to me. Pretty near perfect, actually."

Flattery screamed. "I do not look all right. I look exactly like him. He made me that way. I don't want to be exactly like him. I don't want his face. I don't want his memories. I don't want his thoughts. I don't want his voice, and I don't want his songs. No one can make me say his name or sing his songs. I'll kill him before he tries to make me sing them again."

"Oh, my gosh," Olive said. The realization of exactly who Flattery was dawned on her and made her tremble. "You aren't his son. You're the first creature he made to sing his songs, the one that got him in all the trouble with the Harpers in the first place." Olive knew that many wizards had died in Nameless's bizarre experiments to create living vessels for his works.

"What do you mean the first creature?" Flattery demanded.

"Well, he made another one. Woman. Very pretty. Sings like a bird," Olive said. She kept Flattery's attention fixed on her. Behind the wizard, Cat retrieved Giogi's foil and returned it to him. Olive bragged, "Everyone loves the songs she sings. The songs he wrote."

"You lie!" Flattery shouted, closing on Olive. "I will kill you and slay him with the spur. His name will never be spoken again." His eyes wide with rage, Flattery raised a ring-bedecked hand and pointed at the halfling.

Giogi slammed into Flattery, spoiling whatever magic the wizard had intended to cast at Olive. "Stay behind me, Mistress Ruskettle," the young noble said as the halfling scurried to his side.

"Little present from your aunt," Olive whispered, slipping the wyvern's spur into the top of Giogi's boot. Giogi concentrated on the dream. From behind the nobleman's body the halfling taunted the wizard. "You're too late, you know, Flattery. Nameless's true name is on everyone's lips. Best bard in the Realms—Finder Wyvernspur."

Flattery lunged at Giogi to get at Olive but found himself confronted with a wyvern.

Flattery leaped backward with a snarl. His foil was not likely to penetrate the wyvern's scales, and Giogi's transformed body was immune to his spells. Flattery might have run, but he spotted Cat picking up the finder's stone.

Backing away farther, the wizard drew something out of his pocket. It was a crystal as dark as a new moon. Just like the one Jade had stolen, Olive thought.

"Catling, you want this? Come and get it," said Flattery, circling to keep the enchantress between him and the wyvern, Giogi.

Cat looked with confusion at the crystal. Her eyes shone with desire. She took a hesitant step forward.

"It's a trick, Cat," Olive shouted. "He destroyed the real crystal. He just wants to use you against Giogi."

Flattery was a fast thinker and a faster liar. "I made a second crystal, Cat. It's everything the first was. Just come here, and I will give it to you."

Cat froze, then stepped back, taking up a position behind Giogi. "It doesn't matter anymore, Flattery," she said proudly. "I can make myself new memories."

With that, Olive said, "Time to go," took Cat's hand, and pulled her toward the exit. Giogi backed slowly in the same direction, waving his tail over his head. He had to get the mage and the bard to safety before he finished with the wizard.

The three of them slipped from the audience chamber quickly. Something exploded behind them. Flattery shrieked, and a howl went up from the undead.

"Run!" Olive shouted.

The halfling and the mage pounded down the corridor. Behind them, Giogi continued backing away as fast as he could. Drone, in his human form, stood waiting outside the door.

"Giogi?" said the old man.

"Right behind us," Olive gasped.

The wyvern backed out of the keep door and changed quickly back into a human. "You know, this wyvern form is deucedly awkward enough to walk in going forward," Giogi said with irritation. "I can't see where I'm going at all when I go backward, let alone try to be graceful about it."

Drone took Cat by the shoulders. "Where are my scrolls, young lady?" he demanded.

Cat swallowed. "Gone," she said. "Flattery took them. He's already opened one, I think. We heard an explosion as we fled the keep."

"You knew the scrolls you took were covered in explosive runes?" Drone asked.

Cat grinned slyly. "Except for the few I used," she said.

"The exploding scroll will have destroyed all the others with it," Drone snapped. "All you needed for a booby trap was one."

"If I'd only brought him one scroll, he'd be suspicious," Cat explained. "The more I brought him, the less suspicious he'd be. I had to bring all the ones with exploding runes to make sure he got it by the first one he read."

"Devious. She's very devious, Giogi. She owes me twenty-seven scrolls, though," Drone growled. "I've spent all my power for the day. Without those scrolls, I'm no good to you in battle. I can get the ladies safely to the ground, Giogi, if you can delay pursuit."

Giogi nodded.

A horrendous howl erupted from the audience chamber, and everyone knew Flattery trailed them with renewed fury.

"Lead Flattery away from this rock, as far away as you can get him to go," Drone said.

"Yes, sir."

Drone pulled a small scroll from his sleeve, muttered a few words, and was surrounded by a milky blue glow. When the glow subsided, the old Wyvernspur had been transformed into a pegasus.

"Hand up, if you please, Master Giogioni," Olive said.

Giogioni lifted the halfling onto his uncle's back.

"Be careful," Cat pleaded.

Giogi kissed her once and set her behind Olive. "Don't fall off this horse," he warned. "It's a long way to the ground."

"Wait!" Cat said. "The undead. If they get past the invisible barrier, they can still chase you, as they did your father. The mage untied her yellow sash, dropped the finder's stone in it, and knotted it inside. "Change to the wyvern," she ordered Giogi.

Giogi quickly transformed.

"Bend your head down."

Cat wrapped her sash around Giogi's wyvern throat and knotted the fabric tight. "There," she said.

The finder's stone shone brightly through the fabric.

Drone stamped his foot impatiently and whinnied.

"Good luck," Cat whispered.

Drone took off, flying just high enough to clear the fortress walls. Giogi took to the air and circled over the fortress, near the large iron doors. The moon had just risen high enough to shine on the inner ward.

Flattery came out, just as Giogi knew he would, in the shape of a great sky-blue dragon. The wizard looked no worse for all the injury Cat had done him with her magic missile in the nursery and the explosive runes on Uncle Drone's scrolls. He looked like a dragon in his prime.

Giogi folded his wings and swooped down silently, his moon shadow behind him. Like a wasp, he delivered a stinging blow to Flattery's head. Then Giogi tore off to the west.

When he took a moment to look back, he could see the dragon's silhouette in the moonlight, much closer to him than he thought. Dark clouds and white mist flew beside the wizard.

*　*　*　*　*

Olive squinted through the telescope at the tiny, retreating figures of Giogi, Flattery, and the few flying minions he had left. The minions were already no more than a collection of motes in the glass.

Drone was balanced precariously on the tower roof, chanting some very powerful spell from a scroll. Mother Lleddew was in courtyard below, praying some powerful prayer from another scroll. Their chants intermixed in a toneless song of magic.

Olive looked up at the flying fortress looming over the castle. Suddenly it began to shake then levitate upward very, very quickly, so that it looked as if it were shrinking.

The halfling could hear Drone jumping up and down, shouting, "Look at it go!" and Cat trying to keep him calm enough so that he didn't slip off the tower and break his fool neck.

Drone slid down the kudzu vine and back into the room, still chuckling. Cat followed.

"Did you see that?" Drone asked.

"You made it fly higher," Olive said.

"No, no, no. You don't understand how gravity works. I made it fall up."

"Nothing falls up," Olive said.

"Hee, hee, hee," Drone wheezed. "Not without powerful magic, at any rate."

"Will it fall back down?" Olive asked.

"Oh, I hope so," Drone said.

"But then it will destroy the town," Olive objected.

"Burn up as it falls. Be quite a spectacular meteor."

"What?"

"Don't worry about it, Mistress Ruskettle."

At the window, Cat fidgeted nervously. Mother Lleddew was casting some sort of scrying spell so they knew what happened in Giogi's battle with Flattery. Cat didn't want to miss anything. "Are we finished?" the enchantress asked impatiently.

"Don't you snap at me, girl," Drone told her. "You owe me twenty-seven scrolls. You'll work off every one of them, too."

Cat looked at the floor.

"Oh, stop that. Don't mope. I hate it when pretty girls mope. I suppose we're finished. Lleddew should have her scrying spell set up by now. Let's go watch the show. Don't want to miss Giogi beating the stuffing out of the villain." His voice was light, but Olive could see the worry lines in the old man's face tighten as he spoke.

*   *   *   *   *

My arms are going to fall off, Giogi thought. Wings, not arms, he corrected himself. The cold wind streaming over his scales whistled in his ears. Behind him he heard Flattery's dragon-shape pumping its leathery wings, and he knew that the un-dead must still be with him. Undead fly as fast as dragons—and faster than me, he realized.

This has to be far enough, the transformed Wyvernspur thought.

Giogi rolled and banked to the south, then east, back toward Immersea and his pursuers. Flattery climbed, positioning himself for a dive down on Giogi.

He's still silhouetted against the moon, Giogi thought. He hasn't got any instinct for this kind of fighting. Giogi slowed as the attackers closed the gap between them.

The wyvern waited until the dragon and the undead cloud and mist shapes were almost on top of him, then he pulled up, baring his belly and the scarf-wrapped stone to his pursuers.

All right, finder's stone, Giogi thought, squinting his eyes nearly shut, keep those undead from me.

The finder's stone flared into light as bright as daylight. The wraiths and specters flying with Flattery scattered across the night sky like spooked pigeons. Flattery—momentarily blinded—pulled up.

Giogi banked around again. He was below but behind the dragon now. He increased his altitude while Flattery shook off the effects of the bright light. The wyvern positioned himself above the dragon, careful not to cast his own shadow on his prey.

Flattery tried climbing, too, but Giogi was already diving on him. Flattery tried to swerve, but he moved too slowly for the plummeting wyvern.

Giogi's talons closed on the back of the dragon's neck and he stabbed at the dragon's throat with his stinger. It was like striking the pillar in the crypt. Flattery's scales were as hard as stone. Giogi stabbed again and again, uncertain whether he was doing any damage. The dragon did not cry out, so he doubted it.

They lost altitude, then an updraft caught in both their beating wings and they soared, locked in combat. Flattery raked one of his foreclaws back and upward along the wyvern's neck, clawing a gash in Giogi's scales. Pain shot along Giogi's very long neck, and his flesh burned from the cold wind blowing on it. In a rage, the wyvern began stabbing faster at the dragon's neck until his tail muscles twitched.

The dragon had all four claws free to use, while Giogi's two claws were occupied hanging onto his prey. His tail seemed unable to penetrate any scales within its reach. Still, Flattery was in an awkward position for clawing, even though he had managed it. Giogi could not afford to let go, lest Flattery get a hold on him with his mouth facing the wyvern. Dragons could breathe deadly things, not to mention bite and swallow.

Flattery clawed up along Giogi's throat again, and the wyvern began to feel moisture around his neck. He was bleeding. He felt colder than before. In pain and anger, he bit down on Flattery's blue-plated neck.

Shocked by his action, Giogi ceased suddenly. He couldn't bring himself to chew his opponent.

Flattery's back claw caught and tore one of Giogi's beating wings. The pain of the tear drove Giogi to frenzy. He sunk his teeth into Flattery's neck again and shook it, like a dog baiting a bull. One of the blue dragon's neck plate's came loose, and Giogi tasted blood. He pulled his head up and thunked his tail in the spot. He did it again.

Flattery screeched with pain at last. Then Giogi noticed they were both dropping in the sky. He flapped his wings, but he could feel the tear widening with the effort.

Giogi folded his wings and became a dead weight, his stinger still embedded in Flattery's throat.

The added weight of the wyvern was too much for Flattery to support. Unable to fly together, the gigantic creatures fell faster. The dragon tried to twist in Giogi's grip, to break away, but the grip of the talons was too firm, and the daggerlike stinger kept jabbing him. The ground, covered in a thick forest, came up to meet them.

Flattery tried to somersault, to dislodge Giogi, and they both began spinning as they plummeted.

At the last moment, one of the gigantic creatures pulled away from the other. Its shadowy form spread its great batlike wings and swooped low, skimming the treetops and gliding swiftly to the north.

The other gigantic form smashed into the trees with an impact that rattled cottages miles away. The woods rumbled with the sound of the crash, and all the wildlife within was silent. Then, softly, the spring peepers began to sing again.

❧ 22 ❧

Coming Home

From the journal of Giogioni Wyvernspur:

The 25th of Ches, in the Year of the Shadows
Second Codicil by Olive Ruskettle

Three days have passed since the events I described in the previous codicil to this volume, and Giogioni has still not returned to Immersea. I'm beginning to wonder if Mother Lleddew didn't peer into her scrying font and see what she wanted to see: Giogioni soaring away from his battle with Flattery, when that may not have happened at all.

Perhaps she confused the wyvern with the dragon. I've tried to suggest this to Dorath and Cat, but they vehemently refuse to believe Giogioni might be lost to them forever. They ride up to the House of the Lady daily to consult with Lleddew, who tells them Giogioni will return when he's ready.

Dorath has become very attached to Cat as a consequence of their common anxiety, and Drone is quite pleased to have drafted the enchantress into his service as an assistant, now that Gaylyn's time is occupied with Amberlee. Cat, while very unhappy with Giogi's absence, seems content comforting and helping his relatives.

I caught Thomas weeping over Jade's little silver spoon yesterday. It turns out that two weeks ago she bumped into him in the street, and besides lifting his purse, she'd also stolen his heart. After a whirlwind courtship, he'd introduced her to his closest confidant—Drone—with the results already described herein.

The mausoleum key was in Jade's bag, and I returned it to Drone but asked to keep the gifts he gave Jade as keepsakes. I gave Thomas the silver spoon.

Gaylyn begged me to sing at Amberlee's blessing next week. She's a hard woman to say no to. Drone has invited me to stay at Giogi's townhouse to keep the light in the window for him. After Amberlee's blessing, though, I think I'll leave Immersea. It's too lonely here without Jade.

The front door opened and slammed shut. Olive put down her pen. Thomas usually went in and out through the kitchen, and he never slammed doors. Cat and Dorath would still be up on Temple Hill at this time of the day. The parlor door opened.

"Heigh-ho, anyone about?"

"Giogi!" Olive cried, running to the young man who stood in the doorway. For a moment, she'd forgotten he was a human, well over six feet tall. She drew back before she embarrassed herself by hugging one of his legs. She held out her hand.

"Congratulations on your victory," she said, shaking his hand and smiling from ear to ear.

"Oh. Thanks. Where is everyone?"

"Thomas is shopping. Cat is out with Dorath. They'll be back in a while." Olive looked down at the nobleman's muddy, torn clothes and his scarred neck and his bruised and haggard face, covered with three days' worth of stubble. He looked like an adventurer. "You have just enough time to clean up."

"Good. I must be rather distressing to look at. I wouldn't want to worry anyone."

Olive laughed. "Too late for that. What took you so long?"

Giogi's expression grew as distressed as his appearance. He shuddered as if from some fear. "I need a drink. Would you care to join me, Mistress Ruskettle?"

"But of course. You sit down. I'll pour."

Olive crossed to the tea table and unstoppered the brandy bottle. Thomas does such a good job keeping it full, she thought. She poured two tumblers full and carried them to the fireside, where Giogi slouched in an armchair, heedless of the grime he left on its arms. The nobleman took a hefty slug of the liquor. Olive sat on the ottoman at his feet.

"You want to talk about it?" she asked.

"Would you mind?" Giogi asked. "It's not the sort of thing I could tell anyone else, but you're so, well, worldly. I think it would upset my relatives, and I'm not sure Cat will understand how I feel."

"I'm always ready to listen to a friend," Olive assured him.

Giogi smiled gratefully. "It's two things, really. The first isn't that bad, but I used it as an excuse, trying not to think about the other. The wyvern shape takes a lot of . . . fuel, I guess you could say. I was really hungry after I used it the first time. I was starving after—after the battle with Flattery. I was miles from the road, though, and nuts and berries weren't going to be enough, and it was cold out there. So I stayed a wyvern for the night and ate like a wyvern." Giogi shuddered.

"Uncooked meals can upset one's equilibrium," Olive said, thinking of sweetened oats.

Giogi laughed. "You have such a way with words. I guess that's why you're a bard."

"Among other things," Olive said. "Go on with your story," she encouraged.

"Well, I ate this wild pig, which was completely awful, all hairy and bony. Then I fell asleep. It was too cold to sleep out-of-doors as a human, so I stayed a wyvern.

"The next day, I kind of got lost. I thought I was north of the road to Dhedluk when I was really south. So I flew around as a wyvern for a long time before I found the road. Then I was hungry again. You know, Sudacar told me that my father was allowed to hunt in the king's woods unaccompanied. Now I realize he didn't go in with a bow and arrow. I ate this cow. I tried to get a deer first, but it dove into the woods where I couldn't follow. So I had to eat the cow. I shall have to go back and reimburse whoever it belonged to.

"Anyway, the guardian said I couldn't go all wyverny and forget I was human. I tried, though. I didn't want to be human, I think. I—you see—Mistress Ruskettle, have you ever killed anyone before?"

"Oh, that's it," Olive said with an understanding nod. "Well, yes. Not as many as you might think, but more than I really know for sure. The first two were a matter of life or death, but I was really too scared to know I was doing it."

"Yes!" Giogi said. "I was scared. Then it was over. But it doesn't change things. I killed a man. A man who was sort of a relative. I knew he was going to kill me, as he'd killed my father and all those elves and tried to kill my Uncle Drone, and who knows who else. I didn't think I'd ever kill anyone, and I guess I wanted to blame it on being a wyvern. I had to bite him as a wyvern to kill him. It's easy to kill things when you're a wyvern. Otherwise, you go hungry. I stayed a wyvern for a while so I wouldn't have to think about whether I'd have killed Flattery as a human being."

"What made you come back, then?" Olive asked.

"Well, the guardian was right. I'm not a wyvern. I kept thinking about things that made me human again. I had to think about killing Flattery as a human being. I think I had to kill him. I don't think I wanted to, but I made a decision anyway. It was more important protecting my family."

Giogi had another gulp of brandy. Then he asked, "Mistress Ruskettle, who was Flattery? What did he mean when he said Finder Wyvernspur made him? Is Finder really evil?"

Olive sighed. She'd seen this coming. "Nameless, that is, Finder Wyvernspur, is one of your ancestors. A grandson of Paton Wyvernspur, as near as I can tell. I went through the family histories while you were . . . out. There is a name crossed out in the list of Paton's grandchildren, so I think that must have been his name. He magically created Flattery as a copy of himself. I'm still wondering if he named Flattery, or if Flattery named himself, or if someone else named him. Finder was kind of arrogant. He wanted his songs and his name to live forever, absolutely untouched by time, unchanged by the flow of generations. An interesting idea, but not very workable.

"Anyway, in making Flattery, Nameless—Finder—was responsible for the deaths of two people. I don't know if the Harpers ever actually learned that Flattery had lived, or even if Finder knew, but they sentenced Finder to exile and suppressed his songs and made him forget his name. He didn't age in exile, but his experiences, when he was released, changed him. I'm sure he'd be appalled by what Flattery had become."

"But now the Harpers have forgiven Finder and released him?" Giogi asked, hopeful.

"Well, he's been released. The Harpers are debating what they're going to do about it. I think he's redeemed himself, and not just because I love the man's music."

"Why was Flattery so intent on killing him?"

"Flattery was an experiment gone very wrong. He was too much like Finder. They say, if a mage makes an exact copy of a person, the copy or the person go mad and try to destroy one another. Flattery might have felt he was the one who had the right to exist, since he wasn't the one the Harpers put on trial. Or he might have been afraid that his 'father' was going to find him and punish him for not doing what he'd been made to do."

"Why didn't Flattery want to sing his songs?"

"I don't know. My theory is that Flattery was cursed from the moment someone died to create him, but maybe Finder just forgot to put into him what's in you."

"What's in me?"

"Yes. Whatever it is that doesn't let you forget you're a human. A pretty nice human, as humans go," the halfling said, smiling.

"Is that why Flattery was afraid to go into the crypt after the spur?"

"Probably. He wasn't really sure if he was human. That's why he got so angry when you said he wasn't. If he wasn't human, he couldn't really be a Wyvernspur. So he married Cat and sent her in. If he was a Wyvernspur, she'd live and he'd have the spur. If he wasn't a Wyvernspur, she'd die and he'd have to think of some other way to get hold of it."

"But, I thought you said Jade and Cat were already Wyvernspurs."

It was getting harder to answer Giogi's questions without giving away the secret that Alias, Jade, and Cat were all made by Finder, too. Olive told as much of the truth as she believed. "Well, as far as I know, they are. Flattery didn't, though. Jade would have liked being adopted. She liked being my family. She would have liked being in yours, too."

"Why did Uncle Drone want me to have the spur so badly?" Giogi wondered.

"Oh, I imagine for the same reason he wanted your father to have it. It's a Wyvernspur tradition, and the king expects the services of a wyvern. If every Wyvernspur walked away from destiny like your Aunt Dorath did, you'd be merchants or farmers or something within a few generations."

"If only Uncle Drone had just taken it from the crypt himself, or told me to. So much trouble might have been avoided," Giogi said.

"Apparently, after arguing with your uncle about giving it to you, your aunt threatened to skin him alive if he so much as touched it. So he promised not to touch it. Everything he did was to get the job done without telling a lie. You know, life in your family might be a little less complicated if the men in your family could just tell your Aunt Dorath what they really think."

Giogi laughed. "It not as easy as it sounds. The best any of us have ever managed is to think really hard."

"Hmmph. You better go scrub up. If Mother Lleddew gets her facts straight, she'll send Dorath and Cat right over here."

Giogi swallowed the rest of his drink and stood. "I won't be long. Please, if Thomas gets back while I'm upstairs, could you tell him I'd like lots of things for dinner. Cooked things."

Olive grinned and nodded.

When Giogi had left the room, the halfling drew out her knife and very carefully sliced out the pages in Giogi's journal that she'd written on. "He can tell his own story to posterity," she muttered. She folded the papers and slid them into her pocket, then took another sip of her brandy.

A quarter of an hour later, a clean, shaven, and freshly dressed Giogi returned to the parlor. He had a scarf around his throat to hide the scars, and his arm was stiff from some wound, but he looked much more cheerful.

He and Olive were on their second brandy when they heard the front door open and close. Olive opened the parlor door. Cat stood in the hallway alone.

"Where's Mistress Dorath?" the halfling asked.

"Out in the carriage," Cat replied. "She's very tired. I told her I'd just check in to see if there was any news. Is there?"

"Wait a minute. I'll check," Olive said, turning to face the parlor. "Giogi? Is there any news?"

"Well, I hear that the bishop of Chauntea and the patron of Oghma still aren't speaking to one another. The runaway Princess Alusair Nacacia is still missing. Local gossip has it that that fool, Giogioni Wyvernspur, is home."

"Giogi!" Cat cried, pushing past Olive and throwing herself into the noble's arms. "You're all right? Where have you been? Mother Lleddew told us you'd won the battle with Flattery, but when you didn't come home right away, we were all worried sick about you."

"I stayed a wyvern for a while."

"Was it fun? Will you take me flying again? We could go adventuring this summer and fly everywhere—if your uncle will let me go for a bit. Maybe I can get him to teach me to turn into something that can fly, too. Oh, I missed you."

"I missed you, too," Giogi said. He bent over Cat and kissed her.

Olive slipped out of the parlor and through the front door. She waved for Dorath to come inside.

The driver hopped from his seat, opened the carriage door, and helped the old woman down. Olive rushed to her.

"He's back. He's just fine. Just ran into a little trouble finding the road."

"How like Giogi. That boy has no sense of direction. Is Cat with him now?"

"Yes."

Dorath stared at the house as if she could see through stone, then she said, "Then I'll just head back up to Redstone and tell everyone there the good news."

"Don't you want to come in and say hello?" Olive asked.

Dorath shook her head. "I think I'll just leave them alone together for a while. You know, Mistress Ruskettle, I think Cat is just the girl Giogi needs to take his mind off this wyvern nonsense."

Olive fought hard to control her expression. Wyvernspur men had to learn to say what they really thought to Dorath, but, fortunately, Olive didn't. "You know, Mistress Dorath," she said. "I think you're right. She's just the one."

FANTASY ADVENTURE

1990 Novels by
R. A. Salvatore

THE HALFLING'S GEM
Icewind Dale Trilogy: Book Three

Assassin Artemis Entreri whisks Regis south to Calimport and into Pasha Pook's vengeful hands. If Pook can control the magical panther Guenhwyvar, Regis will die in a real game of cat-and-mouse. Available February 1990.

New Series!

HOMELAND
Dark Elf Trilogy: Book One

Exotic Menzoberranzan is the vast city of the dark elf, where families battle families. Possessing honor beyond his unprincipled kinsmen, young Drizzt asks himself: Can I live in an honorless society? Available September 1990.

EXILE
Dark Elf Trilogy: Book Two

Exiled from Menzoberranzan, Drizzt must live among races normally at war with his kind. And all the while, the hero must look over his shoulder--his people are not a forgiving race. Available December 1990.

FORGOTTEN REALMS
FANTASY ADVENTURE

Pool
of
Radiance

James M. Ward
Jane Cooper Hong

A possessed dragon commands the undead armies of Valhingen Graveyard and the beasts from the ruins near Phlan. Desperate, a spellcaster, a ranger thief, and a cleric join forces to deliver Phlan and the entire Moonsea region from the dark possession of evil incarnate ...Tyranthraxus.

Now an award-winning SSI computer game, too!

DragonLance Saga

HEROES II TRILOGY

KAZ, THE MINOTAUR
Richard A. Knaak

Sequel to *The Legend of Huma*. Stalked by enemies after Huma's death, Kaz hears rumors of evil incidents. When he warns the Knights of Solamnia, he is plunged into a nightmare of magic, danger, and *deja vu*. Available June 1990.

THE GATES OF THORBARDIN
Dan Parkinson

Beneath Skullcap is a path to the gates of Thorbardin, and the magical helm of Grallen. The finder of Grallen's helm will be rewarded by a united Thorbardin, but he will also open the realm to new horror. Available September 1990.

GALEN BEKNIGHTED
Michael Williams

Sequel to *Weasel's Luck*. Galen Pathwarden is still out to save his own skin. But when his brother vanishes, Galen foresakes his better judgment and embarks on a quest that leads into a conspiracy of darkness, and to the end of his courage. Available December 1990.

PRELUDES II

RIVERWIND, THE PLAINSMAN
Paul B. Thompson & Tonya R. Carter

To prove himself worthy of Goldmoon, Riverwind is sent on an impossible quest: Find evidence of the true gods. With an eccentric soothsayer Riverwind falls down a magical shaft--and alights in a world of slavery and rebellion. Available in March 1990.

FLINT, THE KING
Mary Kirchoff & Douglas Niles

Flint returns to his boyhood village and finds it a boomtown. He learns that the prosperity comes from a false alliance and is pushed to his death. Saved by gully dwarves and made their reluctant monarch, Flint unites them as his only chance to stop the agents of the Dark Queen. Available in July 1990.

TANIS, THE SHADOW YEARS
Barbara Siegel & Scott Siegel

Tanis Half-Elven once disappeared in the mountains near Solace. He returned changed, ennobled--and with a secret. Tanis becomes a traveler in a dying mage's memory, journeying into the past to fight a battle against time itself. Available in November 1990.

FORGOTTEN REALMS
FANTASY ADVENTURE

EMPIRES TRILOGY

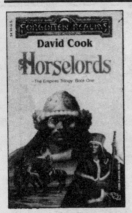

HORSELORDS
David Cook

Between the western Realms and Kara-Tur lies a vast, unexplored domain. The "civilized" people of the Realms have given little notice to these nomadic barbarians. Now, a mighty leader has united these wild horsemen into an army powerful enough to challenge the world. First, they turn to Kara-Tur. Available in May.

DRAGONWALL
Troy Denning

The barbarian horsemen have breached the Dragonwall and now threaten the oriental lands of Kara-Tur. Shou Lung's only hope lies with a general descended from the barbarians, and whose wife must fight the imperial court if her husband is to retain his command. Available in August.

CRUSADE
James Lowder

The barbarian army has turned its sights on the western Realms. Only King Azoun has the strength to forge an army to challenge the horsemen. But Azoun had not reckoned that the price of saving the west might be the life of his beloved daughter. Available in January 1991.

NEW  BOOKS

DARK HORSE
Mary Herbert

After her clan is massacred, a young woman assumes her brother's identity and becomes a warrior--all to exact revenge upon the chieftain who ordered her family slain. With an intelligent, magical horse, the young warrior goes against law and tradition to learn sorcery to thwart Medb's plans of conquest. Available February 1990.

WARSPRITE
Jefferson Swycaffer

On a quiet night, two robots from the future crash to Earth. One is a vicious killer, the other is unarmed, with an ability her warrior brother does not have: She can think. But she is programmed to face the murderous robot in a final confrontation in a radioactive chamber. Available April 1990.

NIGHT WATCH
Robin Wayne Bailey

All the Seers of Greyhawk have been killed, each by his own instrument of divination. And the only unusual sign is the ominous number of black birds in the skies. The mystery is dumped on the commander of the City Watch's night shift, who discovers that a web of evil has been tightly drawn around the great city. Available June 1990.